Penelope's Odyssey

Penelope's Odyssey

Amy Wachspress

Woza Books
Books that Raise the Spirits

Penelope's Odyssey
Copyright © 2025 by Amy Wachspress

Woza Books
Oregon City, Oregon
(707) 468-4118
www.wozabooks.com

Cover design: Anjelica Colliard
Book design: Amy Wachspress

Publisher's Cataloging-in-Publication Data

Wachspress, Amy
  Penelope's Odyssey / by Amy Wachspress – 1st ed. – Oregon City, Oregon : Woza Books, 2025

Paperback ISBN: 978-0-9788350-5-7
Hardcover ISBN: 978-0-9788350-6-4

Summary: This Penelope does not sit quietly awaiting Odysseus's return but instead charts a course of self-discovery to learn the truth about her family and her Native American roots in this telescopic odyssey of stories-within-stories about women in search of identity that explores the power of forgiveness.

1. FIC044000 FICTION / Women. 2. FIC014000 FICTION / Historical / General. 3. FIC059120 FICTION / Indigenous / Women. 4. FIC072000 FICTION / LGBTQ+ / Bisexual.

Library of Congress Control Number: 9780978835057

Printed in the United States of America

10 9 8 7 6 5 4 3 2 1

For those driven from their homes,
for those lost to genocide,
and for those who died because of the cruel, selfish acts
of the ignorant powerful

what didn't you do to bury me
but you forgot that I was a seed

—Dinos Christianopoulos, 1978

Contents

Book 1: Athena
Hoepper's Knee Reservation, 1971

When I first laid eyes on her in the tribal office I knew the full sum of her, A to Z, top to bottom; knew it as certainly as I knew she had no inkling of even the least of it herself. She resembled my mother, only fairer in complexion. Unsettling the way features in a family insinuate their way through the generations to reappear like ghosts. Her mother had an ugly past but I don't consider that a valid excuse. That ruined mother should have told her. Near past. Distant past. A blank. She must have known something about it because she turned up here at the Rez. I figure she had a sense about the ugliness because of the way she came apart. What a mess. Made me tired just thinking about taking it on.

Dita asked her if she knew she belonged to the Tribe, but she could barely speak at that point and I doubt she believed it even if she understood what Dita told her. We wound up with the children. The girl went to Nelson and June. I took the boy. I'm too old to look after a small child, but how could I do otherwise? We checked her into the Plains Clinic. The Plains takes the Natives who crack up. They get money from a do-good foundation to pay for them to glue us back together. It takes a lot of glue.

When they finish with her at the Plains, she'll likely land on my doorstep, and I don't know what I can do for her. Don't know how much she knows or doesn't know about her family. Don't know if she has much spirit left. She might have had it knocked out of her. Ah well, she's my aunt's great-granddaughter, a cousin, and that makes her one of mine. My responsibility. At the least, I should tell her the truth.

I take the decision to the Tribal Council.

"Another half-breed," Podon grumbles. "The minute they patch her back together at the Plains, she'll be up in here sniffing around for a house and yapping about what can the Tribe do for her. Seems like all we got left up in here is greedy half-breeds."

"Yeah, like your grandkids." Hera never hesitates to speak truth. Podon mutters belligerently. He has a temper like the ocean. I pity anyone who gets on his bad side. But even he would think twice about going toe-to-toe with Hera.

"Aren't those children a more immediate concern?" Dita asks. She clacks her knitting needles without pause.

"The children will make out just fine," Nelson replies quietly. "Helen has a strong spirit." He has already fallen in love with the luminous little girl. I can see if he lost Helen, it would cut Nelson at the knees. All the more reason to look after the mother here among our own.

A sharp pang of maternal attachment to Penelope stabs me. If I had known about her when she was yet a child, perhaps I could have taken her and prevented the whole tangle. I still have not said a single word to her. I don't know what pushed her over the edge, don't know the shape of the tragedy I consider stepping into. It would make it worthwhile, I suppose, if I could find her inside it and lead her out. I clear my throat. "We owe it to her and to the ancestors who survived to reclaim her. Haven't we had enough of our children robbed from us?"

"This one is damaged. Leave it," Podon snaps at me with a curt snarl.

Hera ignores him. "Athena, if you tell her about her mother and her grandmother and about the ones who survived, then what? What do you give her? How do you trade bad medicine for good and bring healing?" she asks me softly, woman-to-woman. Can I bring her healing? Dita's knitting needles stop clacking as she peers over her thick magnifying eyeglasses at me sharply. Podon's eyebrows shoot up and he gives me the I-told-you-so look, only, heaven help me, I can't figure why the old buzzard acts so smug.

"What do you mean?" I ask, stalling for time to work out what I intend to do.

We soak in silence.

"When she comes out of the Plains, I can offer her a place to stay. She'll have to get a job. I can't support her."

"Half-breeds *and* lunatics," Podon mutters.

"Hush," Hera says with a graceful wave of her arm that silences even Podon. "I accept Athena's decision. If we have even a small chance of recovering her, then we owe it to the ancestors to try. Those of us who remain have survived on the strength of small chances."

Podon holds his tongue. He frowns, but I can tell he knows Hera speaks truth. Dita clacks and whacks her needles furiously. Nelson bites his lip.

"After the Plains spits her out, we'll bring her home," Hera commands.

Penelope is shipwrecked on the island of her personal pain. I must soon join her on that island and I don't wish to go there.

Nevertheless, I have agreed to take it on. Flesh of my flesh. Blood of my blood. I hope to change her and I fear how she will change me in the process. I know all this. I enter knowingly. I wish I could see how it will end. I wonder if I will live long enough to find out. Ah well, I am not as old as that. Not yet.

Book 2: Penelope
Athens, 1965

I savor this extraordinary reprieve from my oh so ordinary life. Today I am not a receptionist at the student fitness center earning my way through college with a boring work-study job. Today I am a philosopher, an anthropologist, a seeker after truth. I have landed in Athens, summer after my sophomore year, on a trip with my Greek Mythology class; a trip I never imagined I could ever travel but here I am. More than just a world traveler, more than just a tourist, more than a mere survivor of my crazy, sick family. I have become a university student touring the Archaeological Museum and the Parthenon. I have successfully reinvented myself as a person with a future; the only such person to emerge from that disaster masquerading as a family that produced me.

"You must visit the open air market on Sintagma Square," the concierge at our hotel tells me. I trust his advice. I take the bus to the market while my fellow travelers snooze through an afternoon siesta to avoid the heat. I brave the heat to seize the opportunity to explore on my own. I crave an adventure.

The steadfast, white buildings reflect the sun and send it into every corner at crazy angles. Not even the tiniest crevice of stone escapes the blaze of this ridiculous heat. Vendors and buyers squint in this inferno, dripping with sweat. Everyone imagines a cool drink in the shade, a siesta indoors, like my fellow travelers have chosen.

I buy a dress the color of deep blue delphiniums. I stop at a flower stand and fall in love with the calla lilies. I have never seen a flower like the calla lily before. It has but one huge white petal in the midst of enormous, waxen leaves. The rigid yellow stamen stands obscenely erect, rooted at the base of the single arched petal. I buy a dozen wrapped in a cone of newspaper.

As I turn from the flower stand, the heel tears off my shoe and I twist my foot, stumbling. The pain makes me limp. I think I will have to catch a bus back to the hotel because I can't walk that far on this turned foot. The broken shoe annoys me. I lean against the corner of a stand for a moment to rub my foot and I knock a ball off a shelf by accident with my shoulder. It bounces away from me and I can't chase it on my bad foot.

He appears.

He wears only cobalt-blue shorts and dusty sandals. A pair of soccer shoes flops against his chest, the laces tied together behind his neck. He catches the ball and holds it out to me balanced on the perfect, graceful curve of his fingers. His heavy-lidded eyes burn dark and mysterious, with a shadow beneath them. His mane of golden hair catches the sun and glints with a dozen dazzling metallic hues. A slick of sweat glistens on his bronzed skin. He has a smooth, nearly hairless, muscular chest and well-defined shoulders and upper arms that remind me of the statue of Poseidon at the Archaeological Museum. A god heaved up from the depths of the sea.

He holds the ball out to me. His face blossoms in a smile and he asks in English, "Your ball?"

I take the ball from him and place it back on the shelf. The merchant generously does not complain.

He enters my life on a roasting-hot day, surrounded by flowers, fruit, and fabrics at the marketplace. I am too young to fall in love. He should know better, this man ten years older than I. But he cannot help himself. My thick, blue-black hair flows straight down my back like a waterfall. My round behind is as tight as a summer peach. A thousand mysteries sparkle in my eyes. My bare arms are graceful. He cannot resist me. I wear my luscious youth like a strapless gown. I am a new flower, a young woman stepping into the dance, and I want him. I exult in the power I sense that I have over him. Later he would confess that I took his breath away, standing there in the bright, bright light that reflected off the buildings and baked the streets, pulsing up from the sidewalks.

He is dusted in gold, more than mortal, splendid in the noonday sun. How can I resist him? Why would I resist? Even his toes in his worn sandals look delicious. I have dreamed of a man such as this. Longed for it with a virgin's longing.

"Tourist?"

"How could you tell?"

"Your clothes. What you buy. How you walk." He has been watching me.

The heat of the day coils inside me, begging to leap out. Perhaps I will faint. I need water. My knees go weak. I am speechless, a young girl limping on a sore foot with my bare arms full of lilies.

"Those are funeral lilies. They will bring you bad luck."

"They're too beautiful for funerals."

"I will brave the bad luck. Let me buy you a cool drink."

I follow him effortlessly. He wants me and I want him and we both know this. He has no need to seduce me with clever words. He seduced me before he opened his mouth. We can barely make conversation. We cannot concentrate on forming words. I watch his graceful hands move as he lifts his glass to his mouth. He watches my lips, moist and tender, as they draw him to me like a strawberry flower draws a honeybee. He can see he has snared me. I wonder if two people have ever felt more desire than that which blooms in us.

"Let's get out of here," he says. I nod mutely, trembling.

He hails a taxi and I sit beside him with my leg grazing his, my arm brushing against him, my skin electric. We say nothing as we glide through the streets. By the time we reach his apartment, my whole body sings for him. We scramble out of the taxi, drenched in sweat and desire. He pays the driver and takes my hand, leading me into his apartment, practically at a run. We must have each other.

He closes the door behind us and his lips find mine, his tongue warm and wondering inside my mouth. I am completely lost. I do not see his apartment. I do not see his bed. I do not even see him. I am hands and lips and skin and he touches me and I rise to his touch. I explore, amazed that I have permission to touch this man's body. I urgently want him inside me and when he enters, our boundaries fade and we become one. I am entirely full. He belongs to me and I to him. We quiver and moan and cry out in our ecstasy. We become a single, unified flash of pure light.

Later, when we return to ourselves, disoriented and entangled in each other, I ask, "Who are you?"

"I am Odysseus. And you?"

"Penelope."

"Then we are made for each other."

The coincidence of our names terrifies me.

We will get to know each other. We will grow together like intertwined vines on a trellis as we learn the details of one another.

For now, we are abruptly in love. Our bodies sing to one another, each to each. Our blood rises within us in waves, breaking against the shore of our desire. We lose ourselves in one another and become one again and again. I belong to him forever. I have stepped into my destiny on this hot afternoon in Athens.

I have found my Odysseus.

Our love is powerful.

We are resplendent.

We are wandering.

Book 3: Penelope
Berkeley, 1966

I open the door to my studio apartment and with delighted astonishment I discover, on the threshold, Odysseus. The amber light of Athens clings to his hair. He is my best souvenir. I want to keep him.

An electrical engineer, Odysseus has obtained a work visa. He already has a job. I am envious. I aspire to be a writer and yet I have to work my silly work-study job.

"When you finish school, you will find the perfect writing job," Odysseus assures me.

He stays with me in my tiny studio, making me crazy with desire. I can't let him walk past me without touching his chest, his arms, the bulge in the front of his pants. How will I concentrate on school with this man in my bed? I could spend all my hours with him in our secret garden. But I don't. I go to class. I go to work.

When he takes me to Tilden Park for a picnic, we sit on the beach at Lake Anza on a green cotton bedspread and he reads a short story I wrote about my Aunt Beth and me, except he doesn't know it's about us. Only I know this.

"It's a well-written story," Odysseus says, "but depressing."

"Depressing?"

"These characters are so lost. I want some kind of redemption."

"There is no redemption. They have no hope."

"I wonder what happened to this woman to make her so hopeless." Odysseus takes a banana out of his backpack and peels it. The woman he reflects on is the character fashioned after Aunt Beth, who raised me.

"Pass me one." He reaches into his backpack and pulls out a banana for me. "She has no life," I tell him.

"Yes, but why?"

"She never did. She never had a chance. Nothing has meaning for her."

"What about the niece? The niece has meaning."

"Not really. She got stuck with the niece." Suddenly I don't want to discuss this. It will ruin a perfectly pleasant day at the lake. "Forget it." I snatch the story from him and stuff it into my bag. "Let's go for a walk." He shrugs as he pops the last piece of the banana into his mouth. We fold up the bedspread and set off on foot. He matches his stride to mine. I tilt my face to the sun, drawn to the warmth like a flower. I like the present. I would like to stay here.

Odysseus befriends everyone he meets. He talks to our neighbors when he sees them in their yards or walking on the sidewalk, asks them about themselves. He talks to the people we meet at the Laundromat, and the sales clerk at the natural food store, and the necktie salesman on Telegraph Avenue, and the lady who walks past our apartment with her collie in the evening, and the four-year-old twins at the end of the block. Odysseus makes friends easily because he has a genuine interest in what people do, what they care about, and what they have to say. I am too shy to make friends so easily; but fortunately his friends become mine as well. The lady with the collie greets me when she walks past. The twins invite me to play badminton with them.

On Halloween, we don't buy enough candy. When we realize our mistake, I bake a batch of chocolate chip cookies right quick. When the candy runs out we stand at the door with a platter of warm cookies. The moms and dads don't worry about letting their fairy princesses and superheroes take homemade cookies from us. It pleases me that they trust me. I belong to a neighborhood, a community. Odysseus made this possible.

A couple of weeks before Thanksgiving, Odysseus buys a beautiful, two-tone, vintage Chevy. I love it. We don't actually need a car in Berkeley, although it comes in handy for the grocery shopping and the laundry. Once in a while we drive to the coast to see the ocean.

I wonder how Odysseus drags himself out of bed every morning to go to work. We can't keep our hands off each other. All too often I stay up late at night making love and then wind up tired and unfocused the next day. I used to lead a balanced, busy, self-contained life. Now I fall asleep in my seat in class and sometimes I can barely finish my shift at work.

Aunt Beth figures out that a man moved in with me when she calls and he answers the phone. She disapproves, but she can't do anything about it. I don't want to introduce her to Odysseus. My family poisons whatever it touches. I want this to survive. How can I avoid going to her house on Christmas? Odysseus insists. He doesn't know what he's getting into. He says I can't leave her alone on Christmas. Oh yes I can. Why does he have to be so decent?

We go to Aunt Beth's for Christmas dinner. A metallic fake tree sporting a handful of lurid balls stands in her living room. She cooks turkey and sweet potatoes, which we fail to eat because we don't make it as far as the meal. Before we sit down to dinner,

Odysseus informs her that I'm pregnant. She chases him into the street with a meat cleaver, a lit cigarette bouncing on her lip.

"She had a chance. She was gonna make something of herself," Aunt Beth yells at him. "Selfish like all the rest of them." Odysseus runs. He jumps into the two-tone Chevy and drives away. I stand in the street behind Aunt Beth. She lowers her arm. The meat cleaver dangles by her side.

"Stupid idiot," she hisses, tears running down her cheeks. "You had it made. What a waste."

I abandon her without a word and begin to walk. Bad choice of timing to reveal our secret joy, Odysseus. He should have checked with me first about it. I figure he'll circle around and find me. So much for spending Christmas with my family. Aunt Beth cries and cusses me out as I walk away from her. By the next time I see her, many years from now, she won't have any words left in her.

When Odysseus finds me walking, he pulls over and opens the door for me to hop into the car. "Merry Christmas," I say.

Odysseus looks me in the eye unwaveringly and asks, "Will you marry me?"

"You don't have to prove anything to her."

"This has nothing to do with your aunt. I love you."

I finish my sophomore year before Helen is born. I lose interest in school after that. Helen is perfect. I am complete. I am making a functioning family that is nothing like the mangled one that produced me. Odysseus and I are making a real family. He rents a house for us with a white wooden fence around the front yard. I plant green beans and red geraniums. We build Helen a sandbox in the back yard. She is still too young for it, but she will love it when she gets older.

Placid and contented, Helen hardly ever cries. She sits in my lap and pats my cheeks with her firm little hands. She studies my face and Odysseus's face and the faces of the twins down the street and the lady who walks the collie. She wants me to hold her all the time so I can't get anything done.

When Odysseus comes home from work, I apologize. "I bathed her and took her to the park. The day got away from me. I haven't had a chance to make dinner."

He laughs. "Do you want me to cook or to play with her so you can cook?"

"I'll make sandwiches."

He lies down on the floor and tickles her toes. I make tuna melts in the toaster oven.

"Have you written to your mother about Helen yet?"

"Have you called your Aunt Beth?" he parries.

"That's different." I frown. "Or have you forgotten she chased you down the street with a meat cleaver?"

"Not so different. Given the opportunity, my mother would jump at the chance to chase us with a meat cleaver."

"How's that?"

"Because you're not Greek Orthodox, she will never recognize our marriage. So from her perspective we're living in sin. I would love for her to see Helen, or pictures of Helen; but I know she would refuse. She and my father disowned me when I married you. They won't change their minds about us. I am dead to them." He set his mouth in a firm line. "She made her choice. I made mine. I will not ruin my life to please them."

"Try sending her a picture of Helen."

"It wouldn't matter."

"Are you punishing her?"

He looks at me sharply and holds his tongue. I know all about families in which people punish each other.

"We will make it different," I say.

"Yes, we will make it different," he agrees and seals our pact with a kiss.

How could he have agreed that we would make it different, and then gone on to do what he did to me?

Berkeley, 1969

Helen peers into the face of her newborn baby brother. "When will he wake up?"

"When he gets hungry," Odysseus answers. He puts Telemachus into the car seat next to his sister and tells her, "You keep an eye on him for us, OK?"

Her eyes grow wide. "What if he wakes up?"

"Then you tell us he's awake."

A banner greets me when I enter the house: "Welcome Home Mommy and Max." I recognize Helen's scribble scrabble in bright colors around the words.

"You made us a beautiful picture," I compliment my daughter.

"We baked a cake and Daddy cooked lasagna."

"My favorite."

"Do you think Max wants cake?"

"He's too little for cake, but I bet he will like it as much as you do when he gets bigger. We can eat his cake this time."

"Right now?"

"After supper."

She scampers off to her room and sings to her dollies while Odysseus puts the lasagna in the oven to warm up.

Later, as we lie in bed with Max between us, Odysseus asks, "Are you going to be OK with these babies?"

"It's a little bit late to ask."

"Do you regret leaving school? Do you want to go back?"

"Eventually. Not right now. This is more than OK for me right now." I stroke the downy hair on Max's head.

Odysseus peers into my face anxiously. "Just say the word when you're ready. We can get some help. I don't want you to ever resent leaving college." His voice trails off. Is he seeing Aunt Beth running down the street with the meat cleaver, tears streaking her face? Her dream ruined. Not mine.

Mine is alive here in this sunlit house.

Berkeley, 1970

I lift Max up so he can see into the tank. Electric blue and yellow fish dart back and forth. Max shrieks with glee and claps his hands. Helen perches on Odysseus's shoulders. "See the fishies?" she asks Max. "Fiss," Max mutters, his eyes following the trails of color in the depths of the water. Odysseus pushes Max's stroller in which rests our backpack full of lunch. This is what a family is supposed to look like. This is what a family feels like. I marvel over it constantly. So many people take this for granted. For me it is novel and heavenly.

I love the aquarium. I could watch the silver sardines swim in circles like animated coins for hours. The jellyfish drift like lazy, luminous parachutes.

We walk up the ramp into the circular shark room. A shark tank surrounds us. We stand in the middle and turn slowly around. Max is amazed into silence. Odysseus sits on a bench and Helen covers his eyes with her hands and giggles. "Guess who, Daddy."

He peers through her fingers and tells her, "Look at that one with the pattern. It's a leopard shark. Doesn't it look like a leopard?" He swings her up onto his shoulders and turns to follow the path of the gliding shark.

Almost all the fish swim in the same direction. One fish swims opposite. I wonder what law of nature demands that this fish swim against the current in opposition to his companions. What purpose does it serve him?

"Cookie," Max demands.

"Odysseus, would you please get Max's cookies out of the backpack? They're in the front pocket."

"Me too," Helen says. Odysseus gives each of the children a cookie. Helen takes a bite, still perched on Odysseus's shoulders, and drops crumbs into his hair. If someone had told me beforehand that I would find my husband sexy because he lets our daughter drop cookie crumbs in his hair, I would not have believed them.

We leave the aquarium and sit at a table in the courtyard to eat our lunch. After we eat, the children become sleepy and contented. We have seen enough fish for one day. We drive back over the Bay Bridge to Berkeley.

Helen wakes up as we pull into the driveway. Odysseus takes Max out of his car seat. I stop at the mailbox at the bottom of the steps. Glancing through the letters, my heart stops. A letter from Greece. I recognize the return address. Odysseus's parents. It must be bad news. What else can it be? They never write.

I hear Odysseus in the living room talking to Helen. "I guess we can't have tuna sandwiches for dinner after visiting the fish."

Helen giggles. "Oh Daddy," she brushes him off.

"Bah," Max shouts. "Bah bah." He sees his ball.

I don't want to break the magic spell of their delight by handing this letter to Odysseus. Our delight. Fate crouches in this envelope. I smell it.

"My father," he mutters, as his eyes race over the words.

"Is he dead?"

"No."

All these years they want nothing to do with their son, stewing in their disapproval. Yet they know where to find him. He still belongs to them. Was he ever mine?

I go into the kitchen to unpack the backpack. He follows me in when he has finished reading.

"The government has arrested my father."

"What did he do?"

"Nothing. They fabricated a charge because of his political views. My mother is beside herself with terror. She begs me to return to Athens."

"Now that she needs something from you, she deigns to communicate?" I ask, one hand on my hip. In the living room, I hear Max shouting, "bah, bah!"

Odysseus sighs, runs his hand through his hair. He throws me a pleading look. "Please don't be like that."

"Can we afford to go to Athens?"

He shakes his head. I know what this means. He will go to Athens and I will not. He crushes me in his arms. I can hear his heart beating wildly. "Greece is dangerous right now. It isn't safe for you to go. Besides, the children…"

"If it's dangerous," I whisper into his chest, "then you shouldn't go either."

He holds me until his heart calms to a more regular rhythm. "I don't want to go."

"Then stay."

"I can't. They are my parents. My family."

"Your family is here."

"It will only be for a week, maybe two. Until I can sort out what has happened with my father. I have to get him out of jail. He might have to agree to sign a statement, to swallow his pride. My mother can't make him do that."

"And you think you can?"

"I think I have to try." He tips my face to his, kisses me long and hard. "I will return before you can even miss me."

"I doubt it. I already miss you."

"Daddy, Max is eating your wallet," Helen calls from the other room with glee.

"Max is eating your wallet," I echo.

Odysseus squeezes my shoulder and goes to rescue his wallet from Max.

He takes an emergency family leave from work. He explains our finances to me so I can pay the bills while he's gone. I'm terrified. He says I will be fine. I have no experience at managing money. I have never had two nickels to rub together. We drive to the airport in the vintage Chevy with our babies in the back seat.

"Just drop me off. Don't come to the gate."

Crying, I slide behind the steering wheel. He grabs his bag from the trunk.

He leans into the back seat and hugs the children. "Take care of Mommy," he tells Helen. "Make sure she eats her vegetables."

"OK," Helen promises.

I get out of the car. I need to hold him close for one more second. He crushes me to him, kissing me deeply and desperately with the whir of airplanes whining overhead.

"I love you Penelope, more than anything," he whispers. "I carry you here wherever I go." He touches his chest with two fingers as he walks backward away from me into the terminal.

He melts like a dream.

Helen will remember almost nothing about him. Max will remember nothing.

I remember everything. The taste of his sweat, his scent, his voice, his laugh, his touch.

The day after Odysseus leaves, I send him one of Helen's drawings. I send it to his parents' address in Athens, the one on the envelope for the letter he received with the news about his father. I imagine I might not get a letter from him before he returns since international mail takes a long time. I start a letter to him and write a little bit each night. I mostly tell him about the children. After a week I have not heard from him and I mail my letter about the children. Perhaps he will come home before my letter arrives and I imagine his mother opening it and reading about the grandchildren whose existence she denies. Will my news soften her heart?

Two weeks go by and I hear nothing from Odysseus. I work hard to hide my anxiety from the children. They chirp and play and thrive in their routine. They do not seem to miss their father much, although Helen speaks of him occasionally. I show Max his picture.

Three weeks and two days. Helen's drawing comes back in the mail unopened. The post office has stamped on it "return to sender." I have no way to reach my husband other than this address that does not work. Then my first letter to him comes back. On the envelope it says "no such person." As if I could have imagined my husband, the father of my children.

I send a letter, a note, or a card every day. Everything I send comes back marked "no such person." I'm afraid to tell anyone what is happening to me. Odysseus's boss calls and I say that Odysseus's father is dying in Greece. He calls again, concerned. The next week he calls and I can tell he no longer believes me. Why should he? I am lying. He stops calling. He sends a severance note with a check for Odysseus's accrued vacation time.

Four months have passed. The things I held as true have vanished.

"Mommy," Helen calls, "Mommy, get up and make toast."

I can't get out of the beautiful bed that Odysseus built for us. The children are hungry and I lie in bed crying. I can't get up. I can't support my children. What will happen to us?

Helen comes into the room. I wipe my eyes.

"Does your tummy hurt?" Helen asks.

"No, I'm just tired."

"We want toast. Max has a messy diaper."

I have to keep moving. I have to figure this out. I have children to care for and our money will soon run out. My money. "We" no longer exists. How could he do this?

I sell the vintage Chevy.

I have a garage sale.

I can't afford to rent a whole house. I move to a studio apartment in Oakland where the children and I sleep together in one bed. I take a few of my bean plants with me in a pot to die on my sunless windowsill.

How can I support my babies? What am I qualified to do? If I get a job, who will watch Helen and Max? They are so little. I don't think I can find a job that pays enough for me to hire someone to watch them while I work. I lie in bed at night, thinking of these things, unable to sleep, longing for the comfort and security of his embrace.

"Where are we going?" Helen asks on the bus.

"To see our Aunt Beth," I tell her.

Her eyes grow wide. "Aunt Beth?" She turns the words over in her mouth. "Aunt Beth," she mutters to herself.

My feet find the way to the apartment by themselves.

It is changed. The door is painted green. The buzzer works.

A blonde woman about my own age opens the door. Her mouth forms a question mark.

"My aunt used to live here," I mumble. I do not say that I grew up here.

"How long ago?"

"I have not seen her in a few years."

"I've only been here since January. Try asking Ruby downstairs in number one. She manages the building."

I trudge downstairs and knock on number one, which has no buzzer. Ruby has a gray ponytail and a light mustache on her upper lip. I don't recognize her.

"My Aunt Beth used to stay in number five. A few years ago. I wonder, I mean, do you know where she might have gone?"

"Last I heard, the landlord had the police clear her out of that apartment. She went crazy," Gray Ponytail tells me. "She holed up in there. It got to smell bad. The landlord wanted her out. They took her up to the psych unit at Harbor Hospital, I think. Last I heard they moved her up North somewhere. Napa or something."

"What about her things?" It has been years. Of course there are no things. Why do I ask?

"The landlord had to have the place cleaned out and I suppose he disposed of her things. Do you want the landlord's number?"

"That's OK." I shift Max on my hip. I turn to go.

"She got sick," the lady tells me, gently. "They took her someplace safe where she would get help."

I nod, mutely. Doesn't this stuff run in families? Am I going crazy too? Is that what's happening to me? I can't afford to go crazy. I have children and no one to take care of them if. If.

Oakland, 1970

"Where is your husband?" The lady at the welfare office asks me.

"I don't know," I say, barely able to drag the words out of myself. You don't understand. He loves me. I'm not like these other women here. We had a good marriage. I can't fathom why he disappeared. Something happened. I was not betrayed like these other women. I'm different. I'm special. I'm loved.

I'm a single mother with no education, no skills, no resources.

"Fill out this paperwork and bring it back on Thursday at eight in the morning. Go to Window B. Don't come late. The caseworker will get you started. If you have trouble with the papers, the caseworker will help you on Thursday."

On Wednesday Max screams and cries and clutches his ear. I call our pediatrician in Berkeley, who won't see us because we don't have the right health insurance anymore. I go to the emergency room at Highland Hospital. By the time I get the children packed up and onto the bus, it's getting dark. We're tired. Max has a fever.

"Can't we stay home and sing to Max?" Helen begs.

Max whimpers.

"He has an ear infection and he needs medicine so we have to take him to the doctor. Singing won't help tonight."

The minute we walk in the door, I know I'm in deep trouble.

Emergency room workers carry young men covered in blood past us on stretchers. Max hollers, trapped in his pain, and doesn't notice the evidence of violence surrounding us. Helen hides behind my leg and sucks her fingers, trembling uncontrollably. I can't pick her up because I'm trying to comfort Max. All three of us sob as we watch the inhumanity afoot in the world displayed in front of us.

A nurse notices that I stand in the middle of Armageddon with two small children and says kindly, "Come with me." I follow her numbly, practically dragging Helen, who has perhaps gone into shock. The nurse takes us to a little room with a bed and a chair. "I'm so sorry. There was a shoot-out downtown and we're up to our ears in it. That lobby is no place for these little ones. I'll have someone get to you as soon as possible, but it might take a while. Make yourself at home."

Make myself at home?

Helen cries herself to sleep on the bed. A nurse gives Max Tylenol, which helps. I walk back and forth in the room with him. He will not sleep. He moans feebly from time to time.

When the doctor finally sees us, he prescribes an antibiotic for Max. He gives me a sample of the antibiotic to tide me over until the pharmacy opens the next day. We take a taxi home. I can't afford it, but I'm exhausted and the buses are barely running this late.

I have to appear at the welfare office in a few hours.

Helen is a wreck. She is so sensitive to people's feelings that she picked up every bad emotion in that emergency room and absorbed it. She swims through a nightmare of fatigue and trauma. Blessedly, Max sleeps while I sit up and rock Helen. We sing a little.

I arrive at the welfare office for my appointment with a sick, drugged toddler and Helen, who behaves like she is auditioning for the leading role in a horror film about a child possessed by the devil.

The caseworker at Window B takes my paperwork. "Wait here," she tells me.

Does she think I will leave?

She reappears shortly and takes us to a little office. We trudge in and collapse into plastic molded chairs.

The caseworker from Window B lectures me, hand on hip. "If you would think twice about having these babies when you have no way to support them, you wouldn't be in this situation. A little planning. A little restraint." She tosses her head. "Next time, use birth control."

There won't be a next time, I think, biting my lip to keep from crying. Helen spits at the woman. She has never behaved so badly. I am as shocked as the woman, who looks at us as if she just scraped us off the bottom of her shoe. She shuts the door with a snap and leaves us alone. I want to run away.

Helen takes off her shoes. Max's nose runs like a spout.

Our social worker, Betsy, enters the room. Crisp and compassionate, she gives Helen and Max lollipops as green as traffic lights. I persuade Helen to put her shoes back on.

I tell my story. Again. My husband left me. He went to Greece. No I can't trace him. I don't have any way to find him.

Betsy sets me up to receive weekly payments. She says we qualify for food stamps and helps me obtain them. She tells me about a food pantry that will help. She can get me into a program for health care for the children. She hands me a Kleenex because I am crying with relief at her kindness.

Oakland, 1971

How do things get so complicated? So difficult? People just want a clean, comfortable life that affords them time to delight in those they love. Nothing extravagant. Just a chance to live decently and if they have children then to be able to raise them in health and happiness. To learn a little about the extraordinary world around us and to share food and music with friends and family. To belong to a community. To make love with passion rather than desperation. To take pride in their work. To have people who will comfort them in hard times and who will celebrate milestones and achievements with them. And when they get old they want to sit on the porch in a rocking chair and look at the stars in the clear night sky and say "yup." To lie down when they get tired and to not have to work anymore at the end. To know that someone will remember them when they're gone, that people will say their name and tell some of their stories once in a while and think about who they were and put their picture on the wall.

Self-pity tastes like metal.

I lie in bed and taste metal.

The rose-fingered dawn lights the East.

I see Odysseus in silhouette against the shattering morning sun blasting through the window. Of course I know it can't be Odysseus, even as I think I gaze at his image. The loss cuts through me again, as fresh as if brand new. No sleight of hand nor slant of sun can ease his body into my embrace. I long for the length of his thighs, his solid chest, the comfort of his arms, to ignite the fire of my opening to him, petals turned outward by his heat. His image recedes. Only the brilliant sun remains. And my longing. I wish I could go through an entire day and not think about Odysseus at all. Not once.

I can't seem to get myself out of bed. I keep telling myself that I'll get up in just a minute. Just one more minute. I hear Helen in the kitchen. She climbs on a chair to reach the cupboard and takes down crackers. I hear her giving some to her brother.

My children have lost their luster.

Every night my body cries out for his touch.

My sleep is half-sleep.

My mind fills with cotton. It fills with voices. My mind has a mind of its own. I am Aunt Beth. I am losing my mind.

"We want to go to the liberry," Helen demands. "Take us to the liberry."

She remembers that the library has air conditioning. My Helen is such a smart child. Our apartment is hot and she knows where to go to cool off. What a waste to give such a smart child to a half-wit like me. Who thought of this arrangement?

"Put your shoes on and take us to the liberry," Helen tells me.

I can do this for her. I put on clothes, feed the children cereal, and walk with them to the library.

Helen and Max look at picture books in the children's room. They are cool and content.

I wander into the reference section.

"Can I help you find something?" a cheerful librarian asks.

I shake my head negative.

When did I last speak to someone other than Helen and Max?

I pull down an atlas with maps of California and I look up Hoepper's Knee and B'Taka Lake. Just for the heck of it. I have a wild hair. I wonder if these places exist. Aunt Beth and my mother told stories. I have never looked for these places on a map before.

In Mirror County, I see these names in black and white.

I am dropping through the Twilight Zone.

These places in my crazy aunt's stories, in my mother's bizarre stories, actually appear on the map. Aunt Beth and Mom didn't just make them up out of their imagination.

What is real? What is not real?

Did my mother grow up in the arms of a bear? B'Taka Lake she called it. I see it here on a map. According to this map, in the reference room at the library, a place named Hoepper's Knee exists in Mirror County.

I am lost and maybe someone at Hoepper's Knee can find me. I am becoming invisible and maybe someone at B'Taka Lake will see me.

Maybe, like my mother whispered, like Aunt Beth said, maybe the bear will embrace me in its arms.

I take what I can carry.

I pack crackers and juice for the children.

These children are all I have left.

Nothing else matters.

We board a bus. I and my precious children. Helen clutches her stuffed bear with the bright, brown button eyes. Max wears his favorite pajamas with red trains on them. Their eyes glisten with anticipation. They love this adventure, this change, the promise of something better than what we have had. I feel ashamed for making them unhappy for so long.

We ride to Mirror County, to Hoepper's Knee, where we leave the bus and walk onto the Kapa Reservation. A sign says "Tribal Office." I push open the screen door and step inside. I sense that my children are safe here and so I give myself permission to sit down and weep, to break apart with grief for the life I promised myself and the promise I have lost.

Book 4: Penelope
The Plains Clinic, Mirror County, 1971

D r. Esther gave me a journal. It smells of fresh paper. The cover is one stroke of deep-blue shy of the color of the night sky just before the sun disappears at the end of a clear day. I don't want to defile the pristine beauty of the journal with the ugly words that spell my story. I trust Dr. Esther to help me get well so I can return to my children. I can't speak my story but perhaps I can write it. I must sacrifice the beauty of the journal to fill it with the ugliness of my past. I write to save my life.

Oakland, 1953

My sister Carla used to be plump like a brown berry. Now she is thin. Something happened and I don't understand.

Last night our father was in Carla's bed. When I called her name, he told me to mind my own business and he left the room. Carla cried. I asked if she was OK. She told me to go to sleep. At first I couldn't. Then I did.

In the morning I dress quietly. I don't want to wake Carla. I tiptoe past my mother who snores loudly on the couch with her mouth wide open. I want to push her mouth shut.

In the kitchen Sammy eats a bowl of Wheaties. The breakfast of champions. Today is his cartoon day and he can't watch because of Mom sleeping in the living room.

"Why can't she sleep off her damn hangover in her bed?" he grumbles.

I don't remind him not to say "damn" because he is six years older than I am and strong, so I don't want to make him mad.

If I tell Sammy that our father hurt Carla in her bed, will he understand what it means? Will he know what to do?

I pour myself a bowl of Wheaties. I pull out my father's chair at the head of the table and sit down in it, tracing the curve of the armrests with my fingers.

Sammy fiercely shovels Wheaties into his mouth. Between gulps he warns, "Dad will kill you if he finds you in his chair."

"He won't find me and if you tell, I'll tell that you said 'damn'."

I decide not to say anything to Sammy about last night. I am six years old and I have no idea what on earth to do about this situation.

My mother sleeps until noon. She wakes up in a nasty mood. She and Dad yell at each other in the bedroom with the door closed. Sammy says that's how they make a decision. I don't like decisions.

I go to the park. I swing on the swing. I have a stomach ache. I lie down in the sandbox and fall asleep. A lady with a dog wakes me up. "Little girl, are you OK?" she asks. The dog sniffs my sneakers. Sand sticks to my cheek. "I'm OK," I tell the lady with the dog. It's a nice dog; black with a purple tongue. The lady tells me to go home.

Carla smiles when she sees me and asks if I'm hungry. My stomach ache has gone away so I tell her yes. No one else is in the house. She makes hot dogs and macaroni and cheese out of a box. We are still sitting at the table when Dad comes in.

"Your mother and I have made a decision. Penny is going to stay with Aunt Beth for the summer."

"I don't want to," I blurt.

My father says, "Of course you want to. She lives in a better neighborhood than ours and you can go to summer camp over there at the museum."

"I want Carla to come with me."

"Carla has to stay here to help your mother. You're the lucky one who gets to go. Now pack your things."

Carla folds her hands precisely in her lap and gazes straight down at them. Her hair hides her face, like a curtain. A tear drips off her nose onto her skirt.

I am the lucky one.

I stand at the curb with my suitcase as it grows dark. My sister hangs on my neck and we sob, clinging to each other as if drowning. My father is angry. I wish that I said a better good-bye to Carla. I wish that I said a better good-bye to everything before I left my family at the curb on that evening.

Aunt Beth won't tell me how my sister died. "You ain't old enough," she says whenever I ask.

Oakland, 1957

"You can't wear that dress," Aunt Beth tells me.

"Why not?"

"It's a party dress, Penny. This is not a party."

I am wearing my yellow dress with the ruffles at the sleeves. It's my favorite dress. It's a happy dress. That's why I have put it on to visit my brother in juvie. I have not seen him in a couple of months. Not since he and Cousin Jessie stole a car and robbed a store.

"I want to look pretty," I explain, pouting. Pretty is not the right word. I want Sammy to look at me in my bright yellow dress and cheer up. I want the image of me in my dress to change his life.

"I know." Aunt Beth lights a cigarette. "Listen, the boys won't notice how you look. They'll just be happy to see you. But the people who work there will notice how you look and it's not a good idea to wear something that fancy. See what I'm wearing? Not fancy. You don't want anyone noticing you."

"What should I wear?"

"How about your gray skirt?"

No one will notice me in my gray skirt. That's for sure.

I go to my room to change. I have a picture of Carla taped to my mirror. I tell Carla, "I can't wear my party dress, but we baked him cookies. Don't worry. He'll be OK."

Aunt Beth and I take cookies to Sammy and Jessie in juvie.

We sit in a room at a long table. Other people sit at other tables, visiting with their brothers in juvie. A prison guard brings Sammy and Jessie. They wear orange jumpsuits. They sit across the table from us.

"I made you chocolate chip cookies," I say.

Jessie grunts. Sammy smiles at me and says "thanks." When he reaches for a cookie, I see a little black bear on the back of his hand.

"You have a bear on your hand."

"Yup. They got a guy comes down and does tattoos. It's a special program. I was good so they let me get a tattoo."

"Did you get a tattoo?" Aunt Beth asks her son Jessie.

Jessie grins. "Nah, I didn't make the program." He looks at Sammy and they laugh. "I'll get one when I get out if I want one."

"These are great cookies," Sammy compliments me. "How you doin' in school, still a little Einstein?"

I look down at my hands, embarrassed. I'm the good sheep, he's the bad sheep. Carla is the dead sheep. Aunt Beth answers for me, "She does very well in school."

"I don't know how you can stand it," Sammy says. "Boring."

Aunt Beth opens her mouth to say something and changes her mind. She snaps her mouth shut.

"You got a smoke?" Jessie asks his mother. She produces a pack of cigarettes and they each take one and light up.

"When we get out of here, we're gonna work for this guy named Bull," Jessie informs Aunt Beth.

"He has his own business," Sammy adds.

"What about school?" Aunt Beth asks.

"Boring," Sammy tells her.

"We don't get along too good with school," Jessie says.

Aunt Beth nods. She takes a big drag on her cigarette. "You think quitting school is such a hot idea?" she asks them. Jessie shrugs. Sammy looks off out the window. Aunt Beth sighs. "Well you obviously ain't gonna listen to me no-how. What kind of business does Bull do?"

"Insurance," Jessie answers.

"We can make a lot of money if we play our cards right," Sammy comments with an outstanding lack of enthusiasm. He takes another cookie and chews it thoughtfully. "Great cookies, Penny."

I told Carla I thought Sammy will be OK, but actually I don't think he will be OK. I just don't want Carla to worry.

Oakland, 1964

I look at the envelope from U.C.-Berkeley, my first-choice school. San Francisco State and San Jose State already sent acceptance letters, so one way or another, I'm going to college. But I desperately want this one, and I have worked extremely hard for it.

The letter leans against the wire napkin holder on the kitchen table. Aunt Beth sits beside an ashtray overflowing with the stubs of smoked cigarettes. She stares at the unopened letter and then glances at me expectantly.

I put down my bag and shrug out of my jacket. My throat goes dry.

I pick up the letter. It feels weightless. Like a feather.

Aunt Beth has rolled her hair up in sponge rollers and she wears her fraying powder-blue housecoat. The kitchen reeks of cigarettes. I hate that smell, which has clung to my clothing for years. I can't wait to move out.

I sit across from this virtually illiterate woman who raised me when my family blew apart, who raised me in the absence of other options, and I open the letter and read my acceptance.

"I'm in."

She starts to cry. I wonder if she is rejoicing because one of us has the chance to get out alive or grieving because I'm leaving. Jessie is dead. Sammy is back in jail. When I go, she will have nothing left.

Mirror County, 1971

"You have a talent for writing," Dr. Esther says as she returns my journal to me.

"I wanted to be a writer once. I was studying English in college."

"Did it help to write things down?"

I nod affirmative. She waits patiently, unperturbed by my silence.

"I took some of it out of me and put it in the journal."

"And that made you feel better?"

I nod affirmative.

I wonder how she does this for a living; this listening to the tragedies of people who, like me, have families that don't work, that fell apart, that kept terrible secrets and did terrible things. The fall-out from our disastrous families floats down and lands in the plastic chairs in the group therapy room at the Plains Clinic and Dr. Esther cleans it up.

"Where are you?" Dr. Esther asks. "What's going on in there?" She points at my head.

"I'm wondering how you do it."

"Do what?"

"Spend your days listening to the stories of people like me who come from families that are one cog shy of a rusted outboard motor left on the side of the road when it comes to functionality."

Her blonde hair is wrapped in a neat twist. Her face is clear, with no make-up. "I like to help people change their lives."

"How can you stand to hear the stories, though?"

"That's not my favorite part of the job," she confesses. "But I listen to people who have to tell it to someone."

"What's your favorite part of the job?"

"Seeing people recover. I'm sorry you have suffered what you have suffered. You didn't do anything to deserve it. You will probably never find out why your husband abandoned you. If you wish, you can make a perfectly fine life without him for yourself and your children. I would like to help you figure out how to do that."

I nod.

"What else can you tell me about your family and where you grew up?"

"I was raised by my aunt."

"What about your mother?"

What to say?

Dr. Esther waits. "Your father?" she asks after a minute.

Even less to say.

"Talk to me."

I look Dr. Esther in the eye. "My father killed my older sister and they sent him to jail for it. I have not seen him since I was a little girl. I don't know how he killed…" I falter. Why can't I speak her name? Dr. Esther waits. I continue. "Carla. My sister Carla." There, I have spoken her. "They wouldn't tell me how…" I take a deep breath. "My mother was an alcoholic and she died of breast cancer the year after we lost Carla. I have one older brother named Sammy. I have not seen him in a long time. He could be in jail or dead. Maybe I'm the only one left. My mother's sister, Aunt Beth, raised me. She had one son. Gangbangers gunned him down in the street. I heard she went crazy. I don't know where she is."

I expect Dr. Esther to register shock and horror at this account. Her face remains neutral. I want her to understand what losing Odysseus means. I want her to pity me the way I pity myself. "I didn't have a family while growing up, and yet I always thought I had the capacity to make that family. A functioning, normal, happy family. That happy family doesn't work without Odysseus. He knew this about me and he left me."

Dr. Esther hands me a box of Kleenex.

She says nothing while I cry.

When I have calmed down, Dr. Esther prompts, "Tell me about Carla. If you could have a conversation with Carla, what would you tell her?"

I laugh.

"What's so funny?"

"Carla is the only one I talk to."

"That's good," Dr. Esther approves.

"Good that I talk to a dead person?"

"She is obviously not entirely dead for you."

That's true. And it's OK for it to be true. I have never thought of that.

"What is the most important thing that you want to say to Carla today?"

The chatter in my head falls silent. How did Dr. Esther think of this question?

"I want to…" My voice cracks. Dr. Esther waits. The words pour out of me. "I want to ask Carla to forgive me for leaving her in that house to die with my father. To forgive me for being the lucky one who survived. I want Carla to forgive me for making such a mess of things. For surviving and subsequently wasting my life when she didn't even have the chance I had."

"Penelope." Dr. Esther leans forward in her chair, as if sharing a secret with me. "You are twenty-four years old. You are not old enough to have wasted your life. You have two beautiful children to raise. You have not made a mess of anything. What happened to Carla was not your fault and you don't owe her anything. You were one of the positive things in her life. She wouldn't be disappointed in you at all."

The tears freeze in my eyes. Dr. Esther's words strike like lightning.

"Penelope?"

"You're right. I can do it myself."

Dr. Esther looks both puzzled and pleased. "You can do what yourself?"

"All of it. I don't need Odysseus. I can do it myself."

"Yes, you can."

"I just wish it wasn't so hard."

"I do too."

Our session ends. Dr. Esther walks to the door as I stand, turn, and open my mouth. Nothing comes out. I have lost language. Like a guppy gasping for water with the air all around suffocating me, my mouth opens and closes. Somewhere deep inside myself I have lost an entire language that could have precisely taken the shape of my thoughts and instead I must speak an alien tongue merely to communicate. Dr. Esther leaves the door closed, she steps lightly to me and wraps me in her arms and holds me. I cling to her, my heart beating wildly. She holds me until I can collect the shattered pieces of myself into one bundle and step out of the room.

I am finding my way back. I have good days and bad days, good hours and bad hours, good minutes and bad minutes. It gets better little by little. I feel less and less overwhelmed. Soon I will return to my children in the world outside. This both scares me and comforts me.

I call the children three or four times a week now. I only call when I feel OK. I picture my children's upturned faces. Open. Like exquisite flowers.

My journal saves my life.

When I imagine the future, I imagine writing. I imagine my brain becoming so full of wonderful shapes and ideas that they spill over and pour out of me. Dr. Esther says I have the ability to reinvent myself. At her suggestion, I draw a map of my future. On a corner of the map I make a star and inside the star it says, "I will keep Carla's spirit alive." Thinking about that star fills me with peace.

I recognize myself in new women arriving at the clinic, with their eyes full of self-pity and their sense of worthlessness, incompetence, and resignation. They think they can't change things.

I continue to grieve for my losses, while at the same time moving beyond them. I feel my perspective changing.

Esther asks me if I feel stronger. I don't want to say that I do for fear she will tell me I can leave and I don't want to say that I don't because she might think she hasn't helped me. Truthfully, she does her job extraordinarily well.

I love to walk on the paths in the enormous garden at the clinic. I walk and walk and walk among the flowers and trees and I think about Max and Helen. I check books out of the clinic library and read. I read poetry.

"I have hope for the future again and that makes me sad," I tell Dr. Esther.

"How's that?"

"My hopefulness is the first step away from this place, away from you." A tremor creeps into my voice.

Dr. Esther smiles. "Trust me, you won't think about me much after you leave. Right now it might seem like you will, but you won't. We can stay in touch if you like. This is not another abandonment," she assures me.

"Abandonment," I repeat after her.

She says nothing. I love the way she gives me space to gather my thoughts in a conversation. She doesn't jump in and speak right away.

"The hardest thing about his abandonment was that it completely blindsided me," I tell her. "I didn't have the smallest, slightest clue that anything was wrong or that he might not return. If you had known our relationship from the inside, like only he or I could, you would understand my shock and bewilderment when I never heard from him again. I couldn't bear it. After the intimacy we shared. His disappearance altered everything that had gone before. It negated my one true and perfect relationship. I wonder if I experienced a single authentic moment with Odysseus. How long had he been planning to leave me? He poisoned our marriage. I can't look at any of it in the same way now."

Dr. Esther did her job; she helped me heal. My husband abandoned me and that's a shame and now I have to get on with my life. I grew up in a dysfunctional family. Bad things happened that I could not control. Carla's death was not my fault. I fully understand, in my heart, that I could not change what transpired or save Carla. I play this tape in my head. I had no control over these situations. This is not rationalization, this is the truth. The adults in my family should have saved Carla. Oh, Carla, I'm sorry I was so young. Just a child. Powerless. Our parents failed us. I will not fail my children. I will break the pattern. I have internalized Dr. Esther. I listen to my inner doctor's voice. I am ready to face life outside in the world.

I know there is more to the story of my family and I dread finding it out. Athena knows and certainly she will tell me if I ask. What horror lurks in the missing pieces? I fear the truth and at the same time accept that I must ask Athena to tell me exactly how my sister died, who my family is, and my relationship to this Tribe that is obviously more than a fairy story made up by my mother and my batty Aunt Beth. I must leave the Plains Clinic and uncover the truth.

Book 5: Penelope
Hoepper's Knee Reservation, 1972

The shadows lengthen as the afternoon sails for the horizon. I sit on a bench and wait. I hear Athena's truck before I see it, coming down the driveway, a rusted-out tin can wending its way between the precisely manicured lawns of the Plains Clinic.

Athena does not embrace me the way women often do in greeting. She nods her head slightly in my direction. "Do we have to do anything? Sign you out or something?"

"I can just go." I turn for one last look at the clinic before I climb into the truck.

"How are my children?" I ask, eager for any shred of news.

"Can't wait to see you. Helen has surprises for you. Things she made at school to show you. Things she made at home when she missed you. She learned how to read." My Helen learned to read without me. Will I recognize her?

"I enrolled Max in Head Start. He started growing a braid, a small one at the back, like Nelson's. Make sure to notice and say something about it. Nelson wants to teach him the bear dance. He likes dancing and has good coordination; very athletic, that one."

"I know," I murmur. He got that from his father. I remember the muscularity of Odysseus's athletic body; how he loved to play soccer.

Athena gives me comfortable silence the way Esther gave it to me. A place for me to sit and listen to my inner voices, collect my thoughts, and prepare for the words that follow.

"The past can't be changed," Athena says, her eyes on the road ahead. "Let it go."

"It *can* be changed," I disagree. "The present can falsify the past or alter its appearance or make it disappear entirely. The present redefines the past." His abandonment changed my perception of our marriage. Athena glances sideways at me sharply. She mutters something under her breath in a language I do not know.

"What words did you say?"

"Xa-pa-na-ka words. I said that the present has invisible-ized our people's past."

"Invisible-ized?"

"English has no word for it. What you describe. Our experience was erased from history. Our truths invisible-ized. They don't teach our history to children at school. We must prove to our children that it happened. Otherwise it will vanish." She has interpreted my words about redefining the past through the lens of her personal framework.

"If a tree falls in the woods, and no one hears it, does it make a sound?" I ask her an old philosophy question I remember from college.

"It makes a sound," Athena declares definitively.

"How do you know? No one hears it. It's as if it didn't happen."

"Just because it occurs outside human consciousness? Ridiculous. You speak as one ignorant of spirit."

"Perhaps I am."

"You have no idea who you are, do you?" she asks; not an accusation, simply a question.

Does she mean literally or figuratively? I guess it doesn't matter. I do feel ignorant beside Athena because she is as old as snow. "Then tell me." I don't want to hear her answer and at the same time I want to hear more than anything.

"You have the blood of a Native chieftess in your veins mixed with the blood of an Anglo rapist. In 1879, your great-grandmother was raped by John Hoepper, a white invader who bought a ranch up north of Hoepper's Knee. She had his baby. Could hardly tell it was half white. I knew that baby when she grew up. She was your grandmother, who married a man from a neighboring Tribe and they had two children: your Aunt Beth and your mother."

Athena speaks in that flat intonation of hers that at first sounds like a monotone. Deceptive. Sounds flat yet deeper meanings lick at the edges of each word in the hints of inflection. She gingerly wades into the English language as if it is impossible to force any real meaning out of these words, but in the absence of a native tongue it must suffice. Aunt Beth talked like that sometimes.

Athena continues, "In those days the B-I-A, you know, Bureau of Indian Affairs, took indigenous children from their families and placed them in boarding schools where they forced them to abandon their 'Indian ways'. They called it 'acculturation'. The BIA took your mother and your Aunt Beth to such a boarding school. After they came out, they moved to the city. The boarding school beat their identity out of them. We didn't see them for a few years. Your mother came home to the Tribe to give birth to Carla because she had nowhere else to go after the daddy was killed."

"Carla was my half-sister?"

"They didn't tell you?"

"We had different daddies?"

Athena pats my knee with her gnarled hand. "I thought you knew that at least. Carla's father was shot by the police. Nowadays, they'd call it racial profiling or some such fancy name for blatant cowboys-and-Indians garbage. Wrong place, wrong time, wrong color."

"I never knew about Carla or her father. I wonder if she knew. If she did, she kept it from me. I was a little girl when Carla died."

"Your mother stayed for a few months after she had Carla, then she went back down to Oakland. We didn't hear much from her after that. She met your father, had your brother, Sam I guess, right?" Athena asks, one eyebrow raised.

"Yeah," I grunt. "Sammy. Locked him in jail and threw away the key. You won't ever see him up here."

Athena nods, does not pass judgment, continues, "Then she had you."

"Where is my mother buried?" I ask shakily.

"Cremated. Beth brought the ashes up here to B'Taka Lake to spread them on the water. Same for Carla. We spread her ashes on the lake when she passed."

"What happened to my sister?"

She hesitates, glances at me quickly before turning her attention back to the road, "Your father killed her."

"Yes, but how?"

"You sure you want to know?"

"I need to know."

The dark gathers, preparing to pounce on the highway. Streamers of rose, orange, and pale-blue shoot through the sky, streaked with thin lines of cloud. The amber sunset bounces off Athena's face, makes it glow gold.

"What did he do to her?"

I can see a weight drop to her shoulders. She does not want to participate in this telling, yet it has come down to her to do it and she cannot walk away. It's not easy for the one who must tell the story.

"That man was damaged. He had no love left in him. He had sex with your sister." She stops there, gathering her strength to tell the rest of it.

"He raped Carla, you mean."

A tear runs down Athena's cheek and she ignores it. She continues, speaking quietly; as if she makes this terrible event happen again by telling about it. "One night." She swallows hard. I imagine she might choke on the words. "He sodomized her. He was a man. She was a child. She bled to death."

Carla, my Carla. I weep.

Now that Athena has voiced the worst of it, the words seem to tumble out of her more easily. "Anyone could see what happened, but they bungled the investigation and didn't produce the right evidence to convict him at first. Then your mother testified. It was the one thing your mother did for that child. The district attorney wanted to send him to the chair. The media turned it into one of those sensational stories fit only for the tabloids." Athena looks into the distance at the horizon, then at the road unraveling in front of the hood of her truck.

"Did they execute my father?"

"Nah. They were working on finding a way to do it. But a few of the other inmates got to him first. I guess even convicted criminals consider raping and murdering little girls immoral. He was killed in prison before the state could have the satisfaction of putting him to death at one of their media circuses."

Aunt Beth could not possibly have told me the truth. I see myself as a child, wondering what happened to my sister. I can't imagine how Aunt Beth might have framed it into words, explained such crimes to a little girl.

"Do you remember your mother?"

"A little. I remember her telling us stories; some of them about Hoepper's Knee. And I remember visiting her when she was dying. She didn't say much."

"She was broken. You probably remember that part. Broken before she met your father, else she wouldn't have took up with him in the first place. Well she produced you and there's the blessing in it."

I remember my mother strung out and drunk, asleep or in a stupor on the couch. "Did you ever meet Carla's father?"

"Once. He was Navajo. He had integrity. Your mother loved him. After the police killed him, your mother never recovered. She might as well have jumped into the fire with him because her spirit followed his to the other side." That explains the empty husk that was my mother.

"So Carla was practically all Indian, huh?" All except for that small streak of rapist blood from our distant past marring her pure berry-brown beauty.

"Yes. Practically all Native."

My children have Greek blood in their veins that comes down to them from the time of the gods and Native blood that comes down to them from the ancient before-time of the people at B'Taka Lake, the people Athena calls Xa-pa-na-ka.

"Is my Tribe Kapa or Xa-pa-na-ka?"

"Xa-pa-na-ka is one of the Kapa Tribes. The Anglo invaders couldn't tell one Tribe from another, they called all of us Kapa, all sixty-eight Tribes from the Mirror County region. We had different beliefs, different languages, looked different, but to them we were all Kapa. In the old language, the name of the Kapa Tribe of our family is Xa-pa-na-ka," Athena explains.

"Will you teach me who I am?"

Athena bites her bottom lip as she reaches over with her veined and spotted hand and covers my young hand where it lies on the seat. We say nothing. I am like a kidnapped child who grew up among strangers; my face looking out from milk cartons, begging someone to recognize me. Begging someone to point me toward home. Miraculously recognized and returned. Knowing nothing of my family, history, culture.

For a moment, I wish Athena and I were the same age. I imagine us raising our children as contemporaries and growing old at the same time. We would have been great old ladies together. Wrapped up in giant thick sweaters, drinking hot tea on the porch on a misty autumn morning. The steam rising from our mugs. I am momentarily heartbroken that Athena will die so many years before me. I was cheated. I did not have the chance to grow up before the warmth of her hearth, in the embrace of my true people, my true family. I was denied her presence. The U.S. government did this. Children ripped out by the roots. If a tree falls in the woods. I was not there to hear it when it fell, but I feel the shock waves.

"Why did you come to Hoepper's Knee?"

"The question is more like *how* did I come. I'm amazed I found it. When we were little, Mom told us stories about B'Taka Lake. She and Aunt Beth told stories. They told us one story about the she-bear who descended from the high mountains and settled down in the valley and slept until she turned into water. Something about the waking of the bear in the spring and putting the bear to sleep in the fall. Aunt Beth had a lot of bear stories. She talked about a place named Hoepper's Knee in Mirror County. I never thought it was real. I thought she made it up to put us to sleep at night. Fantasy stories. Stories you wish are true."

Athena speaks softly as if sharing a secret, "She told you the stories of her people that she remembered from her childhood. The stories outlawed at the boarding schools. Our children carried those stories in their hearts."

"Those stories brought me here. I went to the library one day and I looked at maps of the North Country. When I found B'Taka Lake on the map, and Hoepper's Knee, I couldn't believe my eyes. I had to see for my own self. I had to come here to fall apart." A hint of peace whispers in my soul. Perhaps one day, down a long road, everything will turn out all right.

"You followed the trail home to your Tribe and you found us."

If I had any more tears left in me I would cry for a day and a night with relief at her words. "Let me drive," I offer. She pulls over at the next exit and gives me the wheel. I drive. She sleeps.

I take some of Carla home to the Tribe with me. I am the lucky one. It is up to me to do something useful with my life for both of us. I am Carla's ambassador to the present. I will go home for my sister, whose ashes sleep in the lake. I will keep her private and close to the bone. My personal ghost, imaginary friend, guardian angel. To the world, she doesn't exist. Only a few elders at Hoepper's Knee remember that her ashes floated out over the lake. Her child-spirit drifts like a wispy cloud over B'Taka Lake. She rests in the arms of the bear.

It's almost night when we arrive. One thread shy of a dark blanket drops across the sky of an autumn evening. I can find my Tribe in the dark. I turn in on the unmarked road and drive head-on toward B'Taka Lake, returning to a place where I belong.

The headlights catch the Kapa Rancheria sign with the silhouette of the bear on it. We drive past the Round House and the tribal office and into the maze of broken-down trailers and patchwork modular homes stuck together with duct tape and plywood patches, old rugs, baling wire, and heavy-duty plastic. Yards full of drifts of junk that no one seems to want to part with or can't figure out how to dispose of. Strollers, car parts, broken toys, tools, kitchen appliances, furniture, wood, metal, plastic, pieces, parts, just plain rubbish, tin cans, paper, yards full of useless, broken junk. A place drowning in the broken, rusted, mangled everyday objects of its past.

Athena wakes, stretches, pats her straight gray hair back into its loose haphazard bun, held in with tortoise shell combs. She sits up straight. We turn at her driveway. Her yard differs from most of the others because there is no junk here. It is clean. The front porch light casts a bluish glow on the truck. The kitchen light spills from the doorway as we arrive. Someone waits for us.

When I open the door of the truck, the scent of Athena's herb garden rolls out to greet me, almost knocking me over. Dill, mint, rosemary, and the strong tang of geraniums. Aunt Beth had a window box with red geraniums. She grew dill too. She couldn't cook without it. Eggs, soup, baked potatoes.

Max races out the front door and onto the porch. He bounds across the few feet of grass that separates us and hurls his muscular little body into mine. I pick him up, his skinny arms wrap around my neck, and I swing him in a circle. He laughs and shouts and I can't keep from crying.

My cup is full of golden nectar. This glowing child is my very own son.

When I put him down and look at his face, I no longer see his father in him. He still resembles his father, but he is an individual person. At last I can look into that face and see my son. Max. Telemachus. I see the little braid starting at the base of his neck, already a couple inches long as it stands out from the rest of his hair, which is cut more closely to his head. I touch the braid and smile and he smiles because I noticed. He is his own self, no longer merely the shadow of his father. We are not destined to be our parents and grandparents over and over again in endless repetitions of the same patterns. We can make ourselves anew. Reinvent ourselves. Max is brand new. He is not his father. He is Kapa.

No-nonsense Athena takes my things out of the truck. I start to turn to help her when a figure on the porch catches my eye. Half in shadow, half a cascade of golden light. A figure in a bright yellow dress with tiny red flowers. I step toward her. Helen. A child with a woman's face. Her skin so smooth, her hair shiny as a raven's wing. Hair black with steely green and smoke-blue whispers threaded in it. Her bones perfect. Her fluid movements render all other creatures awkward. The perfect lift of her eyes at the edges causes my heart to constrict. This child has ever defied credulity with her beauty.

I walk up the three steps to the porch and she throws her arms around my waist. She is too big for me to pick her up, but I do it anyway and hold her tight against me. "It looks like you took care of your brother just fine," I say softly in her ear. "Thank you."

She leans away from me and cups my face in her hands, "Are you happier now?"

"Yes. I am much better. I won't go away again."

"It's OK." Her easy forgiveness stuns me. "We like it here with Athena and Daddy Nelson and Auntie June. Can we stay?"

"We can stay forever," I say, and in an instant, hit with this truth, I rejoice with the same joy my Helen has found in this place.

She wriggles down out of my arms. "I have pictures I made for you, come see." She takes my hand. The family I thought I ruined has sprung back whole and well.

Nelson steps out onto the porch. He is short, maybe only five-foot-six. He is broad-shouldered, stocky, and solid. A man you can rely on. His hair is black as obsidian with silver streaks in it and his eyes even blacker, like the deep galaxy darkness between the stars on a clear summer night in the countryside when you can see straight through the universe. He smiles with his whole face, unlike Athena, and his smile gives the impression that he contemplates mischief. He has such warmth about him. He gives me a welcoming bear-like hug. Helen watches us closely. "I'm Nelson," he says in a deep, chuckling voice as he lets me loose from his arms.

No wonder Helen wants to stay with him. Nelson is the daddy I always wanted. I envy Helen for having him. If I had found Nelson when I was Helen's age, things would have turned out vastly different. No would-have should-haves. Do what you can with what you've got. That's Dr. Esther's voice, my internal doctor. I couldn't have a daddy. I tried to give one to my children. That didn't work out either. They have discovered a daddy on their own.

"Lena and June made pumpkin cookies. Can you smell them? Come into the kitchen. They're the best, aren't they Lena?" Nelson winks at Helen, whom he calls Lena. Helen obviously loves it. She has turned into someone new in my absence. She tells me, "We used June's special secret recipe. She showed me the secret."

Athena and Max put my suitcase in a room set aside and made up just for me.

"Max was sleeping in here," Athena tells me, "and he moved in with Lena this morning so you can have this room to yourself." How can I thank this woman for taking in me and my children?

I ask Max, "How do you like school?"

"Great!" Max shouts. "You can visit. Lots of moms visit."

"They encourage parents to participate in the classrooms," Athena informs me.

"I'd like that."

We enter the kitchen and I meet June and we sit at the table and eat pumpkin cookies and drink milk. Max chatters nonstop. I don't remember him being this talkative. Helen shows me pictures she drew. The whole scene strikes me as surreal. I have stepped into a 1950s family TV show. The upbeat episode when mom comes home cured from the insane asylum. Except this family is brown with black hair and they have secret histories that belong in horror movies.

Nelson can see I am tired. He and June take their leave, with hugs and kisses for the children. After helping them brush their teeth, Athena shoos Max and Lena off to bed. I hate to let them go, even though I can barely keep my eyes open. I sit in Max's bed with him, Lena cozies down in a twin bed next to him. I read them a story. A stack of library books sways precariously on the table between the beds. We read part of *The Velveteen Rabbit*. Max's eyes close and he curls up next to me, drifting off. I slowly disentangle myself from him and go to Helen, whom I kiss on the forehead.

"My darling girl," I whisper. Nearly asleep, she smiles.

I count my blessings. One. Two. Tonight I will go to sleep. Tomorrow I will wake up and start all over again. And the next day I will start again. And the day after. Every day I will conquer my temptation to give up. Every day I will start again. For as long as I breathe.

I will help out in Max's classroom at Head Start. It is an opportunity for me to do something useful. But I need to get my life organized before I visit his school. At the welfare office, I spend hours filling out their papers and talking to a lady with pity in her eyes, just so I can get a little money to help Athena with household expenses. Next I go to the unemployment office and meet with a counselor. She wants to sign me up for a workshop about how to write a resume. Waste of time. I don't have anything to put on a resume. I return to Athena's house and unpack my few belongings.

Nelson offers me the use of a creaky Rambler station wagon that he owns. It's about one shot piston shy of junkyard fodder, but it runs, which is something in its favor. He promises to keep it working for me until I can afford something better. It will do for around town and I'm not going on a road trip anytime soon.

When I finally visit Max's preschool, I find the children making an ocean. They glue fish cut-outs to a giant piece of blue paper rolled out on the floor. Max hops from one foot to the other when he sees me. He takes my hand and gives me the tour, pointing and jabbering in his high-pitched little-boy voice. His teacher, Mrs. Anderson, acts like I'm the best mom in the world for showing my face at school. Her enthusiasm strikes me as exaggerated. Never mind, I like her. I crawl around on my hands and knees to help the children glue sequins to the ocean. They draw on the paper with crayons. I ask, "Do you want me to make an octopus for you?"

"Yes, yes!" They want an octopus.

I draw a simple octopus; one I think they can copy. My octopus multiplies under their eager fingers. We have an ocean full of octopuses, or is it octopi? I ask Mrs. Anderson and she looks it up in the dictionary. "Either one," she tells me and her students. Her eyes twinkle as she starts to sing "You say octopuses and I say octopi, you say tomayto and I say tomahto, you say potayto and I say potahto." We start to sing with her.

I draw a dolphin and everyone wants to draw dolphins. The spacious paper ocean has room for hundreds of sea creatures. We are having such fun that when Mrs. Filbert calls us for lunch we hate to stop. Mrs. Anderson lets us leave our project spread out on the floor until later. She says we'll eat lunch while it's hot and clean up our ocean project afterward. We sit at child-sized tables. Several other moms have turned up and a couple of them have toddlers and one has a baby. We sit together at the miniature tables and eat family-style, passing the food to each other. The children talk about the ocean while we eat and we talk about visiting the ocean and the beach. No wonder Max loves school. I don't want to find a job and go to work; I want to go to school with Max every day.

After lunch, the children help clean off the tables and some of them have special little chores, like wheeling the cart with the dirty dishes into the kitchen. As we finish up with lunch and prepare to put away our ocean, a lady appears in the classroom and introduces herself to me as a "family support specialist."

"So you're Max's mom," the family support specialist says. "Thank you for paying us a visit. I understand you are just getting back on your feet after a tough time."

What did she hear about me and from whom?

"I've started looking for a job. Unfortunately, I don't have any skills to recommend me," I confide, wryly. "I have no idea what I'll wind up doing."

"Do you like helping out in Max's class?" She twirls a strand of her hair thoughtfully.

"I love it. Did you see our ocean?"

"Yes, I did. It's marvelous. Come with me a minute." She leads me through a hallway and into an office. She removes the thumb tack from an announcement on a bulletin board and hands it to me. "We're hiring classroom assistants. You don't need special training, just have to like small children. Drop off a resume at this address by the end of the week. If you don't have a resume, just write a letter describing any experience or education you have that the personnel office should know about." She opens a drawer while she's talking and pulls out a pad with job applications on it. She tears a couple off and hands them to me. "You have to fill out one of these forms, too."

I thank her. I fantasize working in Max's classroom. Must stop that. I don't want to be disappointed. Well, what's wrong with hoping?

The family support specialist puts her hand on my arm reassuringly, "Listen, don't let the form intimidate you. Just fill it in the best you can. We always give preference to the parents of our children, so you have a foot in the door already on this one." I try not to cry.

"C'mon, you don't want to miss playground time. Mrs. Anderson is doing bubbles today." She winks at me and I follow her out.

Two weeks later, Head Start hires me as a classroom assistant in Max's classroom. I have the best job in the world. It doesn't pay much, but since Max and I both eat breakfast and lunch at Head Start, and Athena won't let me pay her rent, and Nelson keeps that Rambler running for me, well, I can manage to get by for the moment.

My journal remains my best friend. I write at night before I go to bed, sorting out my thoughts by writing them down. I also describe people and places on the Rez and I make up stories out of my head.

One damp winter night, after the children go to sleep, Athena and I sit on the porch, side-by-side, warming our hands with steamy cups of hot cocoa. Water drips from the trees and the eaves while on the porch we remain dry and warm.

"Why don't your sons live on the Rez?" I ask Athena. She has three boys. Two are married and one of them has a child.

"They're busy with their interests elsewhere. Jobs. Friends. Families. I raised them to be independent and so they are. Things move too slowly here for them." Athena sips her cocoa and grunts with satisfaction. "Not too slow for you?"

"I need to take it slow. Good cocoa."

Athena pulls her afghan tighter around her shoulders. The rain has washed the air clean.

"I'm going back to school."

"To study what?" I hear a note of approval in her voice.

"I need to earn a living and I like Head Start so I figure a degree in Early Childhood Education. Also English, because I love to write. I hope I can do a dual major. I think I can transfer my two years at Berkeley. I'm going to look into it and in the meantime I'll enroll in a couple of classes at the junior college this summer. I would have to find scholarship money to go to a four-year college."

Athena stands and pats my knee. "That's settled." She takes her empty mug into the kitchen. I smile. She said "that's settled" I tell Carla.

Max and I stop in at the tribal office so I can get a recipe from June. June has woven purple and red embroidery threads in her hair. The threads converge into a thin collection of strands to form a tiny braid.

I admire her handiwork. "Would you do one for me?"

"Of course."

Max pulls a book off the shelf and looks at the pictures.

"Come over this evening. It takes about twenty minutes. Bring Lena and I'll do one for her too."

"Let me see, do I want that girl to look any more beautiful than she already does?" I joke.

"I want to make a fire," Max says.

"A fire?" I ask. Terrific. Is he turning into a pyromaniac?

He points to a picture in the book. Looking over his shoulder, I see a drawing of a fire in the shape of a tipi, with logs and sticks leaning in against each other and coming to a point at the top where smoke lifts in a ribbon.

"I want to make a fire like that." Max touches the picture with a grubby finger.

He hands me the odd-looking book, which seems self-published or something. It has no copyright or standard information at the front. It has a hardcover binding and no publication date and contains many hand-drawn pictures of a variety of fires. It includes stories about fires or perhaps stories told around the fire. I don't have the time to stand here right now and read enough to determine which, especially with Max hopping up and down impatiently at my elbow.

"Can we borrow this?" I ask.

"Of course," June says. "I don't remember seeing that book in here before. I wonder where it came from."

Max takes the book from me excitedly.

I drive to the post office and the bakery. Max makes not a peep in the back seat. Unlike his usual self, he doesn't come into the bakery with me. The fire book mesmerizes him.

In the evening we walk over to Nelson and June's so June can put a braid in my hair and in Lena's. The second we step into the house, Max drills his little rear end into Nelson's lap and opens the book. "Look at the fires." Max shows him.

Nelson reads out loud from the odd book. "Every month, at the full moon, Elk made a fire and invited the Tribe to sit with him to gaze into the flames."

"Elk?" June asks absently as she works on my braid.

"That's his name," Nelson explains. "Before long, word spread about the full moon fire and people came from neighboring Tribes each month to share the fire. It soon became a ceremony, as if a ritual the people could no longer do without. It afforded a regular opportunity for community and reflection."

"What is reflection?" Max asks.

"When people stop running in every direction busy with their own nonsense and take time to think about things," Nelson tells him.

"I want reflection. I want to make a fire like Elk," Max demands.

Nelson turns a page. He and Max study the book.

"I want a drum." Max points. "I want to drum at the fire like here."

"That looks powerful, doesn't it?"

"Read," Max commands.

Nelson obliges. "Looking into the fire each month, the people learned. The fire revealed to them powerful lessons about spirit and the universe."

"I want to see powerful lessons revealed by the fire." Max's eyes shine brightly. He turns another page. "I want to make a drum like this one."

"What a wonderful book," Nelson announces. "It shows how to make different kinds of fires. It shows how to make drums. I can make drums, but I've never tried making one out of a burned log like in this picture." He hugs Max to him. "Where did you find this?"

"He picked it up at the tribal office," I answer.

Captivated, perhaps obsessed, Max pores over the drawings of the fires with Nelson. They study the instructions for making drums.

"Let's do it," Nelson exclaims with a sparkle in his eye. "I'll start inviting people tomorrow. Next full moon. We'll have a fire. We'll have to build a fire ring and collect wood. It'll be hard work."

"I like hard work!" Max shouts with glee.

Two weeks later, on the full moon, we gather in Nelson's back yard at sunset. Nelson and Max build a tipi of wood and light it. A few people turn up. Podon comes with his grandson Thorn. They sit on a picnic bench and pass a bottle of Jack Daniels back and forth between them. June frowns her disapproval but holds her tongue. They remain tame enough, speaking in soft voices, watching the flames leap in the fire ring. A gaggle of children play hide-and-seek in the tiptoeing dark.

June has made fry bread and acorn soup to honor the occasion with traditional food. The soup tastes flat and woody. The fry bread is wonderful; warm, greasy, and probably about a million calories. I didn't realize you could cook with flour made from acorns and I have never tasted fry bread. We sit around in plastic lawn chairs, wearing thick sweaters, sipping soup, and eating the fry bread, licking the delicious oil from our fingers.

Max dances around the fire like a wood nymph. "Look in here Nelson," he shouts, "look on this side. I see a whale swimming on this side."

Nelson looks thoughtfully into the flames. "I see it too, with its fluke flipped up."

"Show me," I demand. I go around to the other side of the fire and sure enough, to my amazement, I see in the flames the image of a whale with its tail up.

"That's really something." Nelson scratches his head incredulously. "There's a story behind that whale."

"What do you mean?"

"I brought this piece of wood from Jewel Beach last March. Been setting here since. The day I picked up this wood, a pod of whales passed by. June and I stood for quite a while watching them blow as they swam. Tonight, when I finally burn the wood we picked up that day, a whale appears swimming through it." He looks at me with that impish grin of his, just plain tickled by the inexplicable mystery of the workings of the universe. "Back in March, I thought those whales were swimming away from me. Now I figure they must've been swimming toward me. Near as I can guess it just took them till now to get here."

"What do you think the whales mean?" I ask.

He throws his head back and laughs. "Don't mean nothin'. Just whales, plain and simple."

Nelson picks up one of his drums. He has quite a few. He makes them. He starts drumming and Max joins him. Podon and Thorn drum too. The thrum of the drum beat reaches throughout the Rez and beckons others to the yard. People pick up drums and sticks. A few people go home to get their drums and then return to the fire. Pretty soon we have a strong drumming circle going. I join in with one of Nelson's handmade gourd rattles.

He grows gourds and dries them and makes them into these rattles. He has a hundred or more laid out to dry on racks in the yard right now. As they dry, molds grow on them, forming patterns. In the spring, Nelson scrubs the gourds and polishes them with brown shoe polish. They become shiny and exquisitely decorated with the mold patterns drawn in the art studio of nature herself. I shake one of last year's gourds, now dry and joyful with loose seeds.

The full moon fire is a great success. I'm proud of Max for dreaming this up. Nelson and Max spread the word that they will do a fire on the full moon every month for anyone who wants to come. Each time, more people show up. The fire becomes a vocation for Nelson; a summons he cannot resist. He considers the fire a great teacher and a great healer. Before long we have people from all around coming regularly. Max loves the festivity of it, the celebration and the ritual. Athena says that Nelson has grabbed onto something and he won't let it go. She predicts he will put the fire to use. I wonder what she means by that. I do not have to wonder for long.

The story of the massacre rears its head after only a few months of full moon fires. If I had known Nelson better, if I had known more about my people, I would have seen it coming, like Athena did. In my defense, I work at Head Start, take classes at the college, and am raising two children, so I'm a little busy, a little distracted with maintaining my life. When the story of the massacre appears on my radar, it hits me hard. Truthfully, ignorance is bliss. Once a person knows about something like the massacre, well, don't we have an obligation to act on that kind of knowledge?

The massacre steps from the shadows on a warm summer night. The crickets chirp loud enough to scare the quail out of the tall grasses. Nelson has a lot of people at his place and a large oak stump embedded in the midst of the flames. Dark arrives late and sneaks up slow as a panther. We float Athena's homegrown spearmint in tall icy glasses of lemonade. Around midnight, Nelson squats down on the edge of the fire pit, the golden glow lighting up his face and making him look young. He has a long, thin gourd rattle in one hand and he shakes it softly. He turns his head slightly and speaks to Athena, who sits just behind his left elbow. "Descendants of all the survivors are here."

"I see it," she replies.

"I figured the fire would bring them together eventually."

"I know you did."

Nelson looks at the ground. He turns his face toward Athena so that the glow of the fire catches his cheek and eye socket in amber light. "I have to tell it." Athena nods her acquiescence.

Watching him intently, I see a crease of pain appear between his eyes where his forehead wrinkles above the bridge of his nose. A hush has fallen over the fire guests. Nelson speaks out in a clear voice that carries to the bear sleeping in the lake.

"I'm going to tell the story of the Massacre of B'Taka Lake because tonight's fire has brought together descendants of all the survivors. These events happened on this land where we stand."

"We live in this town called Hoepper's Knee. The knee itself is not in town; it's here at the Rez. It's that bend in the lakeshore that our people used to call Yopika Bapa, which in our language means the beautiful bend." He gestures toward the lake, his arm moving in a graceful arc. "The invaders renamed it Hoepper's

Knee after a fella named John Hoepper who came in the late 1870s and bought a cattle ranch north of here from the Mexicans. After he bought the ranch, Hoepper and his business partner, Jack Madison, needed people to work the ranch, so they captured or bought hundreds of Kapa slaves. They kidnapped Kapa women and children and forced them to work. They used them as hostages to acquire forced labor from the men. They tortured the women and children if the men did not obey. Hoepper captured Kapa from both the Xa-pa-na-ka Tribe here at Yopika Bapa and also from the Xa-ri-no-ka Tribe that lived above in the hills."

"After they established their ranch, Hoepper and Madison rode regularly with a group of their men to our Tribe to choose young girls who appealed to them, girls as young as ten or eleven. They ordered the parents to bring these girls to them for the night with the threat of a beating if they did not comply. Many parents suffered the beating before losing their daughters in the end anyway. Hoepper tied these parents to a tree and whipped them. Our people could not understand how a man could take pleasure in destroying the innocence of a child. What kind of man would do such damage to a child, a sacred gift from the Creator?"

"One day a woman named Lena refused to send her daughter to Hoepper and Madison. Hoepper had kidnapped and enslaved Lena's husband and her father. Lena would not allow them to take her daughter too. Lena was pregnant, not far from her time to give birth. Hoepper and Madison strung her up by the wrists from a tree and prepared to whip her. This brutality was the last straw for a few of the men from the Tribe, who shot Hoepper and Madison with arrows, cut Lena's bonds, and took her down from that tree before she came to further harm."

"Our Tribe did not often resort to murder, moreover we feared retribution from the invaders. But our men had no choice.

They could not allow the brutality and oppression to continue. After the death of Hoepper and Madison, the slaves at the cattle ranch escaped and hid in the hills. Large-scale massacres had not yet occurred at that time. Sand Creek, Nez Perce, and Walla Walla had not cracked the surface of history. Our people were naïve. They believed that when the American soldiers came, as expected, they would sit down and speak with them in peaceful council and explain the conditions of brutal slavery and pedophilia that had led to these murders. You can read this in the eye-witness accounts of the incident. Our people truly believed that the American soldiers, who had daughters, sisters, and mothers of their own, would be decent men who would understand the need to kill Hoepper and Madison."

"When the soldiers came they did not have peaceful council on their minds. They had retaliation on their minds. They came to punish Indians for killing white men. They found the village of the Xa-pa-na-ka in the bend of the lakeshore and massacred the men, women, and children of the Tribe who were unable to flee, trapped against the water. Killed by gun, bayonet, and knife in a bloody act of genocide. No record remains that identifies exactly how many died. We think they murdered more than two hundred. A handful of children hid in the water. They broke off tule reeds and breathed through the hollow stem so they could submerge themselves in the lake. Soldiers walked through the reeds and stabbed their bayonets into the water to murder any children hiding there. Only three children who hid in the water survived: Athena's mother survived, my grandmother survived, and another little girl who turned crazy after that and wandered among the trees singing nonsense to herself until she died before reaching womanhood. Two boys who hid in the trees also survived. One of them was Troy's great-grandfather and the other was Menny's grandfather."

Nelson pauses in the telling to acknowledge the presence of Troy and Menny at the fire with a nod in their direction. They nod; no words spoken. I look into their faces. Alive because the trees rescued their ancestors. Nelson continues.

"The only other survivor was a baby, a child born to a young girl once forced to go to Hoepper's bed. The baby had half Kapa blood and half Hoepper blood. The baby's mother died in the massacre, but the baby survived, hidden beneath her mother's lifeless body. The baby's mother was the older sister of Athena's mother. And the baby was the grandmother of Penelope, who has returned to her people with her children, Max and Lena."

I attempt to hide the wave of emotion that washes over me, but I am hearing for the first time the history of my people, my own family; I am hearing my past and the source of the blood in my veins. It is more gruesome than I could have imagined. The tears run down my cheeks. I hug myself, ashamed, embarrassed, mortified to have my ignorance publicly exposed.

Nelson has squatted by the fire while telling the story. He sees my face and he stands, steps over to me, and puts his hand on my head as if in benediction as he tells those gathered, "Penelope has not heard the history before." With his words, I no longer feel embarrassed to be crying. It seems like the completely correct response.

Athena says "OH" and the others around the fire echo her in unison with an "OH." The Native amen. Their "OH" tells me they are together with me. Nelson removes his hand from my head and Lena climbs into my lap. I put my arms around her. She is my shield. The fire dances in the eyes of the witnesses who stand, sit, squat, and kneel in the circle of firelight while Nelson continues.

"The children who survived walked a day and a night to the neighboring Xa-ri-no-ka Tribe. Athena's mother was eight years old and she carried her sister's baby into the hills to the neighboring Tribe, who took our Tribe's children in and raised them as their own. Meanwhile, the invaders claimed our land, naming it after John Hoepper, a hero they revered. To this day, our people must say we live at Hoepper's Knee, our land labeled with the name of our oppressor; a rapist, pedophile, and murderer. You will not see this story in any history books. Only one written account remains, handwritten in a letter. In the world outside the Rez, no one remembers or teaches our story. But we refuse to have our history erased so we tell it from time to time. The descendants of those who survived stand here on this ground today. Troy, Menny, me, Athena, Penelope, our children, and our children's children. We survived. We multiply. We remember. We will always remember. We will tell our story. The core spirit of our Tribe will endure. They tried to bury us but they didn't realize we are seeds."

Nelson speaks softly and specifically to me, but loud enough for the others to hear. "This is why, daughter of the Xa-pa-na-ka, this is why we hold you and your children so dear and rejoice at your return." The people around the fire breathe out together with a resounding "OH," affirmation from the deep past. I dissolve in sobs. Lena gently touches my face. Now I understand why Nelson renamed her Lena.

I gaze into the mesmerizing clear blue flame at the heart of the golden orange blaze of the fire. I have found my people.

Later that night, Lena sleeps in my bed. We curl snugly into each other and find comfort for old wrongs. Unfortunately, it turns out to be a rough night for her to sleep in my bed because I have a terrible dream.

I wrestle with a creature that refuses to divulge information I need. I restrain the creature while demanding answers. The creature is a lion with shaggy hair and I grab it around the neck and hold on. It turns into a slippery red snake and tries to slither through my hands. So I tie it around my wrist and hang on and demand that it reveal the information I need. It transforms into a silky black panther that breaks my wrists so I press it between my legs, my thighs clamping it tight, and I ride it as it twists and turns, trying to bite me. It becomes a wild pig, with long tusks, and it bucks me off its back. I jump on again and grab the tusks to keep my seat. "Tell me," I holler, "tell me." It changes from an animal to water, a giant wave washing me under, pulling me into a whirlpool, and I gasp for air, flailing my arms, drowning. I swim up through the whirlpool to the surface and bodysurf on the wave, which turns to fire. I cannot hold onto fire. It burns away from me, escaping, and I shout at it "tell me, tell me." I wake drenched in sweat with Lena shaking my shoulder.

"I'm sorry, baby," I whisper. "I had a nightmare."

"It's OK, Ama," Lena reassures me, her little mouth pressed close to my ear. She has recently taken to calling me Ama, which means "mother" in Kapa. "It's OK. The bad men can't get us here, not at B'Taka Lake. The bear will protect us. The bear always protects us."

We are new. She is Lena. I am Ama. Max has a Kapa braid.

We have found ourselves in the distant past.

I get up and take a shower. When I return, Lena is sound asleep. Perhaps it is the spirit of the bear that has transformed me and returned me to my people and my purpose; given me entry into my history and culture. The spirit of the bear. B'Taka.

Hoepper's Knee Reservation, 1974

Orange, yellow, gold, and blue licks of flame burst from the top of tonight's tipi-shaped fire. A village burned here on this spot. Tipis of flame. I stare into the fire and imagine I am small and following my instincts, like a wild animal, fleeing to the lake to hide among the tule reeds. I imagine I am Athena's mother, breathing through a hollow tule. Hunted. Silent. Would I have survived?

I tried it. I went to the lake, cut a tule, and sat under the water, breathing through the slender stalk. Not much air comes through a tule reed. It felt like drowning. And if the air was filled with smoke? And if the lake was filled with men carrying bayonets? And if my family was screaming and dying on the shore? What manner of child could survive this? And, having survived, walk for a night and a day carrying a baby? What manner of child?

I stare into the full moon fire, a creation sprung from the imagination of my son and Daddy Nelson. They have manifested this sacred space of contemplation, drumming, and friendship. They build the fire on the Saturday night nearest to the full moon. The fire circle continues to grow. The full moon fire has evolved into a community event, with members of our Tribe and other Tribes, and friends, and friends of friends, and someone who heard from someone who heard from someone, and here we have it. People bring food, logs to burn, musical instruments, and drums. They bring small gifts for Nelson and Max, like feathers, shells, rocks, pieces of wood, and other found objects, beautiful in the mystery of their creation. I call these people the fire guests. Max and Nelson ask the fire guests to tell them what they see in the fire. They gaze at the moon with them. They read messages in the smoke that drifts upward. They take them out of themselves drumming. Each fire is different. Different fire. Different season. Different dynamic of people. Different stories. Different mood.

At tonight's fire, Nelson keeps tugging at his braid restlessly and fooling with the fire unnecessarily, poking it with his shovel. He glances up and sees me watching him. Our eyes lock. "Nelson," I call over to him. "You're acting like a cat with fleas." He laughs. "Do you have something on your mind?"

He leans the long handle of his shovel against a tree and walks over to me. I stand, holding a gourd in one hand and Max's drum in the other. Nelson says, "I want to introduce a new fire ritual, but I need your help."

I put the gourd and drum on the picnic table, warily, and cross my arms to protect myself.

Nelson continues, "I want to tell the story of the massacre each time to the people who haven't heard it."

"What do you need from me?"

"I want you to tell it."

"Why me?"

"Because you're a storyteller."

"So are you."

"Not as good as you."

"Thank you, I guess. You know, it's not a cozy-around-the-fire story. It makes people uncomfortable."

"They need to feel uncomfortable. The fires offer an opportunity to tell our history."

I look at the fire, as if it will have something to contribute to this conversation. He wants me to repeatedly tell a difficult, horrific story. I suppose I can do this much for my Tribe, that took me in when I had been discarded. I look at Nelson and I nod. He smiles. He has me. It is worth agreeing to it to see him so satisfied. Nelson has stepped in as a father for my children. It is small repayment to tell this story. Nelson turns away from me and announces to the fire guests, "Who has not heard what happened here at Yopika Bapa in 1880? If you have not heard the story, come over here and Penelope will tell you. Come pay the fire's fee."

He wants me to tell it now? It has to begin somewhere, I suppose. I pull a chair up to the fire. Storyteller, historian, *griot*. What have I become?

Each month when I tell it, the story changes with the contributions of other tribal members who pass through, one month here, next month not, always a different fire family. Soon the story beats inside me like a bird bursting to escape from a box. I want to write it. But I can't. I, who have a gift for writing. It has become a living thing that won't tolerate a cage. Nelson says it will permit me to pin it down in writing when it's ready. The story has a spirit that has not fully revealed itself to me.

In the aftermath of the massacre, our Tribe has evolved as a hodge-podge assortment of stray descendants of survivors with partial Native blood; "half-breeds" as Podon calls us. The "Tribe" at Yopika Bapa includes tribal members from several Kapa Tribes lumped together. At the fires, I tell the story of the massacre of the Xa-pa-na-ka, the Tribe of my mother and Aunt Beth, the Tribe of Nelson and Athena and my children. Although I can't undo the damage done to us, I can learn about my Tribe and teach our truth to others. When I reclaim our history in this way, I prove that those who attempted to annihilate my Tribe failed. They could not invisible-ize us.

Book 6: Penelope
Hoepper's Knee Reservation, 1976

Secretly, I still imagine Odysseus will return one day, like in the classic story. My heart waits for him no matter how hard my mind tries to forget him. If I truly wanted him to find me then I shouldn't have covered my tracks so well. I dare him to find me. Let his heart break like mine did. How can a woman love a man so deeply and hold such rage against him both at once? Some nights I crave his touch beyond endurance. I long to feel the full length of him stretched out along my body. I yearn for him so much that I can barely breathe. I'm still a young woman. I should not waste my youth wedded to an obsession for an absent husband. I should not choose to be without a man to appreciate me and satisfy my desires. I must refuse to be the debris left behind from a tragedy, or, worse yet, a mundane soap opera. I must remain open to possibility.

Phil walks quickly to catch up to me. I sense his presence behind me and, exercising restraint, I resist turning. I have spoken a few times casually to this fine man. I have watched him surreptitiously in our child psychology class. He is tall, has lovely broad shoulders and a well-rounded behind that could fill a girl's hands nicely. He has soft brown eyes, juicy fleshy lips, and glowing mocha-brown skin. He is a sensitive man, a thinker. I love his deep rumbling voice. This lovely man attracts me and it's about time this Native girl came out of mourning. My steps slow.

Phil strides up alongside me. "What did you think about that case study?"

"It was interesting. Honestly, I'm not as interested in the unusual children as I am in the regular ones."

"I hear you."

We look each other up and down in the dappled sunlight sprinkling through the trees.

"I don't really want to talk about class. I want to ask if I can take you out."

I laugh. He looks concerned.

"Tomorrow we have our monthly full moon fire at Yopika Bapa on the Kapa Reservation. Please come."

"That wasn't what I had in mind." I shrug. "What's the full moon fire?"

"We make a bonfire on the Saturday closest to the full moon. People come. We drum, talk, whatever happens."

"Sounds magical." His eyes crinkle in a warm smile.

"It is."

"Give me directions and I'll be there."

"I'll introduce you to my children."

His eyebrows jump up, alarmed, questioning.

"My husband left me."

"I'm sorry," he says. Of course he isn't.

"It's been a few years. Old news." I give him directions to the Rez and we part ways. I float home.

Athena checks Phil out when he arrives. I have mentioned him often enough that she guesses my interest.

A huge tree stump smolders and glows in the middle of the fire ring. Someone has brought Max a large mangled wad of mistletoe tumbled down from the top of a recently felled oak and he throws it over the stump into the fire. It crackles and leaps into flame, twisting and snapping as the fire consumes it.

"What do you see in the mistletoe?" Max asks Phil.

"What do I see?" Phil looks puzzled.

"Any shapes?" Max asks.

"Messages?" Nelson adds.

Phil stares at the mistletoe. "No messages. It looks kinda like tumbleweed."

Phil is the only newcomer at the fire tonight and, as custom dictates, I must tell him the story of the massacre. The prospect of this intense, one-on-one private telling of my Tribe's heart-stopping history makes me anxious. Nelson comes to my rescue. He pulls up a chair and says, "I'd like to hear the story again this month." Is that a hint of amusement I see at the corner of his eyes? Sheesh. Must the whole Tribe know I'm attracted to this handsome, Black man?

In the amber glow of the fire, engulfed in the scent of wood smoke, I tell the story. A couple of other folks wander over to hear it again. I could tell this story in my sleep by now. Phil is a professional listener. He gives me his full attention. At first I'm self-conscious because he watches me so intently. Once I begin, I shift to auto-pilot. My mouth tells the story while I watch Phil listening to my mouth telling the story. When I tell the part about the children hiding in the lake and in the trees and about my grandmother as a baby trapped under the dead body of my great-grandmother, Phil is visibly moved. When I finish the story, nearby listeners give me the amen "OH."

Phil asks, "Can I get a copy of that story?"

Nelson and I laugh.

"What?"

"You just got it," I tell him.

"Isn't it written down somewhere?"

"Nope," Nelson replies.

"You need to get that story out so people know."

"Probably," I say. "I keep trying to write it down but I can't seem to do it. I think maybe it wants to be told, not written."

"It'll come," Nelson says as he pats my knee.

"It would make a great oral history project," Phil suggests. "You know, have different people in the Tribe talk about the massacre. I bet you could get grant money to do it. Oral history is a big deal these days."

"An oral history project," Nelson mutters. I see his amusement, which fortunately escapes Phil. Everyone wants to make a project out of Native people. There's money in it.

"When did the massacre happen?" Phil asks.

"1880," I reply.

"Do you know the actual date?"

"Of course. May 5, 1880," Nelson says.

"Well then that's it." Phil sits up straight on the bench as if we have settled a problem. He's a man on a mission now. "Let's organize an event for that day. It could be a candlelight vigil, a remembrance walk, a commemorative service, or whatever you want. Where did it happen?"

"Here. X marks the spot," Nelson replies. His amusement has evaporated and he suddenly takes Phil seriously.

I watch the fire, which has many blue flames in it tonight. It's a secretive fire, that cloaks the heat within.

We hear the genuine excitement in Phil's voice as he encourages us. "You could do it. You could hold a ceremony to remember and you could publicize it. Get it into the local newspaper. Get the story out. If we put together an event, I bet the newspaper will send a reporter. Penelope can tell the story to the reporter."

I snort. Sure, yeah, so a melodramatic journalist can write up a distorted or watered down version? No way.

"What?" Phil asks. "Don't you want people to learn the truth?"

Nelson reads my thoughts. "Different people tell the same story in different ways. You're right that it's important to make the truth known. But we worry about how the story might be told by outsiders."

This story can't seem to wait until I'm ready to write it down. The story pushes to step out into the world on its own power.

"I would love to help you organize an event, if you'll let me," Phil offers with sincere generosity. "I have experience as a political activist. I've done a lot of organizing for social change. I know how to go about it."

I believe he does know. At Head Start we talk about advocating for our needs and the needs of families with very young children. We must speak up about what we need in order to be good parents and about what our children need to thrive. In school. In the community. I'm not used to speaking up about what I need, about what matters to me, so I have to work at it. Phil's idea excites me. This matters to me. This would be something for my children. I look at Nelson and he returns my look and I see the reflection of the full moon fire flicker in his eyes and I see the flame of perseverance there and I can tell he is up for this kind of ruckus and so am I. Nelson gives me an almost imperceptible nod of the head.

"You discuss it amongst yourselves and let me know what you think and if you want to go for it, then I volunteer to help. I can do this stuff with one hand tied behind my back."

I flash Phil a bemused smile. "We just discussed it and we want to do it."

Phil glances back and forth between us, puzzled.

Nelson grins. "You'll get used to us." He stands up to leave. "Can you come by my house next Saturday afternoon? Have to get a few people together to make plans."

"Sure," Phil says, still sounding a bit bewildered. "What time?" He seems self-conscious now, out of his depth, as he tries to work out exactly what just happened.

"Whatever time suits you," Nelson replies, and in three strides he is on the other side of the fire pit, picking up wood, leaning it into the flame, sculpting the shape of the fire.

"I'm not necessarily opposed," Athena says the next day when I tell her about it. "I'm just worried about the repercussions. Will this make our lives harder?" Athena takes me to the Council to talk it over and see if they approve.

"We should take this idea and run with it. Let's organize a campaign to change the name of this town while we're at it. You know what I'm talking about. On the days when I think about it too much, I could run into the lake screaming mad. Living in a place named after a man who raped and murdered our ancestors?" I argue heatedly.

Podon grunts, "You can't just change the name of a town. They won't let you."

"Who?" I demand. "They who? Who decides? People decide the name of a town. People who live in the town."

"How many of those people do you think know the real story about what happened here?" Dita asks, without raising her eyes from her knitting.

"Then we have some educating to do," I reply. "This event is a place to start."

Hera's eyes squint down to slits while she gives this discussion some hard thought. This is a tough one for her. Close to the bone. Tough for all of us. Do we want to expose ourselves to the wide world in this manner?

"How do you propose we go about it?" Hera asks.

"We could take it to the city council," I suggest, with a level of certainty in my voice not matched by the doubt in the pit of my stomach. "We can make a heap of noise. Perhaps put a resolution on the ballot for the next election. At least it will give us the opportunity to get the story out so people know what happened."

"And why will they care?" Podon asks bitterly. "You think you're so smart," Podon grumbles, "but you can't fool me. This is about that boyfriend of yours, isn't it? He has you all fired up."

That wily fox. He tries to hit me in a soft spot. I blush, but I do not back down. "So what is wrong with that? And for your information, Mr. Busybody, he is not my boyfriend. Yet." Several elders laugh and Athena grunts with satisfaction that I stood up to Podon. "Phil is a political activist. He reminds me to have the courage to stand up for my convictions. The fact that I even know who I am is a small miracle. Now that I know, I figure standing up for myself equals standing up for the Kapa. I don't want to be like my mother, who took everything life dished out and then crawled into a hole and died. I'm not willing to let these people around here get away with noodling along in their comfortable everyday lives, at our expense, out of pure ignorance. I will demand they see us."

"What do you think?" Dita asks Athena.

"I don't for a minute believe we will change the name of Hoepper's Knee. I do believe we can make people ask questions and learn the truth about the genocide. I think Penelope can shake people up and alter their perspective. We have to make people uncomfortable. Comfortable people don't make change. I'm willing to find out where this will take us."

"Our children have enough difficulty at school, in town, living under the thumb. How much harder will this make it for them if we pursue this?" Hera asks.

Nelson says, "It will certainly make things hard out there for our children. But how much harder is it for them to see their parents and elders hold our tongues?"

"We've held our tongues for a hundred years. They've gone numb," Podon says.

Athena sits forward abruptly in her chair and grabs my upper arm, "Do you understand what this will require from our children, from Max and Lena, to go out day-to-day into the town as this unfolds?"

"I don't," I admit. I cannot disguise the note of fear in my voice. "But I think people around here ought to realize that this town bears the name of a murderer and a rapist. When they get it, I think they will agree with me that we should change the name. We don't have to call it Yopika Bapa, but we can't keep calling it Hoepper's Knee. It's criminal."

"Welcome to Indian Country," Dita says flatly. No laughter dances in her usually merry eyes.

Phil holds me protectively in his sleep. One arm cradles my head, the other curves around my side, resting lightly on my hip bone. My back leans against his smooth muscular chest. His embrace shelters me from the dangers lurking in the world. His even breathing is the rise and fall of the sea on which we float, drifting together, in safe harbor. I have found a decent, caring man. A man with integrity. Yet that which I seek in his arms eludes me because the center is missing. Try as I might, and I do try, I am not in love with this man. I may love him, but I will never be bottom-falls-out, hopelessly in love with him. I know what that feels like and this is not it.

Damn you Odysseus, you ruined me. You dropped anchor in my blood. My yearning for you does not dissipate with time. Must I lose you again and again whenever I think about you? Must my enduring love for you deny me the delight of another man? A replacement husband? A man who is present? Must the ghost of you, shot from my spirit like an arrow dead on the mark, kill any relationship I attempt to build with another man? Drive him away?

Sleep twists away from me whenever I think I hold it in my grasp. I gently disentangle myself from Phil's embrace and wrap a blanket around my shoulders. I tiptoe to the porch where I gaze up at the stars. They settle me. I can think under the stars, which render my struggles and trivial concerns inconsequential and prevent me from becoming too overwhelmed by my thoughts, my choices, my decisions. Thousands of years from tonight, who will remember that I passed this way? What difference will I have made? My actions carry little weight. My choices seem less momentous and absolute under the stars.

I thought I had left the bed quietly, without awakening Phil. But he joins me on the porch.

"You worried about tomorrow?" he asks.

I leap at the excuse. "Yeah."

He wraps his arms around me from behind and I lean my head against his solid shoulder.

"It'll go fine," he reassures me. "There's a significant Native American population in Hoepper's Knee plus a lot of liberals. The city council members don't want to appear racist or to offend anyone. They don't want to lose votes."

"Is that all it's about to them, losing votes?"

"Nah. I think it's more like concern for their image. Some of them will take a genuine interest in the issue. But I bet all of them will think, 'These crazy Indians want to change the name of the town?' Because they don't get it. Maybe eventually they will. And if they're decent then it will require they give it some thought. It has to start somewhere."

"And it starts with a conversation."

"It starts with a conversation. C'mon back to bed. My body wants to have a conversation with yours. I'll put you to sleep." His hands move to caress my breasts, his lips find mine, and he leads me inside.

Hoepper's Knee, 1976

Town folk pack the city council chambers and overflow into the hallway. I've never gone to one of these things before. They scheduled our "item" early on the agenda. I figure they want to get it over with. Fluorescent ceiling lights flicker and cast a surreal glow. My mouth goes dry and I have a strong urge to run away and hide under my bed. This public outcry business is not for sissies. They announce our "item." Nelson and I rise and proceed to the microphone. Nelson reads our petition aloud. We suggest that the city council vote to change the name of the town to Bataka. The Tribal Council came up with suggesting Bataka, thinking it a fairly benign and also beautiful name. The city council members listen to Nelson with all due seriousness. I appreciate their attentiveness. They do not take this lightly or indicate that it amuses them in any way. When Nelson finishes reading the petition, the mayor asks, "Can you tell us a little more about your reason for changing the name?"

Nelson steps away and motions me to the microphone. I am scared to death. I focus on the face of the mayor, a woman named Cindy Cadogan. Her daughter is in Lena's class at school and I have seen them in the grocery store. She has bright green eyes that peer at me with kindness, encouraging me. I speak directly to her.

"As stated in the petition, we of the Kapa Tribe have decided to no longer silently go about our daily business in a town named after the man responsible for the extermination of our people. It is a matter of historical record that John Hoepper and his business partner Jack Madison caused the massacre of a Kapa Tribe in 1880. Hoepper was a known pedophile, rapist, and murderer. We view it as inappropriate to name a town after a criminal. We understand the inconvenience it will cause to local merchants and public institutions to change the name of our town, nevertheless we believe this necessary because it damages our community to perpetuate the lie that the man for whom our town is named deserved such an honor. He was not deserving. We owe it to ourselves and our children to have a home with a more fitting name." I have said my speech directly to Cindy, who seems sympathetic. I step away from the microphone.

Cindy speaks to me and the room at large. "Although I have the deepest compassion for your feelings on this issue, I don't think you fully understand how difficult it would be to change the name of the town. It's a complicated legal matter, something which would potentially harm local business, and deeply affect every citizen in this community."

Nelson is ready for this response. Phil prepared him for it. He responds, "We have brought the petition before the city council to draw this to your attention and to pursue this change through proper channels. This is our first step. Our next step will be to put it to a vote as a ballot initiative in the next election."

I lean over to the microphone and add, "In the meantime, we will educate the community about the history of what happened here and the true nature of our town's namesake. On May fifth we will hold the first annual commemoration of the Yopika Bapa Massacre. We brought flyers with more information. I assume we will see city council members there." I look at each of the city council members in the eye, without flinching. Knowledge is power.

Cindy says, "This issue is now open for discussion. We have twenty minutes allotted."

Nelson and I take our seats. A lean, middle-aged man in cowboy boots takes the microphone. "City council," he nods toward them, "folks," he nods toward those gathered, "I'm Frank Hoepper and I'm not so good at speaking in front of people." He rubs his stubbly chin. "I have to say what's on my mind and what's on the mind of most of these people here tonight. If this story about John Hoepper is true then why haven't we heard it before? Our town is named after the fella who founded it, and that's all there is to it."

Podon interrupts, shouting from the back of the room, "How can you found a damn town if it existed already for thousands of years? You think Hoepper discovered this place? The Kapa lived her for centuries before he turned up!"

Cindy bangs her gavel. "I'm sorry, sir," she states with intensity, "this is an orderly discussion and you may not interrupt. You may have a turn to speak shortly."

Podon ignores her and yells out, "Hoepper was a goddamn pedophile!" Thorn takes Podon by the arm and Podon attempts to shrug him off. Thorn holds him more firmly and steers him out the door. I wonder if Podon's been drinking. As Thorn heads through the doorway with him, he yells over his shoulder, "Learn about real history you fools!" He exits the room growling, "My turn to speak! What am I? Two years old? Go teach kindergarten."

Others take their turn to speak. Phil speaks. The conversation remains orderly, though heated. The real story about events in 1880 and the history of our town becomes the biggest topic of discussion. Phil encourages people to attend the commemoration on May fifth to hear the story. That will be me. A great weight rests on my shoulders.

Yopika Bapa, May 5, 1976

I wake before sunrise to the scent of Athena's geraniums and spearmint sneaking in through my open window. The water birds call joyously to one another across the lake. The susurrating tule reeds whisper their secrets. I can't hear them from my room, but I know the sound. Today is the First Annual Memorial of the Yopika Bapa Massacre.

We are ready.

Reporters have been alerted. The public has been invited. The Tribe is prepared. We simply have to hold the ceremony. But I suddenly feel violated. Exposed. This is the terrible thing that happened to my ancestors and I must face its perpetuation. I could not have predicted the intensity of rage and shame rising within me today. I must reveal to the world this event embedded in my history that shaped my being and mangled my family. I will open it up for scrutiny. For comment. For judgement. For common gossip.

I walk to the lakeshore with a complexity of emotions whirling inside me. I am one touch short of dissolving in tears. I am on the verge of either hurting someone or retreating to hide in my room for the day. Others join me at the lake and we light candles. We drum while we chant to greet the rose-fingered sun as it rises in the sky. This centers me and helps me gain a modicum of control.

Max and Lena gather tule reeds with the other children. They need help cutting the fibrous stalks. The children place the long reeds on an altar at the edge of the lake. We say the names of children who died on that long-ago day. We can only say the names of those Athena remembers. The rest are lost for all eternity. Athena says a few things in the old language and we repeat after her. She can't speak it fluently, but she remembers many words. Our ability to define our world died with our language. So we speak these words in a dead language, guessing at their meaning, using them to say things they were not designed to say. We complete our private tribal ceremony. The public ceremony, the one we advertised, starts at ten o'clock.

We walk up from the lake to the Rez entrance, by the tribal office. We have put up a new sign and it is covered with canvas. Nelson burns sage. More drumming. June and Dita take the canvas off the sign. There it is, plain as day, a silhouette of the bear and in large block letters across the silhouette it reads Yopika Bapa.

I look at the sign with satisfaction. Phil squeezes my hand. June and Athena lead the children in a song. Lena and Max sing with the other children. I'm surprised the sign makes me so happy. I run my fingers over it. Others do the same. Over the previous weeks, we have changed many signs and markings on the Rez to remove the traces of Hoepper's name. I have an image in my mind of our Tribe rising out of the ashes of a fire.

I take the children to a pancake breakfast in the community center. Dita sits in the corner knitting as usual. Podon complains about something or other to Nelson while June attempts to soothe his crusty carbuncled feelings. He's a loose cannon if there ever was one. I hope he doesn't go off in the middle of the ceremony and start railing about the betrayals of the federal government, the worthless pledges of the worthless colonizers. A restlessness and anxiety ripples through the room. The thought of having so many outsiders on the Rez unsettles us. We suffer a deep cultural memory of invaders.

Phil crosses the room to sit beside me. He has two plates of pancakes and puts one down in front of me. "You OK?"

"Not really."

Max comes over and asks Phil to refasten his necklace of feathers, which has come untied. It's not a traditional piece of regalia, just something Max made for himself that he likes to wear to ritual events.

Phil fixes it and says, "Go get yourself some pancakes. Hera's blueberry specials. That woman knows how to throw down. Bet you can't eat more than two, they're big."

Max heads to the kitchen for pancakes.

"You should eat," Phil urges gently.

"I have too many butterflies."

"I figured. You'll be hungry later. Besides, you need to stand out there a long time. Not a good idea on an empty stomach."

The pancakes are delicious. Buttery and sweet with those delectable blueberries that just burst open when I bite into them.

"You'll do great. Don't worry," Phil assures me.

"I need to go for a walk before the public ceremony."

"You want me to come with you?"

"I need to be alone. I have this surge of persistent anger this morning. I hope a walk at the lake will help me clear my head. Would you keep an eye on the children for me?"

"Of course." Phil leans across the table and gives me a light kiss.

A little footpath winds around the lake. It starts at the Rez, eventually ending up at the lakefront beach that's part of the city park. I walk around this footpath, talking to the lake, the bear. The lake was, after all, named B'Taka because it once had the distinct shape of a bear. It still has the shape if you look at it the right way from the right spot. The bear and I have one of our typical conversations consisting of whispered secrets. The bear is counting on me to weave a tale that will capture hearts. I promise to give it my best shot.

As I walk back to the house to prepare for the public ceremony, I spot a reporter and her photographer setting up a tripod. People begin to arrive. People from other Tribes, friends of tribal members, and people who come to support us because they heard or saw our publicity. It amazes me that non-Native people come simply as a matter of conscience. I am glad that there are still principled people in the world. I see Cindy Cadogan and her daughter and I wonder if the whole city council came or just the mayor.

Phil and I walk down to the lake together. I imagine opening my mouth to tell the story and having nothing more than a squeak emerge. Phil gives my hand a squeeze.

We stand at the water's edge.

Nelson lights tall candles and puts them on the altar we have built for those who died in the massacre. The drummers begin drumming and this steadies me. The sound of the drums always infuses me with strength. The drums transport me to a sacred place. The Tribe chants. Others chant along, trying to follow.

A local radio station transmits a simulcast. Two reporters hover at the fringes and a photographer snaps pictures. Athena approaches the photographer and explains that he must not photograph a spiritual ceremony. He complies, looking worried.

Soon I will have my turn. I still wonder that I have become the Tribe's storyteller.

The drumming and chanting stops. Nelson introduces me. I tell myself it's like at the fires, only bigger, with a radio station broadcasting my words. I close my eyes so that I don't see the people, otherwise I don't think I can tell it. I pretend I'm standing at the fire. I imagine the flames and the heat in front of me, instead of the water of the lake. I part the flames and begin.

"The Xa-pa-na-ka lived on this land by the lake for twelve thousand years. My ancestors walked the ground we stand on for thousands of years before the birth of Christ. This place is sacred. These people are sacred. In 1876 a man came to this land and desecrated it."

I tell the story simply and humbly. The story comes through me, not from me. The story belongs to my people. I am a conduit. As I tell it, standing here with my eyes shut, sharing it with strangers and simulcast on the radio, it dawns on me how I want to write this story, it comes to me like white lightning piercing my thoughts. I am calm and centered. Peace touches me like the cool fingers of rosy dusk over the ocean. I reach the end, where Athena's mother carries my grandmother across the hills to safety. The surviving children leave their sacred home to seek help. I open my eyes.

Nelson stands at the water's edge, his arms outstretched, as if blessing B'Taka Lake. He wears a leather jacket with fringes that run down the arms so that his arms outstretched make his silhouette against the bright lake resemble that of an eagle in flight. He wears a flicker-feather headdress with a quail topknot. I am not the only one who stands in awe of Nelson. When I finished the story, my people breathed an "OH" of affirmation; but I am no longer the focus of attention. All eyes have turned to Nelson, poised to take wing over the lake. We have strayed from the rehearsed ceremony. In the silence we can hear the bark peeling off the nearby madrone trees in the sun. Nelson calls out a phrase in the old language and it echoes across the lake. My heart leaps into my throat. He calls it again. His hands drop to his sides. June goes to him and puts her arm around him. He has his back to us for a time, lost in his personal moment, as the focus of attention shifts away from him and the ceremony continues with ritual dancing and singing. The children perform the bear dance, even though this is not the correct season for it. The boys snake in a circle. The girls stand across from each other in lines with bright-colored skirts. Podon's grandson Thorn and his friend Buck burn sage.

After the children complete their dance, women hand out turkey feathers, which we float onto the lake. Hera says a few words about retaining our culture, about passing our history and our ritual to our children. Those gathered listen in respectful silence. She asks if anyone else wants to speak. "I have a talking stick to pass around to anyone who wishes to speak." Hera holds her talking stick, brightly wrapped in yarn with feathers and shells woven into it, above her head. "The rule of the talking stick is that only the one holding the stick talks. The rest remain silent and listen."

Podon takes the stick to have his say. He is not antagonistic and is mercifully brief. I am grateful he stayed sober today. He passes the stick to the next person who wishes to have it. In this way it passes through the crowd. A few people sing. Others recite poetry or tell stories. This part of the event unfolds as it creates itself. Cindy takes the stick and talks about the diversity of our community and the richness of our history in this geographic area.

I appreciate the sincerity of her words. After its journey, the stick returns to Hera.

The drummers drum again, many with their eyes closed. Podon, Thorn, and Buck start a simple chant. Everyone joins. We chanters become one for an inch of time. When the chanting fades, Nelson says a final blessing. "Go from this place with the unified strength of those gathered here and with renewed spirit for the work that must be done."

I think it is clear to everyone present that the heart of this beautiful and satisfying ceremony we have shared was the moment when Nelson called out his words over the lake, wearing a mantle of divine grace. He is a holy man now.

"What did he say over the water?" Phil asks me.

"I'm wondering the same. Let's ask Athena." We weave our way through the crowd of well-wishers and participants to Athena's side. I take her arm. Phil leans in close to hear her answer as I ask, "What did Nelson's words mean?"

"He said 'I forgive them'."

Book 7: Penelope
Yopika Bapa, 1976

The day after the ceremony, I stand in the kitchen shoulder-to-shoulder with Athena as we slice vegetables for soup. I tell her, "I want to find Aunt Beth. I want to bring her home."

Athena studies me carefully. "I should have brought her back to the Bapa when I first learned of it."

"You can't do everything, take responsibility for everyone," I remind her. "I think of our history like a bomb going off. The resulting disaster is so total that it's impossible to figure out where to start to pick up the pieces."

Athena nods in agreement.

The onion simmers in the stew pot with a hunk of beef and a handful of barley. I pop pieces of crispy carrots in my mouth as I continue to slice. Cabbage. Potatoes. Celery. We chop and crunch. Athena eats strips of cabbage. She has slowed down in recent months. Lately she uses a cane. Her knees trouble her, especially in damp weather like today. She is my anchor and my rock. How will I manage when she goes? At nearly eighty, every year is a gift. What will we do, me and Max and Lena; what will we do when Athena crosses over into spirit? Long life, Athena, I pray. Stay with us.

"Sit down," I order. "You've been standing long enough. Rest your knees." She doesn't argue as she settles into the rocker. "Do you know where she is?"

"In an institution in Napa. I have the address. The doctor sends me an annual report. The report describes her with words like 'uncommunicative', 'harmless', 'obedient'. She apparently has not spoken in many years." Athena rocks absentmindedly in the chair.

"Do you have a phone number for the place?"

"I have it."

In a little while I'll call Nelson and ask him to send my children home for dinner. He's helping Max with his homework. June is teaching Lena how to sew a dress. Lena is getting so big. I must remember to slow down, to take the time to enjoy the children, to enjoy Athena while we still have her with us. I want to share this family with Aunt Beth. "She has lived among strangers her whole life," I say.

Athena stops rocking and stands. "I'll look for the number."

Napa and Yopika Bapa, 1976

The wildflowers dot the sides of the highway with red, purple, yellow, white, and pink on a late spring day verging on summer. I drive while Athena checks and rechecks her paperwork.

"The doctor seems worried we can't look after her," Athena tells me.

"How do you know?"

"He said on the phone we can bring her back if we run into trouble."

"What trouble?"

"He obviously hasn't seen the people who live on the Rez."

I laugh, thinking in particular of Podon.

"It wasn't a joke," she says, though unable to suppress a grin.

"When was the last time Aunt Beth was at the Rez?"

Athena sucks her teeth, thinking. After a while she answers, "Probably Carla's funeral."

"How old was she when the BIA took her to that boarding school?"

"Five," Athena replies right away. "When's the last time you saw her?"

"Ten years ago this Christmas. Odysseus and I told her I was pregnant and we intended to get married and she chased him down the street with a meat cleaver."

Athena chuckles. She points to a sign on the road and indicates that I have to turn. She has scribbled directions on the back of a grocery receipt. When we arrive at the front gate, a guard with a clipboard peers in the car window and asks for our names. He has me sign and presses a button in his little guard booth that makes the metal gate swing open smoothly on well-oiled hinges.

I park the car and we climb out and stretch. Athena is stiff and bent over. "Give me a moment," she tells me. I lean against the car until Athena straightens her bones out. I wonder if it's just about her back and her knees or if she's afraid to see how bad Aunt Beth is.

We walk into the lobby and stop at the front desk. As soon as I give my name, the receptionist smiles in recognition. "We've been expecting you. Come to take our quiet Beth, have you?"

I would not have described Aunt Beth that way.

"We don't often have one of our patients leave," the chatty receptionist tells us. Athena grunts. The woman rambles on. "Most of our patients have been forgotten."

Have I lost my own mind to want to take this crazy old woman to live with me? Maybe the doctor is right. Maybe we're biting off more than we can chew. I remember her chasing Odysseus down the street. It would give her little satisfaction to know that she was right about him. But if she can comprehend what's going on then it will give her great satisfaction to attend my graduation in December.

The doctor arrives in the lobby, red-faced and jovial. "Dr. Bronkowski, very pleased to meet you," he introduces himself and pumps my hand vigorously and then Athena's. "We packed her up and she's ready to go." He makes her sound like a set of plates. "Come this way." He leads us through a door into a modest waiting room.

There she is, sitting obediently in a chair, with her hands folded neatly in her lap, as she stares straight ahead out of lusterless, vacant eyes. She doesn't recognize me. I doubt she even sees me. Her hair falls in stringy strands and has gone entirely white. She wears a dull gray cardigan over a faded blue house dress and penny loafers that are too big for her feet. She is as pale as boiled spaghetti. I would never have recognized her.

"We packed a suitcase for her. We don't know how attached she is to her things, but maybe she will want them," Dr. Bronkowski tells us.

The suitcase stands at attention beside her chair.

I touch her arm and she does not respond. I pick up the suitcase.

"Come Aunt Beth. We're going home," I say.

She does not respond.

"She is compliant," Dr. Bronkowski says. "She'll do whatever you tell her to do if you give her clear directions. Just take her arm and tell her to stand. Tell her to walk."

I put my hand under her elbow. "Stand," I say. She stands; like a dumb dog obeying a command.

"Call me," the doctor offers anxiously, "if you feel like you're in over your heads. You can bring her back." Athena shoots me a meaningful glance. He's just like she said. I tell myself that he's trying to be helpful. I hold my tongue.

"Walk," I say to Aunt Beth, who shuffles forward in her too-big shoes.

We walk out the door of the room together. She stares straight ahead. We walk across the lobby. The cheery receptionist waves good-bye. I leave Athena and Aunt Beth at the bottom of the front steps with Aunt Beth's suitcase on the ground beside them. I drive the car around. Aunt Beth doesn't move from the spot. I pull the car up to the steps and put the suitcase in the trunk. Aunt Beth looks up at the sky, as if searching for a plane in the distance.

"Walk," Athena tells her. I open the door of the car and Athena orders, "Get in the car. Sit." Aunt Beth obeys. I buckle her seatbelt.

I go around to the driver's side and get in. Athena gets in on the passenger side next to me. We look at each other and smile. I turn around to look at Aunt Beth. She stares straight ahead.

"Breathe," I tell Aunt Beth. "Keep breathing."

Before long she falls asleep, her head bobbling, her mouth open, snoring gently. If I didn't know better, I'd think they drugged her. I keep peeking at her in the rearview mirror.

Everyone at the Rez knows where we went, of course. When we drive onto the Bapa, people try to peer into the car. They wonder how crazy she really is.

"We might as well get it over with," I tell Athena. She nods.

After we help Aunt Beth out of the car, we sit her on the front porch where our nosy Tribe can thoroughly examine her. Athena makes her a cup of tea. We tell her to drink the tea and she does. She does whatever we tell her to do, while staring out of those dead and vacant eyes.

Folks come by all evening. They don't stand on ceremony. They comment about her as if she were a post. "So there she is." "Don't look much worse than Granny May." "Don't seem no different from Cousin Jack." "Does she talk?"

Podon sniffs around her like a coyote. "Another stray to feed," he mutters disapprovingly.

Dita brings one of her colorful handmade Afghans and slips it around Aunt Beth's shoulders. A gift of welcome. Aunt Beth stares ahead of her and slurps tea noisily. Afterward she holds the empty cup in her lap.

"You can put the cup down, dear," Dita tells her. Aunt Beth obeys. She places the cup on the porch. The Afghan slips from her shoulders. Dita puts it back in place. "You're simple," Dita informs Aunt Beth, "and have come from far away. You don't recognize what land this is. You don't recognize your home."

Aunt Beth seems content to sit on the porch wrapped in the Afghan. She doesn't notice the people filing past to examine her. Once they have gawked at the crazy woman, they go on about their business. We are easily entertained here at the Rez.

Max and Lena can't figure what to make of her because she's so unresponsive. You can't have a conversation with her. You wonder if she actually registers anything you say. She must on some level because she does what you tell her to do. Max has the devil in him. He tells Aunt Beth to touch her nose with her thumb. He hands her a peanut and tells her to eat it. Later, when we bring her inside, Max sneaks over when no one is looking and tells her to stand in the bathtub. Athena reprimands him for that. Lena and

I hide in the garage and laugh about it where Max can't see us so that he'll behave and take it seriously.

We converted the little TV room next to the kitchen into a simple bedroom for Aunt Beth with a bed, dresser, nightstand, and chair. It's sunny, with windows overlooking the lake. Athena unpacks Aunt Beth's few belongings and puts them away.

"We have to get her into more comfortable shoes," I note.

"Agreed," Athena replies.

In the morning I head out to work, the children go to school, and we leave Athena to handle Aunt Beth. When we return, Aunt Beth is sitting on the porch.

"How'd it go?" I ask Athena.

"Easy. She just sits as the day is long."

After supper I wash Aunt Beth's hair and put conditioner in it and Athena combs it out and trims the broken ends. It is Kapa hair. It has a mind of its own. It looks tidy when we finish with it. Aunt Beth looks healthier.

In the mornings, Athena puts her out on the porch. After a few days she starts to have a little color in her cheeks. Mostly she just sits. Sometimes she scans the sky. What are you looking for Aunt Beth? A sign? A message from your dead son? Your dead sister? Your dead people? I wait for messages from the dead myself. Perhaps I should scan the sky too.

On Saturday morning I lie awake in bed for a few minutes before I get up. I think about Phil, who has gone to Pittsburgh for a family reunion. I reach to my neck and pull out the chain with my wedding band on it. I dangle it above my face and look at the ring that I no longer wear on my finger, the ring that binds my heart. Before he went to the reunion, Phil asked me about getting a legal divorce. What will I tell him when he returns? In my heart I grieve for you Odysseus and continue to long for your return.

I get up, wash, make coffee. I peek into Aunt Beth's room. She lies on her bed, staring at the ceiling. Same every morning. She will stay there like that until someone arrives to get her up or she has to use the bathroom, whichever comes first. Does anything go through her head? Can she summon even a single thought?

I make her a slice of toast. I have decided that today she will leave the porch. She is starting to irritate me with her nothingness. I wish she would say strange, indecipherable things at inappropriate times. I wish she would spit and curse. I wish she would shout or break something or possibly chase me with a meat cleaver. I want her to holler because she wasted her life.

I watch her as she methodically chews her toast.

Maybe I am crazier than Aunt Beth, married to a ghost, choosing a phantom husband over a real one.

After I finish my coffee and toast, I lead Aunt Beth down the porch steps. I link my arm through hers and walk her along the road in its graceful arc through the Bapa. We walk in silence. She carefully studies the ground under her feet, as if in fear of stumbling. We walk in the early morning, fog-fresh and damp with opportunity. We follow the road to the lakefront. When we arrive at the lake I sit her on a bench and I sit down next to her. She lifts her eyes from her feet and gazes out across the misty lake. She looks up at the overcast sky, as she so often does, and she smiles. I haven't seen her smile since we brought her to the Bapa. I resist an impulse to run up the road shouting to everyone that Aunt Beth smiled. She scans the cloudy sky and then she looks out over the lake. She raises her hands in front of her. It is the first gesture I can recall seeing her make that is not in response to an order she has been given. She stands, and with her arms outstretched, she walks into the water.

I laugh gleefully. What have you done Aunt Beth? Do you still have a little fight in you? She stands in water up to her ankles. Her ill-fitting penny loafers gathering lake mud. I guide her out of the water.

"Aunt Beth, look what you've done. Your feet are wet." Neither one of us actually cares.

She says the first word I have heard fall from her lips. "B'Taka."

"Yes, B'Taka," I confirm gently. "You're home."

Tears run down Aunt Beth's cheeks. Her hands, still outstretched toward the water, tremble. "B'Taka," she repeats again and again. She has come home to the bear. Her life is by no means over. And no telling what will happen next.

Who am I to say that a woman has wasted her life?

Book 8: Penelope
Yopika Bapa, 1976

Phil and I walk along the edge of the lake, sparkling in the first blush of summer. The sky is one sliver of sun short of sunset. The mosquitoes are having a party but we wear insect repellant so I am impervious. We appreciate the cool breeze from the lake after the day's heat. Phil leads me by the hand to a bench. I have started to think of this particular bench as "Beth's Bench" because she likes to sit here.

"Aunt Beth started to make tea for herself this week."

"That's an improvement."

"It is, isn't it? She doesn't do a whole lot on her own volition. Hey, look, a blue heron." I point.

"I see it." He nods. He turns to me purposefully. "Did you make the appointment?"

I pause, I swallow. "No."

"Are you going to?"

Why can't things just go on as they are? I look down at my fingers laced in his and say nothing.

"You're not going to, are you?" He removes his hand from mine. He is talking about the divorce lawyer.

A hot tear drips from my face into my lap.

"Penelope, look at me."

I look into his earnest face, his deep brown eyes and those long eyelashes that I have kissed on countless occasions.

"I love you. I want to marry you. I want for us to be a family; you, me, Lena, Max. I'm hoping I can convince you to change your mind about having children with me; hoping you will take the plunge and carry my baby. Odysseus left. He's not coming back. He has nothing to offer you. Let go of him. Don't let him ruin the rest of your life."

And here it is. "You're right about him, but I can't let him go."

"What is it? Is it the name thing? Jeez! You're not living in a Greek epic. Just because his name is Odysseus and yours is Penelope doesn't mean he'll turn up twenty years later with an outlandish tale of his adventures. That makes no sense."

"No, I don't think he's coming back. Phil, you're a beautiful, good man and I'm grateful that you want to marry me. It's just, I can't give you what you want. I'm not going to change my mind about more children. And you deserve a wife who will give you children of your own. Little Phils with your gorgeous eyes and your luscious lips." I touch his lips gently with my fingertips. "And you deserve a wife who loves you, exclusively, without the intrusion of the ghost of a husband that will not leave."

"He won't leave because you won't kick his ass out. You're torturing yourself for no reason. It's all in your head." He taps my forehead in frustration with a finger to illustrate.

"The truth is that I don't love you as much as I loved him," I confess in a tiny voice. "That didn't come out right."

"It sounded pretty straightforward to me."

"I love you, just not enough. I know what it's like to love someone totally and you should have a wife who loves you that way. I will never be that wife."

"I get it." He laughs a brittle, bitter laugh. "If he turned up tomorrow, or ten years from now, you'd go back to him wouldn't you? You'd leave me and go right back to him."

I stare up at Phil, his face contorted with anger and hurt. "I'm not sure," I answer honestly. "But I might. That's not fair to you."

"Well guess what, baby? Life's not fair. It wasn't fair to you and you refuse to get over it. You won't get a better offer than this."

"You're right." I've hurt him deeply and the guilt is unbearable.

"Think it over. I've got to get out of here. Call me if you change your mind, if you decide to go to that lawyer and take care of business. But do it soon."

He strides up the street to where he parked his car and gets in and drives away in a puff of dust. I sit on the bench for a long time, trying to think how to tell Lena and Max that Phil is gone.

After Phil leaves, I have more time to myself. I have time to write. I am ready to find the words for the story welling up in me. I name this story *Death in Hoper Valley*. I will dedicate it to Carla because she is my muse. But completing it lies far in the distant future. The story has become bigger for me than the events that took place here at the Bapa all those years ago. I want to chart my loss, my mother's loss, Aunt Beth's loss.

I invent the Anderson family who lives on land they believe belongs to them. They are in for a surprise. I have given Molly Anderson a loving husband. I imagine that she met Owen Anderson while at college, where she studied English and early childhood education, of course, like me. And also like me, I have made Molly a writer. Or rather she *was* a writer. She envisioned a Bohemian lifestyle for herself, in which she rented a little apartment in the East Village in New York. She studied in London for a semester and kicked around Europe and the Mediterranean. Italy. Greece. Her visit to Athens turned into quite an escapade and she had intended for that to form the basis for her first novel. While Molly was banging around Europe, she would not have imagined in a million years that one day she would settle down at Hoper Ranch and have a heap of children. But life happens. The things she wanted changed after she met Owen Anderson, affectionately called "Andy" by his friends.

Andy was destined for Hoper Ranch. He fit into the ranch like a seed in loam. Andy saved Hoper Ranch from financial ruin. Straight out of agriculture school, he took the ranch over from Molly's father and converted it from orchards with aging and diseased fruit trees into a range-fed organic beef-cattle operation. He described himself as a grass farmer. "I grow the right feed to raise happy beef." Andy said range-fed beef was the future. It made sense in more ways than one. Hoper Ranch had once been a huge cattle ranch when Molly's ancestors first came to the land and settled there. In fact, Hoper Ranch had put Hoper Valley on the map in the late 1800s.

I will write this story about these kind, good-hearted, homespun people. Molly and Andy. I'm going to make terrible things happen to them. Watch me do it.

From *Death in Hoper Valley*

On the Saturday that Eli gave her the news that tilted the world crooked, Molly noticed the old woman wrapped in the bright red, blue, and green quilt at the corner of the soccer field. She had seen her there twice before. The woman didn't cheer, just watched, while she sipped a hot drink that she brought in a thermos. She was sitting beside the field when Molly arrived and she stayed on after the game ended, which gave Molly the impression that she hadn't come to see any particular child or team.

Molly sat with her husband Andy in their blue folding chairs on the sidelines and cheered like the dickens for their twin fourteen-year-old boys, Mike and Mac, who constituted a formidable offensive assault on the opposing team. "Sat in their chairs" was a euphemism for attended the game. The chair served as a launch pad for Andy, who ran up and down the field spouting advice like "stay on them" and "pass it" and his favorite war cry "take it away, it's your ball!" Molly jumped in and out of her chair as well, but she limited her exclamations to whooping when they scored or made a great play.

Eli and Peg's son Drew played on the twins' team. They were Molly and Andy's closest friends and owned a sheep farm, mostly run by Peg. Eli worked as a family doctor out of a small country clinic in the heart of town. Molly noticed that Eli was subdued and figured he had a hard week in the clinic. After the game, Eli insisted Molly and Andy come by the house for a bite to eat.

"We're going over to Drew's house," Andy informed the twins as they barreled off the field, their faces flushed and sweaty.

"I made three goals," Mac boasted.

"I assisted on two of them," Drew noted as he punched Mac's arm. "I should get credit for those two. I set them up, put the ball right in front of you."

"Yeah, yeah, yeah," Mac replied with a wide grin.

"Pass the cooler," Mike demanded as Andy opened the hatch door of the van. Andy handed him the Playmate and he took a plastic container of water out of it, dumped half of it over his head, and drank the rest.

Eli opened the door of his Dodge and told the boys, "Why don't you guys come with me and Andy will take the girls." The boys piled in obediently, exuberant with the taste of victory. Andy and Molly settled Bethany, their ten-year-old, and Eli and Peg's two daughters into the van. They rolled out of the parking lot. Molly listened to the girls chatting in the back seat. Andy listened to the weather channel, then popped in a Coleman Hawkins tape. Molly leaned back against the headrest contentedly.

They parked at Eli and Peg's and the girls clambered out of their seats and ran off. Molly helped Peg make peanut butter and jelly sandwiches for the kids, who ran around the yard kicking a soccer ball between them, like a bunch of spooked chickens. They put the sandwiches out on the picnic table with a big pitcher of lemonade and paper cups. When they returned to the kitchen, Eli looked up from the table where he sat and nodded at Peg, who locked the back door. Molly's eyes darted from one to the other in alarm. If they were locking the kids out in the yard, they had something serious to discuss. "What is it?" Molly asked.

"Sit down," Eli said, pulling out a chair for Molly. She glanced at Andy as they sat at the table.

"I should really do this at the office," Eli apologized. He was their family doctor and had delivered each of their five children. He had an office at a clinic that faced the single main intersection of their small town. "I got the results of your mammogram, Molly." He put his hand on her arm. "You have abnormal masses in your breasts. We can't determine what these are without a biopsy. We need to do that right away."

"What do you mean?" Molly asked, dumbfounded. She had gone for a routine mammogram the week before. She didn't have any problems. What Eli said made no sense.

"I mean you may have something going on with your breasts," Eli replied.

"My breasts are fine. Maybe they got my records mixed up with someone else's."

Eli looked to Peg for help. Peg, always placid and calm, told Molly evenly, "Hon, you have lumps in your breasts. And they could be any number of things. They could simply be cysts with fluid in them. Let's hope so.

Unfortunately, they could also be tumors. If they're tumors, that's just if, then Eli needs to find out what the hell kind of tumors they are."

"Tumors?" The whole scene suddenly felt surreal, like it was happening to someone else. Molly's face flushed and her heart pounded. This wasn't real.

"Not necessarily," Eli spoke evenly. "We don't know what you have in there."

"How soon can we find out?" Andy asked, his voice cracking in the middle of the sentence.

"I've scheduled you for a needle biopsy in the radiology department at the medical center in Carlysle at ten o'clock on Wednesday. It was the soonest appointment I could get. Peg will go with you. She'll drive."

"I'm going too. Can't they do it sooner?" Andy demanded. "Why can't they do it Monday?"

"It's OK," Molly told her husband in a shaky voice. "I need a little time." She needed to have her body to herself before doctors started inserting needles into it. "What will they do at the biopsy?"

Eli produced a pamphlet, which he slid across the table to her. She took it and did not look at it. Instead she searched Eli's face. She had the bizarre thought that this was a practical joke and in a minute Eli would say "gotcha" and everything would be normal again. "Details are in that pamphlet. Basically, they're going to give you a few shots of Novocain to numb you up so they can insert needles into the lumps and remove a sampling of cells to send to the pathology lab. Since you have more than one lump, they'll do it in a few different places. The procedure isn't painful. In many instances, cysts will simply deflate when the needle is inserted."

"So it could just be cysts?" Molly asked hopefully.

"That is one possibility," Eli answered.

"Can Peg come into the room with me, you know, when they insert the needles?" Molly's voice quavered.

"I don't think so but you can ask. They do it in a sterile environment. Here," he handed her a little envelope. "Valium. Take it in the morning to help you relax. I wrote the directions on the front of the envelope."

Molly tried to imagine herself stretched out on a cold antiseptic table while shrouded doctors inserted needles into her breasts and she shuddered. Glancing at the envelope of Valium, she read the words "for anxiety."

"How long will it take to get the results?" Andy asked.

"About a week. And they'll send them to me. I'll call as soon as I get them," Eli promised.

Bethany's face appeared in the window of the door. She knocked. "Hey, you guys, the door is locked."

Peg pretended it was a mistake. "Oh, sorry, hon," she called as she got up to let Bethany in.

Bethany held the pitcher out. "Those guys drank all the lemonade. You got more?" she asked breathlessly.

Peg took the pitcher. "You run on outside and I'll mix up another batch and bring it out in a minute." Bethany rushed out.

"I don't want to say anything to the children," Molly told the others. "I don't want to worry them when it could be nothing."

"It really could be nothing," Peg repeated reassuringly.

Molly set her mind to remain positive. It was just a scare. A wake-up call to remind them to take better care of their health and to appreciate their good fortune a little more. "It's OK," she told Andy. "I feel fine and I think I would know if something was wrong. I would have a sense about it."

"Worrying won't make a bit of difference." Eli gave his informed advice.

"But it's hard not to," Peg muttered, ever practical.

"It's impossible," Andy said, his voice wavering.

Bataka, 1976

At the Rez we call the town Bataka now. Doesn't a place take its name from what the residents call it? If we put the name into circulation, maybe people will start calling our town Bataka after a while. An organic evolution of nomenclature.

We have an initiative on the ballot for the election in November. Thorn and I sit in front of the grocery store at a card table with flyers protected from the autumn breeze by the weight of a rock. I'm hopeless at accosting strangers. Thorn boldly calls to people as they pass by, attempting to engage them in conversation, to get his foot in the door and make an opening so we can explain the history of the place in which we live together and why the name must change.

I'm tired. I got up at five o'clock to work on my novel, but I didn't get far. I worked a six-hour classroom shift at Head Start. After that I went to a class at the college. I want to eat dinner and put my feet up.

Nelson drives over and parks the car in the no-parking zone in front of the store by our table. He rolls down his window. "Penelope, get in," he calls.

"What is it? Are the children OK?" I ask in alarm.

"They're OK. An incident occurred at the school, though, and it involved Lena."

"But she's OK?"

"Yeah, she's OK, but we have to go to the school. Leave your car here, we'll come back for it later." I grab my purse and jump in beside Nelson. Thorn looks worried.

"What happened?"

Nelson pulls out of the lot. "Some boys at school cornered Lena and Marilyn on their way home. I didn't get the details. Fortunately a teacher discovered them before it got too far out of hand. They are calling the boys' parents in and they called Athena. She went to the school and sent me for you."

"Did they physically harm the girls?"

"The principal told Athena that they're OK."

I want to see my Lena. I'm glad Nelson is driving. I would get a speeding ticket.

At the school, a teacher waits for us at the front door. She leads us into the principal's office. When we enter, Lena leaps off Athena's lap and runs to me. I wrap her in my arms and she starts crying. "He hit me with a rock," she tells me quietly.

The principal says, "We have the boys and their parents in the conference room. If someone will stay here with these girls, I'd like for the others to come with me."

Athena stays with the children. Marilyn's mother, Nelson, and I follow the principal.

When we enter the conference room, a wave of hostility nearly knocks me over. There are four boys and an assortment of their parents. One of the fathers argues hotly with a teacher. "They started this mess with their attack on the Hoepper name." The man is coiled and about one rattler fang short of a venomous assault. "If you want to talk about discrimination then let's talk about smearing a family's name all over town. I'm proud of Perry for sticking up for his family. I'd a done the same, if push came to shove."

"This was not a push-come-to-shove, Mr. Hoepper, this was an outright attack. Your boy and his friends attacked two girls who are several years younger and quite a bit smaller than they are. I caught them throwing rocks at the girls," the teacher says, heroically maintaining her calm.

A doughy woman wags her finger at me and Nelson when we enter. "It's them Injuns what's making this mess. Telling the town my children come from rapists and murderers. We're goin' to get a lawyer and sue you for libel you keep this up," she threatens shrilly. I wince at her use of the word "Injun."

"Be that as it may, the topic of discussion here," the principal tells the Hoeppers firmly, "is the fact that these boys may not under any circumstances throw rocks at other students. We have a zero tolerance for violence policy in the district and the consequence of this incident is that you boys," she speaks directly to Perry and his companions in crime, "will be suspended from school for one week."

The Hoeppers sputter in anger, while the principal turns to me and Nelson and asks, "Do you intend to press charges?"

"Press charges?!" Mr. Hoepper explodes.

"Yes," the principal replies. "Throwing rocks at a person is assault, which is against the law."

I look to Nelson for help. Marilyn's mother smoothes her dress and sits down abruptly in an empty chair. The three of us are at a loss as to how to respond to this situation.

"Come Perry," Mrs. Hoepper says, standing in fury, "we're going home."

The principal blocks the door for a moment and tells the Hoeppers and the other families, "These boys may not come back to school for one week. If you wish to collect their homework so they do not fall behind, you may stop at the office at the end of each day and we will have it available for you."

"This is not over, you're going to hear about this," Mr. Hoepper threatens. The boys and their parents crowd behind the Hoeppers to follow them out of the room. The principal is not ready to let them leave yet. She speaks directly to the children. "We do not throw rocks at other people. I expect you to obey the rules of the school in future. If you have a disagreement with another person then you speak with them about it respectfully. If you would like to have a school-wide discussion about the issue of the history of Hoepper's Knee and the name of the town, that can be arranged."

"Discussion?" Mr. Hoepper is so beside himself with fury that he practically squeaks. "Discussion?! You can put your discussion where the sun don't shine!" The principal has stepped aside and the Hoeppers barge through the door. Most of the others follow, but one woman and her son hang back. The woman tells the principal adamantly, "I assure you that our Bobby will never, ever throw rocks at another child again. This incident will have serious consequences for him at home." Bobby sobs. His mother says to Bobby, "You are not leaving here until you apologize to those girls." She asks the principal, "Are the girls here?"

The principal replies that they are across the hall in her office. The mother prods her miserable son. "Apologize to these people and after that you will apologize to the girls."

Bobby sniffles an apology to us and his mother carts him across the hall to see our daughters. I half expect her to drag him by the ear. She has his upper arm locked firmly in her grip. Well, at least one of these families does not condone throwing rocks at little girls, even if they are "Injuns." After Bobby and his mother have left, the principal assures us, "We take this kind of thing very seriously. If you have questions or concerns about how this is handled, please do not hesitate to call me. Would you like to press charges? If so, we should call the police."

"That won't be necessary," Nelson says. "This has been traumatic enough for our girls." I agree with Nelson. But I wonder if we are running scared.

"If you change your mind, call me. I had expected a more civilized discussion. I'm surprised and frankly dismayed that the parents of these boys have taken the view that they have."

Marilyn's mother stands and I put my arm around her as we return to the principal's office to retrieve our children. She is a reserved, shy person, which makes this situation even more difficult for her. Bobby, still sniveling, and his mother pass us coming out of the principal's office. "Very, very sorry," the mother apologizes as we pass in the corridor.

Nelson motions to Athena. "We're leaving."

I ask Lena and Marilyn, "Did you get hurt when the boys threw those rocks at you?" Athena answers that Lena has a bruise coming up on her hip and Marilyn's leg is scraped, but neither injury appears serious. The girls look at us out of large, solemn eyes. I wonder what they think.

Athena takes the girls and Marilyn's mother back to the Rez. I go with Nelson to pick up my car at the grocery store. After riding a couple of blocks in silence, I turn to Nelson and ask, "What just happened?"

Nelson laughs. He laughs so hard he can barely watch the road.

"What's funny?"

"We really got under their skin, didn't we?"

I don't find it as humorous as Nelson does and I remember when I went to the Council and they told me I didn't fully understand how this name change thing might impact our children. I wish the election was over. We won't win and I'm tired of fighting.

Nelson pats my hand. "We'll be OK. Been around thousands of years. The Kapa are as old as B'Taka Lake."

That night, I can't sleep. I get up and prowl the porch. On an impulse I pick up the phone and dial Phil's number. A recorded message tells me the number has been changed. The area code is different. I call the operator and ask her about the area code. She tells me it's the area code for Pittsburgh, Pennsylvania. I will never see Phil again. I'm sure he will find happiness with some other woman in Pittsburgh.

I slide into my desk chair and place my fingers lightly on the keys of my typewriter, poised to do my bidding.

From *Death in Hoper Valley*

On the way home they listened to the same Coleman Hawkins music while the same vibrant autumn images swept past the windows. But for Molly, the clarity and brilliance of the day had evaporated. She sank into panic. She wanted to have a good cry in private. After Andy parked, she told him she needed to go for a walk. He wrapped her in his arms and whispered in her ear, "It'll turn out to be nothing, just nothing. We shouldn't get ourselves all worked up over it."

She put on her worn cotton gloves and stepped out on the old herder's path that meandered throughout their two hundred acres of rolling meadow and forest. Her thoughts immediately turned to her children. From the moment that Susan parted the curtain of life to make her entrance seventeen years ago, Molly lived with a mother's irrational terror that misfortune might befall her children at each twist in the road. Injury, illness, disappointment, and harm lurked. She feared for the children's health, safety, and happiness, and had not given much thought to her own health or how her health might impact her children's happiness.

A sweet, deep ache sometimes penetrated to Molly's bones at the sight of her firstborn child's youth and beauty. Susan had shiny, thick, chestnut hair, straight as a horse's tail, often braided, her bangs curling ever so slightly inward across her forehead. The muscular competence of Susan's legs gave away the fact that she was an athlete. These days she had a passion for volleyball; in the past she had gone out for soccer and basketball as well. Off the volleyball court, fashion-conscious Susan was the picture of poise and elegance; the diametrical opposite of her younger sister Kelly, who wore overalls day-in-day-out and, at fifteen, already took her school studies as seriously as any college student. Kelly understood how long and hard she would have to study to reach her goal of becoming a veterinarian. A devoted 4Her, from her first guinea pig right on up to raising rabbits and breeding goats, she regularly volunteered to help Andy with the cattle. Last year she inoculated the entire herd. Andy boasted about it at the feed store. Ironically, Andy's boys had no interest in the ranch. Instead his quiet daughter hovered at his elbow. Kelly seemed years older than her brothers even though only one year separated them. Mac and Mike had been a handful, and trailing Kelly by just that one year made it feel like having triplets, as if twins weren't enough. They hadn't meant to space the children so close together. The twins were, as they say, "an accident." And they sure hadn't bargained for twin boys. What a circus. Molly smiled to herself. Well, she wouldn't give up those twin cyclones of enthusiasm and good humor for anything in the world. They were a matched set of pure energy, as pure as light.

Once she and Andy recovered from the toddlerhood of Mac and Mike, and the twins started preschool, she talked Andy into having one more. He almost changed his mind and balked at the last minute. He kidded Molly in private that Bethany got in under the wire. Just about the same day Molly realized she was pregnant, and before she had told him, Andy had asked her if she would go back on birth control until they talked about it further because he was having second thoughts. "Well," Molly told him with a smug smile, "I think the horse has already bolted from the stable."

"You mean it's too late to close the barn door?"

"Too late to close the barn door."

"You get your five."

"They're your five too."

"I just hope you're not carrying twin boys."

Luckily, she was not. She wondered if another set of twin boys would have destroyed their marriage. Instead, they had Bethany, a child so angelic that all of nature stood in awe of her. No dog barked at her. No bee dared to sting her. As a toddler, when she stepped into the garden, the butterflies circled her head like a halo. She was a wise Buddha baby. Now Bethany was ten years old. They grew so quickly.

Molly hiked up toward the ridge. She liked to walk uphill on the walk out and downhill when she came back. She had a habitual loop that took her through a stretch of forest she loved, had loved since childhood. The oak trees had dropped many of their golden leaves and the chalk-green lichens clinging to the branches were more visible, like torn lace dangling from the branches. Many of the ancient oaks and madrones had individual personalities for her and she thought of them as old friends. She had told them the secrets of her girlhood heart, weeping in melodramatic adolescent grief over small infractions and rejoicing over silly successes that meant the world to her at the time. The maternal madrones flowed gracefully into the dips and bulges of their feminine curves. The stout oaks wore their moss cloaks and, in the winter months, their mantillas of delicate lichens. The upper branches twisted into contortions that defied logic. The tough, unyielding flame-orange-red manzanitas squatted beneath the larger trees. Molly loved this landscape, this land. She could not imagine living anywhere other than in this breathtaking northern California landscape in which she grew up, the only child of big-hearted country folks whose family had lived at Hoper Ranch for a hundred years.

Molly knew the story well. Hoper Valley was named after Molly's great-great grandfather, who had been murdered by Indians in the 1880s. Hoper Valley was an all-American down-home town, a Mayberry or Centerburg, where Bessie served fresh-baked apple pie at the diner until midnight and if you were running late to get to the movies you could call Jackson, who owned the movie theater, and he'd hold the movie five minutes until you got over there. How could a person have a charmed life like Molly's, married to Andy, with five smart and talented children, living on this beautiful land, and then out of the blue have breast cancer at forty-five? The hot tears of self-pity, bewilderment, and anger finally flowed as Molly sat on a log and wept.

It couldn't be breast cancer. No one in her family had ever had breast cancer. She ate homegrown food, including organic range-fed beef. She breathed clean air and drank clean water from a three-hundred-foot well. She was not a candidate for cancer. Not so young. They would do their horrible needle tests and find nothing. She felt fine. She was tempted to tell Eli not to worry about it and to decline the needle biopsy. If it were just her, and she had no children, no husband, that's exactly what she would do. But she had to do the responsible thing and go for the test so they could confirm that nothing was wrong. If she had something wrong, then she would feel it, right? And she absolutely didn't. Molly returned from her walk in better spirits.

Andy stood at the stove in his barbecuing apron that said DANGER! MEN AT WORK, frying chicken. He had put potatoes on to boil and grated cabbage and carrots for a coleslaw. The kitchen smelled delicious and felt warm like a living thing.

"It's going to turn out fine," she reassured Andy. "It's just a bad scare."

Yopika Bapa, 1976

The house fills with people eager to congratulate me. I still wear my graduation gown. Aunt Beth holds the mortar board cap, clutching it to her with fierce proprietorship. June and Hera made a huge sheet cake with white icing and ridiculously gaudy decorations. Max hops from one foot to the other in front of the cake, "Can we cut the cake? Can I have a purple flower? Is it chocolate inside or vanilla?" The thought of that cake has him three granules short of a sugar frenzy.

"Go outside and help Nelson light the fire," I tell Max. "We'll cut the cake soon. Here," I hold out a banana, "eat this if you're hungry." He frowns. "Go help Nelson," I thrust the banana into his hand. He takes it reluctantly as he heads out the kitchen door.

Athena and June put food on the table. They made heaps of fry bread; greasy, doughy, and oh so delicious. Aunt Beth hums to herself. I open the leather case and look at my diploma again. Bachelor of Arts in English and Early Childhood Education. I pat Aunt Beth's knee. She waited a long time to see this.

Nelson enters the kitchen with Max trailing behind.

"I just sent him out to help you light the fire," I tell Nelson.

"It's lit. We have a gift for you." His eyes twinkle. Max hops up and down. June and Athena wipe their hands on their aprons and come over to where I sit. Nelson grins like a coyote in the hen yard as he hands me an envelope. I glance around at their expectant faces, fearful that this gift will make me cry.

I open the envelope and pull out a brochure about a resort hotel on Maui. Inside the brochure I find an airplane ticket. I don't have to put on an act to provide the family with the satisfaction of an extreme response. I yelp with delight!

"Ten days on Maui with your typewriter," Athena says. "And none of us to disturb you."

Max jumps into my lap. "Bring me sea shells," he demands.

I give Lena a one-armed hug. "It's a good surprise, isn't it?" she asks.

"A terrific surprise."

"And Max knew and he didn't tell," Lena points out.

"I didn't tell." Max leaps off my lap and goes to the table to gawk at the cake.

"Thank you. Thank you all so much."

"When was the last time you went away on a vacation? Without children?" Nelson asks.

"I can't remember." But I can. I remember too well. I went to Greece.

I imagine the luxury of opening a suitcase in a hotel room, with precious solitude stretching before me as the day is long. I imagine tapping on my typewriter while drinking a rich cup of coffee. No children to look after. No job to go to. No school papers to write. No chores. No obligations. No failed campaigns to change the name of a town. My mouth waters just thinking about those ten days on Maui. "This is the best gift ever. A slice of heaven."

June and Athena laugh and look at each other and say "OH." They are delighted that I am delighted. June says, "We better cut that cake before Max drools on it."

I take the airplane ticket and my diploma into my bedroom and lay them on the nightstand. I am blessed.

I glance at the manuscript piled on my desk.

Poor Molly. How I torture her. It's for a higher purpose, unlike in real life.

From *Death in Hoper Valley*

On Wednesday morning, Molly awoke shaky and anxious. Andy got the kids off to school. He told them Mom didn't feel well. Molly had not intended to take the Valium that Eli gave her. She changed her mind when she found her hands shaking so much that she had trouble tying her shoes. The Valium helped.

Peg dropped Molly and Andy off at the entrance and went to park the car. The receptionist gave Molly a clipboard with a stack of paperwork to fill out. A pen dangled from the clipboard on a metal beaded string. The words on the paper looked like ants marching across a sun-washed sidewalk. She handed the clipboard to Andy. He filled most of the papers out, asking Molly an occasional question about family health history. He passed the papers to Molly and showed her where to sign. She couldn't think straight between the Valium and the residue of anxiety not suppressed by the Valium.

When a nurse arrived to take Molly into the radiology room for the procedure, Molly asked, "Could my friend come in with me?"

The nurse glanced back and forth between Molly and Peg with concern.

Peg put an arm around Molly. "Molly's nervous about this. I'm her doctor's wife and a close family friend."

"I'll double-check, but it should be OK," the nurse said kindly. Peg gave Andy the high sign as she went through the double doors with Molly and the nurse.

In a changing room, the nurse showed Molly a hospital gown to put on and told Peg she would bring her a sterile smock to wear over her clothes. Molly changed into the gown, which made her feel vulnerable and exposed.

After the nurse settled Molly on the table for the procedure, she covered her with cotton blankets that had been warmed and felt as if fresh from the dryer.

When the doctor entered, he smiled and put a gentle hand on Molly's arm. "So we're going to get a few samples today and we'll have you out of here in a jiffy." An older man, he had a fatherly bedside manner. "Do you have any questions?"

Molly shook her head negative, her eyes wide with terror. Peg introduced herself, extending her hand, which the doctor shook. "I'm Molly's friend Peg. You probably know my husband Eli."

"Oh yes," the doctor confirmed. "Of course. Good man your husband."

"I've always thought so. I came along to help Molly out. She's pretty nervous about this procedure."

The doctor turned to Molly. "Do you understand what we're going to do or do you want me to explain it to you first?"

"I understand. Let's get it over with."

The nurse uncovered Molly's breasts and wiped them with a cold liquid. The doctor injected her breasts with Novocain in the spots where he would insert the biopsy needles. He apologized before injecting the Novocain, which didn't hurt much, just felt like a bee sting for a brief moment. Molly had anticipated more pain. The Novocain injections were the most painful part and they weren't bad. Eli had not lied when he said it was a relatively painless procedure.

Peg stood at Molly's shoulder and held her hand. "OK," the doctor told Molly, "I'm going to insert the biopsy needle over here. It shouldn't hurt. If it hurts, you tell me right away." Molly hung onto Peg's hand and squeezed her eyes shut. The doctor talked to the nurse as they methodically collected the samples they needed, tracking locations. Molly felt like a claustrophobic in a small cave, like she had to get out, like she couldn't breathe. The thought of having the biopsy needle in her breast spooked her. It had nothing to do with what she could actually feel. It was all inside her head. It panicked her to think of that needle in her breast and she couldn't wait for the doctor to remove it each time. "Is the needle in now?" she kept asking.

The doctor patiently answered whenever she asked. After he finished at one site, he moved on to the next. "Is the needle in now?" Molly would ask and he would answer that it was in, or out, or that he was about to put one in. The procedure became interminable for Molly. "I can't do this anymore," she informed them. "I have to stop now."

The nurse put her hand on Molly's arm to steady her. "We need samples from all the problematic sites," she explained. "We want a picture of what's going on in there."

"Hang on, hon, they'll be done soon," Peg said as she squeezed Molly's hand and started talking, rambling on about her sheep herd, relating mundane things. Nothing she said registered in Molly's brain, but the droning of her voice soothed Molly. The nurse and Peg conversed about livestock and Molly listened to them to distract herself. Then the doctor said, "That's it, we're done, you did a great job." Molly knew she had not done a great job, nevertheless she appreciated the doctor's kindness.

"Let's get you up and changed," the nurse told her brightly.

"Can I just lie here for a few minutes?" Molly asked shakily.

"I thought you couldn't wait to get out of here and now you want to stick around," Peg teased. Molly produced a weak smile.

The nurse brought Molly a cup of orange juice. It tasted delicious. As she drank it, relief flooded through her.

Peg helped her change into her street clothes and they went out to the lobby where they found Andy forty squares deep into a crossword puzzle. "You OK?" he asked. Molly nodded.

"She was a real trooper," Peg told him. "Just wait here and I'll bring the car."

On the drive home, Molly dozed in the back seat while listening to Peg and Andy talk about breeding rabbits. Back at the ranch, she slept until dinner-time. Andy made her potato-leek soup and Bethany read to her before bed.

"What's wrong with Mom?" Mac asked.

"She's a bit under the weather," Andy told him. The children didn't inquire further.

Molly took advantage of having an excuse to stay in bed. A cattle ranch and a farmhouse full of children left a woman little time to herself, especially when the woman worked as a preschool teacher. Molly had taken the week off work. She didn't want to risk having one of the children in her classroom bump her breasts after the procedure. Her mother came over and looked after the housekeeping and Molly actually spent much of the week rereading a couple of her Jane Austen novels. It felt like an extravagant luxury and reminded her that many years ago she had planned a different sort of life, and with that a tiny dormant seed inside her stirred.

Book 9: Penelope
Maui, 1977

I leave the familiar behind, stepping out of the flow of ordinary days as effortlessly as a bird leaving the sky and alighting on a rock. It's shocking how easily I become another woman, a woman unknown to my family, a woman I have kept private. That woman flies to Maui.

When I arrive, a van driver collects me and other guests, greets us with leis, and shuttles us to a resort hotel. I have no expectations. This vacation has taken me by surprise from the day I opened the envelope and saw the ticket. I admire the exotic flowers and trees visible through the window of the van. I wear a lei of magenta and white flowers with petals as soft and kissable as lips, and I receive another lei as I enter the hotel foyer.

The main event at this hotel appears to be the cocktail lounge, open around the clock. In the evening the lounge sways with live music and dancing; just the place for singles to meet and have a romance. When I get it, I laugh my head off. Nelson, June, and Athena have hatched a stealthy plot to manipulate my return into the dating scene. Their plot will backfire, though, because I have other plans. They have coaxed out a woman in me whom they have not glimpsed.

My first day on Maui, I take a long walk on the beach. Any observer would think I walk alone and would not guess that Molly walks with me. I have set her foot on a difficult path. When I return to my room, I lean into the luxury of having nothing to do other than write. I could accomplish a lot in ten days here by myself. I could create worlds.

From *Death in Hoper Valley*

After Molly's week in bed, she felt refreshed. She went to the soccer field with Andy on Saturday to witness the twins in another triumph. My double trouble, Molly thought to herself with smug satisfaction, as she watched her sturdy boys celebrating their win after the game, high-fiving their teammates and guzzling Gatorade like champagne. As Peg, Andy, and the children left the field, Molly lagged behind. She stood for a moment looking at that old woman in the colorful quilt. The woman fascinated her and held her attention almost like an obsession. She approached the woman. "I see you here every week. You must love soccer."

"I like to watch the children play. It's a new generation. They give me hope," the woman stated flatly in a voice that did not sound particularly hopeful.

"I'm Molly Anderson. My husband and I raise cattle at Hoper Ranch. My boys played on the blue team."

"I know who you are," the woman replied. "Your family lives on Kapa land."

Molly was taken aback. Maybe the old woman didn't have both oars in the water. She said to her gently, "I'm not sure we're talking about the same place."

"The Kapa made a home on that land for more than twelve thousand years before Hoper turned up." The woman looked into Molly with a piercing gaze. Molly sensed deep in the center of her bones that the woman spoke a truth that ran like a hidden vein of precious metal in underground rock. A sliver of doubt about all that she believed about her family and her ranch slid a slender finger through a chink in the armor of Molly's reality. She held eye contact with the quilt-wrapped woman, who saw in Molly's eyes that flicker of doubt.

The woman smiled a smile like fresh rain. Had Molly just passed a secret test? With that smile, the woman tossed her head, and Molly noticed the flash of the woman's silver earrings in the shape of bears as they caught the light and sparkled where they dangled. The sun picked out black-blue and white-gray strands of the woman's variegated hair that matched fabric in the quilt she wore. She leaned forward and held out her hand to Molly. Molly took it. "Teresa Clearwater, pleased to meet you Molly Anderson."

Molly dreamt about Teresa that night. A monster held Molly and her daughters imprisoned in a cave and it planned to eat the children. Molly hid them behind a rock.

She tried to distract the creature so it wouldn't notice the children. Then, out of the corner of her eye, Molly saw Bethany shift behind the rock, and the monster saw it too. He pounced on the children, lifting them in his hand like King Kong examining Faye Ray. He placed the girls in a cage made of closely spaced tall wooden spikes pounded into the floor of the cave. After securing them in this stockade, he left. Molly sat outside the cage weeping and held her daughters' hands through the narrow spaces between the spikes. Teresa landed inside the cave in an airplane. She wore old-fashioned aviator goggles and a bright red scarf. When she put the goggles on top of her head, Molly could see the imprint they left around Teresa's eyes where they had pressed on her skin. "Quick, get in," Teresa commanded. Molly climbed into the plane and they flew over the top of the spiked wall of the stockade. They rescued the girls and flew out of the cave. When they emerged into the sunlight, the airplane disappeared and they rode instead on the backs of sheep, or perhaps cows; the animals kept changing. They rode so fast that the wind whipped past her face. The monster pursued them, throwing large boulders at them. Teresa shot an arrow tipped with fire into the monster's eye. The beast roared in pain and bellowed, "What?! Defeated by a feeble old woman?!" The monster cursed them all;

Teresa, Molly, and the children, "May you never return home."

Molly cried out and woke shivering. Her cry woke Andy and he held her and stroked her hair while she told him her dream. "What a horrible curse; to never go home," she whispered with a shudder.

"You are home," Andy murmured, as his caress moved from Molly's hair to her breasts. He gently ran his fingers over them, cognizant that they were still tender from the biopsy, yet overcome with the desire to touch them. His sensual touch soothed away Molly's terror and dissolved the aftertaste of the strange, vivid dream. They made love slowly and gently in the grainy predawn blue-gray light.

Maui, 1977

I don't want to spend my whole fancy vacation in a hotel room. The evening carries a sweet fragrance inviting me to partake and I can't resist the invitation. I wear a turquoise and aqua rayon dress patterned with flowers. It fits me tightly and I feel sexy. I would enjoy a flirtation and therefore curiously scan the talent on display in the cocktail lounge from atop a bar stool. The bartender, a tall Black man with graying dreadlocks and glowing skin, flashes me a smile. "My name is Bruce and I'm here to serve you tonight. What can I get for you?" he asks in a vaguely Jamaican accent. Affected or real?

"OK, Bruce, I'm Penelope." We're already on a first name basis, I see. I hold out my hand to him and he shakes it. "I'll have a margarita." Why not? If it starts to go to my head, I won't finish it. I can crawl to my hotel room from here.

"Where do you hail from?" Bruce asks as he fixes my drink.

"Bataka," I tell him, with a secret smile.

"Where's that?"

"Northern California."

"Sounds like a Native American name."

"Correct." I think he's flirting with me and I suspect that's part of his job. It wouldn't surprise me if it actually says "flirt with female guests" in his job description. I am upstaged suddenly by a woman in a bright green dress, with green eyes to match, who perches on the stool next to me, or rather lands on it as if making a brief layover between flights. "Beer with lime please, Bruce, and if you have one of those frosty glasses in the freezer I'll love you forever."

"All yours, BJ," Bruce says. The woman wipes sweat from her face with a cocktail napkin. She reaches down into her cleavage and takes a swipe while grinning sideways at me impishly. "Sensational band. Can't stop hopping," she explains, as if this justifies the cocktail napkin down the cleavage.

"You like to dance." I state the obvious in an attempt to make conversation.

"Like Emma Goldman said: If I can't dance to it then it's not my revolution."

"Revolution is a bit more than I can fit into a vacation."

"BJ this is Penelope. Penelope, BJ." Bruce introduces us. "Warning. BJ is trouble. Fun trouble. A scandalous lady." Bruce flashes that brilliant smile again.

"Stow it," BJ warns him. "I've turned over a new leaf."

Bruce throws his head back and laughs. His teeth sparkle. "Must be a fig leaf."

She wags a finger at him and drinks deeply from the cold beer he hands her.

"Hey, BJ, she's a new kid on the block. From California. Why don't you show her around?"

What makes him so sure I want showing around?

I like to watch BJ move. She's graceful and striking, with thick, wavy, brown hair, those emerald eyes, and a sensational, curvaceous figure.

"OK, California, follow me," she beckons me with a snaky hand moving to the beat of the band.

"What have you gotten me into?" I ask Bruce. He winks as I scramble off my seat and hurry to catch up with BJ, who shimmies back out to the dance floor.

Interesting and attractive evening diversions for an aspiring writer with a heavy topic on her hands.

From *Death in Hoper Valley*

On Thursday, when Molly walked in from work, Andy told her Eli had called and wanted them to meet him at the clinic. He had the results of the biopsy. They left a note for the kids, who were still at school, and drove over to the clinic where Eli's assistant ushered them into his office. Soon we'll put this to rest, Molly thought optimistically. They waited briefly for Eli. When he entered the office, he closed the door behind him. Still standing, Eli did not beat around the bush. "They're malignant, Molly. I'm so sorry. You have malignant tumors." Eli's shoulders bowed with the weight of having to deliver the news.

Andy's chest heaved as if a mighty unseen hand had knocked the wind out of him. "No, no, no," he moaned.

"What does that mean?" Molly demanded. She knew what it meant, it just didn't make sense to her. It was just words.

"You have breast cancer," Eli said.

"No I don't," Molly argued irrationally. "I feel fine."

Andy and Eli exchanged a concerned glance.

"I can't have breast cancer." Molly shivered, as Eli's words sunk in. "I have breast cancer? What does that even mean?" Andy reached over and took her hand in his big rough calloused one.

It was not over. It was just beginning.

"What do I have to do? I will not lose my breasts!"

Andy choked down a sob. "Oh sweetheart, it's not about your breasts, it's about your life."

Eli gripped Andy's shoulder firmly. "Let's just take it one step at a time."

"What are my options?" Molly's voice rose dangerously.

"I want to refer you to a breast specialist in Carlysle named Amanda Percy. She's one of the best around and we're lucky to have her in our neck of the woods."

Lucky for whom? Molly wished she had no reason to even hear the name Amanda Percy. "Eli, tell me my options."

"You'd best talk to Amanda about that. I'm out of my league." Eli picked up the phone and called Dr. Percy's office to make an appointment. After that he called the hospital in Carlysle to order a CT Scan. As he hung up he offered, "Would you like for me and Peg to pick up pizza and bring it over for the kids?"

"No," Andy looked at Molly to confirm her response. "We need time alone with the children to explain what's going on."

"We don't *know* what's going on." Molly's voice was edged in anger.

Eli said, "We'll get answers as soon as possible. Amanda will see you tomorrow and she'll arrange for further tests. We need to determine if the cancer has metastasized elsewhere."

"Elsewhere?" Andy echoed. Eli didn't respond. He could tell that Andy understood, he just didn't want to understand.

Maui, 1977

My second day on Maui I stop in at the bar in the late afternoon, hoping to wrangle a few shreds of useful information out of Bruce. Bartenders know everything, right? I want to find out what's up with BJ. She intrigues me. I wonder what scandal she caused last year and what she means by turning over a new leaf.

Bruce sits on a high stool behind the cash register reading the newspaper and listening to jazz on the radio in an empty bar. He looks up and smiles as he sees me approach. "California. What can I do you for?"

I sit on a stool across the counter from him and put my chin in my hands. "You got me tangled up with BJ and she wants to take me to a club in Lahaina tonight. I haven't agreed to go yet. I'm thinking it over. Don't look so innocent."

"Moi?" Bruce blinks his eyes like Tweetie-Bird in the cartoons that Max loves to watch.

I laugh at his performance. "What happened last year?"

Bruce puts a hand on his hip and frowns. "Wouldn't that count as gossip?"

"I don't need the gory details. I just want enough information so I can decide whether to go to Lahaina tonight or not with that woman. I like BJ. She's one horse short of a carousel when it comes to a fun ride. But I'm not up for too much adventure. So is she a drug smuggler or is she a gun moll for the Hawaiian mafia or what?"

Bruce does not answer.

"Am I safe with her?"

Bruce sighs.

"I mean physically safe."

"Depends on how you define that."

"OK, I think that answers my question." I turn away, prepared to spend the night in my room with the typewriter keeping me company.

Bruce hastily calls me back, "Wait. That didn't come out right." He lowers his voice. "Sit. I'll tell you the quick version, if you swear not to tell BJ that I said anything."

"I swear." I pretend to spit in my hand before shaking Bruce's hand to seal the oath. He laughs at my gesture. I sit on a bar stool and lean in. Bruce speaks quietly. "It's not such a big deal, but a lot of people who come down here are pretty conservative so to them it was a big deal. You're from California, so maybe more open-minded? What happened was that she hooked up with a young couple who were honeymooning. The three of them had fun together, until BJ slept with the wife. If it had been a ménage, or even the husband she slept with, I don't think anyone would have batted an eye. But it was just the two women. Holy hell, you would have thought BJ was rabid the way folks acted. Then it turned out the wife was a latent lesbian. She fell head over heels for BJ, decided she had been waiting forever for this moment to arrive. It was way too much drama from there on out. The wife wanted to have the marriage annulled. The husband attempted to strangle BJ with a suitcase leash in the front lobby. BJ disappeared without so much as a peck on the cheek for Miss Newlywed, who promptly tossed all her sandwiches out of the basket and went home in a sorry state. Sad story. Make of it what you will."

I digest the story as I get off the stool and turn to leave.

"Wait," Bruce calls. "I don't like to bad-mouth folks. I like BJ. I hope you'll still go to Lahaina with her. She's OK, just made a bad choice for her vacation romance last year."

"I'll go. She can't do any damage to my marriage. It exploded a long time ago."

I retire to my room to squeeze a little writing in before dinner and the impending escapade into Lahaina with the notorious lesbian seductress.

From *Death in Hoper Valley*

The visit to Amanda Percy left no doubt in Molly's mind that she had only one choice. She had to pick door number two, and behind door number two waited a double mastectomy. Door number one opened on the grim reaper. There was no door number three.

The instant she returned from Amanda's office, she locked herself in the bathroom. Somewhere lab technicians in long white coats were reviewing her CT Scan and looking at biopsies from her lymph nodes under microscopes to determine which parts of her body were infested with alien cells. Only days ago she told Andy that if anything was wrong in her body she thought she would know it. Sitting in her bathroom, she began to hear the hum of cancer cells vibrating in her body for the first time.

Molly stood in front of the mirror and lifted her shirt. She looked at her breasts. Her tender, sensitive, lovely breasts. Molly had nursed five children with her breasts, had enjoyed thousands of nights filled with the pleasure of Andy caressing her breasts; she had admired them on many occasions, pleased with them, proud of them. She loved to tease Andy by giving him glimpses of them or glimpses of the beginning of the rise of the curve of them from a peek-a-boo of clothing, lacy underwear like fancy bras and teddies, old-fashioned fluffy nightgowns. She could still find, deep within her breasts, the memory of the let-down response releasing milk to flow for her babies. Her breasts defined her feminine beauty, her selfhood as mother and woman. How could she live with the gross violation of her womanhood that the doctors proposed?

Amanda Percy would scoop her breasts out and replace them with silicone implants. Filler. Unfeeling matter. Straw. She would never again have the pleasure of Andy arousing her desire by rolling her nipples between his thumb and forefinger, so that, by some mystery, the flame of desire flickered in her thighs at his touch to her nipples. She could not face the thought of their last night together before her impending surgery and his desperate last loving touch of her breasts. She wanted to fight to keep these breasts. But if she refused to submit to their loss, then it would surely open death's door. Perhaps death's door stood open whether or not she lost her breasts. She sat on the lid of the toilet seat and wept.

From deep within, a seductive voice enticed her with the promise of peaceful death. She could slip over to spirit so easily and leave the mess of her body and the mire of physical and psychological pain behind. She did not have to endure the torture of her body's failure. She could choose to pass into the shade.

That was not a viable choice. She had five children who needed their mother, so she would struggle forward in this disappointing body. She would submit to the intrusion of medical treatment. Whatever the doctors required of her, she would do, because she had children to raise. And also because of something else remembered from long ago. She had a mission left unfulfilled. She must survive and persevere because she had lovingly seated the writer in herself in a quiet garden overgrown with honeysuckle and wisteria and she had left her there with the promise that she would return one day. She sent messages to that writer once in a while; messages that soon, when the children had grown more independent, she would return to that other Molly. So far, she had failed to return.

She envied her mother for the years filled with grandchildren she had been given. Molly might never hold a grandchild. Rage at the unseen hand that forced her to this fate engulfed her and she wept for the loss, the injustice, and the fragile, tenuous simplicity of mortality.

Maui, 1977

I meet BJ in the lobby at seven. A tight-fitting shimmery red dress clings to the curves of her exquisitely sinuous figure and she has wrangled her thick mane of hair into a chignon with a large yellow flower pinned in it. I forgot to ask Bruce if BJ is only into women or if she likes men too. I wonder if I have inadvertently agreed to go on a date. Oh well. I'm curious. And, if I'm completely honest with myself, perhaps up for the type of adventure BJ can offer. I'll decide when I want to decide.

BJ frowns, "What's this?" She waves her hand up and down the length of my body as she studies my outfit. I wear a peach-colored rayon shirt and loose-fitting beige linen pants. "Didn't I say we're going out?" She raises an eyebrow.

"I'm comfortable in these clothes."

She pats her hair to see if it's in place, and it is. "Well, don't go dud on me. I want to par-tay."

"Don't worry, I'm up for some late night dancing."

She links her arm through mine and we walk out front to the taxi stand. Her hip bumps gently against me and I smell her perfume, musky and evocative. If I'm noticing her perfume, what does that mean? I have the upper hand because she doesn't know that I know about her. Thank goodness Bruce spilled the beans.

In the taxi she fishes for information, "So, tell me about Penelope. Single? Divorced? You're here by yourself, right?"

I measure my words, deciding how much to reveal. "I have two children, no husband. I just graduated from college with my bachelor's degree. My Tribe (I'm Native), I mean my family, gave me this trip as a graduation present. I'm a writer and this is a writing vacation for me. Ordinarily I have precious little opportunity to write in my everyday life."

"Native? You mean like Indian?"

Vocabulary holds me hostage. "Native American. I belong to the Kapa Tribe."

"Wow, are you full-blooded?"

"Does it make a difference?"

She blushes. "I guess not. Sorry, I don't know much about Native Americans. Just tell me if I put my foot in it." She points at her mouth.

"OK, you put your foot in it. At my Tribe we prefer to be called Native American." I appreciate her candor and her desire to learn.

"Are the rest of the Tribe as attractive as you?"

What a flirt! "Now you're trying to get in my good graces."

"Maybe so."

"What is Maui to you? You come here every year?"

"Usually twice a year. I love Hawaii. I'm saving to move here. I work at an uppity law firm in Phoenix as a legal secretary. In another five years, I expect to have enough saved to buy a condo in Hawaii. Then I'm moving."

"I can't imagine spending my whole life on vacation."

"What to do you mean?"

"This place, this vacation, reminds me of a trip I took to Greece when I was a teenager. It's a step outside everyday reality." This trip is an interlude, a moment to catch my breath, take stock, get on track with my book, refocus. I can't imagine *living* in a vacation destination. I would feel like a tourist in my own life.

"Oh this place is real," BJ assures me with enthusiasm. "The only place I feel real is in Hawaii. Have you ever been to Honolulu?"

"My plane stopped over in the airport there, if that counts."

"No, it doesn't count. I adore Honolulu. I consider myself a born-again Hawaiian. I love everything about the islands. I come to unwind and let my hair down."

"Looks like you put it up tonight," I joke. "It looks lovely like that." I catch a flicker in her eyes as she registers that I notice how she looks.

"This is us," she says as the taxi pulls up to the club.

Disco music mingled with glittery silver-blue light pours onto the sidewalk through the entrance doors when they open and close. I have never gone disco dancing and haven't listened to much disco music. But hey, I'm on vacation and a party is a party. BJ is already dancing as she pays the taxi driver.

Inside the club, a large shiny disco ball spins, casting sparkles of light on the dancers. The volume of the music prevents me from hearing a thing BJ says. She shouts over the music and I shake my head and shrug to indicate I can't hear. She takes my hand and pulls me over to the bar, where I attempt to order. Apparently the bartender can hear us because he sets a beer in front of me and a mixed drink sporting a green paper umbrella in front of BJ, who leads me to a booth where I slide in beside her. Shielded a bit from the music, I can hear her when she shouts in my ear. She asks if I want to dance and I yell over the music that I don't know how to dance to disco. She says she'll show me. We leave our drinks at the booth and snake through dancers who shimmy and shake with smooth moves that rhyme with the rhythm of the music. I don't care what these strangers think of me so I have fun dancing however the mood strikes me. BJ dances like a star and I enjoy watching the glitter of her shiny dress and the slink of her supple figure.

By the time we return to the table, we drip with sweat. I drink half the glass of delicious cold beer in one gulp.

BJ returns from the bar with tall, icy glasses of water. She holds one between her breasts to cool herself off. When she removes the glass and brings it to her lips to drink, the dampness remains in her cleavage. She drains the water. Wisps of hair escape from her chignon and brush her neck. After downing her water, she sips delicately at her mixed drink while she removes the pins from her hair and shakes it out around her shoulders, running her fingers through it in a half-hearted attempt at taming it. She laughs lightly. "So much for looking elegant," she shouts to me over the din.

No apology necessary. She is about one accessory shy of Jackie Onassis when it comes to elegance, style, and grace; with her hair up *or* down.

A tall man with amber-brown skin and thick curls appears and invites BJ to dance. From my vantage point at the booth, I watch them. I am sinfully amused when her dance partner bumps and grinds against the seductive, sensual BJ, because I figure that he thinks she's flirting with him and, in fact, she's more than likely flirting with me. The amber-brown man has no clue. He's having fun because BJ is a terrific dancer.

I'm not the only one watching BJ. I see men checking her out. If I tried to dance like that in those high-heeled strappy sandals, I'd break my ankle. She's a wonder. Halfway into my second beer, I turn a corner in my inhibitions. BJ invites touch with each ripple of her energy-charged body. Half the room, it seems, wants to touch her, and I have the best shot at it. I'm flattered, scared, curious, attracted, and most definitely tipsy.

The band takes a break and a jukebox plays quieter music. I can finally hear.

BJ leans in and speaks into her dance partner's ear. The man looks stunned for a moment and then laughs, revealing his dimples. She gives him a momentary hug and walks to me across the dance floor. Her partner disappears into the crowd.

BJ picks up my beer and polishes it off while tapping her toe to the music. She slides into the booth next to me.

"What did you say to your friend out there on the dance floor?"

"I told him my wife was getting jealous." She giggles.

"BJ! That's mean. And a lie."

"He knew I was joking."

"He didn't follow you to the table."

"I didn't invite him. I can go find him and invite him over. Do you want me to?" she asks, her voice syrupy and teasing.

"No. The next dance is mine."

When the band returns to the stage we hit the dance floor together. I put my hands on BJ's hips from behind and try to hang on while she rumbas and wriggles. Are we making a scene? I think we're making a scene. I have had three beers, which is past my limit. I'm a bit soused.

It's well after midnight when we hail a taxi. I have carried a weight on my shoulders for too long and tonight I feel unusually light. The illusion that I can rewind my adult life and start all over again from the beginning hovers before me like a mirage. I savor it and reject it in the same heartbeat. I would never give up my children for all the carefree existence or writer's solitude in the universe. I don't need to give them up. Here, on vacation, I have permission to play; to briefly pretend I have no weight on my shoulders, no obligations.

In the taxi, I lean back against the seat. As the driver pulls away from the curb, BJ kisses me questioningly on the lips. I find it startlingly exciting and not unexpected. I was forewarned, and besides, I have been flirting with her shamelessly.

"BJ, you're drunk." I laugh lightly.

"Not as drunk as you think," she corrects. She rests her head on my shoulder and hums to herself as we plummet through the streets to our hotel.

"You have to see my room," BJ demands. "I have a luxury suite." Far be it from me to protest.

In the elevator, I find myself trembling. Am I trembling with fear, nervous tension, desire, all of the above?

BJ unlocks the door to her suite. I enter wonderland. She has an ocean view and a huge bathroom with a large soaking tub. Marble pillars stand at the four corners of the tub.

"You weren't kidding when you said luxury."

"I go in style." BJ tosses that honey-colored wavy hair and grins. "Would you like to try the tub?" She turns the water on and takes me in her arms and kisses me with a penetrating kiss. Aroused, I sink into the kiss and drink. She awakens an unfamiliar, fascinating, and undefined desire in me. I am grateful that I met her in Hawaii, where I am relaxed enough to allow the unexpected to happen. I reach up under her dress and touch her thighs and her stomach and slowly move my hands to her breasts. She is soft and inviting, much softer than a man. I love the feel of her skin.

She breathes fast and hard as she leads me to the tub where she jumps in, fully clothed, strappy sandals and all. "Come on," she beckons.

"You're crazy." I kick off my own shoes and hop into the tub with her, laughing.

"Crazy and wet," she replies. We kiss and touch each other in the tub as we gradually leave our clothing floating behind and emerge like a pair of Venuses on the half-shell to climb into her wide bed where we make love until she has me moaning her name.

I fall asleep in her arms and in the morning wake to her insistent, gentle touch.

Making love to BJ is like a ride on a merry-go-round that I could keep riding as the day is long. I have wasted too many years on men.

This woman is exhilarating, provocative, and familiar. This woman could become a major distraction from my writing. When I finally leave her room at midday, I tell her not to bother me until the evening. I borrow some of her clothes to wear as I tiptoe to my room, since mine lay damp around the rim of her tub.

It takes all my writer's discipline to crawl back inside Molly's head when I'm dripping with sex in a tropical paradise. But I need to move Molly along on her journey.

From *Death in Hoper Valley*

Until the surgery, Molly felt fine; after the surgery, she felt like she had cancer. Flat on her back in a dim hospital room, drugged and depressed, barely able to move, she couldn't so much as lift her arms. She felt like she had a huge rock sitting on her chest. She wanted nothing more than painkillers and sleep. Certainly not visitors. If she was awake when people tiptoed in to sit by her bed, she feigned sleep. She did not wish to speak with anyone. She could not even speak to her children. She felt ashamed for being sick. Irrational, she knew. She felt as if she had made some deep blunder on a spiritual level, something she couldn't fathom, that had erupted in bad karma.

She dreamed bizarre dreams. Teresa appeared in all of them; until Molly wondered if Teresa had actually visited her in the hospital. She asked Andy about it. He was nearly certain Teresa had not come, although he couldn't say for sure. Molly became convinced that Teresa came to see her late at night. Teresa's presence infiltrated Molly's subconscious. She could not distinguish real from imagined, experience from dream, until the morning she woke up with a clearer head to find Andy holding her hand and Peg standing near the window.

When she saw Molly open her eyes, Peg asked, "Hey, hon, how you feeling?"

"Like I got hit by a truck," Molly grumbled. "I'm more clear-headed this morning than I've been, though."

"They didn't give you as much painkiller last night," Andy informed her. "You seemed OK without it."

When Dr. Percy entered, Andy and Peg looked at her expectantly. "She just woke up," Andy told the doctor.

"Nothing like a good night's sleep for a body under stress," Dr. Percy said as she walked to Molly's side. "And how do you feel today?"

"Like I have a rock on my chest," Molly replied. "I can't lift my arms."

"Don't worry, you'll be able to lift them soon," Dr. Percy assured her. "You came through with flying colors. I think we got all of it. The margins were clear. There was no cancer in the lymph nodes we sampled. You are a lucky gal. We may well have caught this in time. After a round of chemo, I'm optimistic that you could live to be a hundred."

Andy wiped tears off his cheeks, self-consciously. Peg patted his shoulder.

Dr. Percy asked if Molly had questions. Molly lied and said no. She didn't want to discuss her concerns in front of Andy and Peg. She felt exposed. She told Andy to go back to the ranch and tend to the livestock. She shooed Peg out too.

"You sure, hon? I can stay if you like," Peg offered.

Molly wanted to be alone. Dr. Percy and Peg left. Andy kissed Molly lightly on the lips with a reminder to call if she needed him. He'd drop everything and drive the forty minutes from Hoper Ranch into Carlysle to the hospital if she called.

She felt bad sending Andy away, but she couldn't bear to talk to anyone. She feared that if she spoke with Andy, or Peg, or anyone she loved, that she would let the cat out of the bag. For truthfully, despite Dr. Percy's optimism, Molly knew different. She had a strong soul-deep sense that the cancer continued to crouch inside her, squatting in her body. She could neither pry it loose nor identify its exact location; but she knew with a palpable surety that it would spring again, elsewhere, unmovable, unhindered by Dr. Percy's best efforts. She believed her illness was more spiritual than physical and that it was connected to Teresa Clearwater and the disturbing dreams. She figured that voicing this belief would place her sanity in question, so she held her tongue and kept her thoughts on the subject as private as possible, still discouraging visitors, while she erected a shield between her inner self and the world. She constructed a fence to keep out those she loved, to spare them and to protect herself from their watchful eyes.

As Dr. Percy predicted, Molly could soon lift her arms again, even though they felt weak and she had to take care not to overdo it. When she could stand steadily, she went to the bathroom by herself, locked the door, and removed her gown. Although bruised and framed by incisions, her smaller, perkier silicone breasts looked firmer than her old ones, which had sagged from breast-feeding five babies. She had lost weight and actually looked sort of younger. She hated it. She felt like she no longer inhabited her body. Cut adrift, her spirit wandered, dwelling nowhere.

She dreamed Dr. Percy replaced her with an inflatable doll on the operating table and the real Molly crouched in a hospital broom closet, gagged and bound. Dr. Percy sent the inflatable doll Molly home to her family. They didn't notice the difference. They loved the doll. It was indestructible and perfect. Teresa knew where to find the real Molly. Teresa opened the door to the closet and untied Molly. She wrapped her in a blue-red-green quilt and said, "You know how to get out of this. You know in your bones. You can hear the blood-drenched land." Molly was fed up with dreaming about Teresa. She wished this infernal woman would get out of her head. She wished she'd never seen her at the soccer field, never talked to her.

On the day of her release from the hospital, Molly returned to a house filled with cards, flowers, fruit, mouth-watering baked treats, and well-wishers. She put on a cheerful face for her children, but her homecoming was strained. There was no avoiding the fact that she was deeply depressed.

After a dinner of turkey soup, which she ate in bed, the girls tumbled into her room while Andy took the boys to soccer practice.

"It's just us girls," Kelly said. She held a large gray cat with green eyes in her lap where she sat cross-legged at the foot of the bed. Susan stretched out next to Molly. Bethany had her head in Susan's lap and her feet next to the cat's head.

"Don't bounce," Susan warned Bethany, "it might hurt Mom."

"Mom's in a cocoon," Bethany informed her sisters, "aren't you Mom?"

"I'm in a cocoon?" Molly asked.

"Yeah, you're inside; you've gone inside. You'll come out when you finish changing," Bethany clarified.

"Don't be so cryptic," Susan admonished.

"What's that mean?" Bethany asked.

"Sort of mysterious," Kelly explained, stroking her cat. The purring vibrated the bed.

"I'm not changing," Molly said, although she knew in her heart that her most intuitive daughter had hit the nail on the head. "I'm just trying to get well."

"You'll come out of your cocoon when you're ready to be all better, right Mom?" Bethany twisted her head around so she could look at Molly.

Molly brushed a strand of Bethany's fair hair from her cheek and said, "I suppose so. I hope to get all better, but it will take time."

"The chemo will probably make you sicker, won't it?" Kelly asked anxiously.

"Yeah, it'll make me feel rotten. I'm not looking forward to losing my hair."

"That's going to be pretty awful," Susan agreed. "But it'll grow back. Are you going to get a wig?"

"I haven't decided. Maybe just a scarf or a hat. What do you think?"

"I think a scarf," Kelly said.

"I vote for a wig," Susan declared.

"A hat would be fun," Bethany suggested with a laugh.

"What's so funny?" Molly asked Bethany.

"Everybody has a different idea," Bethany answered. "We didn't help you decide."

"Can we read part of *Little Women*?" Kelly asked. "Dad offered to read it to us, but it's a girls' book. We want to read it with you."

Molly sighed. "I'm not up to reading aloud. I'm pretty tired."

"I'll read and you can just listen," Susan offered.

Molly liked that idea. Bethany ran off to get the book so Kelly wouldn't have to disturb the cat by getting up.

Molly closed her eyes and listened to Susan read. When the boys came in from soccer, Susan stopped reading. Mac and Mike sat on the floor side-by-side and gave Molly a blow-by-blow account of the practice, until Andy shooed the children out to get ready for bed. As he closed the door, he told Molly, "They're happy to have you back."

"I'm happy to *be* back."

After the children went to bed, Andy crept quietly into the bedroom.

"I'm awake. You can turn on the light."

"Should I sleep in here or in the guest room?" Andy asked anxiously. "I don't want to disturb you."

"In here is fine. I'll send you out if I'm having trouble. I've missed you." It would comfort her to sleep in Andy's arms.

He sat on the edge of the bed and took her hand. "I want to hold you, but I don't want to, you know, hurt you." She thought he would never be able to touch her again, only the fabrication of her.

"Are they sore?"

"I can't feel them," Molly replied. She looked away.

Andy cleared his throat. "Can I see? I mean, you know, what they look like now."

She was not ready for this, but he had a right to see what was left for him. She unbuttoned the front of her nightgown. "At least there's something there," she said grimly.

"They're smaller," he noted.

"They are."

"I'll get used to it. It's not the most important thing."

"I'm sorry."

"Not your fault."

"You don't know that." The words escaped Molly's mouth before she could stop them.

Andy looked shocked. "You think you did something that made you get cancer?"

"Not consciously."

"What's that supposed to mean?"

Molly shrugged.

"I'm worried about you."

"You and everyone else. I have cancer."

"No. You don't. You *had* cancer. It's gone."

"Then why am I about to do chemotherapy?" Molly asked belligerently.

"To prevent it from coming back," Andy snapped. "I'm not as worried about the cancer as I am about your attitude."

"Gosh, Andy, I'm sorry I'm not more positive. But I can't just get over it and be an inspiration to everyone. I have these crappy little tits that I hate and can't even feel. I have weeks of chemo ahead of me. I can't get excited about losing my hair and perfecting the sport of vomiting."

"I didn't mean...." Andy tried to interrupt.

"I'm not heroic. Not everyone is, you know. So I might just not get through this, OK?"

"I didn't mean to make you feel bad about the breasts. Screw the breasts, Mol; I want you alive. Stay with me here." He ran his hand through his hair, riffling it backward so that it stuck up. "I'm so damn useless."

"Yeah, well, the whole thing is completely out of our control."

"It's not. That's what I'm telling you. Having a positive attitude could make a difference."

Molly looked Andy in the eye. "It's hard to have a positive attitude when I don't think it's gone."

"You heard Dr. Percy. The margins were clear."

"Well the margins can be as clear as sterilized glass, but I'm telling you that I know the cancer is still in there. And here's the thing Andy, no matter how much you love me, and how positive my attitude, and how much my children want me to live, and in spite of the prayers and healing thoughts and positive energy of friends and relatives, there's a chance that there's not a damn thing anyone can do about it. If it wants me, it will get me."

"You don't know what might tip the balance." Andy's voice cracked.

"You don't deserve this."

"Well neither do you. It's not fair. Life is not fair."

"I would completely understand if you slept with someone else," Molly told him bitterly.

"Are you kidding me?! I can't believe we're having this conversation." Andy smacked the side of the bed with the flat of his hand in frustration.

"Tell me that you're prepared to go the rest of your livelong days without ever, not ever, holding a real handful of a breast. Not ever again. You, the breast man that I married."

Andy looked stricken. He stared at a spot on the floor and swallowed, then he lifted his eyes to meet his wife's gaze. "I'm having a hard time with the loss. Don't make it worse."

"About the only thing worse is death."

"Listen," Andy said. He paused, thought better of it, and didn't continue. Instead he stood and walked over to his dresser. He opened the top drawer. "Here. I was going to give this to you tomorrow, but I want you to have it now." Andy handed her a book. It had a marbled lavender and violet cover. When she opened it, she discovered it was blank inside. She glanced up at him questioningly.

"Back in the day, you wanted to be a writer. And you gave it up. You went to work teaching and we had the children and the ranch and one thing led to another and you didn't have that chance to write. So I was thinking that this is an opportunity for you to have that chance. Maybe that's even what this is all about."

Molly gave a snort. "I don't think it's part of a grand plan or a, a..." Words failed her.

"You are one stubborn woman. Listen to me," Andy rushed on, "you're out on extended medical leave, money coming in from state disability pay, you have excellent health coverage from work, I mean, that's part of why you went to work in the first place, for those great benefits. So look at it this way, you have this bizarre opportunity to take a break from all of it. The work, the ranch, the children, even me. Plenty of people are eager to help, to pick up the slack for a little while. So you write."

He had tossed her a life raft and she knew it. She put the blank book on the nightstand.

"Now's your chance, because once you're well and we put you back in harness, you won't get a chance like this again until Bethany goes off to college."

Maui, 1977

"Don't come down to the lobby," BJ commands. "I want to remember you just like this." I'm barefoot and wearing one of Nelson's old shirts with the sleeves rolled up. I take a sip of coffee from the room service tray at the end of the bed.

BJ is dressed for travel in a navy-blue suit and her bag sits by the door.

"Send me a postcard from Phoenix."

"I will."

"Remember not to write anything revealing or racy on it because my children will probably read it, plus Athena doesn't miss a detail."

"Probably not what she and your Nelson had in mind when they bought you the trip," BJ says with a satisfied smile.

I hold her around the waist and pull her toward me. "I'll miss that cute figure of yours."

"You sure you don't want to meet me in Hawaii in October?" She looks so hopeful that I hate to crush her, but I have to be honest.

"This was a once-only vacation fling, BJ."

"Yeah, I know. An interlude."

"A wonderful interlude with an extraordinary legal secretary. Now go get on that plane and earn your way to your dream." I pat her behind as she scurries to her suitcase and the door.

"Keep at that disco dancing," she calls over her shoulder. She blows me a kiss and she's gone.

So glad I met you BJ. You made my vacation so much more lively, so much more fun.

Now back to work. Nose to the grindstone.

From *Death in Hoper Valley*

MOLLY'S JOURNAL

My name is Molly Anderson and this is the story of my death.

Mom just lost Daddy two years ago. Now me. I can hardly think of anything worse than outliving your own child.

Bethany is ten years old. I can't remember much that happened to me before I was ten years old and what I do remember is vague. For instance, I don't remember what my mother's face looked like when I was ten years old. If I die this year, Bethany won't remember much about me.

What will anyone remember about me? Have I made any difference in the world? What did I contribute? I contributed five good children. That must count for something. I have made a difference in the lives of the children I have taught at Head Start. That must count for something too. As a young woman, I thought I would make a contribution with my writing. That didn't pan out.

I received a gift in my talent for writing and I've squandered it. I raised children, worked as a teacher, canned peaches, milked goats. I filled my days with the activities of a rancher's wife and loved every minute of it. I have procrastinated. The only difference between writers and everyone else is that writers write.

Molly glanced around the dim room in which she had spent many hours rehearsing for her death. She looked at the words in her journal. Writers write.

She got out of bed and opened the curtains to let the sunlight in. It warmed her face. She crawled back into bed. She wanted to write about her trip to Greece. The odyssey of a young woman, full of dreams, with the whole world sparkling before her like Homer's wine-dark sea. The beginning of a parallel life she had planned and never executed. Where to start?

Time is a constellation, not a line.

Maui, 1977

I had a rollicking vacation romance. Now, if I can just have a vacation epiphany. The days left to me on Maui stretch before me like the jeweled water at the beach, inviting me to dive in. I pretend I have the means to quit my job and spend all my time writing on and on and on into the future. Thanks to BJ, I have a spicy romp in mind for Molly's novel. Look out. Here comes Cassandra!

Book 10: Molly and Cassandra

From *Death in Hoper Valley*

MOLLY'S JOURNAL

Last Night's Dream.

I set out from a dock on the edge of Bear Lake in a ship with golden sails, a ship of ancient times. I have a crew of women. Gazing across the water, I see tents that mark the shoreline of Hoper Ranch. The ship does not move toward that shore. It moves across the lake, farther and farther from the Hoper Ranch shore. The ship runs aground at a small island in the middle of the lake. On the island I discover a village filled with children playing. The patriarch of this clan emerges from his cottage to greet me. He leads me into the cottage and gives me a burlap bag bloated with the air of the blustery winds. I return to my ship and set out across the lake again.

The ship sails directly for the shoreline of Hoper Ranch. I see women on the shore tending fires. Abruptly, exhaustion overcomes me and I cannot keep my eyes open. I sleep. I told my crew not to open the bag of winds, but when I awake I discover the crew holding the bag open for each other and standing in the breeze, their breasts bare, enjoying the intoxicating brush of the wind on their skin as it escapes from the bag. The wind from the bag collects over the water. It tosses the ship wildly as if we are in the middle of the ocean. Impossibly enormous waves rise up and crash over the ship. Forty-foot waves, frightening, horrifying. Should I stay on the ship or jump into the water? Miraculously, the ship does not capsize and instead arrives back at the little island. The storm stops. I return to the village where the keeper of the winds listens to my tale of woe. He says, "If you are thus cursed, then I cannot help you."

We sail onto the lake again. Sea creatures rise from the water to pursue us. I move in slow motion, turning the ship, working the sails with my crew, all of us straining to pull the ship away from the monstrous sea creatures. My crew falls over the sides as the ship rolls and pitches in the swirling waters. I grieve their loss and the loss of the sight of their lovely breasts, the breasts they turned to the breezes that escaped from the bag of winds.

Now I walk on a beach. My singular footprints trail behind me in the sand. I come upon a woman with gold ribbons braided into her hair who weaves on a loom with ochre, russet, and umber threads. She is lit from within like a lantern. Without looking up from her weaving, she tells me: you must go under the earth and speak to Teresa if you wish to return home.

Stumbling across the beach, I see a cave in the dunes. In the mouth of the cave stands Teresa surrounded by ocean mist that obscures and then reveals and then obscures her form. Teresa is young, her blue-black hair has feathers, beads, and a leather thong woven into it. She wears a quilted coat of red, turquoise, black, gray, and royal blue. She beckons and I enter the cave. We walk down into the cave together.

I wake.

The dream was so detailed, so vivid.

Why do I dream so much about Teresa?

Today is the day I begin to write Cassandra.

CASSANDRA

When Cassandra stepped off the train upon her arrival in Amsterdam, she told her high school pal Marta who met her there, "I want to see all the great paintings."

Marta's laugh in response was as light and crisp as sleigh bells. "You don't have enough time before we leave for Athens."

"No one has enough time. I'll see as many as I can before we go."

"Where do you propose to start?"

"Rijksmuseum. I want to see the Vermeers and Rembrandts. And there's a Van Gogh museum here."

"You did your research."

"I think the Rijksmuseum has the most Vermeers of anywhere in the world."

"It does, but since he hardly painted anything, that extensive collection boils down to just four paintings."

"Terrific. That won't take long so I'll have time to see a lot more paintings."

Cassandra shifted her backpack and slipped her arm affectionately around Marta's waist. "You look good. Amsterdam must be treating you well."

Marta shrugged her long blonde hair over her shoulder. "I'm having an interesting adventure. You know what Mr. Jackson always used to say."

In unison the girls recited the favorite expression of their high school English teacher: "The world is your oyster."

"And that's exactly why we're going to Greece," Cassandra reminded Marta. Cassandra had just completed a semester of art study in London, and now she wanted to see Athens. Cradle of the ancients. Land of olives and blazing-white stone ruins. Cassandra had not seen Marta in more than a year, but now they were both in Europe and both wanted to see Greece so they had made a plan.

The girls set out early on Cassandra's one day in Amsterdam and went museum hopping.

"There's something about his paintings that bothers me," Cassandra told Marta when she actually stood in front of Vermeer's *Woman in Blue*. "He paints light and air with such perfection that he transports the viewer to another dimension, but it's a dimension lacking in human emotion. His people are distant and stiff. He doesn't know them. Look how much more he loves the dress than the woman wearing it."

"So you think he missed the point?"

"I do. I think Vermeer missed the point. He's all form and no substance."

"A lot of people would disagree with you," Marta argued. "He's considered a master of subtle emotion. Perhaps he's too subtle for you."

"I think he's over-rated."

"Says the student who has completed four semesters of study as an art major."

"Five," Cassandra corrected. "I went summer term last year. And it's a *dual* major, in art and anthropology."

Arms entwined, the girls strolled on to the next gallery. They looked like they had just stepped out of one of the paintings. The blonde and the brunette, linked in female companionship. When Marta tossed her waist-length blonde hair, it flicked like a well-groomed horse's tail. Her eyes were so green, they seemed capable of photosynthesis. She had a lean, slight frame. Her slender graceful hands moved hypnotically to punctuate her words when she spoke. If she had lived at the time of the Pre-Raphaelites, they would have painted her incessantly, for she resembled one of their favorite models, Lizzie Siddal. In contrast, Cassandra was plump and round with wide hips, large breasts, and a couple of handfuls of behind. She had thick, brown, curly hair that played in a tangled mass on her head. Her dark brown, heavy-lidded eyes could have competed with the mystery of those of a da Vinci woman. For their visit to the Rijksmuseum, Marta wore tight jeans and a fluffy grass-green sweater. Cassandra, who did not own a pair of pants, wore a full-length flowing pink and purple dress, a lightweight purple and gold scarf around her neck, and pink cotton stockings. The girls did not notice the heads that turned as they walked through the galleries together, trailing the stares of young art students who sat copying great works of the masters for practice and imagining a pair of models such as these Americans, a painting in flesh and blood walking from room to room, a living Renoir lacking only wide-brimmed hats and dappled sunlight.

Eventually Cassandra wanted lunch. Marta had a tendency to forget about food, but Cassandra didn't let her forget. They found an outdoor café and ordered sandwiches.

"I don't want to leave Europe," Cassandra announced. "I keep trying to think of a way to stay longer. There's so much to do in London. Using the student discounts, I can go to the theater or the ballet or go to hear music for ridiculously cheap admission if I don't mind sitting far away from the stage. Every Tuesday the art museums and galleries admit students for free. When I first arrived, I went to the Tate Gallery every Tuesday for six weeks. It was heaven. They have a replica of *The David* in the Victoria and Albert that makes me so horny it takes my breath away."

Marta giggled. "It's a huge statue, isn't it?"

"Enormous."

"His cock must be gigantic."

"As big as my arm. And he's not even excited."

"Well of course not, he's stone."

"I know, huh? Too bad."

"Hey, what happened with that guy you met at the Camden Market?" Marta asked.

"We had fun. We're still friends."

"I didn't mean to imply that I thought you'd fallen in love with him. The impossibility of long distance romance and all that."

"He's too much in his head. It takes a lot of work to loosen him up. He's a three-beer date."

"I had one of those."

"A guy too much in his head?"

Marta stared off into the street for a moment before casting a piercing look at Cassandra with those iridescent eyes of hers. "No, a woman actually. A woman who was too much in her head. Does that shock you?" Marta licked a dab of mayonnaise from her finger.

"Not at all," Cassandra lied. It did shock her a bit.

"You're blushing."

"And what do you interpret a blush to mean?"

"You tell me."

"I think it means that I want to look at the dessert menu." Cassandra smiled faintly.

Marta got up and waltzed across the terrace to the door of the café, where she scored a menu.

"You were slinking, weren't you?"

"What?"

"You were walking provocatively because you knew I was watching."

"Puleez."

"I'm a woman. I recognize the tactics, and I can tell when a woman is slinking. I suspect it was for my benefit."

"Well you go ahead and suspect whatever you want to suspect."

"I'll do that. Do they have any pie?"

Marta peered at her friend over the top of the menu. "I'm doing the raspberry trifle. Look at the picture. It looks wicked." Marta passed the menu to Cassandra.

The waitress appeared and Cassandra handed her the menu without reading it. "Two raspberry trifles," she ordered.

After they ate their trifles and paid their bill, they stepped out onto the street. Marta put her arm through Cassandra's, just as she had done at the museum, but for Cassandra the connotation had changed. They walked back to Marta's apartment, which she shared with an assortment of international young people. Eric Clapton's *Laila* blasted from the stereo in the living room and they could smell spaghetti sauce cooking in the kitchen. Marta greeted her roommates and headed to her bedroom, with Cassandra following.

"Didn't Eric Clapton write that song for his wife, who ran off with George Harrison? Or was it the other way around?" Cassandra asked as she unwound the scarf from her neck and dropped it unceremoniously on the floor.

"The other way around. Harrison's wife ran off with Clapton," Marta said, as she stood face-to-face with Cassandra. The girls were the same height. Marta cupped Cassandra's breasts in her hands and brushed her thumbs across Cassandra's nipples, which rose in answer through the thin cotton fabric. "You didn't just blush when I mentioned that I had slept with a woman."

"No?"

"No. You blushed and your nipples stood up."

"How could you see them through my clothes?"

"I could see them. And that's how I knew."

"Knew what?"

"That the thought of sleeping with me excites you."

"I wasn't imagining sleeping."

Marta kissed her and Cassandra kissed back.

MOLLY'S JOURNAL

   Holy smokes. Do I really want a lesbian sex scene at the beginning of my novel? How explicit should the sex scene be? Should I describe the details or cut away to a field of daisies? It's my story so I can do whatever I want. I want an explicit sex scene with healthy, luscious breasts in it. Besides, Marcia really did seduce me in Amsterdam and truth is stranger than fiction. Of course she made a botch of things in Athens later because she got jealous. That dimension of the story won't work unless Cassandra and Marta have sex. So there has to be a sex scene between them. It's the nature of the scene that is the question. I want to describe details. I want to describe the breasts. What the heck does "holy smokes" mean?

CASSANDRA

Cassandra kissed back.

   She lifted Marta's sweater over her head. Marta had exquisite small breasts tipped with nipples like the buds of a delicate spring flower. Cassandra had never touched another woman's breasts before.

   "I can't stay on my feet." Marta moaned as she pulled Cassandra onto her mattress on the floor.

   Cassandra laughed. "You started it."

"I didn't think you would be this good at it. Have you done this before?"

Cassandra laughed and shook her head negative. She envied Marta her slender compact body and felt self-conscious by comparison when Marta undressed her, unleashing Cassandra's voluptuous breasts and ample backside.

Marta admired Cassandra's abundance. "Like Astarte, the mother goddess. No one would ever use my body type to represent womanhood. They would carve yours as the goddess statue in the Temple of Gaia." Marta prayed at the temple, kneeling over, bare-chested in her tight jeans, to worship between Cassandra's legs.

Cassandra could hardly believe that a woman had the ability to give her such pleasure. After she recovered from the shock of her own responsiveness, she tentatively explored Marta's body and did her best to satisfy her friend's desire in return. Afterward, the girls lay side-by-side as the setting sun cast bars of amber light across their rosy, flushed skin.

"You sure have changed since high school," Marta noted.

"What's that supposed to mean?"

"You were a prude."

"I was not. I was shy and introverted. No one knew what went on inside my head."

"You seemed like a prude. You won the science fair in ninth grade."

"Are you implying that smart girls don't like sex?" Cassandra bristled.

"No, of course not, just that smart girls in ninth grade didn't seem interested in sex. You were too busy doing chemistry experiments to check out what the boys had in their pants."

"Or what the girls had in theirs."

"Definitely not what the girls had in theirs."

"Did you sleep with girls in high school?" Cassandra propped her head on her hand, balancing her arm on her elbow.

Marta didn't answer.

"You did, didn't you? Oh my god! Who? Who did you sleep with in high school?" Cassandra squealed with anticipation.

Marta hesitated.

"Tell me. I swear, I won't breathe a word. I don't plan to go to any high school reunions. I didn't even like high school."

Marta caved. "Do you remember Patty Ann Bridges?"

"The cheerleader? You screwed Patty Ann?"

"Not technically. I don't have the right equipment to actually screw a girl. We fooled around together a few times in her basement," Marta confessed. "I tried to make it with Ellie Curtis once at a party but she was drunk. She probably doesn't remember what happened. I had such a crush on her."

"I used to wish I was Patty Ann," Cassandra murmured. "She had perfect breasts."

"Not really. She just had expensive padded bras. Mostly, I slept with boys, not girls, in high school. I guess it sounds like I slept around, but I didn't. I only slept with a couple of boys, and they were my boyfriends at the time. I'm not pure lesbian. I like men too."

"I'm not a lesbian either," Cassandra said.

"Of course not, this was your first time." Marta laughed.

"What makes you so sure?"

Marta cast her a doubtful look.

"OK, well it was, but that doesn't mean I haven't thought about it."

"We're still cool to travel together, right? I mean, this won't get in the way?" Marta asked anxiously.

"Why should it? It's not like we're married or anything."

It sounded so simple at the time.

MOLLY'S JOURNAL

I wrote a sex scene while sitting in this bed with my fake little silicone breasts. Me, married all these years and with a house full of teens and pre-teens. What would Susan or Kelly think? I wouldn't allow them to read a book with explicit sex in it like that right now. What if they read it when they grow up? Or after I'm dead? Maybe the scene should end where they kiss each other or conveniently skip to something like "After a two-day sexual adventure with each other, the girlfriends boarded the train to Athens." That would fall as flat as cardboard. Forget it. I'll decide later how to present the Cassandra/Marta affair. Meanwhile, it was fun writing a sex scene. It brings back the wonder of making love to Marcia.

CASSANDRA

Cassandra and Marta boarded a train teeming with young people, off to seek adventure during the springtime height of student travel season in Europe. The girlfriends settled in a compartment that seated six. It soon filled with other young people from all over Europe who spoke a total of ten languages between them. They shared food, translated for each other, swapped travel stories, sang, showed each other pictures of family, slept on one another's shoulders, and became a temporary, fluid tribe as they rolled through Germany, Austria, Yugoslavia, and, finally, the poppy-laden fields of Greece.

Cassandra and Marta arrived in Athens late in the afternoon, eager for a shower and a comfortable bed. They hailed a cab and gave the driver the address of Cassandra's friend Moira. While in high school, Cassandra had participated in a teen drama program that Moira directed. Born and raised in London, Moira had lived in California for a few years while her husband, Alexander, worked there as an architect. Alexander grew up in Athens. Cassandra had written to Moira about her plans to visit Athens, and Moira had invited Cassandra to stay with her, but Cassandra had not given Moira a specific date for her arrival.

When the cab pulled up at Moira's house, the girls discovered no one was home. The cab driver took the girls to a phone booth, where Cassandra called the phone number Moira had sent her. No one answered.

"Let's stay at a hotel tonight," Marta suggested, "and we'll try them tomorrow. They probably just went out."

They asked the cab driver if he knew of a nearby hotel where they could spend the night, something inexpensive, clean, and safe. A decent fellow, he fortunately understood English and soon deposited them at a lovely hotel in an old neighborhood near the center of the city. By the time they checked in and showered, they were starved and it had grown dark. They went down to the small, homey front desk and asked the proprietor to suggest a place for them to eat dinner. He and a friend discussed this in Greek before the proprietor's friend recommended a place a couple of blocks away. He offered to accompany them since he didn't want them to get lost and also, as he put it, "Someone might try to bother you." He said he would walk them to the restaurant and return for them in an hour to walk them back to the hotel.

He introduced himself as Demetrius and offered his hand, which each of the girls shook in turn as they introduced themselves. Marta put her arm through Cassandra's and they followed Demetrius to the sidewalk.

"Is this your first visit to Athens?" Demetrius asked.

"First visit to Greece," Cassandra answered.

"We have friends here," Marta added, "who we're going to stay with. They didn't know when to expect us and they're not home tonight."

Demetrius had dark hair that fell in soft curls, one of them in the middle of his forehead, as in a Michelangelo painting. His eyes were dark brown too. He was average height and roundish, kind of plump. "Do you live in Athens?" Cassandra asked.

"I am steward on boat. I sail at sea for six months and I arrive in harbor last night. I am on holiday," he replied. "I stay at hotel when I am in Athens. The owner is my friend." He drew their attention to their surroundings as they walked down the street, like a self-appointed tour guide; his love for Athens obvious in his voice.

"Here is my favorite restaurant. I suggest the *spanakopita*. I return for you in one hour."

As Demetrius turned to leave, Marta asked, "Would you like to eat with us?"

"I already eat," he said hesitantly.

"Then have something to drink?" Marta suggested. "Is that OK with you?" she asked Cassandra. Demetrius glanced from one of the girls to the other.

"It's fine. Please," Cassandra encouraged him. She thought that Demetrius could probably offer informed recommendations that would make their trip more interesting than the usual tourist experience. "We would appreciate whatever advice you have to offer about our visit to Greece."

Demetrius accompanied them inside the café.

MOLLY'S JOURNAL

I can see Demetrius in my mind's eye as clearly as if we walked into that café together just last night. I wonder where he is now, if he has a family, if he remembers me. We had a special connection. I might have stayed with him a lifetime under different circumstances. He told me he liked my broad shoulders because they revealed that I worked hard. I had swimmer's shoulders then. I should take up swimming again. It relaxed me. If I recall correctly, it was Marcia, not I, who invited him to join us for dinner that first night.

CASSANDRA

In the morning, Marta refused to leave the bed. After three days on a train, she elected to luxuriate in lounging around until check-out time at noon. Cassandra wanted to try calling Moira again and the room had no telephone. She went to the lobby, where she found the manager drinking coffee with Demetrius.

"Good morning, American," Demetrius greeted her with a contagious smile. "How do you sleep?"

"Very well, thank you." Cassandra smiled back. "I need to use a phone." The manager passed her his desk phone, turning it around to face her. She dialed Moira's number. Pick up, pick up, she thought to herself. Where were they?

"Né?" It was a man's voice.

"Alexander? This is Cassandra."

"Cassie!" He lingered on the last syllable of her name, saying it in his British-accented English. Like many friends from her hometown, Moira and Alexander knew her by her childhood nickname. "You have arrived in the land of the Olympians, I take it. Welcome."

What a relief to hear his voice. "I'm here with my friend Marta. We went to your house last night from the train station but you were out."

"Where did you stay?"

"The cab driver took us to a nice hotel. Can we come over? Is Moira around?"

"Moira's not here. She's at the TV station. She's acting in a live circus show on TV this afternoon. Come watch the show with me." Alexander's voice sounded warm and familiar. Cassandra had spent many hours in their home in Berkeley.

"Will it be OK for us to stay with you?" Cassandra asked.

"Of course, of course," Alexander assured her, "didn't Moira write you that it would be fine?"

"Yeah, just checking. Marta is still in bed and we haven't had breakfast so it'll be a little while before we make it over. When is Moira on the TV?"

"At three o'clock. Come over whenever. I'll be here working."

"You work at home?"

"I have a studio here. See you later, OK?"

"Great."

When she hung up, Demetrius asked, "You talk to your friend?"

"Yeah. We'll go over later. When I can get my lazy traveling companion out of bed."

"While you wait for her, will you like to go to breakfast with me?" Perhaps he was coming on to her, but Cassandra didn't mind. She liked him. They went to a café where they sat outdoors on the terrace and ate chunks of white bread dipped in olive oil.

Demetrius ordered a delicious egg dish that resembled crêpes.

"I'm falling in love with Greek food," Cassandra told him.

He said that when he was away on the ocean, he missed the dishes he most liked at the little cafés and restaurants in the neighborhoods in Athens that he frequented. A bachelor, he ate out when in port. He had worked as a steward for several years and didn't have the opportunity to enjoy his beloved Athens often enough. He was thinking of leaving his job.

In the daylight, Cassandra thought him even more attractive than she had the night before. He had heavy-lidded eyes, full fleshy lips, and his hands gestured gracefully to punctuate his words as he talked. He had rolled his shirt sleeves up to reveal his forearms. Cassandra had a weakness for a man's forearms. After breakfast, they returned to the hotel, walking slowly, and he asked her out to dinner for the following evening. "Just me and you, without your friend," he made a point of clarifying. Cassandra gave him Moira's address and phone number and they agreed on a time for him to pick her up there. They went their separate ways in the lobby.

In the hotel room, Cassandra found Marta stepping out of the shower. She wrapped herself in a thick white towel and then flitted about, organizing her things as she repacked them in her backpack. She looked too cute in that towel, and she knew it. Cassandra sunk into an easy chair and followed Marta with her eyes.

"So, did you get your friends?" she asked, fishing a brush out of the backpack and dragging it through her mop of wet hair.

"Uh-huh. Moira's out, but I talked to Alexander. And I had breakfast with Demetrius."

"Oh?"

"He invited me to have dinner with him tomorrow."

"You or us?" she asked pausing in mid-stroke with her brush.

"Me. I hope you don't mind. I like him. I said yes."

"Why would I mind?" Her towel slipped off into a little heap around her feet.

Cassandra got out of the chair and kissed Marta, cupping Marta's tight round behind in her hands. "You're jealous."

"Of course not," she scoffed. "It's no big deal. I prefer men also."

"Are you sure you don't mind?"

"You could easily make it up to me before we check out. We have time."

She was right. They did.

MOLLY'S JOURNAL

Maybe I should shift the narrative into the first person. That scares me a little. It could make it too close to autobiography. Besides, if I write in the first person, I can't get into all the characters' heads. I like being omniscient. It feels powerful.

I wonder where Marcia is today? The last time I saw her was on the roof at Moira's house, when I chastised her and told her to leave Athens. A disturbing parting for us both. She had no business behaving the way she did. Marcia. Marta. If Marcia were to read this book, what would she think? She had a sexy body back in those days. Maybe these days she's fat and out of shape. Or maybe she had her breasts removed and replaced with perky, numb implants.

CASSANDRA

The girls arrived at Moira-and-Alexander's in the early afternoon. Alexander greeted them warmly at the front door. He laughed when Cassandra handed him a bouquet of calla lilies.

"Those are funeral lilies," he informed her. "If you brought them into a traditional Greek home they would freak out. They would be convinced you had brought death into their house."

"I'm sorry. I just love them. I have never seen them before, and they had them at a stand outside the hotel."

"It's OK. I'm not so old-fashioned and superstitious. Thanks." Alexander took the flowers.

He looked great, his white shirt accented his deep tan, his large, brown eyes framed by those long lush eyelashes. He flashed his boyish gap-toothed grin. He seemed much more at home here than he ever did in Berkeley. "Sorry the house is such a wreck. We didn't expect company. Moira has been working hard all week to get ready for the TV circus show."

The house really was a mess. Clothes and newspapers were strewn about; dishes were piled in the sink and abandoned in odd places elsewhere; an ironing board stood in the middle of the living room. Books flung about. Shoes piled in a heap by the door. Cassandra couldn't remember their house in Berkeley ever looking like such a disaster. Alexander turned the TV on and moved a towel aside to make room next to him on the couch. "Moira's show is starting."

It was bizarre to see her friend and teacher again for the first time in two-and-a-half years on TV as a clown. Alexander had to point her out since she was wearing clown make-up and Cassandra couldn't tell which clown she was; although, she should have figured it out by her antics. She was the funniest one, the most expressive.

With one eye on the TV, Marta wandered around the room, examining the art work, books, photographs; checking out the music by the stereo. Touching things. Acquainting herself.

"When Moira gets home, we have a dinner date with my friend Ioannis. He's my best friend from school. We grew up together. Wait till you hear what's going on with him." Alexander paused. On the TV, Moira put her head in the lap of a man in the audience and pretended to go to sleep. The other clowns attempted to move her limp body while she kept tangling her limbs in members of the audience. Alexander and Cassandra laughed. Moira was a master at improvisation. "Hey, anyway," Alexander continued, "Moira and I are going to get married."

"I thought you were already married."

"Well, yeah, we got married in England, but our marriage isn't recognized here because it wasn't performed in the Greek Orthodox Church. We plan to stay here, and we hope to have children, so it seemed like a good idea to make it legal. Since Moira isn't Greek Orthodox, we couldn't get married in the church. Fortunately, we found a corrupt priest. Thank god for making corrupt priests. He actually converted Moira to Greek Orthodox last weekend. In the white robe and total submersion in oily water and the whole deal. She'll tell you about it if you ask her. You should ask her. She'll have you in stitches the way she tells it. She's now officially in the church. So next this priest, this Father Andreas, has to marry us, which he has agreed to do."

"What's the catch?" Marta's voice startled Cassandra and Alexander, who had forgotten about her. Alexander turned sideways on the couch to include her. His eyes wandered rapidly down the full length of her lithe body before returning to her face.

"I mean, how did you persuade this priest to do the conversion and the marriage?" Marta asked. Cassandra knew Marta's body language well enough to recognize the new provocative hint that entered Marta's stance after she saw Alexander look her up and down.

"That's the part where it crosses over into the absurd," Alexander replied with glee. "This Father Andreas is apparently a homosexual and he is attracted to my friend Ioannis, the one going to dinner with us tonight. So we have managed to give Father Andreas the impression that Ioannis will have sex with him if he marries me and Moira. Ioannis flirts with him and leads him on for us."

"That's unethical," Marta pointed out.

"The whole thing is unethical," Alexander exploded. "The whole system is unethical. Totally corrupt! A country that forbids people to marry because of their religious affiliation? Marriage is a sacred, personal matter between two people in love. The government has no right to legislate love."

MOLLY'S JOURNAL

Moira and Alexander's California wedding was so much fun. They had been legally married in a civil ceremony in London just before they came over to America so Alexander could bring Moira into the country as his wife on his work visa. Once they had lived in California for a while and made friends with enough people to populate a proper celebration, they threw a belated wedding reception. Moira wore a Renaissance outfit, low cut in the bust to show lots of cleavage, and adorned with red and black ostrich feathers and gold braid. She dressed Alexander up as Zeus, with a bare chest and a wreath of white and golden flowers on his head. The food at the party was terrific since Moira had friends in the catering business. Goat cheese with pesto and sun-dried tomatoes, warm brie with mushrooms, grilled chicken, small red potatoes in sour cream and chive sauce. I'm hungry. I'm going to call Andy and ask him to stop at Peg's to pick up some of her goat cheese. I haven't craved food since before the surgery.

CASSANDRA

"You saw me on TV?" Moira asked as she breezed in the door like a whirlwind, talking nonstop, racing around from one room to another in a mad attempt to clean up. "Alexander, take the dirty dishes into the kitchen. Be useful," she commanded as she collapsed the ironing board and whisked it away. Rolling his eyes, he obeyed. "We have to meet Ioannis and Sabiya at the restaurant at seven. Call and reserve two more places," Moira shouted from the other room as she collected clothes off the floor and threw them into a hamper.

"Can I help?" I asked, trailing Moira down the hall.

"Yeah," she grinned at me, breathlessly, "tell that bum of a husband of mine to offer your friend a beer. She looks bored. I need to jump in the shower."

I appreciated Moira's tremendous exuberant energy. I gave her a hug. Greece was going to be a blast.

MOLLY'S JOURNAL

That was a mind blip. I switched into the first person singular! Must correct that and keep an eye on it going forward.

CASSANDRA

Cassandra appreciated Moira's tremendous exuberant energy. She gave her a hug. Greece was going to be a blast.

Moira emerged from her shower, her hair damp and skin glowing. Alexander snuck a not-so-surreptitious feel of his wife's bottom and, caught by Cassandra, gave her a devilish wink behind Moira's back. Cassandra laughed. She admired her marvelously lusty friends and their *carpe diem* relationship. Cassandra hoped she would marry a man like Alexander one day; someone who would lust after her the way Alexander lusted after Moira.

They flew hurriedly out the door into a warm golden-green evening scented with star jasmine and drove into the heart of the city in Alexander's Volvo. Abruptly, looming in the distance, Cassandra caught sight of the Parthenon lit up against the night sky. It took her breath away. Marta shot her an excited glance. Turning a corner and seeing the Parthenon glowing and nearly close enough to touch was like bumping into a celebrity at the grocery store.

At the restaurant, the hostess seated them at their table to wait for Alexander's friends.

Moira leaned forward, her hand hiding her mouth as she asked, "Did Alexander tell you how his friend Ioannis is helping us obtain our Greek marriage certificate?"

"If you mean acting as sexual bait for your corrupt priest, then yeah," Marta answered.

"Keep your voices down," Alexander hissed.

Moira flung her hand over her shoulder, as if in dismissal of anyone who might listen. "We're taking Ioannis out to dinner as a little thank you. We'll treat you too. This place is pricey."

"He's one of my best friends. He would do this for me without a fancy dinner as a reward," Alexander assured Moira.

"I know. All the more reason to show our appreciation."

"I forgot to tell you that he's bringing Sabiya."

"I assumed," Moira replied.

"Sabiya isn't a Greek name," Marta observed.

"I'm impressed," Moira complimented Marta on her perceptiveness. "Sabiya is Turkish. And young. And ravishing. I'll tell you about her later."

"Don't be such a gossip," Alexander chided disapprovingly. "Anyway, they're here."

"I'll still tell you later, when my old biddy of a husband isn't around," Moira whispered impishly to the girls. They turned to greet Ioannis and Sabiya, who was magnificent to the point of intimidation. She was tall and slender yet juicily curvaceous, with enormous, deep, brown-green eyes, rimmed delicately in kohl; her upper arm adorned with a triple-twined silver snake, silver hoops in her ears, silver bracelets, and unblemished, brown skin that glowed like pearl. She wore a green dress embroidered with silver, tailored precisely to the perfect contours of her wide hips, narrow waist, and bountiful rounded bust. She took the seat Ioannis pulled out for her with easy grace as she flashed the girls a practiced smile. She carried herself like royalty. Cassandra felt like a bumbling adolescent next to Sabiya, all elbows and stutters. She sensed Marta's immediate hostility toward the woman and wondered about it.

Cassandra assumed Sabiya realized the effect her presence had on the men in the room. Even those who pretended they did not notice her.

Especially those. An electric field emanated from her, following her as she walked, practically making the hair of the men she passed stand on end with arousal. Yet as the meal progressed, Sabiya barely moved her eyes from Ioannis's face. He held her full attention and nothing and no one else appeared to matter to this terrific beauty.

MOLLY'S JOURNAL

I try to imagine being so beautiful that it hurts people to look at me, and yet unable to attain the one thing I most desire. I have everything on Sabiya's list. Husband. Children. Farm. She would probably have given up those fabulous breasts in an instant to have what I have.

CASSANDRA

"She's sensational," Cassandra said later, back at Moira's apartment. "I don't care if it's gossiping, tell me about her." Moira sipped a cup of Earl Grey tea. They sat on a little balcony overlooking the street. Alexander had gone to bed since he had to get up early in the morning for a business meeting.

"She's way too Pre-Raphaelite for me," Marta grunted. "Obviously nothing without Ioannis to admire her."

"Ten points for Marta," Moira responded. "I noticed that you couldn't take your eyes off her, Cassie."

"I happen to be a big fan of the Pre-Raphaelites."

"Those vapid, dependent women," Marta muttered.

"Sensual, mysterious, appreciated down to the least detail," Cassandra countered.

"Guess how old she is," Moira challenged.

"I have no idea," Cassandra parried.

"I mean it, guess."

"Twenty-two," Marta took a stab.

"No way," Cassandra frowned, "I'm nineteen and she's much older than I am. Maybe twenty-seven?"

"Nineteen," Moira said gleefully, "same as you."

Cassandra couldn't believe it.

"Here's the story," Moira began. This is what she told them. Sabiya's mother, Fatima, had been trained from a young age to manage a household, to be a wife and mother. She swiftly mastered the art and craft of wifery. Turkish culture held such mastery in high regard. Unfortunately, soon after giving birth to Sabiya, she lost her husband in a boating accident. The main problem with training for wifery is that it doesn't work without a husband. After her husband's death, she earned a meager living as a seamstress. Deprived of that large house and the many children she had planned to have, she was at a loss. She failed to recover. She feared that she would die and leave her child destitute. But she had no cause for worry about her daughter's future since Sabiya was a superbly gorgeous girl, with eyes that held an irresistible mystery. Eventually Fatima accepted a standing offer and moved in with her sister, despite the fact that she did not get along with the bother-in-law on whose generosity she was forced to rely. She continued to take in sewing work to contribute to the household. Over time, it turned out that Sabiya's greatest gift was inspiring the admiration and, in fact, obsession, of men. She wreaked havoc in her wake.

Ioannis had discovered Sabiya about five years previously on a business trip to Istanbul while buying fabric. He met Fatima and Sabiya at an open air market where they were selling dresses they had embroidered. Fatima took to him at once and trusted him implicitly. He photographed Sabiya and returned to Athens with the images in his suitcase, well aware that he was sitting on a gold mine. Based entirely on the photographs, he lined up work for her as a fashion model. Then he returned to Turkey to fetch the mother and daughter. He set them up in a nice apartment. Sabiya became an overnight sensation. She was Ioannis's Eliza Doolittle. He taught her Greek, and other handy skills, such as how to recognize a quality bottle of wine, how to manage money, and how to drive a car. He had no need to teach her a thing about style, art, grace, music. She was born elegant and discerning. She played the piano beautifully.

"So here's the kicker," Moira closed in on the point of the story. "Sabiya became a smashing success. Made a lot of money. And as she grew up, she fell in love with Ioannis. As for him, well he's not in love with her. He could simply see the potential and wanted to cash in on it. He would like her to become her own woman, but she could care less about success because all she wants is exactly what Fatima wanted. Husband. Children. A comfortable family and a home. You've seen her and the effect her presence has on people. She only enjoys this phenomenon in so far as it will make her more desirable to Ioannis. Everything she does, she does to please Ioannis."

"Has he slept with her?" Marta asked.

"Is he Greek?" Moira laughed.

"Why won't he marry her?" Cassandra wondered.

"Who would marry a woman like that? She's a mistress, not a wife. Who wants a wife that every man in the country fantasizes having sex with?" Moira's cynicism faded and she took on a more genuine tone. "Look, he's actually a great guy. He's Alexander's best friend and he has treated me with extraordinary kindness. He meant well in rescuing Sabiya and her mother and he's fond of both of them. But he's in over his head and he doesn't know how to deal with the situation. Truthfully, he just doesn't love her. At the same time, he doesn't want to hurt her."

"And he likes to screw her," Marta added, with a snort.

"Well, that too," Moira conceded. "After all, he *is* a man."

Later that night, while she made love to Marta in Moira's guest bedroom, Cassandra fantasized touching Sabiya. Afterward she remembered Moira's remark about a wife that everyone fantasizes about.

The next day the girls went to the National Archaeological Museum, returning to Moira's in the early evening so Cassandra could meet up with Demetrius for their date. When Demetrius arrived, he acted oddly formal, as if Alexander was Cassandra's father who needed to approve.

Leaving the apartment, they took a taxi to a Moroccan restaurant where they sat on richly patterned rugs on the floor at a low table. "You better order for me," Cassandra told Demetrius, since she had never eaten Moroccan food before.

While they waited for their meal, Cassandra told Demetrius about a friend of hers in London who had gone to Morocco on a vacation and been arrested for possession of hashish. "They threw him in prison for four months. When he came back, he was a completely different person. He had turned cold. Before he went to Morocco he was a gentle soul. He had long hair, wore Birkenstocks and a silver bracelet. He was soft-spoken and thoughtful. When he returned, his hair was about a half-inch long and his clear blue eyes had turned to ice. He was mean. He would say hurtful things to people just to see them cringe. That prison took his soul. It terrified me to see that a person could change like that in such a short time."

"Enough about your friend in London." Demetrius waved a hand in dismissal. "Tell me about the place you live in America."

"California?"

"Yes. California. Hollywood. Tell me about Hollywood."

Cassandra laughed. "I wouldn't know about that. I've never been there. I grew up in the northern part of the state."

"Then tell me about the northern part of the state," Demetrius demanded, with a note of disappointment. Hollywood was the epitome of the American Dream to the rest of the world.

Cassandra described the college town of Berkeley where she grew up. It wasn't Hollywood, but it seemed to capture Demetrius's interest. He liked to travel, to discover new places and meet new people. He asked questions while slowly enjoying a glass of wine and sensually licking sauce off his fingertips with methodic deliberation. Cassandra liked the languid way he moved, as if sucking the sap from each moment. She wanted him to savor her the way he did his food. So when they came out of the restaurant, and he asked her what she wanted to do, she said she wanted to go back to the hotel with him. He laughed with surprise and delight. That was how Cassandra wound up spending the night with Demetrius, who proved to be exactly the sensual, thoughtful, slow-paced lover she imagined.

Cassandra felt smug about her Greek romance when she returned to Moira's the next day and informed her friends that Demetrius had offered to take her to Epidaurus for the weekend, because she dearly wanted to see the ancient theater there; and afterward on to Korinthos, which he described as a picturesque and romantic harbor by the water.

Cassandra registered Marta's visible displeasure at this development. Was Marta jealous? Not likely. Probably just annoyed to be excluded from the trip to Epidaurus. "It's just for a couple of days," Cassandra told her friend, refusing to feel guilty.

Alexander put his hand on Marta's arm. "Don't worry, we'll find something fun for you to do while Cassandra is away," he assured her.

"You could take Marta to the beach," Moira suggested to her husband.

Marta's face brightened. "I adore the beach."

"Beach tomorrow, then. Today we have a field trip in the works," Moira informed them.

"What's that?"

"The Temple to Apollo at Delphi," Moira told them excitedly. "One of my favorite places. And this is the time of year to go because the red poppies are in bloom."

"Is the Temple the site of the Delphic Oracle?" Cassandra asked.

"Exactly," Alexander confirmed, "and it's your namesake's temple."

"My namesake?"

"The prophetess Cassandra," Moira said.

"The one no one heeded," Alexander added.

"No one ever listens to prophets," Marta commented cynically.

The ruins of the Temple to Apollo surrounded the site of the oracle, which struck Cassandra as one of the most dramatic places she had ever seen. Lives had hung in the balance at this exact spot, where the scales tipped. The walls had long ago disintegrated. Six columns built of stacked stone stood tall at one end, a semi-circle of collapsed rock structures forming natural benches at the other. Poppies, red as blood, studded the grass growing between the missing chambers and walls. It gave Cassandra chills to walk where the priests and prophets had walked, where the people had gathered, after traveling for months, to ask the oracle to foretell their future. Lovers, sinners, the damaged and sick; in pain and hunger, seeking relief. She wondered how many had found their answers in the journey itself more than in the cryptic words of the oracle at their final destination.

Cassandra closed her eyes and listened for messages. She heard only the distant voices of tourists drifting on the warm air and the murmur of the breeze rustling the grasses and poppies.

Cassandra would have liked to walk alone in her reverie among the silent fragments of the temple. But her friends had a different sort of expedition underway. Marta and Moira caught up with Cassandra, laughing and arguing loudly about the properties of the male foreskin. Moira suggested they settle the discussion by asking Alexander, since he possessed the particular item in question. At this point, Alexander retreated behind a bush with his wife to give her a visual aid. They emerged with irreverently lascivious expressions and informed Marta that she had been correct.

"How did you two meet?" Marta asked them.

"He was a one-night stand, but I can't get rid of him," Moira joked. Marta and Cassandra laughed at Alexander's expression of innocence.

"It's true," he corroborated. "She was walking in Sintagma Square and she had the most luscious handful of backside and I followed her."

"And I had a rock so big it felt like a piece of the Parthenon in my shoe so I had to stop and shake my shoe out," Moira interjected.

"Which gave me a chance to catch up with her," Alexander continued. "Otherwise I might have lost her in the crowd. I stopped to talk to her while she emptied her shoe and she agreed to have a drink with me."

"He offered to show me the sights and I consented. He used to be terribly handsome when he had more of his hair," Moira teased, brushing a hand over Alexander's balding head.

"She didn't find out until later that the tour included a few personal sights." Alexander grinned. "Like the inside of my bedroom."

"In retrospect, that was one of my favorite sights during that trip."

"She was only in Greece for two weeks on holiday," Alexander explained. "I missed her when she left. I asked myself this question, 'What keeps me from making a commitment to this relationship?' And the answer was 'Nothing.' So I took the train to London and I knocked on her door and asked her to marry me."

"You're kidding," Marta blurted.

"No, he's serious," Moira confirmed. "He's a romantic. He turned up at my door unannounced. I thought I would never see him again."

"What did you do?" Marta asked.

"Well, I certainly didn't agree to marry him. But I kept sleeping with him. We worked it out. When he landed that job offer in California, it made sense to get married so I could go. California. Athens. Maybe we'll try London again one day. Who knows where we'll end up next?"

"Ask the oracle," Cassandra suggested.

Moira called out to the few remaining columns of the temple, "Where will Alexander and I land?" Just as she threw the words out of her mouth, a gust of wind picked up the filmy red scarf tied around the band of Marta's straw hat and flung the scarf into Moira's face, covering it completely. Startled, Moira clawed the scarf from her nose and it flew to the ground where it tangled itself around Alexander's ankles. Alexander stomped on it to keep it from blowing out of reach while Marta snatched at it.

MOLLY'S JOURNAL

Was I at fault? If I had not brought Marcia to Greece, would Moira and Alexander have made it past that troubled moment in their relationship? Or if I had paid more attention to Marcia? If I had not met Demetrius? If, if, if.

If I didn't have breast cancer. If I could live deep into a prosperous and productive old age. If is useless. Things weren't turning out the if way. Once I was at home in my body, at home in the world, and now I'm lost. Will I ever return home again or will I wander forever, a refugee, a stranger in my own body, a stranger in my own land?

CASSANDRA

Demetrius and Cassandra caught an early morning bus to Epidaurus. The theater, with stone seating carved into a hillside surrounding the famous stage, stood apart and isolated; a destination beyond time and place. Cassandra took a deep breath and stepped through the entryway to the main portion of the stage. Demetrius sat on a stone bleacher in the front row, at ground level, and waited, watching attentively as Cassandra paced the stage from north to south then east to west. She stood in the spaces that marked where the great arched entrances onto the stage once stood. She entered the seating and ascended to the topmost row to take in the full panorama.

Demetrius walked to the center of the stage and projected his voice upward to her. "Listen to this sound. Astonishing, eh?" Other tourists waved to him from their various perches in the amphitheater. Cassandra smiled and nodded in agreement about the theater's splendid acoustics.

Demetrius mounted the stairs, climbing up to sit beside Cassandra. He produced a white handkerchief from his pocket and wiped the perspiration from his face.

Cassandra's eyes shone brightly. "Can you imagine them performing here, thousands of years ago?"

"They still perform here."

"I knew that." Cassandra gazed at the stage. "The human era on Earth is only the tiniest blip in the passage of eternity. In that context, almost no time has passed between the lives of the ancients who performed here and our own. But to me, as this little speck in it all, it feels like centuries. In fact, it *is* centuries. And the work of the ancient Greek playwrights from thousands of years ago endures, and influences how people think and believe today. I wish I could create something that would last like those plays, and make a difference to people for thousands of years."

"Not many people do such a thing."

"I know. But here at Epidaurus, I feel the potential each person has to leave a lasting mark that contributes to the evolution of humankind and the world. An intellectual or scientific contribution or, best of all, a contribution on a spiritual level, like the ancient Greek tragedies." Cassandra waved her arm in a grand arc to elaborate her words.

Demetrius patted Cassandra's leg affectionately. "I like this about you, my friend. You say unusual things. You think deeper than other people." Cassandra shrugged self-consciously.

"When I sit in this theater, I feel very small and very big at the same time. You understand?"

"I do. It's that feeling you have sometimes when you look at the stars."

"Exactly. Sitting in this place, I think perhaps I could do something with my life that matters. Even though I know that one day humans will pass into dust in the enormous cavern of time and all will be lost, I love our noble efforts. I love it that we remember the ancient dramatists for thousands of years and read their words and those words still have meaning in our lives."

"So what do you think we must do here?"

"Like what is the purpose of life?" Cassandra laughed lightly.

Demetrius laughed too. "Yes, my American friend, what you think is humans to do here?"

"Maybe we're not supposed to *do* anything. Maybe we're just supposed to witness, to appreciate this creation."

"You think there is a divine creator? A watcher? We could be an experiment made by quarrelsome, willful gods, like the Olympians, who later got bored and abandoned us to our own devices. Then we stupidly tangle ourselves in awful knots until we collapse and disappear from the planet," Demetrius suggested with a note of sadness.

"Sometimes it seems like that, doesn't it? What if, instead, we change and grow through centuries of greed, power-mongering, ignorant leadership, bad choices, catastrophic damage, stupidity, and suffering into a race of thoughtful creatures capable of brilliant deeds that nurture life on Earth? Perhaps we evolve and adapt together through countless evolutions to a beautiful way of life in harmony with all creatures on the planet. Think positive."

Demetrius placed his hand on Cassandra's cheek and kissed her gently. "Perhaps if you speak it into the world, Cassandra, it comes to pass. Not like your namesake, who spoke in vain, and no one heeded her words."

"They don't need my words. They will hear it inside themselves."

"I hope it is so. Come, we go. We must catch the bus to Korinthos."

They checked into a small hotel overlooking the harbor in new Korinthos, which trailed away from old Korinthos, like the tail of a comet arcing from the bright snap of original energy. They walked to a café by the water in the old city and sat outside on the terrace in the cool evening as the sky darkened and the stars sparkled on the velvet field of night.

"Let me order for you," Demetrius suggested. They ate deep-fried calamari with a variety of mysterious steamed greens in olive oil and garlic sauce accompanied by hunks of freshly baked bread. They dipped the bread in olive oil, licking their greasy fingers, and washing it down with ouzo.

"What exactly is calamari?" Cassandra asked.

"Squid."

Cassandra shuddered. "Why isn't it slimy and rubbery? This is crispy and delicious."

"They snip it and fry it."

"And what on earth are these greens?"

"Do you really want to know?" Demetrius grinned impishly.

"Can't be worse than squid, can it?"

He chuckled. "They are weeds. We call it *chorta* and the dish represents the ingenuity of our women. When families are hungry in hard times, our women hike into the hills and pick wild green plants. Weeds. They steam them and add oil, garlic, and spices. Even though practically nothing, *chorta* fills you up and has good, how you say..., nutrients. Now restaurants put *chorta* on the menu; a dish invented as a desperate measure by starving women."

After dinner, they walked to their hotel along the beach. The slap of the boats docked in the water of the harbor punctuated their conversation.

Cassandra felt comfortable around Demetrius, with a comfort that ran deeper than a chance meeting or vacation fling. It felt as if they went way back together, had a history with one another. She desired him physically, but also because he had strength of character, which took the attraction to a deeper level.

In the hotel room, he played a jazz tape and the light filtered in through the closed drapes so that when he turned out the lamp they could see each other plainly in ghostly moonlight. They danced together, turning in slow circles while they removed each other's clothing. His kisses were urgent and joyful in the warm night. The air was scented with star jasmine.

Cassandra felt relaxed with this Greek man. Open to him. He lay behind her, pressing against her back, touching her with eager, gentle hands, his nose buried in her hair. She could tell he was breathing in her scent. She felt so aroused that she climaxed as soon as he entered her, and he climaxed with her, rippling with his pleasure.

Cassandra thought about how much she didn't know and how much of life stretched before her. Demetrius encircled her with his muscular arms and held her protectively. He held her tenderly all night. He was a sensual man, a man who questioned the gods. She slept profoundly in his caring embrace, as if she had drowned and come to rest at peace locked in his arms at the bottom of the sea.

MOLLY'S JOURNAL

I am no longer writing about Demetrius and my younger self. I am writing about my present self and my Andy. I am writing about sinking into sleep dissolved in the night ocean of my husband's love. I feel no distance between me and Cassandra. Who is this Cassandra character? A seed? A persona? A broken promise?

CASSANDRA

Cassandra returned from Korinthos into the eye of a storm. She found Moira alone when she arrived at the apartment. "Let's go out to a café where we can talk," Moira said. She sounded tired and her voice lacked that vital spark that Cassandra admired in her. On the way to the café, Cassandra described her trip with Demetrius. When they reached the café, Moira chose a table and flung herself into a chair.

As Cassandra took her seat across the table from Moira, her friend said, "Perhaps I flew in the face of the gods by thinking I could transform a summer affair into a lifelong partnership. The Greek dramatists called it hubris. And pride always goes before a fall."

"What are you talking about?" Cassandra went cold as she realized that something unfortunate had happened in her absence.

"Your little friend Marta is more than the perfect house guest. She fit right in like one of the family."

Suddenly Cassandra got the picture. "She slept with him, didn't she?"

"I doubt they got much sleep."

"I'm so sorry. If I hadn't brought her with me, then, oh no, I had no idea. Wait until I get my hands on her." Cassandra wanted to say something that would make it all come right and of course she couldn't.

The waiter arrived and the women ordered sandwiches.

"You can't lay all the blame on Marta. It takes two to tango. In truth, this garbage with my husband has gone on virtually since we met. And now I have to make some tough decisions about what I want for the rest of my life. I have to make those decisions this week."

"This week? Please tell me you're not going to leave him because of this. I'll take her away. We'll disappear from the picture and the two of you can work it out and get on with it. This is no more than a summer vacation for her. For you, it's your marriage."

"Exactly. It's my marriage. Do you think he hasn't done this before? Or that he won't do it again? Only a few weeks ago he ended an affair with a friend of Sabiya's that lasted for seven months. He didn't lie to me. He told me about it from the start. I have to decide if I want to have a marriage that goes like this. He was faithful to me in California. Maybe because we were trying to have a baby and infidelity didn't mix with trying for a baby. I miscarried. I wonder if things would have turned out differently if I had gone to term and had a child."

"I didn't know you had a miscarriage."

"No one did. We kept it to ourselves. I had three miscarriages actually and then we stopped trying. We decided to wait until we returned to London where a visit to the fertility specialist would cost nothing on the National Health. The American doctors thought I had a hormone imbalance, which they assured us was manageable. They encouraged me not to give up. Then Alexander took this job, we moved to Athens, and we put off trying again. We talked about it, but first he wanted me to marry him in the Greek Orthodox Church for his family. He talks a convincing line about being forward-thinking, Cassie, but he's pretty conservative. And like a traditional old-world male, he wants to have a wife and also an affair now and then. The only difference between him and his father's generation is that his father kept his infidelities secret. In our generation, we're progressive and talk about an open marriage. Would I be any less hurt, angry, or jealous if he had lied? I doubt it."

"An open marriage only works by agreement," Cassandra pointed out. "He has to allow you to do the same thing without complaint."

"Theoretically. He says he doesn't mind if I have an affair. But it's easy for him to say that because he knows I'm not interested. I don't have the energy for it. Or the time in my busy schedule. I still want to have children, if I can get my body to cooperate. And if that's not possible with my body, I could adopt children. But not with Alexander. I don't want to raise children in this sort of marriage. So I have to decide if I want him and a career and a very adult lifestyle with no children or if I want to cut my losses, go home to London, and try my luck at meeting a nice family man before my clock runs out. Alexander says he wants to live in London again, but his heart's not in it. I keep pretending to believe what he says, instead of admitting what I see in his heart. That's the part about the hubris. I thought I could make this relationship work out, this multi-cultural, inter-continental relationship. But lately I think it maybe won't work out. The only place we were completely good together was in California, on neutral ground."

"You two are great together. I've seen it. Please don't give up," Cassandra begged. "I'm going to give Marta hell when I get my hands on her."

Moira's lip trembled slightly. "It's not Marta. If it wasn't her it would be a different sweet young thing. It's us. Don't blame her for our failed marriage. However, I would appreciate it if you would take her away. We scheduled this sham priest to marry us in two weeks and I'm going to call it off. We may not have another opportunity to marry in the Greek Orthodox Church once we cut this priest loose. So Alexander and I need to talk about all of this, without distractions, and to redefine our marriage. Or maybe to let it go."

By the time the sandwiches arrived, Cassandra had lost her appetite. She wrapped her sandwich in paper and took it with her.

When they returned to the apartment, Cassandra watched Moira, the actress, put on a cheerful mood, like a mask, the moment they stepped across the threshold.

"How did you like the movie?" she asked her husband and his lover.

Marta yawned and stretched like a cat. Cassandra had an urge to slap her. "It was boring. We left and went for a walk," Marta informed.

Alexander turned to Cassandra and inquired, "How was Epidaurus?"

"Great."

Alexander frowned. He knew that Epidaurus meant a lot more to her than that. He glanced at Moira, who assiduously avoided his gaze.

Cassandra put a hand on Marta's arm. "Marta, come up to the roof with me for a few minutes. I want to talk to you in private."

Marta's face clouded over with defiance as she followed Cassandra out the door. Cassandra led her up the service stairs to the roof of the building in stony silence. Cassandra sat on the edge of a rooftop flower box and looked out at the city. She patted the spot next to her, indicating that Marta should sit. They had a nice view from the roof, although neither one of them actually looked at it.

"What do you think you're doing?" Cassandra began in a confrontational tone.

"Oh don't be so puritanical. Moira doesn't mind as much as you do."

"How do you know?"

"Because she told me."

"You don't know the first thing about Moira. These are my friends. And they're going through a rocky stretch at the moment and you're making it much worse. How can you possibly do this to these people who have offered us their hospitality? Just so that you can have a little fun in Athens? Don't you think about anyone other than yourself?"

"You need to have a talk with your friends, because I don't think this is a problem."

"Why do you think we're up here having this conversation? I did have a talk with Moira. She asked us to leave. To get out of her house. And frankly I don't want to travel with you anymore. I'd rather travel by myself. So I'm asking you to leave Athens."

Marta looked shocked. "If she has a problem with this, why did she pretend it was OK? I'm not a mind reader."

"Marta! You're screwing her husband. Who needs a mind reader?"

"Why are you so bent out of shape? Is this about us? Because I could care less if you sleep with Demetrius, or run off to Korinthos, the romantic fishing village, with him. Do whatever you please. But don't holler at me for having a fling of my own.

Did it not occur to you that I might want to have some fun too?"

"Did you sleep with Alexander to get back at me for going to Korinthos with Demetrius?"

"That's not why I slept with him. I like him," Marta asserted with a pout. "He's good in bed. And he set it up for me to sleep with that model."

"Sabiya? You slept with Sabiya?" Sabiya, the unearthly beauty. Cassandra had wrestled with her secret desire to sleep with Sabiya; even though such a thing was entirely out of her reach. Apparently it wasn't out of Marta's reach. Or maybe it wasn't true.

"Yeah." Marta could see she had finally exacted the revenge on Cassandra that she craved and she twisted the knife. "Ioannis wanted her to experience a lesbian encounter. He and Alexander set it up. She didn't want to at first. After I got her to relax, she got into it."

"You're lying."

"Ask Alexander."

"All the more reason for you to leave. You need to get on the train tonight before you hurt anyone else. Moira wants you out of here. I want you out of here."

"And what will you do after I leave? Seek comfort in the arms of your Greek lover?"

"That does not concern you. Actually, I hope I can help my friends salvage their marriage."

"Spare me the melodrama. Their marriage is in no danger."

"That shows how unperceptive you are. You were pretty much the last straw for Moira." At this news, Marta's eyes grew wide. "Moira is going to back out of the Greek Orthodox marriage deal. She's thinking of leaving him." Cassandra took her turn to twist the knife.

"I don't believe you. Why would she do that after all the trouble they've gone through to get this priest to agree to do it? And you must realize that Alexander does this all the time, has affairs I mean. It's not like I'm the only one."

"Do you ever think about anyone but yourself?"

"I could ask you the same question."

"This thrilling vacation drama of yours is real-life misery for my friends. You think you can breeze through and impose yourself on their lives for your personal satisfaction or amusement, or a titillating quip to write on a postcard, or whatever. You're a self-centered, emotional imperialist."

MOLLY'S JOURNAL

Self-centered, emotional imperialist? Where did that come from? Where am I going with this story? It seems like beach reading. Has my writing ability atrophied this much? I have taken this story out of the deep freeze of my youth because I meant to do something with it and never did and now I'm dying. As a young woman on the verge of my life, I set out to write and I wandered from the path. I got sidetracked. I had a family. Excuses.

I imagine a hypothetical situation. What if I lived in a dictatorship maintained by terror and I wrote to change it? What if I wrote to expose the truth? And what if, in this hypothetical terrorist dictatorship, the government arrested me and told me that if I wrote another word then they would murder my children, but if I stopped writing forever, my children would remain unharmed? There is no question which option I would choose. But here in my reality, within the parameters of my safe, insignificant, narrow world, I have chosen to raise my children instead of writing. And if I had to choose between Andy and publishing a novel? Andy. No contest. Fortunately, I can choose to raise a family and also write. Some women do both. Although many of those women have more money than I and don't have to work a day job. Even so, I have not cultivated that ability. How do I become one of those women? I want to make a difference for other people the way writers have made a difference for me. I want to leave something behind. I resolve to make a difference in someone's life. That would be a transformative act.

In Flight above the Pacific Ocean, 1977

A self from long ago went on vacation in Maui; a self I left behind when I married Odysseus and had my precious children. I say good-bye to that other woman as I return to the woman I chose to be instead, the self who tends to the details that swallow my hours. Details I love, like reading bedtime stories to Max and Lena. Details I hate, like doing the laundry. Details that render it impossible to carve out sufficient reflective time in the still core of reverie that is necessary to write.

Book 11: Erica
Yopika Bapa, 1977

You may ask who I am and how I secured a voice in this narrative. I assure you I belong here and I deserve a turn to speak.

I fell in love with Penelope at first sight at a luau. OK, so it wasn't exactly a luau. A luau is a Hawaiian pig roast, right? This was a Kapa pig roast. What do I know from pig roasts? You take a dead pig, you put it on a stick, you hang it over a fire, or you bury it in a pit. Whatever. It's still a dead pig. All pigs look the same to me. I have no sympathy for pigs. I have my reasons.

I don't eat pork. I grew up in a kosher Jewish home and as a teenager I became a vegetarian. My mother was inconsolable. ("What, no chicken soup? Whatsa matta wid chicken soup?") This makes me the diametrical opposite of a person you would find at a pig roast. Like if you look up "pig roast participant" in Webster's I think it says "antonym: Jewish vegetarian." So don't ask what I was doing at a pig roast. It happens. Once in each century a nice Jewish girl winds up at a pig roast. OK, so I also confess that I'm not a nice Jewish girl. I mean I'm not the kind of catch that Isaac Rosenberg's mom in Yonkers meant when she told him to bring home "a nice Jewish girl." In fact, also according to Webster's, I'm probably the definition of a not-nice Jewish girl because I have no interest in nice Jewish boys. I'm not interested in boys of any denomination. This means, apparently, according to an ancient Talmudic text entitled "Oy Vay Such a Headache That One Gives Me," that I'm in danger of going to hell for breaking the commandment "Thou shalt not disappoint thy father and, especially, thy conniving mother."

What was I saying? It doesn't matter. One Jewish story leads to a hundred Jewish stories. Don't blame me for the interconnectedness of things. I can't possibly explain about one thing without explaining about a heap of other things, without context. That context always takes me the long way around. But the context is the heart of the matter. I mean what's the point without the context? We're born, we have context, we die. The context is the best part. And because everything connects to everything else, a simple event like meeting a beautiful woman at a luau contains multiple levels of meaning.

One glimpse of Penelope riveted me. Admiring her surreptitiously from across the yard took my mind off the macabre primitive scene unfolding in front of me as they roasted all of that pig except the squeal. The stench of the fat dripping into the fire pit made the dogs slobber. People waded through a film of dog saliva and dirt while watching the pig cook. Good thing I didn't wear spiked heels. That was a joke. If you knew me better you would have gotten it. I'd need a parachute to wear heels of any ilk. I have an innate talent for spraining my ankle, even in sneakers.

It must be a Kapa custom to witness the killing of the pig before eating it. Witnessing the death of the pig ensures that the pig-eaters consciously recognize that an animal died for the sake of their dinner. It teaches the children to show their gratitude to the pig spirit for sacrificing itself so they can eat. I've always wondered how they get those tots to eat that thing after they witness the slaughter. If I were a child, I would have nightmares for months afterward. I'll stick to squash. It doesn't scream when you chop it up for dinner. This ritual begs the question: Does a pig have a spirit? Does a squash?

Despite the pig carnage, I was happy to be there that night. Frankly, I would have walked through a week of evenings of flaming pig to meet Penelope. That sounds like a bad acid trip. Or a Disney movie. The evening of the flaming pigs. Can you just see them dancing in tutus with their curly little tails on fire? Sorry. My imagination has its own agenda.

I felt sure from the moment I laid eyes on Penelope that she had never slept with a woman. (So much for women's intuition. I could not have made a more erroneous assumption. Whatever.) And I have strong inhibitions about coming on to straight women. I feel too much like one of those guys who whistles at women on the street. Who needs that? Who needs a whole construction site imagining them naked? I wouldn't want to make another woman uncomfortable in the wake of my desire. Comfortable, yes. Uncomfortable, emphatically no. Plus, mainstream culture views a gay woman coming on to a straight woman as a pervert corrupting a "normal" person. Yuck and double yuck. I don't want to feed a bad stereotype.

When I know an attractive woman is gay then the situation is natural and easy. I can flirt like crazy and rest assured that I'm not embarrassing her or confusing her. I'm flattering her. With Penelope I felt like a klutz at Tiffany's. Don't touch anything. Don't break anything. Put your hands in your pockets. So I stole glances at her; shy in the shadows, hoping she wouldn't notice the obsession in my eyes.

That first night, just looking at her made my ribs ache with longing. She had a depth to her that spooled in the bottomless pools of her eyes. Her hair, dark as a raven's wing, shining blue-black in the firelight. Her skin like amber honey. The fluid grace of her movements. She had me at "Max, that lady might not want you to put your snake so close to her."

She took me to another level of yearning when she told the story of the massacre of her people. The liquid smoothness of her voice seemed to emanate directly from the fire. I know about oral tradition. My people live by it. We descend from wandering Tribes; passing our history and our laws down from one generation to the next in the telling of stories. Penelope said the story of the massacre has not been written. It therefore escapes definition and slips in and out of the unfolding present moment created by the teller and the listeners.

When I think of the Kapa, on this land for 12,000 years or more, I try to imagine walking on land my ancestors have walked for that long. Sinking my feet into that earth and looking at B'Taka Lake where my people have stood for centuries. OK, I don't think I can imagine this. My people dwelled in tents. We pulled up stakes and moved. We continue in diaspora to this day. I have no attachment to any particular landscape. What does it mean to belong to a place?

On that first night at the Rez, I panicked. I had to escape the pork fat and Penelope. The combination of a roasting pig and an incredibly attractive woman was making me crazy. I slipped into the shadows and went for a walk by the lakefront to clear my head.

It's not fair to think you have fallen in love with a woman based entirely on how she looks. I wouldn't want someone to do that to me. Forcing me to attempt to fulfill the expectation of their image of me; their fantasy of who or what I am. So I didn't want to do that to Penelope. My mind tried to talk reason to my heart, my blood, and my stubborn hormones.

I sat on a bench and watched the silver ripples of water reflecting the light of the full moon, which hung above the lake like a single, luminous all-seeing eye. B'Taka Lake was peaceful on that night. It has ever brought me peace since. The bloody history of this spot hides its face behind the water's gentle veil. So much lies beneath the surface of things. Remember that context stuff I mentioned earlier? The water smelled a bit swampy and I heard a frog or two croaking. Mallards swam by and gathered at the water's edge to fluff their feathers and settle for the night. A breeze riffled the air and chilled me. I heard footsteps on the path and I stared straight ahead, trying to appear lost in my thoughts so whoever approached wouldn't bother me. I focused on the lake. Footsteps stopped at the bench.

"Do you mind if I sit here with you for a minute?"

I looked up. My heart stopped. I reverted to humor, my go-to in a tight situation. "Are you stalking me?"

"Huh? No. You took off right after the story of the massacre and after you left I realized I know you. Erica Kaplan, right?" I nodded. She sat on the bench next to me. OK, so then I started frantically running through my mind asking myself, where did she hear about me and what did she hear? How did she know me? Should I know her?

"So you finally caught up with me. I knew it was all over when they put the WANTED poster up at the post office." I shivered from the cool breeze and the desire that I had to hide.

She chuckled at my joke. "Are you cold?"

"I should have brought my sweatshirt."

"Here, take my jacket," Penelope offered.

"No, that's OK." I shivered.

"I'm used to it here. It's not that cold to me." She took off her jacket and put it in my lap. It was deep purple and made of woven cotton. Why protest? The jacket was deliciously warm and smelled like her.

She looked out across the water silently. A frog sang. I'm not good at silence. I'm good at talking. Talking is what I do for a living. Silence makes me uncomfortable.

"So what have you heard about me?"

"Oh," she said, as if she had just remembered I was there. "I teach at Head Start. You've had some of my children. I mean you've treated them. You have a reputation as one of the best. One of my children is in therapy with you right now. Jasmine White. She's doing much better at school. I can see a difference."

"Yes, Jasmine." God help me, I sounded like Sigmund Freud. I might just as well have rubbed my chin and put my pipe stem in my mouth. I told myself to relax. I can be pretty flat-footed in social situations when I get self-conscious.

"She's had a hard time, that one." Penelope continued to gaze out across the lake, leaving me stranded in silence. I wanted to say something and I couldn't. Then the patron saint of geek possessed me and I started whistling Beethoven's Fifth.

With a twinkle in her eye, she said, "I think we should get to know each other better."

I practically swooned and fell over in the water with the mallards and the frogs.

Athena liked me from the start. If Penelope and I went for a bike ride or out to the movies, Athena would always invite me to eat dinner with the family before or after or whatever. And she was certainly not inviting me to eat because she thought I needed feeding since I'm built short and *zaftig*. *Zaftig* is the way they call it where I come from. It's kind terminology for a person with meat on her bones. The Jewish equivalent of when Black folks say a girl's "got back." I've got back, alright. Anyway. Athena could surely see I didn't lack for food. I needed more bike rides. Even though we said nary a word about it, I could tell that Athena had me figured out and that she approved. That blew me away. I knew in my heart I could make Penelope happy and in those early days Athena knew it too.

The thought of confessing my love to Penelope terrified me. I figured I had only one shot. Until I took my shot, I could pretend that it could happen. After I took my shot, if she declined, then I would sink into despair. I wanted to know and didn't want to know, both at once.

In the end, Athena forced the issue. I swear, old people think they can get away with saying anything. I had driven over to the Rez, or Yopika Bapa as Penelope calls it, and I took my bike out of the car. Penelope and I liked to ride on the bike path that meandered around the lake. I picked up my helmet.

Athena emerged from the house. "She'll be right out," she greeted as she scrutinized me with one of her unreadable looks. "When do you plan to tell her the truth?"

There was no use pretending with Athena. "What makes you so sure she hasn't already figured it out?"

"She probably has. That's not what I asked." Athena crossed her arms on her chest.

I wondered if I should put the helmet on to protect myself from Athena. "What are you afraid of?" she asked.

"Isn't it obvious?" I didn't know if Penelope had figured me out at that point. That might sound hard to believe, but the inside of a relationship can get pretty confusing, no matter how straightforward it may look from the outside.

"Maybe I'm stupid," Athena said, "because I don't get it." How did she expect me to respond? Where was she going with this conversation? "You two are in love with each other. Life is short. Do something about it." She turned and stomped across her porch and into her house, exasperated, as I stood flabbergasted. I lifted my bike back into my car and drove away.

When I got home, I sat down on the couch and didn't move. The phone rang in the motionless house. I did not answer. Dark gathered outside and still I sat unmoving on my couch with a million thoughts bumping into each other in my head. The doorbell rang.

When I opened the door, I found Penelope on the doorstep. "What did she say to you?"

"She didn't tell you?"

"No." Penelope looked me up and down, top to bottom, realized I had been sitting in my bike-riding clothes with my helmet in my lap, and asked, "What the heck are you doing?"

"I'm thinking. I sometimes do that."

She stepped inside, closed the door behind her, and sat down on the couch next to me. "You're hiding," she accused.

"OK, I'm hiding. I'm hiding from you and you came and found me. Now it's your turn. You hide and I'll find you."

She studied me with those penetrating dark Kapa eyes.

"You want me to count to ten?" I demanded. I started crying and I couldn't stop. What if this is it, I thought, what if this is my shot and I've blown it already?

She took my face in her hands and kissed me. The forever inimitable perfection of the first kiss. She tasted like vanilla and smelled like fresh rain.

Whenever I had imagined that first time, I had imagined myself seducing her. Never in my wildest imaginings had I considered that she would make the first move. But there she was and there we were and she kissed my neck and my ear and pulled my shirt off over my head and expertly rolled my nipples between her fingers while I cried and moaned and perhaps went into shock at how easily it happened. She had her hand down the back of my pants and I took off her blouse and her bra and felt her gentle breasts and tangled my hands in that blue-black hair that I loved and kissed her hard and she laughed and slid her hand between my legs and I wanted more than anything to be in that moment touching her, having her touch me. We wanted each other like refugees in the desert craving shade and cool water. So we crawled into the tent of each other's touch and we drank from the well of each other's longing.

I thought she was straight! She's about as straight as a pretzel.

Penelope is my winning lottery ticket and I'm her three wishes granted. I give her pleasure in the privacy of our shared bed, hands and mouths and tongues painting ecstasy on the canvas of the night. I make her laugh. Not a flimsy twitter but a deep, solid laugh, substantial as a hunk of warm bread. I love her strength. She survived a childhood as macabre as a Grimm's Fairy Tale. I think of her like one of the children I see in therapy, only full-grown and healed, wearing the mantle of survival, able to experience joy again. I accept her inability to shake her grief at the loss of her husband. Fortunately, she pushes past that loss to offer me the best of herself.

I have landed in the country of love, too far from my source to return for a warmer coat or sturdier shoes or to prepare myself better against hardship. Penelope and I arrived here together with the clothes on our backs and what we can make from what we have at hand. For me there will be no other. But that is not the case for her. I agree to her unspoken terms, which I read in her heart. She's bisexual. I am all the woman she will ever need; but I am not all the man. I must forever share her with Odysseus, who continues to possess her in absentia. We do well with each other. Even so, she remains incomplete. Deep within herself, she still waits for him. I rarely speak his name. As if I might conjure him with the saying of it. I whisper it to myself in fear. My greatest dread: his return, her release, my nightmare.

Book 12: Penelope, Molly, Cassandra
Yopika Bapa, 1979

Looking for the phone bill in my desk, Erica comes across the manuscript for *Death in Hoper Valley*. I discover her sitting in my desk chair reading.

"You wrote this?" I feel as though she read my private diary.

"It's not finished." I struggle to keep my voice neutral, to control my unwarranted surge of anger.

"When did you write this?"

"Hawaii. Then I came home and there was work and the children. And I met you. So, no time to continue." I shrugged.

"Don't blame me and the children with that lame excuse. Are you trying to guilt-trip me? You couldn't even pass Guilt Trip 101. I was raised by a woman who has a Ph.D. in the subject." She puts her hand on her hip and tilts her curly head to one side. How does she manage to make me laugh like this? To lighten up, even when I'm hopping mad?

"I don't have the time to keep writing. I have other priorities." My anger diffuses.

"You mean you don't make the time. Same as changing the name of Hoepper's. You let this stuff fall by the wayside. Important stuff and…" She makes a *pffft* sound and tosses away an imaginary wisp with her hand.

"I lost heart with the name change, Erica. Cut me some slack. It endangered the children and it wasn't going anywhere."

"Do you think it was easy for the Black children to get on the bus to an all-white school to begin integration? You know how you change the world?" Erica wags a finger at me.

I know, and I also know she is going to tell me again.

"One person at a time you change it."

I say nothing.

"Don't pull that Native poker face with me," Erica snaps. "You should finish this story. Make this a priority. It's important for you. Besides, I want to find out what happens."

So Erica starts driving the children to school in the morning, which gives me an hour to write before I leave for Head Start. I go back inside Molly's pain, my pain. I go back inside it for the sake of change, one person at a time, starting with myself.

From *Death in Hoper Valley*

On Saturday, Molly went to the twins' last soccer game of the season. The weather had turned the corner toward winter and a chilling brisk wind ripped through the bystanders on the sidelines. Andy wrapped Molly in a heavy gray wool blanket that had belonged to Molly's father. She imagined it smelled like Dad, or perhaps his scent still really clung to it. She wore a deep-blue, thick, handmade, cotton hat pulled down over her ears, one of several Peg had given her when she hacked off her hair in preparation for losing it to chemo.

As Molly waited for the game to begin, Teresa appeared at her elbow and set up her folding chair with a perfunctory nod in Molly's direction. Molly's heart raced. Teresa pulled her colorful quilt around her shoulders and took out her thermos from which she poured a cup of steaming, hot cocoa. She handed it to Molly without a word. Molly took it from the woman's wrinkled, steady hand. She sipped. It infused her with a comforting warmth, and tasted so wonderfully sweet with hints of flavor she did not recognize. Something root-like and perhaps medicinal. It warmed her to the bone, driving out the chill and making her feel cozy, cared for, and even healthy. For a split second, she wondered if she was in another one of her dreams about Teresa.

"Thank you."

Teresa poured cocoa for herself then returned the thermos to her bag. She leaned back in her chair and drank from her steaming cup. After a while she turned to Molly and said, "I hope your boys win today," as if they were old cronies and had sat together all season, swapping stories and sipping spiced cocoa.

"I hope so too, it's their last game of the season."

"I'm sorry you're unwell." Teresa gazed out at the field.

Molly had the urge to put her head in Teresa's lap and have a good cry.

"You'll figure out how to make yourself well. It'll come to you."

No it won't, Molly thought. She opened her mouth to ask Teresa how to do such a thing, but at that moment Andy returned.

"Teresa, this is my husband Andy," Molly introduced, "Andy, Teresa Clearwater."

Teresa scrutinized him with that penetrating gaze of hers. Andy shifted his weight uncertainly and placed his hands on Molly's shoulders, massaging them gently. "You've made an impression on our Molly," Andy informed Teresa.

"Have I?"

"You like to watch even if you don't know anyone playing?" Andy asked her curiously.

"Oh I know them. They just don't know me. These children in their youthful bodies that can do such miraculous things. And the parents, with big dreams for these children. Their parents who love to watch those perfect, little bodies perform. Parents and children, so hopeful. I can't stay away from that hopefulness."

Molly listened, transfixed, with her cup of cocoa halfway to her lips. Her heart jumped into her mouth when Andy told Teresa, "Molly dreamed about you." She wished he would hold his tongue.

Teresa nodded her head slightly. "Of course," she said as if she already knew. How could she possibly? Molly blushed.

Teresa pointed at the field. "Game's starting."

Molly left the cheering to Andy. Occasionally she glanced sideways at Teresa, who watched the game contentedly from the warmth of her quilt and her cocoa.

"Did you make that quilt?" Molly asked after a while.

"It was a gift. I don't know how to quilt."

"I know how, but I haven't done it since I started having children."

"Perhaps while you're recovering," Teresa suggested. Molly wasn't sure she would recover. She found it reassuring that Teresa thought she would.

"I have cancer."

Teresa reached over and covered one of Molly's hands with hers. The wrinkles around the old woman's eyes deepened as her face crinkled in a Sphinx-like smile, a smile built in the eyes and not much in the mouth. "I know, dear. It's a tough row to hoe." Molly's eyes welled with tears.

"It's so unfair to my children," Molly told the woman quietly. "And my husband."

"And to you."

"And to me."

"If I were you," Teresa said quietly, "I'd ask the spirits for guidance."

"Spirits?" Molly weighed the possibility that Teresa was perhaps crazy.

"Sometimes people become ill because of random and unfair physical reasons. But sometimes illness happens because of a spiritual imbalance. If you become ill from a tipped spiritual balance, and you set it right, then the outlook may change," Teresa answered with maddening obfuscation.

"I don't understand."

Teresa looked into Molly's face attentively. "Perhaps this is not the time."

"No, wait. I want to understand."

"I know you do, dear. Let it unfold as it will." Teresa patted Molly's hand again. "Watch your children play." Teresa pointed at the field and fell silent. She continued to hold Molly's hand as they watched the game and Molly felt comforted.

When the game ended, the boys pelted off the field triumphant and flushed with the power of their athletic prowess.

"I was yelling for Spencer to pass it to me because he didn't see I was open," Mac told his brother.

"Well it didn't matter because he just kicked it in himself," Mike replied.

"He should have passed it," Mac complained.

"We killed them anyway," Mike pointed out.

The boys grabbed their soccer bags and headed for the car, still debriefing the game play by play.

Andy folded Molly's chair and took the wool blanket from her. Molly turned to Teresa and extended an invitation. "Please come to our house for lunch. Our friends and neighbors are wonderful. They've brought heaps of food. We can't possibly eat it all. I'd like to talk with you further."

"If you would eat a few slices of Mrs. Donnelly's exceptional and abundant banana bread you would do us all a great favor," Andy added.

Teresa looked bemused as she declined. "That's very generous. Not today. I'll come another time. When I'm needed."

"Thanks again for sharing your," Molly broke off, not knowing how to thank the woman for the warmth and encouragement she had provided simply by holding Molly's hand during the game. She concluded, "for sharing your delicious cocoa." Molly took Andy's arm for the walk to the car. Once out of earshot, she asked Andy, "That was cryptic, don't you think?"

"You mean the 'when I'm needed' part?"

"Yeah."

"She's a bit odd."

Molly turned at the edge of the parking lot to scan the field. Teresa had disappeared.

On Tuesday, Molly started chemo. She submitted to having toxic chemicals poured into her veins until her plump fluffy cells drowned in a swamp of noxious soup. She visualized cancer cells, glowing with evil, phosphorescent glee, until the glug pouring into her body coated them in goo and squeezed them to nonexistence. As she created this image in her mind, she believed she could hear the humming of the cancer directly behind her left breast. It knew she could hear it and feel it, and even though it didn't like the chemo, it refused to leave. What person in her right mind can hear cancer cells humming inside her body? None. None in her right mind.

Andy drove her home after the chemo and settled her into bed. She slept for a couple of hours before abruptly waking up overtaken by nausea. She retched into a bucket for nearly two hours before Andy called Eli in a panic. Eli talked to the oncologist, who prescribed a medication to help with the nausea. Friends and neighbors came and went, quietly, softly, bringing flowers and food. Molly couldn't bear the sight or scent of these earthly delights.

On Thursday night, Susan stretched out in the bed next to Molly and begged, "Don't die, Mom, I can't do senior year without you." Molly held Susan in her arms and they wept together, while Molly thought to herself that senior year was the least of it. A furious voice within Molly raged against the cancer, the malevolent presence pulsing in her body. My children deserve better than this. My husband and my mother deserve better. There should be a rule that bad things can't happen to good people. But there didn't appear to be any order to the universe and chaos brought a steady stream of bad things to good people.

One week after the first chemo treatment, Molly returned to the oncologist for a consultation. The trip into Carlysle exhausted Molly, who arrived at the doctor's office raw and irritable. The doctor had intended for her to go to the hospital for more chemo, but cancelled because he could see that she had not recovered sufficiently from the last treatment. "Your body doesn't tolerate chemo very well, does it?" It was a rhetorical question.

"Just coming to your office exhausts her," Andy told him anxiously.

"I won't keep you long. Let's figure out what to do here," the doctor replied. He looked at Molly's file, reading to himself for a long moment. "You have help with your children, I presume?" he queried.

"My mother lives on the property with us," Molly answered. "She gets the children off to school in the morning and stays in case I need her. She and Andy take turns cooking dinner for the children. But my mother's not young. This is tiring for her."

"I understand."

"Molly has no energy or appetite," Andy informed the doctor.

"I can prescribe something that will improve your appetite," the doctor told them.

"That would help," Andy answered for her. "Mom is going crazy trying to cook something that appeals to Molly."

Molly's voice wavered and tears pooled up in her eyes. "The chemo makes me feel one breath away from dead. I think it will kill me before cancer can do it."

"Your body has more difficulty with chemo than most. Unfortunately, it's the only way to kill any cancer cells still percolating in there and looking to gain a foothold. Let's reduce the intensity of the dose and leave more time between treatments for you to recover. We have to find a level of treatment that you can tolerate and stick to it for a few months. I intend to do everything in my power to keep you here with us, little lady."

"I've seen people who carry on as usual the best they can while undergoing chemo. How do they do it?" Andy asked.

"Different people respond to chemo in different ways," the doctor explained. "Molly's body has elected to rebel more than is typical. So we'll take it slow and easy. I want to try a milder dose on Friday. We'll revisit this plan after that."

Friday. Chemo. Molly disappeared into a dim world of twilight shadow. Nausea. Exhaustion. Lethargy. Apathy. Despair.

On Saturday afternoon, she opened her eyes to find Teresa sitting next to her humming softly. She reached over and squeezed Teresa's hand. Molly shivered.

Teresa stopped humming. "You mustn't give up."

"It would be easy to do that," Molly confessed in a faint voice. "It doesn't seem real. This doesn't feel like me. Perhaps I've disappeared."

"You're still here, I assure you. And a lot of people are depending on you to put up a fight."

Molly clung to Teresa's hand like a lifeline and spilled her thoughts. "If there is a reason for things and a purpose to everything that happens, then why do humans suffer? What conceivable purpose does suffering serve? I can't believe that the suffering of good people fits into some sort of plan. On the other hand, if we live in chaos, and things happen with no sense or order, then what's the point to any of it? We delude ourselves into thinking that we matter when we don't. We're dust floating at the whim of a breeze. I want to believe there is an order to the universe, but I can't believe that the bad things that happen are part of that order. I want to believe that we invite goodness into our lives, yet if we have the power to invite goodness then why can't we reject badness? I certainly didn't invite cancer into my life. Yet some people would say I created this karma, even chose it. I don't buy that. The randomness, the senselessness of my illness infuriates me. So tell me, how does suffering fit into a grand scheme? Because I can't make sense out of it."

"It makes sense in a way that we can't see, a way that eludes our limited comprehension," Teresa responded. "A universe of order and a universe of chaos must coexist, but we have such limited vision that we can't see how. What we see in the material world is but a tiny part of the infinitely enormous whole wrapped up in spirit world. It is all so much larger and more complex than we can imagine."

"And do you think there is a reason in that complex, unimaginable wholeness for humans to suffer?"

"I have faith that the order as well as the chaos fit together in ways we can't fathom and that a purpose exists beyond our understanding."

"You have faith or hope?"

"Both."

Molly closed her eyes and changed the subject. "Tell me about your people. The Kapa, right?"

"Yes, the Kapa. It's another story about bad things happening to good people."

"I thought it might be. Go ahead. I'm a captive audience."

Teresa told.

The Xa-pa-na-ka lived in the embrace of the valley by B'Taka Lake since the beginning of time. B'Taka means "bear" in the old language, named because the lake has the shape of a bear. The Xa-pa-na-ka are one of the Kapa Tribes, the name outsiders call us in modern times. Once, more than seventy Tribes shared this land, and each Tribe had a distinct culture and language.

The Xa-pa-na-ka Tribe lived on the wide peninsula jutting into B'Taka Lake and called in the old language "the beautiful bend." Today that beautiful bend goes by the name Hoper Ranch and it's owned by your family, who have possessed it for a hundred years. Before that, no one owned it. The people joined with the land in connection during thousands of years of before-time when land, water, natural resources, and people were never possessions.

At first, our people were curious about the hairy men in big boots who appeared abruptly and built a fence around a section of forest just north of the beautiful bend. The Xa-ri-no-ka Tribe, who lived closest to the fence, withdrew and didn't interfere with the hairy men. The children of our Tribes described the men as "anpa," after the pale and hairy worms that could be found under rotting logs. Their hair and skin lacked color, like the worms, and they had abundant hair on their bodies such as we had never seen.

The anpa leaders, John Hoper and Jack Madison, claimed a piece of land and declared it their ranch. Kapa avoided that land after they took it. The anpa cleared it and built their fence and cabins, then disappeared for a time. They soon returned with more men and animals. When Hoper and Madison each brought a woman, we knew they meant to stay. Although we stayed away from the anpa, they had us in their sights. They needed slaves. And Hoper's eyes glittered with hunger for our young girls on the verge of blossoming.

Our Tribes each numbered about three hundred in size. To the anpa, our lives appeared simple. These outsiders failed to see the complexities of our relationship to and knowledge of the limitless natural world surrounding us. They neither saw nor understood that natural world. When they looked at oaks, they saw trees. All oaks looked the same to them. They referred to us as primitive. They soon showed us what it meant to be civilized.

How does a free people become enslaved? Hoper and Madison kidnapped Kapa women and children. They locked the children in cages to make the women work for them. As long as the women worked, the children remained unharmed. When our men came looking for their women and children and found them locked in cages, they were forced to work to keep the women and *children unharmed. If the men did not do as told, then Hoper and Madison beat their women. The anpa at the ranch had guns. Our people discovered that a gun had the power to separate a body from its spirit in the time it took for a hawk to take wing. Many nights the tribal elders sat in council discussing the situation that faced us, which lay outside the realm of our experience and defied comprehension.*

One day Hoper and Madison came to our Tribe and took three girls at gunpoint. Two were young mothers and the third only eleven years old, not yet a woman. They took these girls for the night. The anpa at the ranch used the older two to satisfy their hunger. Hoper kept the youngest for himself. When he returned her to the Tribe, she had lost her spirit. After that Hoper often sought our young girls. Madison wanted our women, while Hoper lusted after our children. These men came with guns and whips and their anpa workers. If Kapa parents refused to relinquish their daughters then they tied the parents to a tree and whipped them. They had their own anpa wives so why did they take our girls? One time, when we had warning of his approach, we hid our girls. In his fury at their absence, Hoper whipped one of our elders to death.

Our Tribe's only relief was when they raped the women and children of the neighboring Xa-ri-no-ka Tribe instead of us. We could not continue to live this way. Our elders decided we must kill these evil men. We did not take this decision lightly. The next time Hoper and Madison arrived to seize our children, we were prepared. Our braves waited, concealed in the trees. They shot their arrows true to the mark, killing these men who had poisoned us with grief, vengeance, and shame. We strapped their lifeless bodies to their horses and sent them away.

When the horses arrived at the ranch with the bodies, the anpa men killed their Kapa slaves and barricaded themselves inside, fearing we would attack them. They could not grasp even the slightest thing about our people. Hoper's wife rode from the ranch to seek help. The history books describe her as a brave heroine. That is a lie! Those anpa at the ranch were never in danger. We killed only Hoper and Madison. We killed them to protect our women and children.

How naïve we were. We could not grasp even the slightest thing about those people. We didn't doubt that more anpa would come. We planned to explain to them why we had killed Hoper and Madison. Surely the things Hoper and Madison did would horrify them as much as they horrified us. We did not yet understand that to the anpa we were less than human, beneath them in intelligence, put on the earth for their use, diminished spirits.

Magdalena Hoper rode to the nearest telegraph station and sent a message about the murder of her husband. Soon afterward, a U.S. Army detachment, led by the governor of the State of California, arrived in the valley with the sole purpose of punishing the Indians for killing white men. They trapped our Tribe on the shore of B'Taka Lake against the water. On this sacred site, they slaughtered us. They sliced through our children and babies with axes and bayonets. They burned our village. The exact number of people slaughtered went unrecorded. We estimate the U.S. Army massacred at least 260 people on the shore of B'Taka Lake that day. Another 30 or 40 Kapa slaves had been murdered at Hoper Ranch. They destroyed our Tribe.

Six children survived; all of them under the age of ten. My mother was one of these children. She hid in the lake. She broke off a tule reed, poked it above the water, and breathed through it. My father hid high up in a tree, clinging to the branches. I am the last full-blooded Xa-pa-na-ka. After the army left, five surviving children searched the bloody land and found one baby still alive. The children walked a night and a day to the Xa-ri-no-ka Tribe, who took them in. You will not find that story in any history book. That is the story of my Tribe and the story of your ancestors, Molly Hoper.

Molly held Teresa's hand and asked, through her tears, "Your Tribe's history has never been recorded?"

"Unwritten. It is engraved in blood on the land."

"Why haven't I heard your version of the story before?"

Teresa didn't answer.

"It's not that I don't believe what you have told me. I do. I just wonder why most people don't know what happened."

Teresa stood and put her bag over her shoulder.

"You must go?"

"I have another commitment."

"Promise you will come see me again soon."

"I will."

After Teresa left, Molly slept.

I am drowning. Fires flicker above me on the surface. The weight of my clothes drags me down into the water. My feet stick in the muddy bottom as I step among the reeds. I desperately rip at a reed, which bows with flexibility in my hand. I must tear it, break it. I rise to the surface to fill my lungs with air. Quickly. Before I am seen. Under again, I wrestle with the green reed. It comes in half in my hand. I sink into the mud. I poke the end of the broken reed above the water and hungrily suck down air. It tastes like the smell of burnt bark. Above me I hear the men searching for me with their guns. The screams of my family cannot reach me. I do not hear my mother cry out in death. B'Taka Lake is my mother now. The bear. My protector. The fire of my home as it burns reflects on the surface of the water above me. The men walk in the water in big boots. I close my eyes tight against them. I breathe through my reed and send my spirit away from this place to fly high above with the spirit of the eagle, the spirit of the hawk. We fly together in a clear,

*clean sky. My family has become purely spirit and we fly
together with the bird spirits who dip their graceful wings in
and out of the air currents around us. I fly for a long, long time.
If my body falls asleep, I will die. I must keep my body awake
sucking air through a reed while my spirit flies high above me
in the clear sky.*

Molly startled awake from her dream, her mind lucid.
The dream left a residue of grief and loss that weighted
her down into herself.

In the amber-and-honey light of sunset, Andy came in
from the cattle barns and grain fields with his
shepherding dogs at his heels. He washed up and took a
plate of broiled salmon, rice, and asparagus upstairs to
Molly while the children ate with his mother-in-law. He
could hear the twins complaining about the asparagus as
he mounted the stairs.

To his surprise and delight, he found Molly sitting up
in bed reading a magazine and listening to music. She put
the magazine on the nightstand when he appeared and
informed him that Teresa had visited.

Andy put the plate of food in front of his wife. "She
worked magic on you."

"She set me thinking." Molly put a piece of fish into
her mouth absently and filled her fork with rice. "She told
me a disturbing story."

"What was that?" Andy asked, pleased to see Molly eating.

"She told me a different version of a famous episode of local history."

"Interesting."

"I'm curious. Would you do me a favor and read something to me?"

"Anything, as long as you keep eating your dinner."

Molly pointed to a high shelf. "See that grayish book up there, the skinny one, next to the Sherlock Holmes?"

"I see it." Andy took the book down.

"Give it here a moment." He handed it to her. She sunk into her mountain of pillows and thumbed through it until she found the page she wanted.

"Would you read this part to me? Start here," she instructed as she showed him the spot. How many times had she heard this story? Pieces left in. Pieces left out. Pieces altered, converted to flat-out lies. Whoever controls the narrative controls the history. The truth is a chameleon. The truth is our individual creation; whatever we perceive, believe, narrate; changing day-by-day.

Andy settled in the chair next to the bed and read the title MAGDALENA HOPER'S ACCOUNT OF THE EVENTS PRECIPITATING THE BATTLE OF BEAR LAKE. He glanced up from the page and threw his wife a puzzled look. "You already know this story."

"Read it to me again."

He read aloud from Magdalena's account.

When John Hoper brought me out to the Northwest Territory as his bride, there was no more here than Hoper Ranch, which he and Jack Madison built with their bare hands. They hired and transported Mexican laborers from San Francisco to work the ranch, and they compensated them appropriately. John was an honest man who treated the ranch hands with fairness. He offered work to the Indians hereabouts, who had no income and lived under primitive conditions. Typically lazy, the Indians did not work as hard as the Mexicans, but John remained patient with them. As the ranch prospered and John had need of more workers, he recruited Indians who lived nearby before sending down to San Francisco for more men. Some of the Indians worked for him. Most did not. You can lead a horse to water, as is said.

One day John and Jack rode to that piece of land that protrudes out into Bear Lake. They knew some Indians lived over there. They carried bibles to give to the Indians and they planned to offer them work. Jack's wife Becky and I worried when the afternoon passed and our husbands failed to return. We sat on the porch, where we worked our needlepoint and sang hymns to shore up our courage.

At evening's first shadow, a wail rose at the entrance gate and we knew a terrible calamity had befallen us. Becky and I embraced one another as the horses proceeded into the yard with their gruesome burden. Thrown across the backs of the horses rested the bodies of our husbands, riddled with arrows.

Becky collapsed and we laid her to bed. The strength that came to me then could only have come from the Lord. I instructed our men to remove the arrows from the bodies. What they could not remove, they sawed off. I sent the Indians from our ranch away for their own safety because of the rage of the other ranch hands. I bathed the bodies and dressed them for burial. In the morning, our men dug two graves. Becky died of a broken heart in her sleep that night. We buried her in the grave with her husband.

Terrified, the men barricaded themselves into the dining hall with their weapons. I refused to sit quietly and wait to be murdered, or worse. I was in the family way and thus had more than just myself to consider. I saddled my Arabian mare that John had given to me as a wedding gift, I took provisions, and I rode to the nearest Mission where they had a telegraph, from which I sent a message to the U.S. Army in San Francisco. Captain Lyons rode up straightaway with a host of troops. He stopped at the Mission to speak with me before proceeding to Hoper Ranch. Then he rode with all haste and determination to avenge my husband and Jack and to bring justice by punishing the Indians who perpetrated this despicable deed.

I returned to Hoper Ranch at a slower pace with an army escort for protection. When I arrived at the ranch, I learned that Captain Lyons and his men had killed those responsible for the *murder of my husband. Many of the men who worked at the ranch chose to leave after that. A few stayed on and I gave each of those who stayed their own piece of land. They settled here and later brought wives. We called the town that grew up "Hoper Valley" after John. He would have been proud of what he started by coming into this wild land and building that ranch.*

I bear witness that the Lord truly rewards his faithful servants. Captain Lyons declares he fell in love with me for my bravery. We were married at the Mission before John's baby was born. Captain Lyons raised Esau as one of his own. Although he insisted that Esau take the Hoper name. The Captain and I settled at Bear Lake and built our ranch on the bend where the Indians once lived. They had melted into the mountains without a trace. The Captain and I farmed that land and raised our boys here. All boys. And every one of them left that ranch except for Esau. He farms the land still with his son. I praise God for delivering me from my ordeal and I count my blessings with each passing day that I continue to draw breath.

Andy gently closed the book. "Great-great-grandma Magdalena. She was the last woman in the family to own land before you came along, wasn't she?"

"All boys," Molly confirmed.

"Until you. First female heir," Andy said, as if Molly didn't already know.

"First female heir."

"Everyone who grew up in Hoper knows that story. I've heard it over and over again. Your Magdalena is quite the local heroine." Andy lifted the food tray from Molly's nightstand.

"She's not *my* Magdalena."

Andy gave his wife a curious look. "Be right back. I'll take this downstairs."

Molly rested against her pillows and tried to imagine the real Magdalena Hoper, who was probably a frustrated, tormented woman trapped in a place she viewed as a horrible wasteland and married to a man who openly committed adultery with his child victims. Did he beat Magdalena? Did he pay her any attention at all? Magdalena, who lived with the shame and the horror, trying to figure a way out, which became more impossible when she found herself pregnant. Did she consider it a stroke of luck when the Kapa murdered her degenerate husband? If Teresa's story was true, and Molly believed it was, then Magdalena had taken control, written the history, and invented herself as a heroine. Molly wondered how many people knew Teresa's version of the story. How many mourned the loss of the Xa-pa-na-ka? An entire people, culture, and language obliterated in a massacre that had been erased from memory by white historians. Obliterated except for the memories of a handful of children who returned from the land of the dead to appear in the stories of an old woman.

On the night after Teresa's visit, Molly asked Andy to sleep with her. He had refrained from sleeping with Molly for fear of disturbing her. That night, he held her, drifting off to sleep with the light weight of his fragile wife floating on his chest. Meanwhile, Molly lay awake. She rode the rise and fall of Andy's even breathing. She felt the cancer pulsing behind her ribcage and she had the urge to reach her hand inside her body and tear it out and throw it away from her. Despite Dr. Percy's assurances that the cancer was gone, she felt the tenacious cancer cells beneath her fake breasts and she was certain that the ghastly malignancy would not give up. It would consume her, sweeping through her body like a hurricane. She heard Susan's pleading voice in her head, "Mom, please don't die. I can't do senior year without you." She didn't want to fail Susan or her other children; to fail Andy, her mother, her friends; but she felt thoroughly ineffectual in her efforts to battle the cancer throbbing within. She wondered how much time she had left. What could she possibly do, in the brief allotment given to her, to make any difference? Because that's what she wanted. To make a difference. She didn't want death to render her irrelevant.

Her mind returned to Teresa's story of the massacre; a story long suppressed and denied. As she replayed the story in her mind, an idea crept quietly into her thoughts. An idea for the first female heir. She could choose to make restitution for the crime of the massacre. Her father had willed the land to her and her alone. She had the power to return the land to the people who belonged in its embrace. She could do this one thing before she died. She could bring justice to Hoper Valley.

Andy would fight it. The children would hate it. Her mother would never understand. She hoped that eventually they would see the need and the reason as clearly as she saw it. That process of journeying to understanding of the need and the reason would be their inheritance from her. It would be her ethical will.

The next day she returned to her journal, which she had set aside when the chemo flattened her.

MOLLY'S JOURNAL

Cassandra, my darling girl, we need to talk. I made a mistake. You're not my legacy. I've given it much thought and I've decided to go in a different direction. I would have loved to complete you. It breaks my heart to let you go; but I am learning to accept many things that break my heart. So, the thing is, it's over.

Wait a minute, you can't abandon me! You can't stop writing me. I am Cassandra, full of prophecy. I have things to say, things you have not yet imagined, that will bubble up from the well of your creative reverie.

My reverie has bubbled and the bubbles have burst. I am done with you.

Don't be so selfish. What about *my* needs? What about the needs of your readers?

What readers?

The readers who would like to find out what happens to the people in my world.

Let them make up their own ending. Let them make up whatever ending they need. Let them control the narrative.

You can't create a world and then leave the people in it to their own devices with no pattern, plan, or purpose. No reason or meaning. No redemption. That's cruel. It's chaos. It's abandonment.

Have I not been abandoned in just such a manner?

Oh ye of little faith. My story has a purpose, which depends on both of us, and is bigger than either of us. Stay with me. I will change the course of your life.

You would have to change it quickly because the sand is swiftly sifting through my hourglass.

There are stories unraveling around me that you must finish. You have an obligation to finish, to tell what happens to us wandering through the Greece of your creation. You must decide how it turns out. You must answer big questions. You can't give up before you answer big questions.

Since when did my little story become such an epic work? I don't have the answers to the big questions, and I never pretended I did. I don't know what our purpose is here as humans. How could I know that?

Pull yourself together and make an effort. Ask yourself, "What would Zora Neale Hurston do?"

That's funny.

I'm serious. In truth, you need me as much as I need you. I'm the magnificent story bursting full-blown out of your youth. I'm the counterbalance. You were once me. Secretly you adore me and you want to reveal me. I'm the razzle-dazzle, the rock star of this jaunt. I have the artistic lifestyle and juicy sexual adventures. I take the risks, travel, see it all, do it all. I will make it possible for you to pack politics, philosophy, human relationships, and the kitchen sink into this shindig. I will keep them reading.

You flatter yourself. No one needs you.

Oh but they do. And most of all, you need me. You need me left standing after you die. I'm the you who sang and danced barefoot under the stars, ate creamy goat cheese on fresh doughy bread, and drank ouzo, threw my head back and laughed freely with friends in a circle, and made love so profoundly as to defy death, refusing to accept less than the full measure of life's abundance. I'm your proof that you touched the pulse, that you seized your opportunities and did not squander your youth. We're intensely connected. You need me. So pick your pen up. Write my name again. Finish my story. Listen to the voice of Cassandra, the voice of remembrance and prophecy, the endless yearning whisper, the prayer of the human heart.

Oh my darling Cassandra, star of my girlhood, prize of my imagination, dream of my desires, climax of my sexual adventures, fantasy, poet, interrupted future, prophetess. I cannot argue with my own heart. I would dearly love to complete your story, but dare I even hope to be graced with the gift of time needed to do so? A reprieve? Stay of execution? Or will your words scatter like grain thrown out in the hen yard? Your prophesies neither believed, nor heeded, nor merely understood.

"It's my body and the decision is mine."

"The chemo will kill any cancer cells that may have eluded detection," Andy argued. "You owe it to the children to fight with everything in the arsenal."

"The chemo makes me feel awful, it's poisoning me, and I believe it won't make any difference either way."

"How can you possibly say that? What makes you think you know better than the doctors?"

"I know my body. I know I'm done with the chemo."

"Please don't stop fighting. You can win this."

"I'm not so sure about that."

"That's the kind of negative thinking that gets people killed."

"Just listen to me. I still have cancer. The doctors can say whatever they like, but I can feel the cancer inside me."

"That sounds to me like a strong reason to continue the chemo."

"Andy, shut up and let me finish. This isn't easy."

"For either one of us."

"The ultimate outcome of this remains unclear. I have to face the fact that I might die. Whether or not I survive, there's a task I've set for myself and I can't do it whacked out on chemo." Her heart was in her throat. She dreaded Andy's reaction. "You know that woman Teresa?"

"Of course."

"She's from the Kapa Tribe that used to live on our land. She told me the truth about what happened to her people right here where the captain built this house. Her people were massacred and her Tribe was wiped out. An entire Tribe, gone just like that. When you hear the details then you'll understand why I have to return this land to the Kapa." Molly trembled. Her plans would explode their whole life. But hadn't it already exploded on the day Molly was diagnosed with cancer?

Andy sucked in his breath and shook his head in disbelief. "What do you mean? I think that old woman's insanity must be contagious. Did she put you up to this?"

"No, she only told me the real story. My decision is what I have chosen to do with the knowledge."

"A story you have yet to confirm as true."

"Oh, it's true. I've thought about it a lot while lying in this bed."

"While lying here in delirium."

"I'm in my right mind."

"Then how did you manage to forget that our income derives from a cattle ranch on this land you want to return to the Kapa?"

"Andy, a terrible thing happened here. I have the opportunity, the insight, to make reparations, and I want to do that. If I don't act on what I know then I'm complicit. I'm complicit in many wrongs in my daily living in ways that can't be helped. But here is one enormous wrong in my own backyard that I can make right."

"Nothing will make it right. You and I and our children did not kill the Indians here. It's not our responsibility to make it right."

"It's easy to keep telling yourself that."

"What do you propose we do about our cattle ranch? Where do you suggest that we live?"

"We can move to the farm house across the stream and keep the forty acres with the old orchards on it. Mom's cottage is on that parcel," Molly told him determinedly.

"And the grazing lands? The lakefront?"

"We give that to the Kapa. With this house."

"Do you have any idea what this property is worth? Two hundred acres, with good grazing and substantial agricultural land?" Andy exclaimed. "You can't just give that away. That's your children's inheritance, their birthright."

"No it isn't. It isn't ours. It doesn't belong to us because it didn't belong to those who gave it. They seized it after slaughtering the people who lived here for thousands of years."

"You would give away your children's home?" Andy raised his voice. "What the hell are you talking about?"

"How can I explain it so you see?" Tears sprang to Molly's eyes.

"What do you expect from me?" Andy defended himself, exasperated. "Go ahead, go ahead, hit me with the worst of it." He ran his hand through his hair, trying to calm down so he could speak rationally to his crazy wife.

Molly took a deep breath. "I want to throw in the towel on the cattle ranch."

"Did I hear you correctly? Because I think you said you want me to give up cattle ranching, which is how I support our family."

"It's not as if you haven't thought about it. Often."

"That's true," he conceded, "but I would need a compelling reason to do it and I'm not seeing one here. Thinking about it and doing it are totally different."

A vein in Andy's forehead pulsed visibly. Molly winced at the pain she saw in his face. He had suffered so much, this decent man she had married. She wished that she could take his pain away and instead she had heaped

more on him. Even so, she held her ground. "Harsh
reality, Andy? Here it is. If I die, then the family will lose
my health benefits through Head Start. So you'll need a
job with good health benefits, not to mention disability
and retirement, and it's not like you can't find such a job
or do one." Andy folded his hands in his lap and looked
down at them. She continued. "If I survive, I've decided
to give up teaching. I'm done. If I survive then I want to
pursue a career as a writer."

"So this is about your interrupted writing career?"

"Of course not. It's not that simple. The massacre of
the Kapa is one thing. What I do for work if I survive is
another. It's a bridge to cross if I make it there. I want to
change my life if the future holds life for me. I want a
different career, one that is frankly incompatible with
running a cattle ranch. One that requires room for
reflection. I'll need a low-maintenance lifestyle, without
livestock, without land, without fields. So far we have
followed your dream, Andy, and I want my turn to follow
mine if I live. For my turn, you need a more secure,
practical, ordinary job."

"Like what?" Andy asked, maintaining a poker face.
She couldn't read him. Was he open to possibility?

"Talk to them at the field station. You know full well
they have an interim director who can't cut the mustard
and they would hire you in a heartbeat. You could keep

working outdoors, with animals, and have a lot of independence. I called Cherie. She's eager to talk to you about it."

Andy held up a hand and closed his eyes for a moment, processing. Then he asked, "You called Cherie? You talked to her about this already? Before even asking me what I thought?"

"I wanted to offer you the possibility of an alternative," Molly said softly.

"Good of you to think of me."

"I'm looking for a way to work this out. Will you talk to Cherie?"

"Does it matter? It sounds like you've got it all figured out already. A done deal."

"I wish I could to this without hurting you, Andy. You're my sun, moon, and stars. Forever."

Andy's shoulders sagged. "This is a lot to digest." He stood and walked to the door. "Get some rest. We'll discuss this further." As he left the room, Andy turned for a moment, his hand on the doorknob, and said, "This whole country was taken from the Indians, Moll, and you don't see anyone else giving their house and land away to the nearest Tribe. I don't get why you think we have to do it."

"We have an obligation to do something to help heal the world, to act on what we know. This is my something."

"I wish you had chosen a different something." He closed the door.

The next day, Molly's mother pleaded with her to continue the chemo. By evening, Andy had called in reinforcements. Eli and Peg arrived to "talk sense to her." Refusing to budge from her decision, she sent them home with a loaf of Mrs. Donnelly's banana bread. After they left, Andy sat in the chair by the window, rested his elbows on his knees, and put his head in his hands. "What more can I possibly do to save your life?" His words caught in his throat.

"That's beyond your control and mine."

"It's not beyond your control. Do you want to live?"

"I've told you what I want," Molly said gently. "Return the land. Take a new direction in our lives."

He looked out the window at the fields beyond. "Do you have any idea how much I love this land?"

Molly followed his gaze past the twisted familiar oak tree that guarded her window, past the sturdy forest ascending the hillside and the comfortable pasture that sprawled casually on the slope leading down to the lake. The setting sun flung marigold-yellow waves across the lake and rose-orange flames across the sky. The beauty of her corner of the world, where she had grown up, called her home, exceeded the beauty of distant lands with its splendor. She doubted Andy could love the land any more than she. "Yes, actually."

Tears glistened in Andy's eyes. "I'm not sure you do."

"I was raised here," she reminded him. "And this was my home until I met you."

"Until you met me?"

"Now my home is in your arms. Wherever that takes me. It is not a place."

He stood and walked to the bed where he took her hands in his calloused work-worn own. He turned her palms face-up and he placed a kiss in each palm before closing them on themselves. "Such a steep price to pay for loving you."

When he left the room, she called after him, but he didn't return. Not that evening, not in the morning, not until the following evening, when he brought her the news that he had gone to the field station and talked to Cherie.

After abandoning the chemo, Molly regained her strength and could sit at the dinner table with the family. Her presence made a huge difference to the children.

On the evening when she announced to the children her decision to move to the farm house and give up the cattle ranch, Molly sent her mother home in the afternoon and made dinner for the family herself. She fixed one of their favorites, which was tacos with ground beef, beans, cheese, guacamole, lettuce, tomatoes, onions, sour cream, and salsa. Somewhere between the guacamole and the beans, Molly related to the children an abbreviated version of the story of the massacre and informed them that she had decided to return their house and most of their land to the Kapa to right an old wrong. The girls stopped eating mid-taco; however, nothing could interrupt the relationship between the twins and their food.

"Mom, that is the stupidest thing I have ever heard," Susan exploded, pushing her chair out from the table. "Dad, tell her how stupid that is!"

Before Andy could respond, Mac said, "I don't get it."

"We have to move across the creek to that old farm house because we have to give our house to the Indians, knucklehead," Mike said as he punched his brother in the arm. "What part of giving our house to the Indians do you not get?"

"Because why?" Mac asked, helping himself to more sour cream.

"Because there was an Indian massacre a hundred years ago," Mike told him.

Susan rolled her eyes and said, "Because Mom says so."

Kelly had frozen with her fork halfway to her mouth. A piece of tomato dangled from the end of it precariously. "What about the cows?" she asked.

"We'll slaughter most of them this year. We'll sell the bulls and the best breeding sows," Andy told her.

"Aren't the cows your job, Dad?" Bethany asked, her forehead furrowed. "I mean like isn't that what you do for work?"

"What about the goats?" Kelly asked. "And the rabbits? What about Ginger? We need the barn for Ginger." Ginger was her horse. Kelly burst into tears.

"First of all," Andy said to Bethany, as he reached over and rubbed Kelly's back, "the cows *were* my job. Not anymore. I took a new job that I start in a couple of months. I'm going to work as the director of the university extension field station in Bridgewood. It's a great job and it pays well enough for me to take care of our family same as always. It will be a lot easier and more dependable than running a cattle ranch." Kelly crawled into Andy's arms, sobbing. "Kelly, Kelly," Andy soothed her, "don't you worry. We'll build a little barn on the other side of the creek for the horses and goats. Rabbits are easy to move. It's mainly the cattle that will have to go."

"It'll work out," Molly reassured the children. "You'll see. Kelly, you can still have animals."

"There's only three bedrooms in the farm house," Susan stated flatly, coldly, her face rigid. "I'm not sharing a room."

"How's that going to work?" Bethany asked.

"Boys in one room and girls in the other," Molly said.

"I'm not sharing a room, Mom. I can't share with Kelly and Bethany. You're nuts." Susan fumed.

"You mean I have to share a room with Mike?" Mac asked through a mouthful of beans and beef. "He snores."

"I do not!" Mike protested.

"You already share a room with him," Molly pointed out.

"So?" Mac answered. "I think he should sleep in the garage when we move."

Molly put her elbows on the table, folded her hands in front of her face, and leaned her chin on them. "Just listen for a few minutes. Like a story."

"Listen to Mom," Andy said, while still attempting to comfort Kelly.

Susan stuck her lip out even further, if that was humanly possible. Kelly wiped her eyes on her napkin. Mike and Mac continued to attack their tacos. Bethany pushed her food around on her plate with her fork.

"OK," Molly began, patiently, gently, "just imagine that a man came to our house. A stranger. Say his name is

Mr. Smith, and Mr. Smith killed all of us except Bethany, who hid in the woods."

"How come Bethany gets to be the one who isn't killed?" Mac asked.

"OK," Molly told him, "let's say you and Bethany escape. Then Mr. Smith and his family move into the house and you and Bethany run away to live with strangers in a different place."

"I'd go live with Grandma," Bethany interjected.

"Imagine that they killed Grandma too," Molly pushed. "Only you and Mac escape. And you grow up and you get married."

"Gross, she's my sister." Mac cringed. Mike made kissing sounds behind his hand at Mac.

"Not to Bethany, to someone else," Andy clarified. "Just listen and quit interrupting."

"So you and your own families live somewhere else, meanwhile you always remember this house that belonged to you and it makes you mad because the people living in it killed your family. And you never have enough money to buy a house as beautiful as this one. One day a strange girl knocks on your door. She tells you that she just learned that her father killed your family and she wants to return this house to you. Because it's really yours and she realizes that."

"And what that means," Susan spat out, "is that I'm supposed to share a room with Kelly and Bethany."

"We're not giving them the beach are we?" Bethany asked anxiously.

"Yes, honey," Molly told her sadly, "we're giving them the beach. My ancestors, who are yours too by-the-way, slaughtered these people and took away their home. That beach belonged to..."

"You're giving them the beach?" Mike interrupted incredulously as the joking tone evaporated from his voice.

"See? Mom's crazy," Susan said to her brother. "If you guys move, then I'll go live with Rachel."

Andy suggested, "Maybe you can stay with Grandma in the cottage, if she's OK with that."

"I want to go live with Grandma!" Kelly exclaimed immediately.

"Keep the beach, and me and Mac could live in the boat house and Susan can have our room, right Mac?"

"Dad, how can you agree to this?" Susan confronted Andy.

"This is OK with you?" Mike demanded of his father. "You agree with Mom?"

The children turned to Andy. He looked at Molly apologetically. He couldn't lie to the children. "I think it's a little crazy," Andy answered.

"A little?" Susan asked.

"Actually, a lot," Andy admitted. "It's hard for me to swallow too. But I understand why Mom wants to do this and the truth is..." Andy stopped there and held his hands up in front of him as if in defense. The children held their breath. "The truth is that your mother owns this property, I don't, and she can do whatever she wants with it. Grandpa left her this land in his will. Mom has decided she received the land for a reason and that this is the reason."

"Don't you have any say-so?" Kelly asked. She turned to her mother, "Mom, doesn't Dad have any say-so? Don't we have any say-so? It's our house too. It's not fair."

"Yeah, it's not fair," the other children chorused.

"We should all have some say-so," Mike said. "We should vote on it."

Molly thought she might as well tear out her heart and throw it on the ground and stomp on it. Whenever she had told herself *maybe I don't have to do this*, she couldn't shake the knowledge of the massacre, the wrong done, and the impossibility of failing to act on that knowledge. She should do more, give all of the land back. But she couldn't bring herself that far or hurt her family that deeply. They would never come back from something that large. She wasn't sure they would recover from this much. What damage had she chosen to do to her children?

"Often," Andy told the children, his voice husky with emotion, "when a person is near death, they see things more clearly than the people around them."

"Mom isn't near death," Bethany said quietly. "She's making a new life."

Molly's eyes filled with tears.

"She's making a new life without a beach, without cows, and without this ranch," Andy stated flatly. And then he had the only dry eye in the house.

MOLLY'S JOURNAL

My babies discovered their world in the laboratory of this yard. If I close my eyes and clear my mind, I can still hear their toddler selves shouting in the wading pool. Mac and Mike chasing lizards. Kelly putting a chirping bug into her bug viewer to have a better look at the pattern on the creature's folded wings. How many nights have I stood on the porch and clanged the triangle to call the family to the dinner table? Watched Kelly and Andy amble up from the barn while Mike, Mac, and Bethany clambered along the trail from the beachfront? Susan in the hammock reading. And the land stretching to the sky in all directions like a giant ship that we sail on, just us, our family, insulated from the strife of the world. Safe in our good fortune.

How can I relinquish the walk up this driveway in the early morning mist when the residue of creation mingles with the scent of pine needles and promise in the air? The tall, tall trees at my gate have watched over me and guarded my loved ones from harm all my days. They are my dear friends and advisors. How does a piece of land become a part of one's soul?

If I truly love this land, I must let it go.

I remember the phrase "sins of the fathers." The displacement of my family will not pay for the sins of my ancestors. The suffering of my children is not an equal trade for what happened here. Our entire nation is soaked in blood, our world built on the backs of the oppressed, so that something as simple as buying a bunch of grapes or a pair of shoes contributes to the anguish of people who live miles beyond the scaffolding on which we have built our lives. None of us is pure, none free of sin.

I don't feel self-righteous. Far from it. I don't feel "better." I feel inadequate. Returning this piece of land is inadequate. And heaped on top of that, this action has made me a horrible wife and mother because I'm causing the suffering of my family. Nevertheless, I must do this. It's a small thing and a big thing both at once. It matters. It confirms that spark of the divine in us humans as we grasp for handholds on the treacherous and incomprehensible climb through the earthly world.

I quarrel with the children over my decision as I pack up our belongings in boxes, work on the legalities, open up the farm house and have it repaired and painted. Out of the reach of the devastation of the chemo, I feel well enough to attend to the things that need attention to make this transition. I don't have time to write more of Cassandra. That will have to come later if my health holds. After I pave the way for the Kapa to make their return.

On the evening before Molly was to sign the final papers, she asked if anyone wanted to go with her for a last walk-through of the ranch house. The twins and Kelly declined. Andy said he would stay with the children at the farm house. The new wrinkles around his eyes betrayed the depth of the loss he was struggling to accept. Susan had moved in with Molly's mother at the cottage and was barely speaking to Molly. Only Bethany wanted to go with her for a final look around. So Molly and Bethany drove to the ranch house on Andy's four-wheeler.

In the yard, they passed the recently installed electric box that would provide power to the trailers that would arrive in the coming days to house Teresa's family and the remnants of the Tribe, such as it was. Teresa, her son and grandchildren, a niece, and a cousin would move into the ranch house.

Molly walked up the wide steps and across the verandah, where she used to sit in her rocking chair to sip tea or cocoa in winter and lemonade in summer. She remembered playing Monopoly with her friends for hours on this verandah as a child.

She and Bethany opened the heavy front door, with its beveled glass. They had not once locked this door. Molly didn't even have a key for it. Soon this door would lock against them. Molly flipped on the light and headed upstairs. The rooms echoed, empty for the first time in over a hundred years. She and Bethany walked through the children's old bedrooms. Molly left Bethany behind and stepped by herself into the room she had shared with Andy through the days and hours of raising a family. She looked out the window at the enormous live oak tree a few yards away. She had conceived her children in this room, under the watchful gaze of that oak, well all except for maybe the twins, who may have been conceived on the beach by the lake. She couldn't say for sure. She herself was probably conceived in this room; and her father before her. She turned her back on the oak and walked down the stairs.

In the kitchen, only a table and chairs remained, left there for the official signing of the deed in the morning. Molly went weak in the knees. She sat down in one of the chairs and bowed her head. The farm house was perfectly adequate for their family's needs, but it wasn't home. She hadn't been sleeping well there. Neither had Andy. He left the bed at night and wandered. In the past he had slept like a rock, even during Molly's illness. Once asleep, he was usually out for the night. Now he sat on the screened-in back porch or stood in the yard, looking, or else he took a book to the easy chair in the living room. The stress of Molly's illness showed in his face more than it had before the move. Andy was beginning to look old.

She crossed her arms on the table and laid her head on them. *What have I done?* Thanksgiving. Christmas. Nothing would ever be right in the farm house. She could never go home again. None of them could. She went looking for Bethany and found her sitting on the floor in the middle of her former bedroom. Molly sat down next to her. Bethany put her head in Molly's lap. "Is this what it felt like to the Kapa Indians for a hundred years?" Bethany asked.

"Worse." Molly stroked Bethany's hair. "It felt worse for them. We still have each other. They lost even that."

"Do you feel good giving them the house?"

"I feel pretty awful," Molly admitted as she brushed Bethany's hair away from her face. "But even if I still could, I wouldn't change my mind."

The next day, after signing papers, shaking handshakes, appeasing local reporters with quotable sound bites, and completing formalities, Molly crawled into bed and slept. She woke up just as sunset sprinted across the lawn and she went into the kitchen to prepare a nice meal for her bruised family. After she put the chicken in the oven, she turned from the stove to see an apparition at the back door. She caught herself and choked back a scream when she recognized the apparition as Teresa.

"You scared me half to death!" She told the old woman as she opened the screen door to admit her.

"It's not the first time you've been halfway to death," Teresa pointed out.

"What're you doing here? Tonight's the big night. Your first night in the ranch house."

"It is. Tonight I sleep with my ancestors."

"I hope they don't talk in their sleep and keep you awake," Molly teased.

"How are you doing?"

"Honestly?"

"Honestly."

"Rotten. My children are furious with me. Susan won't even speak to me. My husband is depressed and insomniac. And I'm inconsolably sad to leave my childhood home."

"I meant in terms of your physical health."

"Oh. That. I'm feeling surprisingly healthy, for a change. I like having my hair again."

"Would you join me for a little walk on Kapa land?"

"I'm rather partial to Kapa land. Give me a moment to tell Andy where I'm going."

The two women stepped out into a clear night overflowing with the brilliance of stars pointing the way to galaxies unexplored, possibilities unfathomed. Teresa's footsteps guided them toward the lake.

"You want to hear something strange?" Molly asked.

"I'd love to."

"Even after everything, I mean the move, leaving my home, uprooting my family, and all that, I have this calm inner peace. As though I've settled into myself after many unsettled years. In important ways, only a part of me lived in my life and today the whole me lives here."

"You have made a settlement," Teresa said with a touch of amusement.

The two women walked through the crisp, cool night to the beach at the edge of Bear Lake and sat on a wooden bench where they could hear the susurration of the tule reeds swaying in the gentle breeze drifting across the water.

"For as long as I can remember, I have awakened from sleep with a weight on my chest like a rock," Teresa said, putting her hand flat across the space below her collar bone. "Every morning I roll that rock off of me to draw breath. It is the rock of anger. The rock of oppression. The rock of revenge. The rock of despair. I must remove the rock to release hope, gratitude, forgiveness, and, the crown jewel, love. I have struggled all my days to move that rock, again and again. This morning, when I woke, the rock had vanished." Teresa wrapped Molly in her arms and whispered in her ear, "You did a good thing Molly Hoper. May you be blessed, and your children blessed, and those born to the Hoper family for generations to come. May you prosper." Teresa released Molly from her embrace.

Tears shone in Molly's eyes. "Thank you. A person rarely receives the opportunity to turn a place of curses into a place of blessings." Then she added with a sigh, "It's stunning how much pain can inhabit a blessing."

Molly turned her gaze across the water.

Teresa patted Molly's hand, "I hear the ancestors singing under the lake. They rejoice in the return to our sacred land. I can finally rest these old bones of mine. My life's work is done."

"Your life's work, as it turns out, is my life's work."

"Not at all. You have much more ahead of you. You will live a long, long time Molly, and you will do many more miraculous things." Teresa left Molly with that promise of miracles ahead. During the night, her ancestors gathered Teresa's spirit to them; she shed her aged body, and she did not wake the next morning.

MOLLY'S JOURNAL

The cancer no longer hums inside me. If I believe Teresa's last words to me, the cancer has fled and I have a long life ahead. I hope she was right, because I have millions of words clambering to tumble out of me onto paper, I have a husband who deserves to grow old with a loving wife, and I have five extraordinary children who need their mother.

I found my future in the distant past.

Book 13: Penelope
Yopika Bapa, 1981

Now that we have brought Aunt Beth home, she treads lightly in the margins of our family life in Athena's house. Wearing her faded blue sweater with patches at the elbows and her flowery cotton housedresses, she quietly makes herself chamomile tea in her special mug with the images of cats on it and takes it to the wicker rocker on the porch where she rocks for hours while the tea goes cold. She often shuffles down to the lakefront to sit on a bench and stare out over the water. She silently prepares food, usually just for herself, occasionally and without warning for the whole household. Like the Sunday morning we woke up to find her in the kitchen producing a tower of blueberry waffles. Lena and Max pronounced them the best waffles ever. It took Erica an hour to clean the waffle iron afterward since the blueberries stuck. Being Erica, she was happy to do it, tickled that Aunt Beth had cooked breakfast. My darling social worker.

Aunt Beth rarely speaks. It seems like she has forgotten English, but we can tell she understands even though she refuses to speak it. She speaks Kapa. Only Athena understands her, although Lena has learned some words. When Aunt Beth remarkably says a whole sentence in Kapa at dinner one evening,

Athena sets her fork down on the table and studies Aunt Beth, who stares with those half-empty eyes.

"What did she say?" I shiver with foreboding.

"She says Sammy must come home."

It takes me a moment to figure out what Athena is talking about and when I do figure it out I surely don't like it. "My brother Sammy the criminal?"

Athena gives me that look of hers over the top of her bifocals. Why is she wearing the bifocals to dinner? There's nothing to read on the broccoli.

I tell Athena, "He's in prison. Locked up and they threw away the key."

"How do you know? Maybe he's out. Maybe they didn't throw away the key."

Aunt Beth speaks to Athena, who turns to me and translates, "She says, literally, that in this season Sammy must come home."

"She can't remember if she tied her shoes or not. She's rambling."

Erica and the children stop eating and their eyes follow the conversation back and forth from me to Athena as if we are engaged in a tennis match.

"Don't be so sure. Maybe she kept track in that rat trap of a brain of hers of when he gets out. We should check into it. If he's getting out of prison, where else will he go?"

"Don't touch this one, Athena. He's damaged."

"He's one of ours. Just like you."

"It is *not* just like me. He's dangerous. You think he's a Native son? He's not. He's my father's son. He knows nothing about the Kapa." My voice quavers despite my effort to remain calm.

"Neither did you," Athena reminds me pointedly.

"That was very different." Sammy? Here? In my home? With Lena and Max? Athena has no idea.

"I'm collecting lost children," Athena says softly. Meanwhile, I'm thinking, *Wait until Podon gets wind of this. He'll have kittens.* Athena doesn't care if Podon has a whole cat. He can bluster and storm as much as he wants. Her mind is apparently as made up as Aunt Beth's. She talks to a friend of hers who is a probation officer and he helps her wade through the bureaucracy of the prison system to locate my worthless brother.

I refuse to have anything to do with it. Sammy was packing a gun when he was thirteen and running the streets raising hell with those other little gangbangers; selling drugs and defending territory by beating up guys who they thought looked at them funny. Does he even know what happened to Carla?

I tell Erica, "I hope he doesn't get parole. I hope they keep him in jail forever so Athena can't bring him here to ruin our lives."

"You haven't seen him in so long that you can't say he's one thing or another," Erica points out. "People can change. They can turn themselves around. I've seen it happen. I wouldn't do what I do for a living if I didn't believe that."

Still I pray they keep him locked up. Although, why I bother to pray for anything anymore is truly a mystery. I should get it by now. "The Great Spirit waits to see what I pray for just to do the opposite," I tell Erica in the privacy of our bed.

She laughs and holds me tight. "Haven't you had even one teensy weensy prayer answered?" She rubs my back, between my shoulder blades, in just the right spot.

"Well, maybe one," I concede. I get her point. I should count my blessings instead of complaining. I have much in my life for which to be thankful. I don't trust it to last.

As soon as Athena locates Sammy, she and Aunt Beth visit him. They wrap chicken salad sandwiches in wax paper and pour Constant Comment iced tea into mason jars. They bundle up a whole tray of chocolate brownies while Aunt Beth hums happily. They get up early in the morning and drive to the prison. It's as if they're going to visit Sammy at summer camp on parent visiting day. They return just before dinner, Aunt Beth asleep in the front seat, oblivious to the catastrophic chain of events she has set in motion by finding Sammy and inviting him into our lives. None of us know what is to come, but I sense we are now living dangerously.

Erica has made spaghetti, Caesar salad, and garlic bread and we sit down to eat together.

Max asks, "Did you see him?"

"Sure did," Athena answers.

Aunt Beth hums. Ordinarily I would enjoy seeing her so uncharacteristically happy. At the moment it annoys me.

"Does he have tattoos?" Max asks.

Athena and Erica laugh.

"A couple," Athena tells Max.

"What'd he do?" Lena asks.

"You mean to wind up in jail?" Erica clarifies.

"Yeah," Lena and Max both answer at once.

"He sold crack cocaine," Athena states brusquely.

Erica shakes her head and helps herself to another piece of garlic bread as she comments, "That's bad stuff. Is he in any type of rehab program?"

Athena nods her head affirmative. "He comes out in a few months. The terms of his parole will require him to find a suitable drug-free living environment."

I explode with wry laughter. "In that case they won't let him live at the Rez. Blue Wolf alone is one capsule shy of a pharmacy when it comes to selling drugs, and none of them legal."

Athena shoots me her sharp, no-nonsense look.

"Well it's the truth," I defend myself.

"I figure that trailer in the front yard is a suitable drug-free environment," Athena says as she points in the direction of the trailer with her fork.

Max's eyes go wide. "You're going to bring Uncle Sammy here?"

"Seems crazy, doesn't it?" I ask Max, without interrupting the glare I have going at Athena. Aunt Beth's humming drones on, like a herd of bees stampeding through the kitchen.

Athena looks down at her plate and sidesteps the question. "Nobody calls him Sammy anymore. They call him Snake."

I snort. "That should tell you volumes right there."

Athena points her fork at me and her eyes flash. "He carries the same burden you do. Show some compassion."

That does it. I push my chair out and stand. I hate to do this in front of the children. I don't wish to frighten them. But Athena is pushing my buttons. "He does not carry the same burden. You don't know what I do and do not carry." Lena starts crying and Erica puts her arm around her while making soothing sounds. Max stares wide-eyed. "You're playing with fire. You're jeopardizing our safety, the safety of my children. What can I say or do to stop you from bringing Sammy, or should I say Snake, to the Rez?"

"You can't stop me. This is my house."

"Yes, it is your house. Maybe it's time for me and mine to move out of it."

"Mom, we *live* here," Max blurts out.

"It's OK, Max," Erica reassures him, "she's just angry. We're not moving."

"Oh shut up," I snap at Erica, who gives me a reproachful look. I walk out.

It's cool down at the lake. B'Taka. Spirit of the Bear. If ever we will need the Bear's protection, it will be now. I'm sorry my brother had such a horrible childhood, such a difficult life. I wish it weren't so. But he made his choices and I resent having to live with his choices. I have enough trouble living with my own. I must be cursed.

I'll apologize to Erica and the children for my behavior. But I will not apologize to Athena. She's a stubborn old woman and more than I can handle. I wonder if she's going senile.

Yopika Bapa, 1982

"Guess what?" I exclaim, as I burst into the kitchen juggling a grocery bag and a bottle of laundry soap with my purse, the mail, newspaper, and a pair of Max's sneakers. "I heard an Anglo guy refer to Hoepper as Bataka today at the gas station. He said to a customer 'Come back to Bataka' and now that guy will drive on up the highway and in his mind he'll forget the writing on the road sign and he'll remember Bataka."

Erica takes the grocery bag from me. "Power to the people," she mutters absently. "Go on in there." She nods her head toward the living room.

"What's going on?"

She doesn't answer, just starts unpacking the grocery bag.

I go into the living room and there he is in the flesh, sitting on the couch, talking to Athena and holding Aunt Beth's hand.

He's still skinny, although more muscular, with a grown man's physique. He has thin, stringy hair. He smiles at me, revealing a mouthful of bad teeth, which make him appear older than he is. He has the eyes of a feral cat. He stands and swaggers over to me, smiling. I recognize that swagger. It's a disguise. He hates himself.

Maybe he thinks he's supposed to hug me or make a show of affection. I give him no opening. The thought of his touch repels me. He returns awkwardly to the couch and sits down again next to Aunt Beth.

"So, Sammy, you're out." I state the obvious. Then my eye falls on Aunt Beth's face and the unabashed joy radiating from it hits me like a blow to the chest. She follows Sammy's slightest movement with her eyes. It occurs to me that maybe she can't distinguish him from her dead son. Does she think he is Jessie? In a way, I guess he is.

"Shit, yeah," Sammy says with a half-laugh as he takes Aunt Beth's hand again. "I got to behave or Athena will string me up by my balls." He grins.

"I'm raising two children in this house," I say curtly, "and I will not have them listening to X-rated language. Whenever they're around, you watch your mouth. In fact, you can watch it when I'm around too."

He grins belligerently. "Well she's a tough nut, ain't she Athena?"

"She's right," Athena backs me up, "no foul language in my house."

Sammy gives her a salute and a "yes ma'am."

He's humoring us. He's using us. Athena thinks she can control him. I go out to the car to collect the rest of the groceries and return to the kitchen to unpack them with Erica. Athena, Aunt Beth, and Sammy join us in the kitchen.

Aunt Beth takes a plate of cookies off the stovetop and uncovers them. She places them in front of Sammy. She opens the fridge and gets out the milk and pours him a glass. She sits down next to him and watches his face like a puppy watching its master.

"Aunt Beth baked for you," Athena tells Sammy.

He takes a cookie and bites into it. "Thank you, Aunt Beth. Delicious."

Aunt Beth continues to stare at him. I hope it unnerves him.

"She understands what I say to her, right?" he asks Athena.

"Yeah, but she only speaks Kapa."

I'm self-conscious putting the groceries away because he's watching me. Athena and I lack the talent for small talk. I cannot think of one single question to ask him to be polite, but honestly I don't want to be polite.

Lena bounds in the back door. The glow of the setting sun behind her infuses her hair with a golden halo. My angel. I don't want Sammy to cast his filthy eyes on her. He has tipped back in his chair and when she enters he leans forward and places the legs of the chair on the floor gently. He folds his hands in front of him and sucks in his breath and I see that he is filled with awe as he gazes at my daughter.

"This is your Uncle Snake," I tell Lena, who has glanced at me questioningly. "Snake, my daughter Lena." I call him by his criminal name to warn my daughter that he's dangerous. I note with relief that he's not looking at her body the way a man who has spent many years in prison might look at the body of a beautiful young woman. He's studying her face. She smiles at him tentatively and nods.

"Pleased to meet you, young lady," he says quietly, almost formally. "You look just like your Aunt Carla. Have they told you that? I would have recognized you anywhere." His words cause my eyes to prick with tears and I'm angry that he has touched me like this. There's no one left who knew Carla except for Aunt Beth, who hasn't spoken of her, perhaps doesn't even remember.

Lena blushes and tells Snake tentatively, "thank you, I guess." She hurries to my side. "Ama, I'm going over to Daddy Nelson's; what time is dinner?"

"I'm making enchiladas in a minute." I glance at the clock. "Hey, does anyone know where Max went after school?"

"He's playing basketball," Athena answers.

"When does he get done?" I ask. I want us to sit down at the table together tonight. I want Snake who used to be Sammy to see that we're a functional family, and he better think twice about disrupting this family. I also want Snake to see what a functional family looks like. Does he have the capacity to participate in a functional family?

"I'll send Max over to Nelson's to get you when we're ready to eat," I tell Lena. She dances out the sunset-drenched door.

"Penny," Snake calls me by my childhood nickname.

I glance over at him and my eyes lock with his. He's looking at me with a furious intensity, his jaw clenched. "I would never harm a hair on her head. So don't worry that I would. I've made a lot of mistakes, but I'm not Dad."

Aunt Beth beams brightly into the leaden silence that follows Sammy's words.

"Did you hear him, girl?" Athena demands.

"I hear," I whisper.

So he knows. I wondered if he did.

I sit on the couch with Max, reading out loud to him from our latest adventure novel, when I hear the ruckus in the yard. "You

stay right there," I order Max and I give him the I-mean-it look. I
go onto the porch. Snake weaves his way into the yard with his
drinking buddies Buck and Thorn, who is Podon's grandson.
They laugh and talk way too loud for this late in the evening on a
week night.

"Snake," I call to him from the porch. He stops and sways in
place. I wonder if he has the capacity to make sense of whatever
I say. "Go to bed. You have to get up for work in the morning."
He works at a deli.

He turns to Buck and Thorn and flails his arm to the side. I
see he holds a square bottle in which amber liquid sloshes.
Probably whiskey. "Y'ear tha?" he asks. "Havta g'up in the
mornin' to make san'wiches. Very impor'an job." Buck and Thorn
laugh. Thorn bends over double with laughter and has trouble
bending back up.

I go into the house and find Athena. "You're project just
wandered in fall-down drunk," I tell her. "Maybe you should put
him to bed."

"He'll go to sleep in a few minutes. At least he's not doing
drugs."

"What makes you so sure of that?"

"I'm sure. Alcohol is legal."

"Yeah, well, in his case it's a bad idea."

"It's better than crack cocaine."

"That's a reassuring thought."

I return to the couch where I continue reading to Max, who
wisely refrains from commenting or asking questions.

Snake and his friends go inside the trailer where they remain
relatively quiet until they pass out. Athena will go wake Snake for
work in the morning so he doesn't mess up the conditions of his
parole.

I am disappointed in Athena. I thought she had higher standards.

I remain vigilant against the day when Snake uncoils. Although I can't prove it, I suspect he has a gun, even though he is not allowed to own one.

"Cut him a little slack," Erica pleads with me later. "He wants to be a normal person, a person who belongs to the community. He just needs to figure out how."

"I wish he would figure it out far away from my children."

"That's not going to happen."

"Have you seen how he is with Lena?"

"OK, that's a little weird," Erica concedes. "But it doesn't seem dangerous."

"He acts like her self-appointed protector. Heaven help us if she decides to go out on a date. Heaven help the date."

"It's because she reminds him of Carla," Erica says softly. I suddenly have a lump in my throat the size of a grapefruit. "I think," she continues, "that he feels guilty that he didn't protect Carla and he's making up for that by looking out for Lena. It's like it's his job, like he's hired to do it."

"Damn, you're good at what you do," I choke out. She shrugs.

Yopika Bapa, 1983

I drop everything and run to the tribal office the minute Nelson tells me.

I find Lena out in front crying while her friend Marjorie comforts her. I am about to breeze past her into the office, I'm that furious. Lena grabs my arm. "He hit Kiki," she says.

"Are you OK?"

She nods. "He hit Kiki because he was flirting with me, Ama. You've gotta tell him he can't do that."

"I will."

"You've gotta make him understand, Ama. He doesn't get it. What if he saw someone actually, I mean, well, like what if he ever heard that nasty Perry Hoepper who calls me 'Injun girl' when no one is looking? He'd kill him."

"Perry still does that?" I can't believe it. "That boy is such a jerk."

Lena wipes her eyes on her sleeve. Marjorie has an arm around her shoulder. "Yeah, sometimes. The point is that if Snake goes ballistic when Kiki just talks to me then..." She doesn't finish.

"Marjorie, take Lena home." I turn sharply on my heel and swallow the steps into the office two at once.

Snake sits scowling, his arms folded across his chest, and his jaw set stubbornly. One of our young men from the Tribe, Kiki, holds an ice pack to his eye while Dita and June fuss over him.

"What the hell is going on?" I demand of Snake, who doesn't answer.

"He hit me," Kiki explains heatedly, "up and hit me. He's crazy. They should lock him back up."

"Well?" I round on Snake, wondering what conceivable explanation he can dredge up to account for this display.

"He was looking at her," Snake growls through clenched teeth.

"He looked at Lena?"

"Yeah. He was looking at her."

"Of course he was looking at her," June explodes. "He was talking to her. People look at each other when they talk to one another."

"He knows what I mean." Snake jabs a finger at his victim. "He knows exactly what I mean. He was looking at her, you know, *that* way."

Kiki jumps up and hollers at Snake, "You mean like a guy looks at a pretty girl? Hell, yeah. That doesn't mean I'm gonna make a pass at her. She's a kid! Back off." He stomps out of the office.

"You have no business looking at her like that," Snake yells at Kiki's retreating form.

"You'll be lucky if he doesn't press charges and put you back in jail," June tells Snake.

"I don't care," Snake mumbles.

"You need to care," Athena says from the doorway. She has just arrived. I half expect her to drag Snake up to the house by his ear. He skulks lower in his seat. Lena appears in the doorway behind Athena. She goes directly to Snake and takes him by the hand. I resist the impulse to intervene, which vibrates throughout my body.

"I appreciate that you want to look after me, Uncle," Lena says, "but I wasn't in danger, and you've totally embarrassed me." It's as if no one else in the room exists, just the two of them. The rest of us are voyeurs.

"I didn't mean to embarrass you." Snake acts like a stray dog, taken in by a kind lady, faithful to the end; a dog that snarls and growls at anyone who comes near his mistress because he has found a warm place to lie down in her house.

"Kiki is a friend of mine. You have to apologize to him."

Snake looks down at his feet. "OK, if you say so."

"You have to make it up to him," Lena presses.

"Not right now," Athena intervenes, "not while he's angry at you. C'mon, let's go."

Does Athena think it's resolved? That it won't happen again? That Snake is reformed, getting his act together? Does she imagine that he'll stop drinking? If she were younger, she wouldn't fool herself like this. She is an old, old woman and she notices less that goes on around her. As I trudge up to the house, I wonder what happened to the perceptive, intuitive, feisty Athena who kept me honest and on track for so many years. Where is she? What will our Tribe do when Athena passes into spirit? I fear for all of us. Mostly, selfishly, I fear for myself.

I retreat into my writing. After I finish Molly's story, where will I find an island in the storm? I have the ending for Molly, but it scares me to complete it.

Book 14: Molly and Magdalena

From *Death in Hoper Valley*

"W hat is that?" Molly asked her mother. "An antique writing desk," her mother replied. "It belonged to Magdalena Lyons. Her husband had it sent from New England as a gift. You've seen it before."

"If I did, I forgot about it."

They were in the attic looking for a quilt, which they told Bethany they would find for a school project about family legacy.

Molly blew the dust off the top of the dainty desk and ran her hand over the wood. It had complicated cubbies and little drawers with abundant Victorian detail. "I like it. I think I'll take it down and clean it up and use it."

"It's not sturdy."

"I'm not going to play Ping-Pong on it. Help me get it down the stairs."

Molly lifted one side and her mother picked up the other. When they neared the bottom of the flight of steps,

Molly's mother let out a sharp cry as she lost her grip on the top end of the desk. Molly stumbled and the desk cracked against the wall.

"It got away from me. I'm sorry, honey. Are you OK?"

"I'm fine. I've got it. It's not that heavy," Molly reassured her mother. She worked the desk down the last step and set it in the hallway. "The bottom fell out. I can glue it back together," she reported. "In fact, I think I can jiggle it back into place."

"I warned you it was fragile," her mother called down the stairwell, as she returned to the attic for the quilt.

Molly noticed a yellowed envelope protruding from underneath the desk. She crouched on her hands and knees and looked at the desk bottom. The piece that had detached itself was not the actual bottom of the desk at all, but rather a false bottom. The envelope had been secured in a hidden compartment.

Molly's heart raced as she slid the envelope into her pocket. She hoisted the little desk onto her hip and carried it to her bedroom, where she put the envelope inside her top dresser drawer. Family secrets? She couldn't wait to open that envelope.

After she helped her mother find the quilt for Bethany, and her mother left to work in the garden, Molly hurried back to her bedroom to open the envelope from her great-great-grandmother's desk. It was sealed with red sealing wax. On the front, in flowery old-fashioned handwriting, it read FINAL CONFESSIONS OF MAGDALENA ELDON HOPER LYONS.

Molly broke the seal and read.

Gentle Reader,

Hear my words and forgive.

I locked the Truth within me long ago. That Truth bubbles to the surface and seeks to sing me out of sanity at unexpected moments so that I surely would have broken, shipwrecked on the rocks of remorse, if not for the strong timbre of my husband's love to which I lash myself for safety and salvation. The Captain cannot accompany me on my final journey, although I hope to see him on the other side. Whether or no depends on God's acceptance of my Repentance and abundant prayers. I would carry the Truth crouched within me to the grave, but Repentance requires confession and I fear for the Salvation of my immortal soul. I must soon answer to God directly for my sins. I entrust my confession to Him, to be revealed at His choosing in future days. Thus, if you are reading these words, then by the will of God you have found them where I secured them in my writing desk and perhaps you may take this disclosure as a sign that the Lord has allowed me to rest in Peace. I entreat you to provide this confession to my heirs that they may know their Heritage and know me and perhaps understand what I endured, why I sinned, and the price I paid. I pray that one day my distant daughters will read this document and understand what truly no man could understand, for no man could share my pain, comprehend my motives and my burden of shame, or appreciate my Triumph over circumstances.

They say that the magnificent Helen caused the death of multitudes in ancient Troy with her Beauty. My face did not launch a thousand ships, though many who looked upon it came to grief. I assure you that had my husband done his marital duty, such grief would never have befallen any of us. Why he married me remains a mystery to me. In my youth, I was a vivacious woman who desired intimacy, which he refused me. Through no cause of my own, I repulsed him and inspired him to Violence against me. I was foolish to accept his marriage proposal. I put forth the excuse that I was young and inexperienced. Apparently not young enough to satisfy his perversion, however, for he lusted after children. Damaging a precious, pure, untouched child aroused him. He possessed a Criminal Mind. He belonged in prison.

As a young bride arriving at Hoper Ranch, I imagined I would be mistress of a large, prosperous frontier house, filled with the children I would have, hardworking ranch hands, good food, and Joy. In Reality I was trapped in the Big House with that simpering idiot Becky and no diversions. What did John expect of me? He could have predicted what would happen if he left a woman like myself alone; a woman in her

prime, passionate, full of desires, and resourceful beyond
measure.

The first one was attracted to me. I knew immediately that
he wanted me. He was a fine specimen, with a smooth
muscular chest, tight thighs, and gentle hands. He spoke a
little English, though not enough to sound civilized; just
enough to sound Poetic. We met in the corn fields, lying
together on the cool earth between the rows. How could I have
guessed such Ecstasy existed in this world? He disappeared
just as abruptly as he had appeared and I never did find him
again. He told me his name, but I could not pronounce it and
remember only the feel of it passing over me.

My desires consumed me as a wolf devours its prey. So I
took what was not given willingly. I made it clear to them,
each one of them, that I would have their wives killed and
enslave their children if they failed to satisfy me or if they
breathed a word to anyone about what we did, and they knew I
had the Power to do it too. Their fear of John was complete. I
liked to watch them pretend they were not attracted to me
while their bodies betrayed their Desire. Men are so easy to
excite. They served my needs. Perhaps they pitied me or
laughed at me behind my back, although that did not prevent
them from performing for me. I became addicted. I craved
them, with their alien, exotic ways, and their silence, their
stillness and their Animal Sensuality.

John paid so little attention to my activities that he did not suspect. He was preoccupied with his own obsessions, his penchant for torturing their young girls, and with his efforts to turn a profit with the cattle business. We were strangers to one another, John and I. Becky knew my secrets since we lived virtually alone together in the Big House, with our husbands constantly away. She prayed fervently and pointlessly for my soul. I hated her for being such a righteous imbecile and even more for what she knew about me.

Then I discovered that I was with child even though I had used all the remedies to prevent such a thing. I was terrified, for John would see the minute it was born, just by its color, that the child was not his. I stopped my activity with my stable of men and I prayed, desperately, for the Salvation of my soul. I prayed for a miracle and God turned his countenance upon me in my time of need and took pity on me in a most unexpected way. One day John rode off to harvest one of those little girls, and by the will of God he came home dead. I laughed so hard when I saw the body, with one arrow through the heart and one through the genitals. It served him right, that lecherous pederast.

Please try to understand about what I did after that. I was trying to Survive. I had my dream of that prosperous family ranch and I aimed to get it, with an aim as True as those arrows in John's body. I could taste it all: the ranch hands and the children, the adoring husband who welcomed my bed, absolute control over a thriving household like one of those big Southern Plantations. I would be mistress of it all, right down to the border collie at the foot of my bed. I made a poor choice when I married John, but a Miracle befell me and granted me a second chance so I seized it. One must not ignore a Miracle.

You have to understand that I could not let the Indians out of there with their knowledge of the Truth about me. I had to silence them. My ranch hands were eager to do it. They hated them and their glaring women. The sight of John and Jack shot to death like that angered them. I could use that anger to avenge my worthless husband, protect my reputation, retain the ranch, accomplish everything at once. Most great accomplishments require a Sacrifice. Do not think this did not hurt me; after all, I had lain with many of them and they were magnificent creatures. I missed them terribly afterward and I have moments when I miss them still. It was the most difficult thing I ever did.

Once the Indians were silenced, that just left the matter of Becky since she was the only one living who knew my secret. I had no choice. I assure you that had you been there you would have seen that it was a Merciful act for truly she was dead from the moment she saw Jack's body atop that horse. That woman lacked a frontier constitution. She belonged in a parlor in San Francisco, sipping tea and embroidering. She did not struggle and I did it gently with her pillow while she slept drugged with laudanum so that she had a Peaceful end.

Then I rewrote my history. I rode to the Mission and telegraphed Captain Lyons, whom I had met the previous winter when he passed through on his way north to the logging camps. I thought him so handsome with his dashing little mustache. We flirted heavily with each other and he swore to me that I could call on him if ever I had need and he would come to my aid. Well I certainly had need and he rescued me like a true gentleman. He brought in his troops to resolve the whole Indian problem.

When I returned to the ranch, it felt like the air had cleared and the land was pure and begging for a fresh beginning. So I turned my back on the past and made a new start. The Captain was mine as easily as cutting butter. He did not so much as give pause when he learned of my pregnancy, which simply caused him to extend greater Compassion toward me. He is a generous man and I am grateful that he remained ignorant of the Truth about me and John and that filthy mess that transpired before he arrived.

I had a plan for the baby. If the baby looked Kapa, I would confess to the Captain that I had been raped. He would have believed me. As it turned out, the need did not arise, for my son looks like me. No one would guess he's a half-breed. The Captain wanted to name him John, and of course I could not allow that. I chose Esau, a solid, old-testament name. The Captain insisted he keep the Hoper name to honor John. He raised Esau as one of his own, treated him the same as our boys. *All boys, not a girl among them, and they each left Hoper Valley to seek their fortune elsewhere, lacking interest in the land. Except Esau, who stayed. Esau, who never knew that this land flows in his blood stretching back thousands of years. It is fitting that he inherited this land.*

I love all my boys, make no mistake, but I love that firstborn half-breed with a fiercer love than I have for any of them, try as I might to shake it. He has the wisdom of the Earth in him and an intuition that surpasses Logic. Though they do not know it, he and his boys, my grandsons and great-grandsons, carry the spark of their vanished Tribe. I see what no one else can: the Kapa in them. Now you know of my mortal sin and my secrets, all save one, and here it is: I did not merely desire the Kapa men, I loved them. They were the most perfect creatures. Gods among men. And I brought about their Annihilation. May God have mercy on my soul.

Dear Reader, please deliver my Confession into the hands of the children of Esau, that they may know Kapa blood flows in their veins and they are the last descendants of their Tribe, the Tribe that I loved, betrayed, and destroyed. Every day of my life I struggle to repent of my sins. Their eyes haunt me. Your eyes. Forgive me.

Magdalena Eldon Hoper Lyons
July 22, 1924

Yopika Bapa, 1983

"That ending is a keeper." Erica waves the last page of my manuscript at me.

"You like it?"

"I love it. The irony is perfect." Erica's smile turns to a frown. "It works for Molly, but what about Cassandra? You can't leave Cassandra hanging. We want to find out what happens in Athens."

"Who's 'we'?" What does Erica know about writing anyway?

"The audience. Me. The reader wants to find out what happens to Cassandra and those people in Greece."

"I don't know what happens."

"You have to know. They came out of your head."

"Like Athena from Zeus."

"Like what?"

"The Goddess Athena sprang full-grown from Zeus's head. My characters sprang from my head."

"Well ask them what happened to them," Erica suggests, her voice edged in frustration.

"Have you been talking to Cassandra behind my back?"

This conversation is one dripping Dali clock shy of going totally surreal.

Erica gives me "the look."

"Just drop it. I have nothing else in me right now, OK?" I shut the door on the conversation. Erica rolls her eyes.

I place the manuscript inside my desk.

Set aside again.

For now.

Book 15: Penelope
Yopika Bapa, 1985

S leep eludes me in the gray night, neither dark nor light, through which I drift in semi-consciousness. No dreams to escape into. No productive activity to distract me. Alone with the empty space left behind when Athena slipped out the door. Our beautiful, beloved Athena, beyond the touch of our hands. I listen to Erica's even breathing beside me. The familiar view from my window comforts me. Literally my window because Athena gave me this house in her will. I rise quietly and tiptoe through my house and onto my porch where I sit on my top step. Before me stretches the vast absence of her. I imagine that she will appear in the kitchen. I wanted her to see Max's graduation. I hoped she would live to see Lena married one day, maybe live long enough to hold Lena's first baby.

Our age difference was a cruel trick. Athena and I would have made great old ladies together. I hear her contagious cackling laugh inside my head. The days ahead of me without her unspool like endless miles of highway. I can't bear to imagine how often I will wish for her presence. Of course I can depend on her presence with us in spirit, but I want her physically here, interfering. I want her cooking, I want her advice, her green thumb, her common sense, her stubborn know-it-all attitude, her self-righteous, ornery, meddlesome, tough love. Our beautiful beloved. Gone. So many years ahead without you.

Not long after sunrise, Erica finds me on the porch. She says nothing, disappears inside, and returns a little later with a cup of coffee, which she puts into my hands. I can't think of any words to say. Nothing seems appropriate or important enough to slice open the sacred silence. Erica leaves me to myself. Bless her for refraining from asking questions or attempting insignificant conversation.

From the porch I see Nelson arrive at the water's edge. Although he is a small figure in the distance, I recognize his gray ponytail and his short muscular body. He lifts a large canoe off his car. Someone helps him. I think it's Snake. How many people will fit in that canoe? We will certainly need more than one canoe to take Athena's ashes out onto the lake. A lot of people will want to accompany her ashes.

I go into the house and take a hot shower. The water cascades in rivulets down my body. The room fills with dense steam. I scrub myself with Athena's Coco Hardwater Castile Soap until I smell like her. I expect to see her any minute, standing by the sink. Or climbing down from that rusted-out heap of a truck of hers. Or sitting in her rocker on the porch wrapped in her frayed Afghan that Dita made for her years ago when they were young women raising children and gossiping in the garden.

When Erica told Max that Athena had died, he asked her in disbelief, "What happened to her?" and Erica replied, "Nothing happened, sweetie. She was old, she just died."

Athena went upstairs. She lay down on her bed to take a nap. Her heart stopped.

She had a good run and now it was over.

I've spent so many years speaking to an absent husband that I should take to communicating with an ancestor spirit like a duck to water. Not so. It feels awkward speaking to Athena when she doesn't speak back to me. Or grunt or nod or shoot me one of her looks.

I dress slowly and descend to the kitchen where June is making breakfast. She embraces me wordlessly, wrapping me in her arms while I cry. Everyone treats me as if I'm breakable.

Lena rubs her eyes and sits sleepily at the table. We moved her to Oakland last month for her first semester at college.

"Will you have trouble catching up? Are you missing too many classes?" I worry.

"It's OK, Ama. This is Saturday; no classes. I'll be fine." She certainly will be fine. My little girl has become this competent young woman who sits before me. Capable and talented.

"Where's Max?" I ask.

"Helping Nelson with the canoes," June answers.

"I saw Nelson by the water unloading a canoe from the car," I say.

"He has more," June informs.

"How many people do you think will go out on the water?" Erica asks, as she pours herself more coffee from the pot on the counter.

"Not sure." June scrambles eggs in a big cast-iron skillet. Athena's skillet. "How about putting butter on that toast, Lena." Lena obliges.

Erica pours another cup of coffee for me and places it in front of me. Shaky from lack of sleep and nothing to eat, I should wait until I eat breakfast to have more coffee. I must remember to take care of myself. I hear Athena's voice in my head saying her standard, "If I'da known I'd live this long I'da taken better care of myself."

I stand with Erica and Lena on the shore of B'Taka Lake as we watch the flotilla of canoes gliding like a flock of geese on the water. Max and Nelson man the lead canoe. Snake went out in a canoe with Thorn. I remain on the shore. I can't bring myself to go out on the water with the ashes. June holds Aunt Beth's hand. Aunt Beth moans softly. It seems as though the whole Tribe stands on the shore with us.

Athena's sons have assembled for the memorial. These men whom she raised, who went out into the world away from her, away from B'Taka. They have returned today with their wives, their sons, even a couple of great-grandchildren. Athena would have loved to see those mischievous brown little boys. This would be a party if the guest of honor would show up. She won't be arriving.

We follow the canoes with our eyes.

It's dangerous to stand in a canoe. That's the first thing you learn about canoeing. Keep your body weight low. If you stand, you can easily capsize. So I suck in my breath when I realize that Nelson is rising to his feet. The canoe wobbles. Fortunately, Max is an excellent swimmer. Nelson is a short, dense man with a low body center. I think he'll be OK. Gray clouds drift ominously across the sky and I hope it doesn't rain. Nelson wears his distinctive fringed suede jacket and when he raises his arms, his silhouette against the clouded sky resembles a huge bird on the verge of taking flight. Nelson casts Athena's ashes across the water. His canoe wobbles and I can't see Max's head or shoulders. Max must have stretched out in the bottom of the canoe to keep it steady.

The Bear, who holds Carla in his embrace, gathers Athena's ashes lovingly, carrying her back to the before-time with the same ease as words from the old language tumbling one over the other like a song.

I close my eyes and wish myself into last week or last month. Are my best years behind me? Are the fat years over? The children are raised and the elders are passing into spirit, leaving the Bapa. Soon I will be an elder.

Tribal women sing a traditional mourning song. Lena cries on Erica's shoulder, wrapped in Erica's arms. Aunt Beth wails like a wounded dog and June comforts her. Athena's sons lean against their wives and weep. These sons have remained so often absent from our lives that it surprises me, although I suppose it shouldn't, that her death affects them so deeply. Even though they made their lives elsewhere, Athena and the Tribe are their roots and they have come home sometimes to see their mother.

The tule reeds along the shore whisper their secrets in soft susurration. The tules saved the life of my great-grandmother, and that is why I exist. My children live and breathe because of the tules. The tules rustle against one another in the breeze, as if a spirit passes among them. In my mind's eye I see Athena walking on the lake. I can almost hear her voice. I see her form threading its way among the tules.

As the canoes turn their noses toward the shore, Podon, Marjorie, and Hera begin drumming. Podon thumps on the large standing drum with the deepest sound. The reverberating beat of the drums is the voice of our people lamenting the loss of Athena and it calls my heart out of me. Oh our beautiful, beloved Athena. Hearing the deep beat of the drum, I go completely to pieces.

Some time later, as the sun glides down to the lake, Max lights the fire that he and Nelson have built. It looks like a tipi, with long sturdy upright sticks surrounding the outside, leaning in on each other at the top. Inside the tipi of sticks, a large round of wood rests on smaller branches with newspaper and twigs underneath. Nelson would call this a "one-match fire" and Max's one match sets flickers of flame dancing at the edge of the tipi sticks, then underneath. The fire takes its course. Remarkably, the tiniest flame has the power to create a roaring blaze.

June and Dita distribute pouches of fabric filled with tobacco and tied shut with string.

"When you throw your tobacco pouch into the fire, send blessings and messages to Athena to carry with her on her journey into the spirit world," Dita instructs as she distributes the pouches to people.

One of Athena's sons helps his grandson throw a pouch into the fire. "Send love to your great-grandma," he tells the little boy. The child throws the pouch and runs off into the yard to play hide-and-seek with the other children, vibrant and full of energy.

I gaze into the flames. Athena has left a lifetime of accomplishments behind. Trees planted. Children raised. Children of children welcomed into the world. A Tribe held together against all odds. A woman and her children rescued. A family recreated. Athena's magnificent footprint on the earth.

June has set out fry bread and hearty turkey soup on the picnic table.

Lena snuggles against me in silence. We gaze into the fire from the circle of each other's arms.

Nelson walks over and assures us, "She was such a fully evolved human being that she will make an easy transition."

"I'm not concerned about Athena," Lena replies. "She's fine. It's us, the ones left behind, that I worry about."

The heat radiates from the fire. My face flushes. I step back, out of Lena's reach, away from Nelson. One person begins drumming on a small hand drum. Another person plays a dulcimer. More drummers join. I can't listen to drums. They tear my heart out.

I slip quietly from the fire circle.

My feet lead me to Snake's trailer. I knock on the door and enter without waiting for his invitation. I know he has strong medicine. He says nothing. I take a dirty glass out of the sink and wash it. I put it down on the table and sit across from him. I turn the bottle on the table around to read the label.

"That's fine," I say. I crave a little quality time with my big brother Sammy (not Snake) and his old friend Jack Daniels.

He looks so surprised it makes me laugh. "You sure?" he asks as I pour myself a drink. The divine burn of whiskey going down my throat makes me want to shout with glee. Blessed, blessed oblivion.

"Turn out the light," I tell him and he obeys. "I don't want my children to find out I'm in here drinking hard liquor." The trailer is lit by the moon and the glow of the Rez.

"I don't think they'd judge you harsh tonight."

I take another deep gulp from my glass. My whole body grows warm. Better. Much better. The weight lifts a little from my chest. I can breathe.

"So Sammy. You don't mind if I call you that, do you?"

"Not a problem."

"Sammy, do you remember when Daddy took us to that drive-in movie?"

He nods.

"He bought us popcorn and M&Ms. What movie was that? It was funny."

"Yeah, we laughed our heads off."

"What movie was it?" I help myself to another glass of Jack. He shrugs.

"I think it had a sheep dog in it." I try to jog his memory. I was too little, can't remember much of the movie at all.

"Do you remember when he stood on Mom's little cardboard china cabinet to change that light bulb and it collapsed under him?" Sammy asks me with a chuckle.

"I do! I do remember that. You and me and Carla, we laughed so hard. He could have gotten mad at us for laughing at him, but he didn't. He looked so funny standing in the wreckage, imagining what Mom would do to him when she saw it."

"He taught me to swim," Sammy says quietly. "I was scared. He was patient. No one would've described him as a patient guy. But I knew he had a lot of patience in him."

"He put me in his lap to tie my shoes in the morning. Did he do that for you too?"

"Yeah, he did." Sammy remembers. No one else would remember that.

"He made the best pancakes." Tears run down my cheeks.

"With chocolate chips in them." Sammy takes my hand across the table. Our hushed voices tell secrets in the dark. We don't want anyone to guess that we remember good things about a man who raped and killed our sister.

"I remember how Daddy combed my hair," I whisper. "He would talk in a silly voice while he combed, more gentle with the tangles than Mom."

"He always came to my baseball games. He even took me to see the A's play once." Sammy's shoulders heave up and down. Sammy's voice breaks. "In a lot of ways he was, well, a good dad."

"He loved us. Maybe he just didn't...."

"He was sick. He needed help."

"How could he do that?"

"He didn't know how to ask for help."

"But he loved us," I repeat. "Even Carla, he loved her too." I have trouble focusing my eyes. Too much Jack too quickly.

"I loved him. And then I hated him," Sammy says practically inaudibly.

"I loved him and hated him too."

I have never seen Sammy cry before. He cries now. We cry together as we share our memories. We are two small children, hiding in the closet, abandoned and alone. We whisper so no one will find us. No one will ever know what only the two of us know about our family.

How good it was.

And how bad.

In the morning I wake up on Snake's bed and he's nowhere in sight. I have a whopping headache. I crawl to the house, dreading a confrontation with Erica. She wouldn't understand.

But she isn't there. No one is.

Everything is way too bright.

I need to get out of here. I wish I had a ticket to Maui.

I need to be alone. Away from the Rez. Away from Athena's house. Away from everyone. I have a crazy thought. I can check into a hotel where no one will find me. Just for a few days. I like this thought.

I swallow a couple aspirin and take a shower. I put a few things into a travel bag and write a note to Erica. I tell her I'll call when I get wherever I'm going. Not to worry. I'm OK. She'll worry anyway. She's Jewish, worrying is in her blood. And I have a history of clinical depression.

I drive. I roll the window down and the air runs its fingers through my hair.

He loved to tangle his hands in my hair. I hear his voice. "I'll be back soon. Before you have time to miss me." I had plenty of time to miss you. Lena is grown and gone to college, Odysseus. Max is a self-sufficient young man. He'll leave the Bapa soon. Nelson stepped up. He more than filled your shoes. They hardly noticed you were missing. We have Nelson, Athena, and the Tribe. Had Athena.

The gracefully twisted oaks and voluptuous madrones of the Northern California landscape dance outside my car windows. This is the land I love, the land of my people for twelve thousand years. I hear Athena's voice: "The land is a friend who lives forever. The trees are teachers. B'Taka Lake will always listen to you. Go to these friends when you have need of them. Men think they can own land. They forget how quickly the land will escape their grasp the instant they turn away. In a second, the land will do what it pleases. No one owns land. We are lucky to partner with it."

"I am in the lake," Carla says. "Visit me in the arms of B'Taka. Whenever. I am always near you."

"We welcome Athena into spirit with celebration," my mother tells me. "She has made a fine transition. She loves you and so do I and we remain with you."

"And I," Carla says. "I'm always by your side."

Where did this chatter come from? I can't hear my own thoughts with all of these voices jabbering in my brain.

"At least no one is telling you to put a beaver hat on your head and shoot at people from the steps of the library," Odysseus jokes. I think I'm about one beaver hat shy of climbing those library steps and making a fool of myself.

I need to shake these voices out. I pull off the road into a little town in wine country to put gas in the car. I see a sign that offers tourists the opportunity to taste locally grown olive oils. Tasting olive oil strikes me as an extremely decadent activity.

As I pump the gas, I get a flash of insight about what I want to do; where I want to go. I drive further into this town until I find the quaint and picturesque Blackberry Bed and Breakfast Inn. It's painted white with deep purple trim and has wooden shutters with quarter-moon shapes cut out of them. It looks like it was transplanted from New England. I have never stayed at one of these places. I want to have a maid put fresh-cut flowers in my room and I want to have a bubble bath and use blackberry-scented guest soap and jojoba shampoo from a little sample bottle and I want to have an employee bring me strong coffee and a croissant for breakfast in my room. I want to wrap myself in a fluffy white guest bathrobe left hanging in the closet just for me.

I check in at the front desk. The key is attached to a wine-bottle opener. I'll be sleeping in the Cabernet Room. The first thing I see when I go into my room is a mauve, maroon, burgundy, and dusty rose handmade quilt on the bed. Starburst pattern. I know that from Dita, who used to quilt. If it rains I bet I could hear the rain on the roof above the high-beamed wooden ceiling. I'll stay until it rains.

There is no phone in the room. I use the phone at the front desk. No one answers. I leave a message for Erica and give her the name of the Bed and Breakfast and the name of the town. "I'll come back to the Bapa in a couple of days. I'm OK."

Like an injured animal, I crawl under the house alone to lick my wounds.

I trust Erica to understand.

Book 16: Erica
Yopika Bapa, 1985

Penelope left me a message on the answering machine. She says she's OK. I'm pretty sure I can believe her. I want to believe her. I'm not up for drama right now. How come she gets to be the one who loses it and checks into a hotel to pull herself together? Why can't I be the one to check into the hotel to pull myself together? It's tough being the stronger partner. I'd love the luxury of coming apart at the seams. Even for just one day.

The house feels empty with only me and the shadow of Aunt Beth slipping from room to room with no one left to speak with her in Kapa.

I'm making enchiladas and I have my hands covered in enchilada sauce when the phone rings. I hastily rinse a hand off and grab the phone, hoping it's Penelope.

"Hello?"

"Erica?" It's Lena.

"Yeah, what's up?"

"Is Ama there?"

"No, sweetie. She's taking a few days off. She went away by herself. You know how she is, needs privacy to sort herself out." I don't want to worry Lena.

"Can you tell me where to find her? It's important."

The parental alarm bell goes off in my head. "Is everything OK?"

"Yes, well, I mean I'm OK. I need to talk to Ama."

"Lena, she wants to be left alone right now. What is it? What's going on?"

Silence. I wait. Lena tells me softly, "I found my father."

My knees give and I sit down abruptly. My heart races.

"Erica? Are you still there?"

Yeah, I think, still here, but for how long? Banish that thought. "Yes, yes, I'm still here," I manage to say.

"It's so not what you think, not what any of us thought. He... Do you have a moment?"

"Of course, sweetie. Talk to me." I wipe my hands on a towel. The enchiladas will have to wait. This might take a while.

"Losing Athena got me started thinking, and, well, whatever," Lena begins, and she tells me the whole story.

I had this idea to find the house we lived in when I was a baby, before my father left. I remember the address. I memorized it when I was little and it popped into my head. So I looked on a map and I found the street. I wish Max had been with me. I thought I remembered a small stone wall in the back yard. Either I didn't remember the front of the house or it changed, because it didn't look familiar when I found it. The house is beige with turquoise trim. It's small and tidy. Four steps lead up to the front porch and there are herb pots on the steps, along the edge, one on each step. A vintage car was parked in the driveway. I couldn't tell you the model. I walked up the steps. There was no doorbell. I found a sort of knocker-thingy, which I used. I heard the sound of chimes from within. Not mechanical door chimes. Balls tapping on strings on the other side of the door.

A lean, older man, muscular, with graying, golden-brown hair, opened the door. His eyes widened with surprise and curiosity. "Yes?"

"Hello." I had to think for a moment of what to say. "I'm Lena and I used to live in this house. When I was little. I was hoping, maybe, that I could see what it looks like now. If you don't mind." I probably should have worried about my safety alone in that house with a strange man, but it never crossed my mind.

He smiled and I liked his smile, even though it lacked something, like an otherwise hearty soup missing the onions. "I'll give you the tour, shall I?" He opened the door wide enough for me to pass inside. "It's just me here. And Icarus." I figured Icarus to be the enormous black cat with green eyes lounging on an easy chair by the fireplace. "Does anything look the same?" he asked me, as I followed him into the kitchen, which was loaded with gourmet cooking paraphernalia. This guy was probably a terrific cook. Center island with a cutting board. Pots hanging on a wrought iron rack. Shiny utensils in a jug on the counter. Herbs and spices in a tidy row in a wooden holder mounted on the wall. A fancy bottle of olive oil on the stove.

I was thinking about that stone wall, so I asked if I could see the back yard. He looked puzzled as he led me to the back deck through a pair of glass sliding doors. From the deck, I saw it instantly. A stone wall about two feet high. I sucked in my breath sharply.

"You remember something?" The man asked.

I pointed. "That stone wall."

He brushed a lock of hair out of his eyes with a trembling hand as he shot me a piercing look. "When did you live here?"

"About fifteen years ago."

"Did your father build that wall with you?" A sigh escaped him as if all the air had left his body. He grasped the railing so hard that his knuckles turned white. He looked as if his legs were about to buckle.

"Yes," I whispered, afraid that if I spoke too loudly the air around us would shatter into a million shards.

"Your mother," he began. His voice cracked. He swallowed. "Is she still living?"

I nodded affirmative. I understood. He has Max's eyes and jaw line and he has Max's hands.

Tears ran down his face. *"You look just like her, Helen. So beautiful."*

His eyes are my brother's eyes, except that they hold such pain in them. This man before me would not have freely chosen to leave my mother. Those many years ago, something must have happened that left him wandering, cut off from us.

This man, my father.

Odysseus.

"So you found him."

"Yes."

"Something happened, you say?"

"Yes. Something happened."

"Let's hear it. What sorry excuse did he give you?" The hair on the back of my neck stands up, electrified. What if he has a viable explanation?

"Long version or short version?" Lena asks.

"Short version." I want to know the damage as quickly as possible.

"He was disappeared by a military dictatorship. Do you know anything about Greek history or politics?"

"Not really."

"Neither did I. They had a military dictatorship in Greece for a while and he spent three years in prison. They tortured him, Erica. His family couldn't locate him. They feared him dead until the government miraculously released him in some sort of amnesty."

"Miraculously," I echo as I try to digest this information. It's nothing like what I might have guessed. "Why didn't his family contact your mother?"

"They didn't approve. She's not Greek Orthodox. So they returned her letters unopened and didn't tell her he was in jail."

"That's what he *says*."

"That's what happened," Lena tells me firmly.

"Then why didn't he come back after he got out?"

"He did. He couldn't find her."

"Why didn't he hire a private detective?" That's what I would have done. Left no stone unturned. I desperately want this tortured man, this hero, to still be the bad guy, even as the image slips through my fingers like sand.

"I suppose he didn't think of it."

"Somewhat lacking in imagination."

"Don't be like that. Ama loves you. That won't change. We're a family. You raised me. You're my other mother, Erica; and Max's."

I'm glad we're on the phone so she can't see the emotion in my face. "Now what?"

"I'm bringing him home this weekend so Max can meet him."

"Your mother isn't here, and she probably won't be here by the weekend either," I warn. "She left instructions not to be disturbed."

"That's OK."

Lena doesn't know Penelope like I do. She knows her as her mother. I know her as a woman, lover, partner. I know Odysseus's grip on her heart, her soul.

I know how a firm relationship can transform itself into a fragile connection in a heartbeat.

Book 17: Penelope's Dream
A Bed and Breakfast at an Undisclosed Location, 1985

The Round House is larger than I remember. The ceiling is higher. The windows let in more light. Dita sits next to me, her knitting needles clacking. I ask her, "Is this the real Round House or the Round House in my dream?"

"The Round House in your dream," Dita clarifies.

The Round House expands. I can no longer see the walls.

The edges of the room disappear into tule reeds. The edges between B'Taka Lake and the Round House blur.

The tribal elders and I sit at a long, heavy, oak table that squats on fat legs carved like totem poles.

Artifacts, such as cradleboards, baskets, tools, and regalia, hang on a huge wall rising above the head of the oak table. I admire a water basket, woven tight enough to hold water without oozing a drop.

My attention, along with that of the others in the room, leaps to the doorway where a man enters, lit from behind by the sun, his hair a halo of glowing, golden light. From around the edges of his silhouette, the sun pierces my eyes with diamond shards of brightness.

His face remains hidden.

Nelson stands at the head of the table and demands, "State your business."

The man responds, "I must prove I am true. Set up the Great Bow."

Podon springs to his feet, in his haste overturning the stool on which he sat, and he grabs an arrow from the wall behind Nelson. Nelson methodically places on the table heavy metal stands crowned at the top with rings. June helps him straighten the metal stands into a row.

Podon hands the arrow to Nelson.

Nelson passes the arrow to the stranger. "You'll have to lift the Bow," he says. "You know I cannot do it."

The enormous Great Bow dominates the wall of regalia, the most prominent object on it.

The stranger strides down the length of the room and reaches up to lift the Great Bow from off its peg, leaning it against his shoulder like a standing harp.

He looks familiar. I know him, but from where?

Nelson guides me by the elbow to the head of the table. He positions me with my back against the huge wall and aligns my body with the metal rings on the table.

The stranger stands at the opposite end of the table from me. In one swift, smooth motion he strings the Bow.

The elders gasp in unison as if they share one set of lungs.

The golden stranger balances the Bow against his shoulder, nocks an arrow to the string.

My body is heavy. I am weighted to the spot. Unable to move.

With an encouraging smile, Athena touches my arm lightly.

"I didn't think I would see you again," I tell her, elated by her presence. I long to embrace her, but my arms remain too heavy to lift.

Athena assures me, "He won't harm you; trust him; the arrow will shoot straight and true to the mark. It won't be what you think. It will be better."

Her words make no sense, although I'm filled with delight by the sound of her voice.

"I thought you died."

"Never." She places her hand gently on my head. "I am one of the immortals."

"I wanted to talk with you again."

"You can talk with me any time. Look for my reply in the lessons of the land, in the changing fingerprints of the days and hours, in the images that enter your imagination when you make no effort to harness them. I speak the language of the mystery. Watch for something you knew for certain to transform itself so that you did not know it at all and have more to learn from it. When this happens, you have heard my voice."

Athena evaporates in a streamer of smoke.

The powerful, muscled shoulder of the golden stranger who wields the Great Bow pulls taut as he aims at the heavy metal rings.

He shoots.

The arrow travels its course straight and true through the middle of the rings without touching a single one.

I see it progress toward me in slow motion as it clears each of the metal rings and emerges from the last to follow its path directly through my heart.

The arrow enters my body painlessly, filling me with a warm glow that transforms into an overwhelming sexual desire.

I recognize the golden archer.

Odysseus.

None other.

The room disappears as we drop through the bottom of the floor, leaving the Tribe behind.

We fall and fall until we land on a soft heap of blankets on a boat on the open ocean where we float together, naked to the sun-laced air, our bodies tangled, skin to skin, electric and responsive to each other's touch.

I flow out of myself like water.

I am the ocean and he is the penetration of light into my depths.

He is the one who strings the Great Bow and shoots.

I follow him to the home of marriage, which I always remember, even in my dreams.

When I wake, his touch lingers on my skin and in my hair. I catch his scent on my shoulders.

I forgot the precise feel of making love to a man. It comes back to me. The firmness and the physical force gentled by thoughtful caring. I remember the excruciating longing for him, the overwhelming absence, how desperately I desired what I had lost. That yearning has not diminished. Not a fraction. Only its frequency has dissipated. I have locked it away into the basement of my dreams where it ages like wine growing full-bodied and poignant.

Desiring one who is always distant.

Forbidden taste.

Passion fruit.

Lost pleasure.

Love of my youth.

Husband.

Book 18: Lena
Yopika Bapa, 1985

Ama went into hiding after Athena passed into spirit. Erica knows where she is. She says she'll be OK, that she'll come back home when she's ready. I remember when June gave away Daisy's puppies and Daisy hid under the house for three days after her puppies disappeared. June had to coax her out with waffles and plum jam, her favorite. It's kind of like that for Ama. She needs to hide under the house for a little while. Maybe Odysseus will be her waffles and jam. Or maybe she will go back under when she discovers he has returned.

I seize the opportunity of Ama's absence to bring my father home to meet Max and Erica. It will be a good thing for Erica and Odysseus to meet each other before Ama knows he has returned. I don't want them to think of each other as rivals.

I rarely see Max now that he has left the Rez to go to college. I know he will return home for the first full moon fire since Athena passed over. It will give me an opportunity to introduce Odysseus to the Tribe, for if he truly hopes to re-enter our lives, he must learn about our people.

We arrive at the Bapa together on a Friday as the evening light drags streamers of orange and blue across the sky. I feel like a princess in Odysseus's elegant vintage Mercedes. At the same time I feel conspicuous riding onto the Rez in such an expensive car.

Daddy Nelson has been my father for so long that I can't wrap my head around the idea of Odysseus as my father. I don't think of him that way.

"So Lena, back to the Rez with your latest find," Erica comments as she crushes me to her in a hug. "It's good to have you and Max at home. I don't know what to do with myself in this empty house."

"You smell delicious, like pizza."

Erica laughs nervously. "I made spaghetti. Just for you. The way you like."

I turn to Odysseus, who emerges from the other side of the car. "Erica makes the best spaghetti." He nods. He sizes up Erica. He's tongue-tied. He has no guidebook for this situation.

"Jewish spaghetti," Erica quips.

"Has Ama come back yet?"

"Not yet. I warned you about that," she points out. "Come inside. Dinner's almost ready."

As we turn to enter the house, Max appears on the porch, all six feet and youthful virility of him. On the threshold of manhood. A father's best dream, I imagine. Odysseus leans weakly against the car for support. His mouth forms the word "Telemachus" but no sound comes out and I worry for a moment that he will collapse. But he stands up straight. Max looks Odysseus up and down and then steps off the porch and approaches him with his hand outstretched, awkwardly, inviting a handshake. Odysseus grasps the hand and pulls his son into his embrace, like a man falling down the face of a mountain who drags himself up on a safety rope. A soft sob escapes his lips and rattles his shoulders.

Max barely returns the embrace. He shifts from one foot to the other and pulls away uncomfortably. Nelson is his father, not this stranger. But he is curious. Max is always curious. And compassionate. "Pretty amazing that Lena found you. How long have you been living in Berkeley?"

"Two years," Odysseus replies as he wipes his eyes with the heels of his palms.

"What are you again?" Max asks. We walk to the porch and then up the steps.

"What am I?" Odysseus cocks his head quizzically to one side.

"What's your profession?" Max clarifies.

"I work as an electrical engineer."

"Oh yeah. I knew that." Max turns to Erica on the porch, "You need me to set the table?"

"Sure."

"What'd you do, paint with the sauce?" Max looks at Erica's apron, which has patches of tomato sauce doused on it.

"For your information, Wisenheimer, it splattered when I took the lid off to check it."

Max reaches out with a finger and pretends to take a swipe of sauce from the apron and pretends to taste it. "Could use a little more pepper."

"Don't get fresh with the cook. If you get on my bad side, I'll slip you a spoonful of Aunt Beth's Metamucil in your O.J.," Erica threatens, laughing.

Max feigns worry.

I laugh at their antics.

This is the tight-knit family we have, Father. Don't imagine you can take this away from us. Don't imagine that you can take our mother away from Erica. How will we make room for you in this family? Even though Erica jokes with me and Max, like usual, I can tell that underneath she is anxious about Odysseus, anxious that he has reappeared on the scene. Yet she acts calm and cheerful. I can also see under the surface to where it hurts her to have Max and me home this way with Ama in hiding and Athena gone to spirit. I can see it in her face when we sit at the table where there are too many empty seats.

After dinner Max pushes himself back from the table and informs, "I have to help Nelson collect firewood for the full moon fire tomorrow night." He picks up his empty plate and deposits it in the sink. "Thanks for dinner. Delicious."

The phone rings. Erica answers. She points at me. "For you. Marjorie."

"Max," Erica calls to him, as he heads out the door. Max turns. "It's chilly out. Take a jacket."

"I'm not cold."

"You might be later. Just take a jacket. You can leave it in Nelson's truck if you don't need it."

Max looks to Odysseus and rolls his eyes. "Because she's cold, I have to take a jacket." He grabs his jacket from a hook by the door. "Are you warmer now?" he asks Erica.

"Yeah. I'm terrific."

Max and his jacket head out the door.

"I made a noodle *kugel*. Tell Nelson to stop by for some later," Erica calls after him.

Max's muffled "OK" drifts in from the yard.

Marjorie is dying for an ice cream cone and wants me to go with her into town to get one. I inform Erica, "Marjorie invited me to go with her for an ice cream."

"I made a *kugel*," Erica repeats accusingly. "Maybe Marjorie would like to come over for *kugel*?"

"She has a craving for pistachio ice cream."

Erica flashes me a pleading look that says "don't leave me alone with him."

Odysseus jumps to his feet and hurries to the door. He calls after Max. "Hey, can I go with you? I'd like to meet Nelson." He vanishes. Erica sighs with relief.

Aunt Beth pokes her head furtively out of her room where she has been hiding from the strange man in her house. "He's gone," Erica tells Aunt Beth, "you can come out and make your tea."

Aunt Beth pads into the kitchen on slippered feet, humming to herself.

"I'll be back early," I promise as I peck Erica on the cheek and head out the door.

Marjorie and I walk into town to the ice cream shop. We take the forest road, a path fragrant with fir needles that meanders through a small forest adjacent to the Rez. The forest road opens onto the lake, where it follows the shoreline until it arrives at the Bapa. The little forest surrounding the forest road provides a buffer, a decompression zone, between the Rez and the town. We proceed along the forest road, arm-in-arm.

I point at a large decaying tree on the ground. "Whenever I see that tree, I remember when you tripped over it playing hide-and-seek."

"Twelve stitches in my knee for that one."

"I almost passed out from seeing you lose that much blood."

"Short-lived drama. The scar's imperceptible. You'd have to know where to look to see it."

"I know where to look."

At the ice cream parlor, Marjorie orders a double scoop of pistachio on a waffle cone. I go for one scoop of vanilla on a regular sugar cone. I know that I have a piece of *kugel* with my name on it in Erica's kitchen so I had better save room.

We choose a table.

Marjorie is devouring her pistachio with gusto when Perry Hoepper saunters in the door with a few friends yapping at his heels. She abandons her assault on the ice cream to watch him. She shoots me a worried look and says quietly, "He gives me the creeps. Ever since that time, with the rocks."

"Me too."

Perry spots us and his face splits open in a fake smile the way a jack-o'-lantern splits in a forced grin, cut by a knife. "Hey girls," he calls out. "Haven't seen you around in a while." He hovers over our table, ringed by his entourage of loser-followers.

I study this former torturer, the bully of my youth. A stubbly growth of unshaven beard gives him a grizzled appearance. He wears a blue bandanna around his neck and a dusty cowboy hat over his sandy brown hair. I feel as if I am hallucinating a character from an old Western movie. My cosmopolitan colleagues at art school would view Perry as an anachronism from the last century, a creature crawled out from under a rock on the prairie.

"I heard your old granny died," Perry says with mock seriousness. "Too bad. She had balls." He laughs a laugh like sandpaper scraping the skin off a smooth piece of madrone wood.

I nod faintly.

"Didn't you jump ship and move to the city?" Perry squints his pale eyes to slits.

"I'm visiting," I reply. "And I have to get back." I rise from my chair and Marjorie hastens to join me as I breeze past Perry and out the door.

I fill my lungs with the crisp evening air and admire the exquisite bluish tint of dusk. I exhale and release the bad feeling left clinging to me by the encounter with Perry. We walk in silence until we reach the forest road, where I hear Marjorie sigh with relief as the trees engulf us. We finish our ice cream cones while we walk and Marjorie licks her fingertips delicately to savor the last few hints of pistachio.

"That was a super-terrific ice cream," Marjorie announces with satisfaction.

I glimpse B'Taka Lake through the pattern of trees. "You have no idea how hard it is to be away from here," I confess. "I miss the people and the land. I miss the whole place. I'm coming home the minute I graduate. I love art school, my classes, studio, the teachers, my classmates; but it's enough of the wide world for me. I didn't imagine I would feel so homesick."

"Great. I'll look forward to your graduation."

When we reach the heart of the forest, I hear a rustling behind me and I stop walking and glance worriedly at Marjorie, who hears the sound too. It is not a benign sound. It is not the sound of a breeze in the upper branches. It is not the sound of squirrels foraging for acorns. It is the sound of a person with harmful intent.

Someone is following us and we know who it is.

The skin on the back of my neck prickles.

We both begin to run toward the lake, trying to escape the swiftly darkening woods.

Arms wrap around my knees from behind and tackle me to the ground, knocking the wind out of me. I roll over and struggle to stand. Two of them restrain me. They pin me to the ground. I scream, but the layers of leaves muffle the sound. I wonder how far my scream will carry. Marjorie fights to free herself from two others. She tries to kick them in the balls. They warily avoid her dangerous feet and knees. One of them has straw-colored hair that glints ghostlike in the gathering inky twilight. The other is darker and a whisper away from invisible.

Perry stands apart and watches his thugs take a battering as they cling to us, their prey, trying to find handholds and footholds on our bodies as they struggle to press us to the ground. Perry smiles crookedly.

"Perry go home," I yell at him. "Don't make this mistake."

"Should I go home to Hoepper or Bataka?" Perry taunts me.

Marjorie bellows and bucks like a wild mare. The assailant with the straw-colored hair hits her in the head with a rock and she slumps, motionless.

"What did you do? You're crazy! Is she OK? Marjorie, are you OK? Marjorie! Did you kill her?" I shriek.

Perry slaps me across the face with the palm of his hand and stars flash across my vision as he commands, "Shut up." I ignore him and call for help. He removes his T-shirt and stuffs it into my mouth. I gag. Perry forces the fabric in place with his hand as he kneels on my shoulder.

"Little miss Injun girl," Perry rasps. "You always spoiled all my fun."

The one with the straw-colored hair and the invisible assailant strip Marjorie's clothes off her. All the hair on my body stands on end. The rough, uneven ground digs into my back. I must concentrate to prevent myself from gagging and suffocating on the material crammed in my mouth.

Perry produces a hunting knife from a pouch on his belt. If Perry kills me tonight, so soon after Athena's death, it will send Ama over the edge. I cry and make noises deep in my throat, uncontrollable primal noises.

Perry slips the knife up under the bottom of my shirt and cuts it off me. I try to kick him.

"Come here you guys," Perry beckons to the straw-colored and the invisible who stand over the unmoving, nude form of Marjorie. "Hold her legs for me."

I have already lost the feeling in my arms because they are holding me so tightly. Perry cuts the rest of my clothing off me so that I lie naked on a heap of slashed fabric.

"You've been asking for this for a long time," Perry snarls. His hands tremble as he unzips his jeans. All of them are breathing hard and I realize that this excites them. How can something so nauseating, so brutal excite them?

As Perry Hoepper kneels between my legs, his face changes before my eyes. It is his face while at the same time it is the face of a much older man, more grizzled. He has stubble and wears a cowboy hat and a bandanna around his neck. I see this clearly in the light of the nearly full moon. His face looks like Perry's but altered, revised to the features of a similar but other Hoepper. We have become another Kapa and another Hoepper and we enact this charade in the present moment while at the same time we enact it in the long-ago.

An explosion that seems to originate in B'Taka Lake crashes from behind me. A look of supreme surprise erupts on Perry's face and a dark dot appears in the middle of his forehead. His eyes film over. He crumples on top of me. More explosions rip the air.

My captors release me and spring away. I remove the T-shirt, which smells of deodorant and gasoline, from my mouth and I gulp air. The weight of Perry's inert body crushes me and I shake so violently that I can't control my arms or legs to move Perry off me. There are splatters of blood on my arms. Cries of pain and fear tangle in the crisscross of branches above us.

Straw-colored lies on the ground not far from my head, his mouth twisted in anguish as he clutches his stomach. I see his features clearly and recognize him as one of my high school classmates. I remember that he loves horses and that his mother bakes delicious gingerbread cookies. I hope for her sake that the woman's son will not die in the forest next to me.

Marjorie remains as still as the deep center of a lake in midsummer. Her motionless arm, flung across the ground, points a finger accusingly at a barely visible person curled up in a ball of agony beside a moss-covered log.

I am crushed under the weight of Perry's body, which I cannot move. Uncle Snake kneels beside me and ferociously hauls Perry off me.

"He didn't do it to you, did he?" Snake demands. "I got him before he could do it, didn't I? He didn't do anything, right? Tell me he didn't do it."

"You stopped him before…he didn't…" I sob, clinging to Snake, who pushes me away awkwardly and proceeds to unbutton his shirt with shaky fingers. He removes his shirt and clothes my naked body. The blue denim brushes softly against my skin. After covering me, Snake puts his arms around me. He weeps as he strokes my hair gently and rocks me like a beloved child, or a sister.

"Marjorie," I squeak. "Is Marjorie OK?" Snake and I ease out of our embrace and turn toward her inert form.

Thorn kneels beside Marjorie and places his fingers on her neck. "She has a pulse," he calls out.

The bodies of Perry and his accomplices surround us. Straw-colored continues to quiver silently. Someone a little way off in the trees moans. Perry and another body sprawl unmoving. The fifth has fled.

"Oh Uncle, what have you done?"

Buck materializes from the shadows. "It was self-defense," he says, his eyes wide. He rakes his hands through his hair nervously as he surveys the battlefield before him. "You have witnesses. It was self-defense."

Uncle pulls me to my feet. His long shirt hangs to my knees. My trampled clothing cascades in streamers on the ground.

"We have to get her out of here. She needs help." Snake hovers over Marjorie.

"Fireman carry," Thorn suggests, and Buck immediately links arms with him. Uncle lifts Marjorie's body into the sling Buck and Thorn have formed while I collect Marjorie's clothes and trail behind. Uncle puts his arm around my shoulders and my trembling subsides.

"We'll send help soon," I call to the dim forms of Perry's gang, in case any of them are conscious and can register my words. I wonder how many will die this night.

We emerge from the forest and Buck and Thorn carry Marjorie to Nelson's house. We enter without knocking and they place Marjorie gently on the couch. June gasps at the sight of me covered in blood.

"This isn't my blood," I reassure her. "Not most of it, anyway." I have not allowed myself to fully comprehend the carnage Uncle left behind in the forest. The blood makes it real.

Nelson covers Marjorie with a blanket. "Whose blood is it then?" he asks.

"We need to get help for Marjorie," I say. Indoors, in the light, I see a gash on Marjorie's head. "They hit her with a rock."

"Who? Who hit her?" June demands. She crosses to Marjorie and examines the cut in the girl's scalp. Caked blood clings to Marjorie's face.

"I have to go," Uncle announces. "I killed some of those men who tried to hurt Lena." That's how he phrases it. They tried to hurt me. He prevented them from gang raping us, in truth.

"Where?" Nelson asks. "How many?"

"I don't know how many," Uncle answers.

"On the forest road," Thorn informs.

"They need help. We need a doctor at the forest road right away," I tell Nelson.

"I have to call an ambulance for Marjorie," June announces. "She's out cold."

"Here are her clothes." I thrust the bundle at June.

"I'll put them on her before the ambulance arrives," June says, untangling the bundle and then realizing it is cut to shreds.

Uncle instructs Buck and Thorn, "You guys stay here. You didn't do anything. I'm the one who did the shooting. It was my gun. Just tell the police what happened."

"Where are you going?" Buck asks.

"I don't know," Uncle replies. He heads for the door.

"We should go with you," Thorn says worriedly.

"No you shouldn't. I already have a police record. I already screwed up. You guys are young. You have stuff to do. You're not in trouble. Just walk away," Uncle entreats his buddies.

"Wait." Nelson grabs Uncle's arm urgently. "Listen. Let the tribal police bring you in. We don't want the city police out here. They get crazy and they don't think. They just bust skulls. We can do this without anyone else getting hurt."

Uncle shakes his head. "I don't think so. I need to go." He's in the doorway, about to flee. Nelson's words bounce off him like marbles flung at a metal wall.

I race over to him, wrap him in my arms, and squeeze him tight. "Uncle Sammy, I love you."

"I can't remember anyone ever telling me that," he replies gruffly. "I love you too." He smiles so deeply that even his bones smile, and then he releases me and melts into the night with Buck and Thorn trailing tentatively behind.

Nelson remains on the porch, gazing after them. His shoulders sag. "The young people don't listen to the elders," he says to no one in particular.

June hands me a towel and a washcloth and sends me to take a shower. "We can't tell where you're hurt until you wash off that blood," she says. She hands me a shirt and a skirt to put on after I clean up.

"What about Marjorie?" I ask with concern. "And the guys in the forest?"

"I'm calling an ambulance right now," June replies.

In the shower, I can't banish the image of Perry with the bullet in his forehead from my mind. His face hovers above me, as if I still lie underneath him on the forest road. I don't understand exactly what happened back there. I lean my forehead against the cold tile of the shower and sob. Where does bad energy originate? How does it persist? Why can't people make it go away?

I scrub myself with June's lemon soap. I rinse off and step from the shower. I dry my bruised body gingerly and don June's clothing. I fold Uncle's bloodstained shirt tenderly and tuck it under my arm. Looking in the mirror, I cautiously touch the swelling on my cheek where Perry hit me. There is a small cut on my cheekbone where the skin split.

The moment I return to the living room, Erica runs to me and bursts into tears. Erica pats me all over. "Look at your cheek." Erica touches it gently. "June, we need ice for Lena's cheek."

Marjorie's mother sits next to her daughter on the couch. June has managed to get some clothes onto Marjorie, who moans softly as she begins to regain consciousness.

Odysseus appears in the doorway, breathless. He winces at the sight of my cheek. "I called the police," he announces to the room at large. "They should be here any minute."

Nelson steps backward as if struck a physical blow and slaps the palm of his hand hard on a doorframe. "What the hell'd you do that for?" he shouts at Odysseus.

Odysseus casts a bewildered glance around the room. "A crime was committed. Helen and her friend were assaulted. I called the police. That's what people do."

"Idiot. We have a tribal police. They are the first line," Nelson bellows in fury. "We don't *invite* the city police onto the Rez unless it's a 'let's-all-get-along' picnic or some-such nonsense."

"I'm sorry," Odysseus apologizes, taken aback, "I didn't realize. I thought I was helping."

"You thought. White people call the police. Brown people avoid the police," Nelson informs him bitterly.

Two ambulances pull into the driveway, one behind the other.

Erica and I step out onto the porch. I hold an ice pack against my throbbing cheek. Erica calls to the ambulance paramedics who jump out of the first ambulance, "In here."

I walk to the second ambulance and point to the forest road, describing where they will find the ones Uncle shot.

Police sirens wail in the distance.

Book 19: Beth
Yopika Bapa, 1985

I gaze upward at the sky filled with dazzling stars. The stars would guide me if I needed to flee somewhere, but I don't need to go anywhere. I am home.

I hear Max on the porch exchanging words with Sammy. I recognize the urgency in their voices. I have heard this urgency before and I lost my son to it. Max hurtles through my door like a spear, propelled by news he will not share. "Going to the tribal office, Aunt Beth. Back soon."

I am quick when I want to be. I grab his arm and lock it in my grasp. He starts to speak, then he looks into my eyes, and he knows I am going with him whether he wants me to or not. My Jessie. I am going with you into it this time.

They think I am crazy, that I am confused, because I call him Jessie. "She thinks Max is her dead son," they say. Let them think what they want. I don't care. I know he isn't my son, who came from my body and nursed at my breast. He is the spirit of my son. Jessie is in him. Anyone who knew Jessie would recognize this, but there is no one living who knew Jessie well enough to recognize it.

Max walks fast and I struggle to keep stride.

Hera stands on the top step of the tribal office, hugging a burgundy-colored sweater around herself, eyes spilling with worry. "They locked themselves in the conference room."

"Who's with him?" Max asks.

"Buck and Thorn," Hera answers. "They have guns."

They have guns. I shiver.

"Stay with Hera," Max orders me. But I clamp my hand like a vise on Max's arm and will not release my grip. I understand the new language, but I cannot speak it. I say in Kapa, "I'm going with you into it this time." Of course Max doesn't understand the words, only the hand locked on his arm he understands. He takes me with him. He cannot shake me off.

"Uncle, it's Max." He knocks on the door, tries the locked doorknob. "Let me in. I want to talk to you. It's just me." Then he adds, "and Aunt Beth."

The door unlocks, we are admitted. The door is locked again. They do have guns.

"What the hell happened out there?" Max demands.

Sammy is agitated, jittery, practically incoherent. Buck is young, almost as young as Max, and his eyes are full with the terror of whatever he has seen this night. The three of them breathe hard. They are jumpy. I recognize the hand of violence passing over the Bapa. The Angel of Death. Which of these men will leave this room breathing and which will be carried out like my Jessie? He had so much good in him. Good that leaked out on the ground and soaked into the earth. There is no happy ending to the story of a people slaughtered to an inch of annihilation.

"Sons-of-bitches tried to rape her," Sammy says through clenched teeth. "Would've done it too. Maybe killed her. Not in my family. Not now. I'm a man now and I don't let that shit happen in my family. You hear?" He waves his gun around. His heart growls. "I'm a man."

"You're a man," Max repeats, soothingly. "Explain to me. What happened?"

Thorn brushes his thick hair off his forehead with a trembling hand before speaking. "It was that guy Perry. Remember him? Like he was gonna be somebody, except he turned into a big zero. He and his buddies tried to gang rape your sister. They would've done it. They would've hurt her too." A proud glint lingers in his eye for a second. "Snake stopped 'em. Stopped 'em dead so to speak." Thorn chuckles nervously.

Max asks incredulously, "You killed Perry Hoepper?"

"He might not be completely dead," Buck replies.

"Probably is, though," Sammy interjects matter-of-factly.

He's proud that he killed a man. That's not our way. That's not our people. This is where violence leads, to more violence. Visited upon our ancestors. Unable to forgive, we visit it upon others. We visit it upon ourselves again and again. The violence breeds and swells inside us. It is inside Sammy. It is the violence that climbed inside Jessie and took him. But now my Jessie has climbed inside Max and he has not taken the violence in there with him. Only pure, unadulterated Jessie is in there. The best part of him. The heart.

"Is Lena OK?" Max asks.

"Yeah. I stopped them before they could hurt her," Sammy's lip curls in a satisfied smile.

Sirens sound directly outside the building. Blue and red lights flash through the windows.

I can tell we are about to crash on the rocks.

"Put the guns down, please," Max pleads urgently. "Meet with the police and explain what happened."

What is he thinking? Those ones in the uniforms have no use for explanations.

Sammy looks Max in the eye. "I have a felony record. I'm not allowed to have a gun."

"There's nothing else you can do," Max points out with a note of desperation in his voice.

"He's right," Buck agrees. "We're in a box."

The police pound on the door. Like on the TV they shout, "Put down your weapons and come out with your hands up and no one will get hurt." Sammy trains his gun on the door. Buck and Thorn hold guns in their hands, which hang at their sides.

A minute becomes an hour.

Sammy looks straight into my soul with the eyes of a small boy who is unable to protect the ones he loves from grown men. Sammy says softly, so that we must strain to hear him, "No one will ever again harm her while there is breath in me. Lena is safe. And Penny. And Carla."

The door explodes like a piñata full of police officers. Sammy turns, Thorn and Buck turn, and they hold guns, which I think they forget they have in their hands. A police officer hollers to put the guns down and they would have, in a minute, in a hair of a second more, but first and last and forever Sammy howls with a howl that reaches back twelve thousand years.

The police officers don't hear the years or the despair or the longing for another way, they only hear the howl. They hear what sounds to them like a war cry.

Thorn and Buck follow their reflexes and raise their arms in defense and in their hands are guns. In Sammy's hand is a gun. The police officers shoot. They fail to notice that Max does not have a gun. But I take care of that oversight. I am so fast. I step in front of Max. This is what I am here for. They will not kill my

Jessie again. I wish I could have saved them all; all of our beautiful, sad, outraged young men.

I touch the spot of blood on my sweater and I smile.

I am grateful to stand in this room in this moment to protect one of our native sons. A good one. A keeper. Jessie. Max.

My heart fills with gratitude.

My heart fills with forgiveness.

My heart fills with love.

My heart fills and fills and fills; and it will not empty.

Not ever.

It will burst.

And now I can lay these old bones down.

Book 20: Penelope
A Bed and Breakfast in an Undisclosed Location, 1985

I am hiding from the empty space where Athena used to be. In the center of a park down the street from the Blackberry Bed and Breakfast Inn is a fountain where birds bathe in the water. I watch flocks of bright yellow-and-black (with just a dot of red) cedar waxwings dip and dance in the fountain as they stopover on their way south. This land once belonged to Natives. Even if we got the land back, the culture would still be decimated. We are all hostages to history. The world has become tangled in a complexity of our creation, a complexity that eventually will strangle us humans. I imagine the flowers and forests will remain, outliving us, powerful in their vegetable wisdom, resilience, and adaptability. It comforts me to think that when humans no longer walk the earth, persistent nature will endure. I sometimes tell the trees, "Be patient. Soon we will be gone and you will have it to yourselves again."

After watching the birds bathe and take wing, I return to the Blackberry. In the parking lot, I recognize Erica's green Honda. I hate her for loving me so fiercely that she can't restrain herself. Leave me alone, my love. I'll return to you when I'm ready. Leave me alone with my anguish. I fight the urge to slip under the front porch to hide; to crouch down in the damp underside of the building; unseen, a wild animal.

Erica steps out onto the wide, gray porch with the white railing. She has seen me approach. Nelson hovers at her elbow. Reinforcements? Moral support? They walk reluctantly down the steps toward me, dragging their feet. Reluctantly? If they don't want to see me then why have they come? My heart hammers in my throat. I told Erica not to contact me unless there was an emergency. What now? My children? I don't want to know. Leave me ignorant.

Erica takes my hand in hers. "Hey babe. We miss you."

No words come to me. That's OK. Erica will understand. She turns to Nelson, who puts his foot up on the bottom step and looks at me.

"We need you at the Rez," Nelson says quietly.

"What happened? Is everyone OK?" I ask desperately. If everyone was OK, they wouldn't be here. I'm afraid to voice the names of my children. Oh please, not my children.

"Max and Lena are OK," Erica assures me quickly.

My legs go weak with relief.

"Some guys tried to rape Lena," Nelson starts.

I suck in my breath. Erica quickly adds, "They didn't do it. Sammy stopped them." I think it odd that she refers to him as Sammy when she usually calls him Snake.

"Sammy stopped them," Nelson continues, "by shooting them. He killed two of them, paralyzed another. The rest ran."

"What guys? How many?"

"Enough," Erica says. "They ambushed Marjorie and Lena on the forest road. These guys gave Marjorie a pretty bad blow to the head. One of them was Perry Hoepper, the same one who used to call Lena names and bully her at school."

Nelson says flatly, "He's dead. That Hoepper."

"Lena is OK?" I need to hear it again.

"Sammy stopped them," Erica reiterates.

"Sammy?"

Nelson clears his throat. "Sammy is dead. Police shot him."

"The police?" I can't make sense of this. Sammy can't be dead. I just drank a bottle of Jack Daniels with him a few nights ago.

Erica begins to cry softly. Barely audibly she says, "and Aunt Beth."

"The police shot Aunt Beth," Nelson clarifies, but there is nothing clear about this statement. Why would anyone shoot Aunt Beth? She is the most harmless creature on the planet. She is one turnip shy of a vegetable patch when it comes to being benign.

"Where?" I mean what part of her body. "Is she in pain?" I ask.

Erica sobs and Nelson puts his arm around her. "They shot her dead."

"Are you sure?" I ask. It's a stupid question. I will remember it later and wonder at myself for asking it. I simply can't believe Nelson's words. They make no sense. I am already struggling to remake my universe with Athena missing and here they tell me that Sammy and Aunt Beth are also gone.

"The police shot her by accident," Nelson continues.

"How can someone get shot by accident by the police?" My voice rises. Nelson's words sound irrational to me.

"They were aiming for Max and she stepped in front of him," Erica explains between sobs.

"She saw what was coming." Nelson shakes his head.

"How did Max wind up in the line of fire?" I can't imagine Max with a gun.

Nelson sighs. "It's complicated. The police misunderstood what was going on. Aunt Beth shielded Max and saved his life. The police killed Sammy and they also killed Buck and Thorn."

My eyes are dry. It has not sunk in. I don't realize in my heart that I will never see gentle Aunt Beth and fierce Sammy again. I don't fully understand that Podon's grandson Thorn, whom he adores, is also lost; and Buck. The truth must sink its stakes into my bones before I will feel it.

Aunt Beth. My mother's sister. She took me in when my family imploded. My Aunt Beth is gone? I'm truly an orphan now. There is no reason or order in the universe. Only chaos. No redemption. I thought I could sneak away for a moment of respite from the drama, and what happens? Another bomb goes off. I'm so weary of living with the ongoing accumulation of losses. But there is no rest for the weary. Another massacre has taken place at the blood-drenched Bapa. When will it end? Oh when will it end?

"We need you at home." Erica weeps inconsolably.

"Give me a few minutes to pack my things and check out." I clench my teeth and reach for the railing. Erica places a restraining hand on my arm. I look at her questioningly and her eyes fill with such desperate fear that it takes my breath away. "There's something else," she says. What else can possibly have happened? Her voice splits when she hits a dryness in her throat as she informs me, "Lena found Odysseus in Berkeley. He's very much alive and well."

I sit down on the steps abruptly. "Odysseus?" I look from Nelson to Erica, trying to comprehend this further news. "How?" I ask.

Erica sits on the step next to me, sobbing and shivering, hugging her knees to her chest.

"He's waiting for you at the Rez," Nelson informs. "He's the one who called the town police out to the Bapa last night," he adds, unable to keep the bitterness out of his voice. "He had no idea." Nelson's dark eyes flash with fury. "We could have handled it. If the tribal police had dealt with it first then…." He shrugs.

"If," Erica chokes out, "is not what happened." Erica is dissolving right before my eyes. I hold my hand up to stop Nelson from saying more, and I take Erica in my arms. "It's OK, baby, it's OK," I croon to her.

"He's your husband," she stutters. "What will you…?"

"He left a long time ago. I have a life and he is not part of it."

"You don't understand." Erica hiccups. "He tried to come back to you and he couldn't. He still loves you. So do I."

"As I love you, Erica." Which is true; but I am relieved that she cannot see how my heart leaps in secret at the news of his return.

I welcome the silence and the indifferent scenery passing outside my window as I drive to the Bapa, which I find eerily quiet upon my arrival. Yellow crime-scene tape that says DO NOT CROSS surrounds the tribal office. I wonder, morbidly, if they have cleaned the blood splatters from the conference room.

Erica meets me at the car window when I pull into the driveway. "Lena and Max are at Nelson and June's."

I go with Erica immediately to see Lena and find her in the kitchen with June, sipping tea and drawing. High on her cheekbone she has a swollen bruise fanning into her eye. Her eyes well with tears as she greets me. "Ama." I embrace her and she cries softly for a minute. "I'm OK," she assures me. "Just sad about Aunt Beth and Sammy and the others."

"I don't think Aunt Beth would regret what she did," I tell Lena. "She would do it again if she could. Where's Max?"

"In back with Nelson." She motions to the back porch.

I touch the bruise on her cheek with my thumb. "You sure you're OK?"

"Yeah, Aunt June is taking good care of me."

June nods in my direction, says nothing, doesn't need to.

Lena continues, "Remember how he used to call me Injun girl when I was little, said he would get me? I thought it was just talk. Unpleasant, ignorant trash and nothing more. 'I'm going to get you Injun girl,' he'd say. Until that once when I finally complained to the principal and they gave him a warning. He had it coming to him, Ama. Maybe not getting shot dead, but he deserved punishment."

"Perry?"

"Yeah," she confirms, "Perry. He started it."

"It started two hundred years ago, Lena. Perry and your uncle are the most recent casualties," I reply angrily.

"OH," June voices in affirmation.

"I know, Ama, I know that."

Recklessness. Lack of respect. Violence. No recognition of the sanctity of life. A country built on genocide, enslavement, and bloodshed. That is the basis for most countries; and how can that possibly lead to a positive outcome?

I go to my son; to see him, to touch him and reassure myself that he is whole. He is on the porch carving pumpkins. He flashes me a grin that makes me weak with relief. He's not a casualty this time. I am so grateful for this fact that it is all I can do to restrain myself from dropping to my knees. He walks to me slowly and folds me in his arms. His embrace envelopes me. He is a man grown. The tears that have eluded me flow. Not tears of loss or grief; tears of relief.

"It's OK, Ama, it's OK now," he hushes me and rubs my back while I weep, so grateful to have him warm and alive in my arms. "Aunt Beth took a bullet for me," he says; the wonder of it and the gratitude reflected in his voice. His flannel shirt rubs softly against my skin. He is tall and sturdy. Firm and strong. Thank you Aunt Beth for your sacrifice, for giving me back my son. Forgive me for ever thinking you had wasted your life.

After I have seen my children and reassured myself that they are well, my thoughts turn to their father.

"Where is he?" I ask Erica.

"At our house. I'll stay here with the children."

"I'll be back soon." I brush her cheek with my hand.

She watches from Nelson's porch as I walk up the road to Athena's house, now my house, to see my husband who has returned to me fifteen years too late.

Odysseus sits in a chair in my living room, doing nothing, waiting for me, which is an activity unto itself for him. He stands when I enter.

We reshape our image of one another.

He left when I was a mere girl and he has returned to a woman. Since last I saw him, I have waded through desperation, depression, shame, loss, grief, discovery, recovery, a college education, exhaustion, motherhood, anger, protest, and triumph. I have raised children, buried elders, fought city hall, found a loving partner, reconnected with my Tribe, and made a difference for struggling families through my work. I have wrestled with my demons. I am no longer that girl he left behind and it shows.

He appears physically strong and muscular. Not much gray infringes on his golden hair. His eyes have changed dramatically. They are bottomless and flecked with tragedy. They have become the eyes of a man tormented, a man bereft. I don't want to hear about the terrible things he experienced that changed those eyes.

He approaches me with his hand upraised to touch my face. I flinch. He steps back and sits in the chair again abruptly, covers his face with his hands, and sobs.

Embarrassed, I sit silently across from him on the couch and fold my hands in my lap, waiting for him to get a grip. I have talked to this man in my head for fifteen years. Here he is in the flesh and I can't think of a single thing to say. Perhaps I have been talking to myself all these years.

"I'm so sorry," he chokes out. "There was a reason."

"I'm listening," I reply, shocked at the cold-stone tone of my voice. My anger rears its ugly and unwelcome head. Do I have the capacity to let go of my anger for this heartbroken man in front of me? I'm sure nothing he can say will convince me that there remains in him a substantial measure of the husband I married those many years ago.

I am wrong.

"If it had not happened to me, I would not believe it," he begins. "Do you know about the Time of the Colonels in Greece?"

I shake my head negative.

He continues. "I didn't think so." He gazes out the window into Athena's fall garden overflowing with squashes, pumpkins, kale, collards, onions, and carrots. For a moment, from the side, he resembles the man I first met in Athens. When he turns back to me, his eyes betray the lash of the years he spent wandering. He wears his age in his face. "It's quite simple. I was arrested and tortured by a military dictatorship in Greece. They detained me in prison for many years, during which time I had no communication with the outside. My mother returned your letters in my absence.

I could explain why but what's the point? Excuses are lame. It happened. After they released me from prison, it took me some time to regain my health. My mother never told me what she had done. I worked, saved money, and returned to look for you. I couldn't find you. I went back to Athens empty-handed. Many years later, my brother told me the truth about our mother sending those letters back. After that I moved to Berkeley. I had the opportunity to buy our old house and I took advantage of it. I lived in the house and waited. Until one day...." He looks down at those magnificent strong and gentle hands of his; he takes a deep breath. "Helen walked through my door."

I digest his story in silence.

"Talk to me. What are you thinking?" he asks.

I imagine a powerful roaring god rearing up from the sea and slashing at us in his wrath, orchestrating the precise devastation of our lives. We humans are precarious beings, balanced on the fragile thread of existence. It's a wonder any of us survives at all; each one of us a tentative miracle.

"Look, it's true." He stands and unzips his pants. I avert my eyes and protest.

"Do not be so modest. We are still married, are we not? I want to show you the scars from prison. The proof." It's true that we are still married. He rolls his pants down to reveal a long jagged mark on the inside of his thigh. It looks as though a beast with tusks gored him, like the slash of a wild boar. But a man, not a wild animal, did this to his flesh. "And these," he begins to open his shirt to show me other scars, proof, the tracks of torture.

"Please. I don't want to see." After the years of anger, confusion, and self-blame, I arrive at the truth. He did not abandon me. We were robbed. The love I trusted was real and he has suffered as I have suffered. In fact, he has suffered more. I had the children while he missed seeing them grow up. I found my Tribe, my true family, while he lost his family. I found meaningful work and a community, while he wandered alone enduring torture, loss, grief. His hands are empty and mine are full. I pity him.

"I should have stayed with you," he asserts vehemently. "I should never have gone to Greece. To leave a wife with two small children and go into the uncertainty of a country in the midst of political upheaval. What was I thinking?"

"You were thinking of your father." The sound of my voice startles him.

"I wasn't thinking at all. Ironically, I never saw my father again. I couldn't save him. I acted as if I was impermeable, like a god, like I could walk through unscathed and immune to the grinding teeth of history. It was a fantasy. I can't begin to imagine what you did to survive with those children when I didn't return."

"Maybe one day I will tell you what I did," I say, simply stating a fact, as the bitterness I spent years cultivating begins to dissolve.

"Forgive me."

"What am I forgiving?" I ask, because his account has truly diffused my anger.

"If I had done things differently, I would not have left you destitute."

If he had done things differently. I consider this alternate reality for a moment. I might not have found my people or returned to my Tribe and my land to raise my children in their Native culture. I might not have found Athena and grown in the shadow of her spirit to become the Kapa woman I have become. Would I have discovered my calling teaching children? Would I know the story of my Tribe? If so, I doubt I would have become the keeper of the story as I have. I would certainly never have fallen in love with my precious Erica. I am rich beyond measure.

Odysseus sits next to me on the couch, trembling. He puts his hand against my jaw and neck, fingers splayed. I do not flinch from his hand this time. He runs his thumb over my lips. The way my blood leaps to his touch terrifies me. Desire overwhelms me and I realize that I can't handle this, not with Sammy and Aunt Beth dead, the Tribe in crisis, Athena gone. Not with the trauma Lena and Max and Erica have just endured. I will shatter.

I take hold of his wrist and stay his hand. "I can't do this right now."

"Tell me what to do."

"Go home."

"My home is wherever you are."

"I belong to this Tribe and we have a tragedy unfolding here. I have a partner. Erica. You can't just insinuate yourself into my life. People I have lived with for many years need my attention. I'm part of a community that has no connection to the relationship from which you set sail those many years ago. Go back to Berkeley. I'll come see you when I'm ready."

"When will you come?"

"I said when I'm ready."

He reaches into his pocket and removes a mauve envelope. He passes it to me. "During the years when I thought I had lost you forever, I took a lover. When I left her to return to California, she gave me this letter and requested that I give it to you should I find you. It was the only thing she asked of me. How could I refuse?"

I take the envelope. "Have you read it?"

He shakes his head negative. "The seal remains unbroken."

I turn it over in my hand and see an old-fashioned red wax seal with the word CALYPSO stamped in it.

I stand. He rises without taking his pleading eyes from mine. He wraps me in his arms and I do not resist. When he kisses me I lose myself to him. For a moment I am a young girl and he is my heaven and earth. He kisses me deeply, thoughtfully, with penetrating resolve, with tenderness and yearning and the white heat at the center of a star. He leaves me breathless and retreats through the door, climbs into his car, and starts the engine.

He looks up through the windshield at me where I stand on the front porch. Our eyes lock. He smiles. It's a delicious smile that starts in his eyes and spreads in a wave across his face. He backs out of the driveway and disappears up the road.

He is a loving man, blameless and righteous. He deserved better than what befell him. He still deserves better.

I have it in my power to grant it to him.

After he leaves, I slit open the mauve envelope and remove the letter from its sleeve. It is penned in black ink on pale gold paper in conscientiously rounded penmanship.

Book 21: Calypso

Penelope:

If you are reading this, then he found you. Believe his story. He has suffered enough. The torture of rejection from you would supersede all others he has suffered. It would kill him. I write this letter because I love him and for that reason I wish for his sake that you believe him, that you take him back. If I can't keep him with me, at least I wish for his happiness. This is what happened. I tell it to you woman to woman.

Nearly seven years ago he began sharing my bed and never for a moment stopped thinking about you. You might ask how I lived with that, why I kept on with him. I have asked myself the same question. The answer is simple and obvious. Would you have given up any of the time you had with him before he left, even if you had known he would leave? You understand then why I would redo every minute of it, even knowing I would lose him in the end.

I met him when I was nineteen. He was larger than life. You, of all women, know exactly what I mean. He had been out of prison for a couple of years by then. Many people thought of me as his project. In those days he had forgotten how to smile. He smiled with his mouth only and not with his eyes. I fell in love first with the intensity of those eyes. He suffered unspeakable horror, wandered through hell, and survived. He is a man who kept his integrity in a godless place. He is a man who could not be broken by the inhumanity that men inflict on each other, but who was broken by the loss of a woman.

He found comfort in my arms. I don't care that you don't want to hear about our lovemaking. I want to tell it. He was an imaginative, exciting, and uninhibited lover. Water play. Fancy underwear. That trick he does in the hammock. Flowers, candles, romance. No, don't stop reading. Hear me out. I suspect he thought about you when we made love, although I never asked him if he did. What did it matter anyway? When we made love, we escaped out of ourselves, out of time. I could do anything in the world if I could go home afterward to lie down in that bed beside him. Remember how he made a woman feel like that?

I write to confirm that what he tells you is true, although it sounds unbelievable. He returned to Athens during a shameful chapter of our history, what we call the Time of the Colonels. His father had been arrested. Our people were foolish; we thought the colonels would not last long. Dictatorial government in Greece? The situation seemed absurd. It became less absurd as the terror spread and families lost loved ones. Our Odysseus returned like a raging bull, determined to free his father. He spoke to the international press, embarrassed the government, aired the dirty laundry, and swiftly got himself disappeared. They locked him up,

*made him wish he was not a principled man, made him wish he
was dead.*

*I won't tell you what his mother was because I try not to
speak ill of people. I try not to generate negative energy. I'll tell
you this: you can thank that woman for taking him from you.
His mother erased you from the family while he was in prison.
She turned back your letters and cut you out like a tumor. She
preferred to lose her son to fascists than to a heathen wife. Maybe
she thought he would survive prison and then she could marry
him off to a Greek Orthodox. That woman does not know what
love is. I know what love is.*

*Odysseus went into prison in 1970. He did not see the
light of day again until 1973, when he finally had a shred of
luck and was included in a sweeping amnesty for political
prisoners. After his release, he first had to regain his health.
After that he found a job and worked long enough to earn his
passage to California. He couldn't find you. Where did you go?
He tracked down old friends and acquaintances in Berkeley, and
tried, unsuccessfully, to gain help from local government agencies.
He even dug up some crazy aunt of yours in an insane asylum.
She told him that if he couldn't find you it meant you didn't want
to be found. That's when he gave up. If you are reading this,
consider it a miracle.*

*I met him when he returned, hopeless, to Athens. Don't
be jealous. He thought he had lost you. And I was irresistible,
with my hair in a hundred golden braids. I could sing like the*

wind in the trees. I smelled of cedar and citron. He floated to me on his raft of pain, shipwrecked on the island of his desire for me. I gave him pleasure and a place to rest from the world. I gave him the desire to live. I loved his hands. I loved his eyes. He has a splendid body. Other women envied me. Ignorant women. He was damaged and I paid a price.

He told me about you of course. He made it no secret that he longed for you. He wept over the loss; a grown man, built like Atlas, his head in his hands. I knew he would never be mine. He himself warned me, told me he would make me unhappy, that he would leave me in the end. I took what I could get with no regrets for a single moment I spent with him.

You have to understand that I was not always Calypso. I became Calypso because he feared for my future. He engineered my career. That's why they say I was his project. Because he made me famous. He knew the right people and just how to go about it. Singer, dancer, high fashion model. My name became a household word in Greece. My face is plastered on billboards and in magazines. Odysseus made me into a celebrity, a goddess in a land that knows how to worship goddesses. Wherever I go, people recognize me, gawk dumbstruck, ask for autographs. I am Calypso. Men dream of me with desire. Women copy my look: my braids, my clothes, the silver vine bracelet I wear on my upper arm. I would have been so ordinary, obscure, undiscovered, forgotten, if not for the clever work of Odysseus.

It was Hermes, his brother, who ended my years with Odysseus. They went drinking one night and Hermes got drunk. He told his brother how their mother had returned the letters from you, how she had refused to write to you to tell you what had happened to your husband. She forbade the family from writing. She wanted you to believe that he abandoned you. That night Odysseus made love to me more tenderly than he ever had, and afterward he told me of his intent to return to California. The next day he left the island of my embrace. I asked him to take this letter to you, should he find you.

In the future I will choose desire over love. Desire is more powerful and gives the type of pleasure that I crave. Love is too painful, unpredictable, uncontrollable. If I learned anything from Odysseus, I learned that.

Do not contact me. I have moved on. I commanded him not to write to me when he left. I fear that if I open a letter from him I will catch the scent of him on my fingers and I will be undone. I took what I could have from Odysseus. I am grateful. I have no regrets. I walked away with fame and fortune, my image, my reputation, my very self. This is my truth: Nothing, not even death, can take from me the dances I danced with the one I loved.

I have seen his suffering and have longed to ease it. Please, whatever the circumstances of your life, find a way to take him back to you. Otherwise, the torturers win.
Sincerely,
Calypso

Book 22: Penelope
Berkeley, 1985

Time is the smile of a child in a photo album, a circle of dancers in the grass, the green-gold light of the evening, a feather on the road. Time transforms intentions to yearnings and converts joy to wistfulness. It brings unexpected moments of startling recognition. Time is the mother of memory and the farmer of the familiar. It swallows me whole and spits me out with a strange face in the mirror. It surprises me when I bump into myself coming around the corner of yesterday. And time sits in the passenger seat as I park my car in front of the Berkeley house in which I grieved and panicked at the loss of my husband long ago when I was a girl.

Despite the rain hammering the earth, Odysseus sits on the porch, wrapped in a warm sweater, waiting for my return, as I once waited for his. When I pull into the driveway, he hurries to the car with an umbrella. "Let me take that," he offers as he reaches for my travel bag in the back seat. I sling my handbag over my shoulder and duck under the umbrella with him. I inhale the fresh scent of the rainy afternoon that clings to his hair and shirt.

He ushers me up the steps under the protection of the umbrella. It's not raining that hard. The umbrella isn't that necessary. Nevertheless, he fusses and bustles.

Inside, he sets my bag down near the door and turns to shake the rain out of his umbrella, which he leans against the railing on the porch. He has lit a fire in the fireplace and I gravitate to its warmth. I put my handbag on a chair. "This fire is nice," I say.

"Especially on a rainy afternoon." He smiles. "Do you want the tour?"

"Sure."

"Well, this is the living room." He laughs nervously as he waves his arm to encompass the room. When we lived here together, we had sparse furnishings picked up at flea markets and thrift shops. He has furnished the house with expensive antiques. Framed art prints from around the world decorate the walls. A print of calla lilies hangs above the fireplace. An arresting batik of African dancers demands attention above the couch. A large pottery urn stands in one corner. He leads me into the kitchen, which boasts all the cooking gear a gourmet could desire.

"You must like to cook."

"It's a hobby of mine, and I prepared a special treat for this evening." He's embarrassingly eager to please.

We take a peek at the back yard while remaining inside the shelter of the house. Then we go to the bedroom.

I whirl around to look at him the instant I see it. "The bed."

"Still here. I didn't believe it either. I couldn't wait for you to see." He built this bed inside the bedroom and it couldn't be moved without tearing it apart since it wouldn't fit through the door. Subsequent occupants must have chosen to keep it in tact. Seeing it is like seeing a ghost. In the heavy wooden headboard, Odysseus had carved an enormous olive tree, with branches outspread. That tree burns in my memory. We had a purple, ivory, gold, and silver quilt on the bed. I sold the quilt for grocery money before I left the house. I see a similar quilt on the bed. I recognize the quilting pattern. It's called sunburst. This particular one has at least fifteen shades of purple and five of gold in it, as well as silver and ivory colors.

"I commissioned the quilt." Odysseus clears his throat. "I couldn't remember exactly what we had. This one was made by an expert quilter."

I run my fingers over it. "Dita would love to see this. It's more beautiful than the old one."

"Nothing is as beautiful as the old one," he says, his voice husky.

The rain pours down in torrents, as if threatening to wash us away as irrevocably as a sandcastle. One of the things I loved the most about this room was that I could hear the rain on the roof. In a rush, I remember lying in this bed with Lena and Max when they were babies. I made love to Odysseus in this bed, in other rain. "I have often thought about this bed," I say faintly, as I try to banish from my mind the image of his splendid younger self, his firm and virile body kneeling in this bed between my legs. "I have imagined other people, strangers, using it while ignorant of its secrets."

"What are its secrets?"

"That my husband built it for me with his two hands. That we conceived our son in it. That when we, when my husband…" My lungs feel so flat that I can barely force air into them.

He takes my face in his hands and I lace my fingers in his golden curls. Our souls join within a still-familiar, deep kiss; as if we are exchanging vows. The kiss goes on for some time. When we separate, breathless, he says, "When I was in prison, I would close my eyes and transport myself to this room in my mind. I would picture you and I would picture myself touching you. I wondered if you could feel it. I wondered if the power of my love was that strong."

I brush the tears off my cheeks. "I didn't feel it." I touch his lips with the tips of my fingers. "I wondered if anything I thought I had experienced was real. If not for the children, I would have thought I had imagined you."

"I am very real and I am here now." He brushes my hair away from my face. "I've cooked you a traditional Greek meal." He leads me into the kitchen by the hand.

"Can I do anything to help?"

"Sit. You can enjoy, and admire my skill in the kitchen, that's what you can do."

"I have a talent for food admiration," I say with a laugh. He has set the table for two with candles, flowers, and a bottle of wine. I light the candles. He brings plates loaded with stuffed grape leaves; *spanikopita*; a salad of tomatoes, Greek olives, feta cheese, and fresh oregano; a cucumber salad; and homemade rosemary bread. The flowery fragrance of the oregano mingled with that of olive oil fills the air. The cucumbers crunch crisply and the *spanikopita* melts in my mouth.

"I feel transported to Athens."

"That means I did my job. I have baklava for dessert. I confess I bought it. I didn't make it myself."

"I won't complain about store-bought baklava."

He pokes an olive with his fork and before putting it into his mouth he asks, "So what's going on up there? I've seen a few things mentioned in the news. It looks like you've become a national flashpoint for Native American rights."

"You really want to hear the saga?"

"I do. I want to learn everything about you, your Tribe, and my children. I have missed too much. I need to catch up. I want to be here now." He puts his fork down altogether and crosses his arms on his chest. "Please. Tell me."

Where to begin? "It has been a bit of a media circus, which is OK in some ways because it makes it possible for us to draw attention to issues we would like people to confront. It's not OK because the timing is off. Our people are in pain, after recent events." I think about Podon, who has not spoken since the death of his grandson Thorn. Blustery, irascible Podon. Silent as a cave. "One of our elders lost his grandson. He's not doing well. Normally, he would have given the media people an earful."

"About what?" Odysseus has resumed eating while listening intently.

"It's a story that's about one verse short of an epic when it comes to length." I pause. Odysseus waits. "For many years we've worked to change the name of Hoepper to Bataka. The town is named Hoepper after a notorious rapist and murderer responsible for the slaughter of my Tribe."

"What does Bataka mean?"

"It means bear. The lake is called B'Taka Lake because it has a bear's spirit." He looks puzzled and I'm not sure how to explain this to him, so I sidestep his puzzlement for the moment and continue. "Many years ago, we put a proposition on the ballot in a local election to change the name of the town to Bataka. It was voted down. So we did it again. Year after year, for five years. After that, we gave it a rest. It was like rolling a rock uphill. The whole process was about one stick of dynamite short of an attempt to blow up Mount Rushmore when it came to difficulty. And it made us Natives unpopular with a certain element in the town."

"And now?"

"Now we're media darlings. Changing the name of the town and spreading the story of the 1880 massacre of our people has become the politically correct flavor of the month. Our moment has arrived. We didn't even need to press for a vote on it. The city council actually made a decision to change the name all on their own. The signs are coming down. We're officially Bataka. And we are suddenly becoming a destination tourist location, which helps the local economy and all that."

"It seems like money is always the bottom line."

"True, and a shame. But we'll take the name change any way we can get it."

"This should make your Tribe happy."

"Oh, it certainly does. But it doesn't eliminate other internal issues we need to resolve."

"Like?"

I'm chewing a tomato drenched in olive oil and red wine vinegar and a chunk of *spanikopita* that dissolves in butter and spice on my tongue. "This is beyond delicious."

He nods with satisfaction. "I'm glad you like it. Continue."

"No one will set foot in the tribal office. Bad spirit energy because of the shoot-out. So we have to figure out what to do about the building. It's just a pre-fab modular. I'm tempted to suggest that we toss the whole thing into the lake." I laugh wryly.

"That would solve it, I suppose."

"I'm not actually going to suggest it."

"I didn't think you would. Will they listen to any suggestion from you?"

"I do think they would listen to a suggestion from me. I've been sitting with the elders lately. Nelson keeps bringing me along. If I make a viable suggestion, they would hear me."

"More of anything?" Odysseus asks.

I put my fork down on my nearly empty plate. "No more. This is up there as one of the best dinners I have ever had. I'm full. No baklava until later, please."

I take my plate to the sink. "Here," I reach behind, "give me your plate."

Odysseus stands and crosses to me. He has no plate in his hand. I have put mine in the sink. He wraps his arms around me. "Do you remember that evening, here in this kitchen, when the children slept and we ate that chocolate cake with raspberries?" His eyes sparkle.

I laugh. "Of course." That cake had been ecstasy and with each successive, sensual bite I had driven Odysseus more and more wild with desire until he made love to me on the kitchen floor.

"I can't stand this anymore. It's like that cake. Watching you talk, watching you move. Your lips. Your hands. The sweet, graceful lines of your body." When he kisses me I plummet out of time. He has his hands on my bottom and then up my back and then on my breasts and I want his hands exactly where they are. It is no use pretending I have come to him now for any other reason. I am still his wife. We have longed for each other, like shipwrecked swimmers long for land; or even a large enough piece of floating debris to cling to in order to gather strength to swim further.

I unbutton his shirt. My hands seek the touch of him like starved creatures searching for bread. He lifts my shirt over my head and releases my breasts from my bra. We are swimming to each other, we are skin to skin. I cradle his manhood in my palm. Husband from whose loins my beloved children found entry into my womb. Thigh to thigh. Breast to chest. Taut against one another. Enter me again. Fill me. The female scent of my body calls and the seed of my lover replies. Odysseus, you are all the man I have ever desired. We bury new secrets in our marriage bed as the rain pounds and pounds outside the circle of our embrace.

I awake in the dark, floating on the chest of my husband as it rises and falls with his even breathing. He strokes my blue-black hair where it fans out like a bird's wing resting on his skin. I lift my head and search for his face. He turns on the light, which casts a soft amber glow.

"These years apart, I have spoken to you even though you couldn't hear me. I told you about my little struggles and triumphs in great detail." I lay back down on his chest and he resumes stroking my hair. "When you left, it took a long time for me to believe you were gone, that you weren't coming back. It took too long because by the time I believed it, we had hardly any money left. I sold things. Like the car. I was depressed of course. I was scared and depressed and panicked."

He continues to stroke my hair and doesn't interrupt me. I tell him the story of how I found my way to B'Taka Lake and how I found my way back to myself. He will have to wait for stories about his children. As the rain continues to pour down outside our nest, I match the deluge by pouring out words. I am not telling the story of my people or a story I made up out of my head, I am telling the story of me. The words trapped inside for so long tumble down. I can't stop. He strokes my hair and I tell my journey from the day he left until this moment in his arms. The shadows gather. Night encircles us. Odysseus listens.

It's past midnight when the words stop rolling from my tongue. The silence left in place of my words startles us both.

"How about that baklava?" he asks.

"Yes, yes, I'd love a piece." I'm hungry again and the thought of the honey-soaked sweetness of baklava sounds wonderful.

"Here." Odysseus hands me a fluffy white bathrobe from behind the door. He pulls on his jeans with no underwear underneath and I want him all over again. Now. But we're going into the kitchen for baklava. He'll have to be my dessert after dessert. I can hardly believe he is within the realm of my touch.

The rain stays with us through the night as we make love again, more slowly, enjoying the details more. And the rain greets us with its persistent tapping at mid-day when we awake.

Odysseus makes strong coffee with cream and a touch of cocoa and he pours it into large mugs. We retreat with our cocoa-coffee to the bed, our bed, our ship floating on the ocean, far from the chaotic and conflicted din of the peopled world. We have wandered, starved for each other. Now we feast. Denied of the fruit of each other's presence, we have put it up in jars and saved it for this rainy day when we open all the jars.

We swim back to our interrupted marriage.

"I want my life back, my life with you and the children. Nothing else matters to me. The Colonels robbed me of my father. They tried to rob me of you, of my family. I refused to allow them to take my love for you and the children. This belongs to me." He pounds his chest with a closed fist, fierce and determined.

"Much as I tried, I could not stop loving you. Even when I hated you, I loved you," I confess.

"I would give up this house, this job, in a heartbeat to move up there to live with you. You realize that, right?"

"Yes. But this isn't a simple thing. I belong at Yopika Bapa. I belong to a Tribe. And it will take time for them to accept you. Try to understand. Some of my people at the Bapa are angry at you for calling the police that night. Nelson is a forgiving man. You have no idea how forgiving. Just give him time to move past this. Whether you like it or not, he is the father who raised Lena and Max in your absence."

Odysseus bows his head.

"The other thing, of course, is that I'm eight years deep into my relationship with Erica. I love her. I won't quit her." I have asked a difficult thing of Erica. I wonder how much she loves me, if she loves me enough.

"So how do we do this?"

"Carefully. First of all, you can't move to the Rez. Stay here. Keep your job. Your daughter would like to live with you while she's in college. She gets homesick and this would help her."

"That would make me very happy, indeed. But what about you? How will I see you?"

"For now, come up on the weekends, or I will come here. We'll take it slow. My people need time to get to know you, to get used to having you around. Don't rush them. Sometimes they seem as unchanging as a rock."

"And what about us." He points to me and to himself and then swirls his hand in a circle. "And Erica. How can this work?"

"I've given it a lot of thought. Erica and I have given it a lot of thought, and discussion. This isn't going to be easy for any of us. She's willing to make an effort at expanding our family to include you if you're willing to accept her relationship with me on our terms, mine and Erica's."

"What does that mean?"

"It means that we're an unconventional family. It means that you'll have to share me with Erica. And don't get any perverted male ideas about a threesome because that's not what we're talking about. She doesn't want to sleep with you. She's a lesbian."

"And what are you?"

I look him in the eye unflinchingly. "I'm bisexual. Erica is all the woman I will ever need. And you are all the man."

"What if you have to choose between us?"

"That's not how a healthy family works, is it?" I refuse to play his game.

I no longer know exactly who Odysseus is. I know who he was. He and Erica and I have the potential to become something much larger than ourselves in this situation. Larger than a family. What shall I call us? Perhaps we will become a constellation.

"I think you and Erica will be pleasantly surprised by each other."

I have lived with uncertainty about a great many things for as long as I can remember. This feeling of certainty that things will work out between the three of us is new to me. I have to get used to it. With Athena gone, I have to rely on my own instincts. Athena isn't here to confirm my intuition so I'll have to trust it on my own, let it parade as certainty. I'll have to go on faith.

"It'll work out. You and Erica were made to share me."

He laughs his head off at what I'm sure he takes to be my conceit. One day he'll understand what I really mean. His eyes have a new twinkle to them that reminds me a lot of an old twinkle I remember.

"You know what?" I ask.

"Of course not."

"Of course not," I confirm.

"Well, what?"

"I just had an idea about how to finish my novel. Erica will be pleased. She's dying to find out what happens to Cassandra," I muse.

"What novel?"

"That's literally another story."

Book 23: Molly and Cassandra

From *Death in Hoper Valley*

MOLLY'S JOURNAL

You win Cassandra. In the turmoil of change and the re-visioning of my life, I return to you, to finish what I started. Perhaps it is writing you that has transformed me. That, and the truth, and acting on my knowledge of the truth. You have your wish. You are not abandoned. I will complete you.

CASSANDRA

When Marta and Cassandra descended from the roof, Alexander had made himself scarce and Moira stood at the kitchen sink washing dishes. When she saw the girls, she turned the water off and picked up a green-and-white-checkered dish rag to dry her hands.

"You lied to me," Marta accused, her jaw set hard in anger.

Cassandra opened her mouth to speak but Moira held up a hand in warning.

"You told me it didn't matter, that you didn't mind. According to Cassandra, it does matter, which makes me the villain."

"You're not a villain. It doesn't matter any more than any of his other infidelities. It's cumulative. It's our problem, not yours. But it would be helpful if you would remove yourself from the equation."

"So I hear." Marta turned, flicking her thick shimmering hair behind her, and went into the living room. "I'll be out as soon as I pack my things," she called over her shoulder.

Moira scrutinized Cassandra. "I gather that whatever you said to her lacked tact."

"I'm angry with her. You're my friends, you and Alexander, and she abused her privileges as your guest. I want her gone. I don't ever want to see her again. She has trashed the friendship she had with me."

They could hear Marta in the living room speaking on the phone, laughing. Cassandra shot Moira a puzzled look. "Who does she know in Athens? Other than us. You don't suppose she's calling Alexander, do you?"

"He's on his way to see a client. She can't reach him."

"I don't really care who she's talking to. I'll leave also. I'll go to the hotel where Demetrius stays."

"You like this Demetrius don't you?"

Cassandra looked out the window briefly before answering. "I do actually. I'm comfortable with him. He thinks about things, about the things I say. He's thoughtful and gentle."

"And a good lover?" Moira teased.

Cassandra blushed. "That too. Listen, I'll leave you the number of the hotel. I'll be around for at least a few more days. We can get together for lunch. I'm worried about you."

"Don't. I'll land on my feet."

"What will you do?"

"I'll probably leave him and move back to London. I can get a real job there teaching. I love London; it's in my blood. I have friends there, my sister, my parents. It's my home. This," Moira made an arc with her arm as she encompassed the kitchen, the house, her marriage, Greece, "isn't my home. I don't fit here. I never did. I want a life more suited to me."

"Maybe he'll follow you to London and stay with you there," Cassandra suggested hopefully.

"Been there and done that." Moira bit her lip. "I don't think it'll happen again." A shadow crossed Moira's face. "I'm making this up as I go. I couldn't tell you what's the best choice for me. Alexander and I..." She paused and raked a hand through her hair. "We need to talk things through together before we make our decisions."

Cassandra nodded. "I'll go pack."

After saying goodbye to Moira, Cassandra took a taxi to the hotel. Demetrius's friend was working the front desk. He appeared infinitely amused by her arrival. She checked in, took the room key from him, and turned away from the counter. When she turned back to the counter, he stood with his arms crossed on his stout chest and a gap-toothed grin on his face. Cassandra blushed, but remained undeterred. "Have you seen Demetrius?" she asked.

"Room 102. Do I tell him you are arrived?"

"No. I'll tell him myself," Cassandra said, trying to keep her tone light.

She loaded her things into the elevator. Her room was much nicer than her previous room at the hotel, even though the price remained the same. This room had a lovely view and a large bathroom with separate shower and bathtub. It occurred to her that the friend at the front desk had given her the royal treatment. She would have to remember to thank him for the nice room. She washed her face, combed her hair, and went downstairs where she knocked on the tall wooden door of room 102.

Demetrius opened the door. His dark eyes with the heavy lids had become so familiar to her that she felt certain she could draw them from memory. She had memorized the way his hair curled over his forehead; his hands; his enigmatic half-smile, that made him look like he knew things, secrets, that no one else knew. Seeing him felt a little like coming home after traveling on a long dusty road.

Demetrius reached up and with his thumb gently stroked the crease between her eyebrows where the day's events had settled into a knot of worry. "What bothers you, my little American?"

Cassandra wrapped her arms around him and pressed her face into his neck, breathing in the musky male scent of him.

"Oh dear," he muttered, closing the door behind her. "Come." They sat down side-by-side on his bed and she told him what had happened. Marta sleeping with Alexander. Moira's decision to cancel the wedding. She even told him about her previous affair with Marta and Marta's seduction of Sabiya.

When she finished, Demetrius commented, "It sounds like one of those soap operas on American TV."

"No kidding. Some vacation, huh?"

"The most astonishing part is yet to come."

"What's that?"

He paused and looked at her intently. "I think I fall in love with you."

"I know."

"Will you give it a chance?"

"What do you mean?"

"Will you continue with me to see what happens? If we have a relationship worth to keep? I would go with you to London and after that to America. To give us time together to see what we have here."

"Can you do that? What about your job?"

"I will quit the job. I can get a visa. I save money. My family will help me. They have money. I maybe go back to college in America to study business so I can make a real job. A philosophy degree has no use to earn money."

Cassandra took his hand in hers and turned it palm up. "I like that you're a philosopher. I like it very much."

"Does that mean you let me come with you? To see what happens?"

Cassandra looked into his eyes and saw how eagerly he hoped for her to agree to his proposal. She thought for a moment about Moira and Alexander, how they had tried to build a relationship on a summer fling and what seemed to be happening with that. A difficult relationship that spanned continents and cultures. Did she have a better chance at happiness than Moira? Should she give herself permission to fall in love with this Greek beauty?

"Yes."

"Yes?"

"Yes. I want to see what will happen."

He kissed her, his lips as gentle as rose petals; his sensuous hands on her throat. And she had that sensation again, that she was coming home, that she could rest safely from the brutality of the world in the cradle of his arms.

A few days later, Cassandra arrived early for her date with Moira. The restaurant hostess seated her at a table from which she could see people entering. She glanced at the menu and kept an eye out for her friend. She remembered her first night in Athens, when Demetrius had taken her to this restaurant with Marta. Where had Demetrius come from, appearing out of the blue? One heartbeat not there, the next heartbeat there. Changing the cast of her future on a moment's notice. Was it random? Was it design? She had such a limited comprehension of the why and how of things. She wondered if the answers would come to her eventually and if she would grasp any more about how the universe worked when she reached old age.

She glanced up from the menu and saw Moira running across the street. The traffic parted for a moment as she passed and swarmed back behind her.

Cassandra rose from the table and walked to the entrance of the restaurant. She met Moira at the door. "I have a table for us."

Moira hugged Cassandra. She was out of breath and her hair smelled like lavender, vanilla, and fresh air. Cassandra led Moira to the table.

As they sat down, the waiter brought a menu for Moira.

"This is Demetrius's favorite restaurant. He took me here the night I arrived in Athens."

"So what's happening with you and Demetrius?"

"He's coming to London with me. Then America probably."

Moira raised an eyebrow. "Excuse me for sounding jaded. I warn you; you have to watch these Greek men. They want a wife and a family, but they also want, well, a little Marta on the side now and then. If that's going to bother you, give it up." Moira shrugged. "Take a lesson from me."

"Demetrius isn't like that."

"Whatever you say." Moira plucked her napkin from the table and laid it across her lap.

"He's a little old-fashioned. And romantic. Besides, we haven't made a commitment. We just want to see what happens. To see if maybe there's something there."

"So he quit his job?"

"He had planned to do that anyway. He wants to go back to school. He might go to school in America. His family can afford an American college. He's going to apply."

"What does he want to study?

"Business. He already has a degree in philosophy." Cassandra laughed. "He says the philosophy degree won't take him far."

"It got him pretty far with you."

A subtle smile snuck across Cassandra's lips as she replied, "I suppose it did."

"Hey," Moira said with a glint in her eye, "guess what your little sidekick Marta did?" She didn't continue because at that moment the waiter appeared and Moira ordered lamb kebabs with rice and a bottle of *retsina*. Cassandra ordered her favorite Greek dish, *spanikopita*. She couldn't wait for the waiter to leave so Moira would tell her what happened. As soon as he pocketed his order pad and walked out of earshot, Moira leaned across the table and delivered the news, "Marta took Sabiya to Amsterdam with her!"

"You're kidding." Cassandra flushed with anger and a healthy dose of envy. Marta had made off with Sabiya-the-beauty. Sabiya-the-prize. Marta didn't deserve Sabiya.

"Dead serious."

"What about Ioannis? What about Sabiya's career?"

Moira scrutinized Cassandra. "You're jealous aren't you?"

"What makes you say that?" she asked, a little too hastily.

Moira picked up her water glass and took a slow, deliberate drink. She set the glass down and peered at Cassandra. "You were sleeping with Marta, weren't you?"

"What difference does that make?"

"What difference?" Moira shook her head. "It made a lot of difference to me, for one. What do you think that business with my husband was all about? You dumped her for Demetrius so she had to find someone to hop into the sack with too."

"It wasn't like that. I didn't dump her. We weren't an item. It was just for fun. Neither one of us is a lesbian," Cassandra defended herself.

"Oh really? I would say Marta is a bit more inclined in that direction than your portrayal, considering she just spirited one of the hottest up-and-coming pop female sex symbols of Athens off to Amsterdam. She must be pretty terrific in bed. Everyone wants to sleep with her," Moira pointed out bitterly.

"I didn't travel to Athens to make trouble for you," Cassandra reminded Moira. "I came to visit you. Because you're my friend. I think you and Alexander are great together. I'm upset about everything that's happened. I want you two to be OK. I want you to be happy."

Moira pointed her fork at Cassandra. "Tell me the truth. Are you jealous that Marta is sleeping with Sabiya?"

Cassandra measured her words. "I'm in awe of Sabiya, that's all."

Moira laughed. "You and the rest of Athens. Ioannis is terrific at marketing."

"Oh my gosh," Cassandra yelped, "Ioannis. How is he taking this?"

"He's more upset than he imagined he would be if she took off. I'm not sure if he's more upset about losing the money or the model."

"What do you mean?"

"She was the goose that laid the golden egg. He was making a lot of money off her career. Now," Moira waved her thumb over her shoulder and made a *pffft* sound. "Gone."

"Poor Ioannis."

"Poor Ioannis my ass. He's fine. He has plenty of income. Actually I would say it's more of a relief to him than anything. He finally got his exit opportunity. He doesn't feel responsible for her anymore."

"What about her mother?"

"Whose mother?"

"Sabiya's mother."

"Oh that. Fatima went to Amsterdam with them. You don't think Sabiya would leave her behind, do you?"

"Marta took Sabiya *and her mother* to Amsterdam?!" Cassandra could hardly believe it.

Moira burst out laughing.

"What?"

"You look shell-shocked."

"Well, you have to admit that it's a bit difficult to swallow."

"Not as difficult as Demetrius quitting his job and moving to London with you." Moira shrugged and lifted an eyebrow. "Greece. It's a transformative, magical place."

"And what is Sabiya going to do in Amsterdam? She's a famous model here. Not in Amsterdam."

"She already has work. A beauty like that? Her face is her ticket anywhere. She's shrewd, multi-talented, and highly manipulative. She's a handful. I wish I could see your conniving friend Marta when she realizes what she's gotten herself into." Moira looked somewhat satisfied.

"So maybe you got your revenge after all."

"I don't want revenge but, if I did, I certainly got it."

"What's going to happen with you and Alexander?"

"I'm leaving him."

A tear ran down Cassandra's cheek. She couldn't help herself. Another tear followed. "I'm sorry." She wiped her cheeks with her napkin and took a deep breath to calm herself.

"Nothing to be sorry about. Now that I've made the decision, I'm excited about going back to London. I'm ready for a new life. Honestly," Moira assured her. "I'm so relieved we don't have the complication of children."

"Maybe with a different man one day."

"I hope so. I hope I meet a proper Englishman with a heart of gold who can keep his best friend in his pants and bring him home to his wife." Cassandra opened her mouth and Moira held up her hand to stop her from speaking. "Don't. I don't want to hear about how great we were together. We were great together and now we're not. We're still friends. He made me happy for a long time, until I outgrew him."

Cassandra nodded mutely.

"I believe things happen for a reason," Moira said. "I think we invite things into our lives on a deeper level, a spiritual level. I think I invited this marriage into my life. I invited those miscarriages into my life. I needed to go through that experience for a larger reason not apparent to me. I needed to marry Alexander and now I need to leave him."

"Hold up a minute. You didn't ask for those miscarriages. Not on any level," Cassandra argued adamantly. How could Moira blame herself for something like that? "Things happen randomly and not necessarily for any reason. Sometimes bad things happen to people who deserve much better. It's not your fault."

"I'm not saying it's my fault. What I'm saying is that I believe there was a lesson in here for me on a karmic level. There was a purpose that I can't see from where I sit. I believe there's an order to the universe that we just don't comprehend. Not in this dimension anyway."

"So you believe in fate?"

"Yes and no."

"Fate makes no sense because then why make a choice about anything if it's all pre-ordained? We have to have free choice. That's why it's important for us to take the high road and make positive choices. OK, OK, I sound like a therapist. But you get what I mean," Cassandra protested.

"I don't believe in fate, not like the Greeks define it. I believe in destiny. Destiny is not the same as fate. Destiny is fluid. It can change based on our choices. Because we don't know what our destiny is or why, because we don't know exactly what impact our choices or actions may have, it is incumbent upon us to try to take the most positive, constructive route. To be true to ourselves, to cause the least harm to others, to contribute to creating a better world. All that stuff. Because, when push comes to shove, we simply don't know."

The waiter brought two glasses and a bottle of *retsina*. He poured the amber resin wine into the glasses. Cassandra took a sip and relaxed into that sharp edge that bounced off her taste buds. She wondered if *retsina* would ever taste so delicious to her again when she left Athens.

"I believe in divine design," Moira continued after taking a drink from her glass.

"Like god?"

"If you mean an old white guy with a long beard, no, not at all." Moira laughed. "I believe there is a spirit realm in which things have a meaning and we just don't understand it in our limited reality, our limited perception."

"Then it's not a benevolent spirit realm because how would a benevolent spirit realm allow the horrible things that happen to people? Like, how do you explain the genocide of Native Americans, for instance, or even, on a smaller scale, a senseless event like the death of a young child? Or a person like you who would be a great mother having miscarriages? I don't get how horrible things can happen to a good person and have that be part of a design in which things happen for a reason. I believe it's all random."

"You will do extraordinarily well in a relationship with a philosopher." They both laughed.

"Obviously I can't answer your question. I have no concrete basis for an explanation. I can only tell you what I believe, which is that there is an intentional pattern and that a meaningful positive plan coexists with the seemingly senseless chaotic events that occur. We can't comprehend how they coexist. We don't have a broad enough vision. Everything is so much larger than we imagine. It's a mystery and a miracle. We go on faith."

Cassandra stared into her glass of *retsina* and swirled the drink before looking up into Moira's face. "I think we have the vision to see it. We just haven't done that yet: seen it. It's common knowledge that we don't use our whole brain. We have to learn how to use more of our brain. We have to learn how to access our whole brain and our whole spirit."

"That sounds like sci-fi."

"Not sci-fi. The future."

"Yes, the future. Let's drink to the future!" Moira lifted her glass of *retsina* and held it out toward Cassandra for a toast. "To London, and beyond," she said, without a hint of regret, just a glint of pure adventure in her eye.

Cassandra touched her glass to Moira's. The glasses clinked against one another. Cassandra thought for a moment before offering her toast: "To the mystery and the miracle."

Book 24: Peace
Bataka, 1987

Recently, in a little park thirty miles east of San Francisco, a botanist found a dozen pale pink wildflowers known as the Mount Diablo buckwheat. This flower had not been seen in sixty years and botanists had declared it extinct. The little pink buckwheat means everything in the world to me. Sometimes something we think we have lost forever returns. Something we think permanently damaged recovers. The tiny buckwheat flower reminds me to hope for those returns, for those recoveries.

I have heard it said that intelligence separates humans from other creatures, but I don't think we're very smart. I think what separates us from animals and plants is hope. While animals and plants merely persist, humans hope. Certainly, of all creatures, we need hope the most. I have lost hope more than once in my life. Now hope is a talisman I carry with me.

Time does not heal all wounds. Grief changes but never leaves. We grow accustomed to living with the pain of loss and grief. We thrust it into the periphery of our lives. Whenever it steps into our main field of vision, it takes our breath away as completely and precisely as the first moment.

Odysseus wishes he had known those we lost before his return. Athena, Aunt Beth, Sammy. I think about Sammy differently now. He saved my daughter, my precious Lena, and her friend Marjorie. He avenged Carla in a round-about way by protecting Lena. I don't condone violence. Yet a part of me is grateful to Sammy for pushing things over the edge. In the end, his anger produced a transformation that changed the name of our town. Nelson told me once that Sammy was, after all, a true Native son. I wish he could have heard Nelson say it. Because of Sammy, we live in Bataka at last.

Yesterday evening, when Odysseus, Erica, and I walked by the lake, Erica said that Athena, Aunt Beth, and Sammy are sleeping in the arms of the bear. I reminded her that Carla sleeps with them too.

Odysseus defended her oversight. "She didn't know Carla. It's easy to forget someone you never knew." Erica threw him a grateful look.

"It's OK." I patted Erica's arm. "I'll remember Carla for all of us."

Then Odysseus asked me, "Can you forgive him?"

"Forgive who?"

"Your father."

"Can you forgive your torturers?" Erica asked Odysseus. My Jewish sweetheart, always ready to answer a question with a question.

"Humans can't move forward collectively as a race if we refuse to forgive one another," Odysseus answered.

I remember Nelson on that silver shining morning of our first commemorative vigil, when he stood at the edge of B'Taka Lake and called out in the old language "forgive them." At the time I couldn't grasp the compassion that allowed him to call those words. Now I think I do.

I told Odysseus and Erica, "The blood from the massacre of the Kapa will never wash from this land. I can choose to wallow in the horrific history or I can choose to transform its meaning. When a whole country is built on genocide, slavery, and racism, then we have to move through it and beyond it and find our way to forgiveness, since nothing else will give us hope for a future for our children. If I can forgive John Hoepper and the other colonizers, then I have to also forgive my own father."

"They were damaged and suffering themselves," Erica reminded us softly.

"And ignorant," Odysseus added.

"Yes," Erica agreed.

"In the end," I said, "I think forgiveness is our only hope. We have to forgive and move forward to trust one another again. And if the trust is broken, we go back to square one and learn to forgive again. Again and again. Until the trust finally holds."

Until we become brothers and sisters on this earth. For truthfully the land was never robbed from indigenous peoples because we never owned it. No one owns it. We are residents in the house of nature that belongs to no one and to everyone. And in the end the land does as the land chooses. Nature has its own agenda. We humans simply pass through, wandering each on our individual journey.

"Let's face it," I told my two lovers, "this planet is our only home and there is no other. If we can't make a life here together then we have no future. Perhaps making peace is our deepest work here."

"Easy to imagine, infinitely hard to accomplish," Odysseus pointed out. "What do you suppose happens if we fail? What if we pass through and out and become extinct?"

"When I pause to look at the way people make one another suffer, I think we humans haven't moved forward even a hair in our evolution. Maybe we've been moving backward, losing touch with what matters," Erica said. "In that case, we deserve to become extinct."

"Remember that you work with abused children. Not all children have been abused," Odysseus reminded her. "It can distort your perception."

"He's right," I added.

Erica gave me one of her looks. "This is what makes me crazy in this love triangle; two can gang up on one. Why couldn't I be in a traditional relationship?" Erica laughed that laugh of hers that reminds me of the sound of water in a stream running over stones. Odysseus combed his hand through his golden hair and grinned.

I love them both, beyond measure.

I could never choose between them.

My ancestors believed that everything has spirit. There is spirit in the trees and rocks and all that surrounds us. There is spirit in things seen and unseen and all spirit is inter-related. I would like to think that the contribution of my spirit has made a difference; that my presence leaves a trace that matters within the incomprehensible vastness of time, a tiny positive smudge upon the trees and the soil, sand and water, a fleck of progress toward healing and evolution. And I pray, with all the heart of human hope, that the smudge of my tiny spirit contributes to the possibility that we have not passed this way in vain, that we endure in a positively meaningful way, throughout the wide reaches of eternity.

I'm blessed with my beautiful beloved children. Blessed with the magnificent people who have materialized out of the blue and helped raise me up when I stumbled. When I drift on the broad chest of my brave, enduring Odysseus or when I rest in the caring arms of my generous, laughing Erica, I dwell comfortably in this place. The story of my Kapa people and the story of how my husband returned to me remind me that within the wandering that falls to each of us lies the kernel of promise that one day we will arrive. Return is possible. Recovery is possible. Witness the recovery of the Mount Diablo buckwheat. Inside the quiet miracle of these ordinary moments with those I love, I am able to summon compassion and am most able to find forgiveness in my heart for my father, for those who massacred my Tribe, and for all those who harm others on this tilted planet spinning under the stars.

I suppose I am one prayer shy of tempting fate by saying so, but I have made my peace. I have known the hard labor of holding out hope and I have known the bright wonder of finding home.

Acknowledgments

It has been decades since I first began making notes for *Penelope's Odyssey*. I have worked on this tale on and off for decades, and the world has changed a great deal in the meantime.

I owe a debt of gratitude to Edwin Lockhart, the original firekeeper of the full moon fire. I began attending Edwin's full moon fire (he called it "the Burn") each month on the Pinoleville Reservation at a time when I much needed his bonfire ritual. Edwin unexpectedly passed into spirit in August 2003 at the age of 54. After Edwin left us, *Penelope's Odyssey* changed. Edwin had his own ideas about where the book should go and he became my spirit guide as I wrote the first version of the book. I thank him for making the journey from the Elysian Fields to look over my shoulder.

I am grateful to Homer for writing *The Odyssey*, one of the most beloved and magnificent classic narratives ever told.

I must confess that I manipulated timeframes with regard to the Mount Diablo buckwheat just a bit. The flower was believed to have become extinct in 1936 and it was rediscovered in 2005. The closing chapter of *Penelope's Odyssey* takes place in 1987, many years before the flower was rediscovered. Forgive me for bending time to my own purposes.

I wish I could say that all the events described in *Penelope's Odyssey* are fictitious. Unfortunately, the cruelest of all events is the one that is closest to the truth. The story of the massacre of indigenous people, recounted several times in the book, is based on an actual massacre that occurred in Lake County, California in 1850. The Bloody Island Massacre annihilated one of the Eastern Pomo Tribes that had lived for more than 12,000 years on the shores of Clear Lake. I first heard the story of the massacre from Clayton Earl Duncan when he spoke at the Ukiah Players Theater. I heard him speak the story many times after that. Documentation of the massacre is held by the Lake County Library System. Some of the few remaining descendants of the massacred Tribe live mostly in and around the Robinson Rancheria in Kelseyville, California. Kelseyville is named after Andrew Kelsey, the pederast who raped and murdered tribal members, particularly children, and the man who precipitated the events that led to the genocide that occurred on the shores of Clear Lake.

Clayton tells that he remembers as a little boy seeing his great-grandmother, Lucy Moore, frequently standing at sunset on the edge of the family's front porch with her arms outstretched to the heavens. In her Eastern Pomo language, she called upon the Creator to forgive those who had slaughtered her Tribe. Her capacity for forgiveness is the lesson that Clayton teaches and the difficult lesson that I have learned from him and his people. Clayton's story has always moved me deeply and the role it plays in *Penelope's Odyssey* is a tribute to him for having the courage and perseverance to speak the truth in a nation built on lies and injustice during an unforgiving and vengeful age.